SYMPATHY BETWEEN HUMANS

Detective Sarah Pribek has worked every-thing on the streets of Minneapolis, from vice to missing persons. But six months after the death of a criminal, Sarah is still protecting his killer. And a zealous D.A.'s investigator is determined to make an arrest ... She immerses herself in two cases — a young man missing from a troubled family, and an unlicensed doctor whose patients are the disenfranchised. She finds her professional honour and personal feelings challenged ... Crossing one ethical line after another, Sarah fears that a misstep on her part will result not only in her disgrace, but also in the death of one of the people she has promised to protect.

JODI COMPTON

SYMPATHY BETWEEN HUMANS

Complete and Unabridged

CHARNWOOD
Leicester

First published in Great Britain in 2005 by
Hodder and Stoughton
a division of Hodder Headline
London

First Charnwood Edition
published 2006
by arrangement with
Hodder Headline
London

British Library CIP Data

20131197

Compton, Jodi
Sympathy between humans.—Large print ed.—
Charnwood library series
1. Women detectives—Minnesota—Minneapolis—
Fiction 2. Suspense fiction 3. Large type books
I. Title
813.6 [F]

ISBN 1–84617–270–5

Published by
F. A. Thorpe (Publishing)
Anstey, Leicestershire

Set by Words & Graphics Ltd.
Anstey, Leicestershire
Printed and bound in Great Britain by
T. J. International Ltd., Padstow, Cornwall

This book is printed on acid-free paper

1

It was late afternoon on Spain's Atlantic coast, the sun turning golden in the lower layers of atmosphere over the water. At the ocean's edge ran a seawall, not a barrier of rocks but a solid stone wall that broke the gentle surf. A section had been cut away to let water feed into a bathing pool, a dark-watered rectangle about half the size of a swimming pool, submerged stone benches cut all around the sides.

It was like something an ancient Roman city builder might have created, both simple and decadent. Egalitarian, as well. There were no fences, and locals seemed as welcome to come here as the well-heeled vacationers. Sunbathers came in to cool off, and children swam, darting across and back from one bench to another, like birds changing roosts in an aviary.

Genevieve Brown had brought me here, Gen who'd once been my partner in the Hennepin County Sheriff's Department. On the job she'd been measured and cautious, and I'd expected the same from her here. But she'd taken the lead, stepping down onto a bench and immediately from there into the center of the pool, tucking her knees to let the water cradle her cupped body as her dark, shoulder-length hair made a cloud around her head.

Now Genevieve sat next to me on one of the benches, her face tipped up into the sun. Her

1

skin seemed already to be turning a warm, creamy brown. Genevieve was of southern European extraction, and while she'd never been a sun worshipper, her skin would tan in the weakest early-spring rays.

'This is nice,' I said, raising my face into the late-afternoon sunlight. Already the salt water was drying on my face, tightening the skin. I wondered if my face would have a faint salt glaze, a shimmer under light, if I decided not to rinse in fresh water afterward.

'You're overdue for some good times,' Genevieve said. 'Last year was . . . difficult.'

It was an understatement. Last spring Genevieve's daughter had been murdered, and last fall I lost my husband to prison. At the end of that extraordinarily bad year, Genevieve had quit the Sheriff's Department, reconciled with her estranged husband, Vincent, and gone to live in his adopted home of Paris.

We'd talked about me coming to visit, of course, almost from her first transatlantic call in December. Five months had passed, though, before I did. Five months of snow and subzero temperatures, of heating my car's engine with an extension cord and myself with bad squad-room coffee, of the double shifts and extra assignments I'd volunteered for. Then I'd taken Gen up on this invitation, to meet her down the coast.

'Have you heard anything about the Royce Stewart investigation?' Gen asked, her voice casual. It was the first she'd mentioned it.

'I heard a little about it early on, in

December,' I said, 'but then nothing happened. I think it's stalled.'

'That's good,' she said. 'I'm happy for you.'

I hadn't told Genevieve about the investigation into Stewart's death, much less that I'd been suspected of the murder. That was curious. If I hadn't told her, who had? She'd said she wasn't in touch with anyone else from her old life in Minnesota.

'Who told you I was under suspicion?' I asked.

'Nobody,' Gen said. 'It just stands to reason.'

A small drop of seawater fell from my wet hair onto my shoulder. 'Why does it stand to reason?' I asked.

'Because you killed him,' she said.

I looked quickly at the trio of women sitting at the other end of the bathing pool, but they gave no sign they'd heard.

Quietly, I said, 'Is that supposed to be some kind of a joke? I didn't kill Royce Stewart. You did.'

'No, Sarah,' Genevieve said softly. 'It was you, remember? I would never do something like that.' Her eyes darkened with pity and concern.

'This isn't funny,' I said, my voice low and stiff. But I knew this wasn't some mean-spirited joke on her part. Her tone communicated nothing but compassion. It said that her heart was breaking for her friend and partner.

'I'm sorry,' she said, 'but someday, everyone's going to know what you did.'

A siren went off beyond the horizon, piercing and almost electronic in its pitch, relentless in its one-note anxiety.

'What's that noise?' Genevieve said.

I opened one eye to see the glowing digits of my clock radio, the source of the electronic wail, then raised my hand and squelched the alarm. It was late afternoon in Minneapolis; I'd been sleeping before my shift. Through the windows of my bedroom, the elms of Northeast Minneapolis cast greenish shadows on the warped wooden floor; they were in the early leaf of spring. It was early May; that much was true.

Also true: Genevieve was in Europe, and my husband, Shiloh, a cop once recruited by the FBI, was in prison. All this is because of what happened last year in Blue Earth. You might have read about it, if you follow the news, but you didn't read all of it.

At the root of everything that had happened in Blue Earth was a man named Royce Stewart, who'd raped and murdered Genevieve's daughter, Kamareia, and gotten off on a technicality. Months later, Shiloh had gone to Blue Earth, intending to run down Stewart in a stolen truck. But Shiloh had found himself incapable of murder. It was Genevieve who, in a chance encounter, had stabbed Stewart in the neck and burned down the tiny shack he'd lived in.

It was Shiloh who'd gone to prison, though, for stealing the truck, while Genevieve, her crime unwitnessed by anyone but me, had gone to Europe to start a new life. I didn't blame her for that. My husband was already behind bars; I didn't want my old friend there, too.

It wasn't until Genevieve was virtually on the plane for France that I'd been tipped off that I was a suspect in Stewart's death. Disturbing as it was, it made sense. I was the one who'd been in Blue Earth, looking for my husband. It was me who had been seen having unfriendly words with Stewart in a bar, just before his death.

Two Faribault County detectives came to the Cities to interview me, recording my carefully rehearsed, evasive answers. They didn't appear convinced by anything I'd said.

I didn't tell Genevieve what was happening, because I feared she'd fly home to bail me out by confessing. Nor did I seek Shiloh's counsel, because at the prison his mail was almost certainly being monitored, and it was impossible to explain the situation without referring to Genevieve's guilt.

But a strange thing happened, or rather, didn't happen. One month passed, then two, but I was never arrested, nor even questioned again. The investigation seemed to have stalled.

Then the *Star Tribune* ran its investigative piece.

THE SUSPECT'S DEATH, the headline had read, with an extended sub-headline below: *Royce Stewart was suspected of killing a Hennepin County detective's daughter. Seven months later, he died in a suspicious late-night fire. A former MPD cop has confessed to planning his murder, but not to carrying it out. While the case is still technically open, the answers may have gone up in flames.*

5

It was the *Star Tribune* piece that had mentioned what all the other stories hadn't:

> In an unexplained sidelight, several documents note that Shiloh's wife, Hennepin County Detective Sarah Pribek, was in Blue Earth the night Stewart died. Faribault County officials have refused to answer questions about whether Pribek is suspected of involvement in the death and the house fire.

Just two sentences, but they acknowledged at last the rumor that had been circulating in Minneapolis's law-enforcement community for months. The Monday morning after the article ran, there was a very awkward silence when I arrived at work.

What bothered me most was this, though: after the *Strib* story ran, I saw something in the eyes of the young male rookies when they looked at me. I saw respect. They believed I'd killed Royce Stewart, and they thought better of me for it.

It would have been an easier burden to bear if it had been shared by my ex-partner and my husband. I didn't blame them for not being here. Genevieve had been wise to get away, safely out from under the growing cloud of suspicion and speculation. And Shiloh, of course, had been imprisoned; he was not gone by choice. But I felt their absence every day. They were more than my immediate family. They were my history here in Minneapolis. Shiloh and Genevieve had known each other before I'd met either of them. That was why, even when the three of us weren't together on a daily or even a weekly basis, there had been a web of interconnectedness between us that gave me a sense of stability. Without them, I had lost something deeper than daily companionship, something I felt the lack of in conversations with co-workers that were polite and pleasant and nothing more than that.

As two months turned into three, four, and five, still I wasn't charged with anything, and I realized that the investigation was stalled, perhaps forever. But I understood something else: if I would never be outright accused of Stewart's murder, neither would I ever be exonerated. At work I sensed a silent verdict: *probably guilty by reason of persistent rumor.* My lieutenant did not assign me another partner. The major-crimes and missing-persons work that Gen and I had done dried up, replaced with interim and odd assignments. Like the one I had tonight.

★   ★   ★

'Excuse me, have you seen this boy?'

A middle-aged woman was showing a photograph around on the avenue where I was working. She was flagging down passersby, trying to find someone who'd seen a runaway teenager.

Out of professional interest, I moved to intercept the woman. She registered me coming and turned to make eye contact. Then her face quickly shut down and she turned away. She didn't see a kind, interested stranger, much less a cop. She saw a hooker.

I couldn't blame her. It's what I'd intended.

Prostitution-decoy work was more commonly done by metro police departments, but there's often a need for fresh faces, so I was on loan. Tonight I was posted on a heavily trafficked avenue south of downtown Minneapolis, not far from the business district, where undercover officers like me vacuumed up out-of-towners looking for a good time, as well as local salarymen leaving the bars after their end-of-day cocktails.

A civilian might have been surprised at how simply I was dressed. That's one of the first things you learn: no miniskirt, no high heels, no seamed stockings. Genevieve had explained it to me, years ago.

'Street workers can't afford to advertise themselves to cops,' she'd said. 'Besides, I think a lot of them are just too tired. Psychologically, they can't bring themselves to treat this like a job.'

So, early this evening, I'd pulled on a pair of jeans and boots, a white V-necked T-shirt, and a cheap reddish imitation-leather coat. The makeup, more than wardrobe, was important. I used a thick, pale concealer stick, not in trouble spots, as prescribed, but all over my face, creating an unhealthy pallor. After that came mascara and eyeliner pencil. 'Eyeliner's the best,' Genevieve had said. 'Nothing ejects you from the ranks of the Camry-driving middle classes like eye pencil.'

8

The number one tip-off out on the street, though, isn't your clothes or makeup but demeanor. It's that guarded little bend from the waist that street workers do, looking through car windows. That's what tells the men who you are.

But tonight, I was having no luck. Men passed on the street in cars, on the sidewalk on foot. They looked at me, some of them, but none stopped, and I didn't try to stop them. The idea to commit a crime has to originate with the arrestee, not the officer, otherwise it's entrapment.

At least it was a pleasant night to be outside.

May weather in the Twin Cities is anybody's guess. It could bring a record heatwave. Or a series of bone-rattling, drenching thunderstorms, the kind that started up in the mornings and worsened as afternoon came on, until they shaped their anger into destructive tornadoes outside the city, on the farmland and the prairie. Conversely, it was possible that a freak storm could blow into Minnesota in the next few days and dump inches of snow on us.

The latest had been two days of storms, rains that were fitful but kept coming back, often torrentially, overloading the gutters and the drains. Tonight was a pleasant exception; the clouds had parted to reveal a polished twilight sky. But the aftereffects of the rain were everywhere: the roads were still dark with it, and the air smelled clean and damp.

A bus swept to the curb, picking up a teenager in a wheelchair. When it wallowed back into traffic and away, I saw that I'd attracted someone's attention. A late-model, midsize car was pulled to the curb across the street. Mentally, I wrote up the man inside: white, mid-thirties, hair color brown with some gray on the temples, eye color unknown, no distinguishing marks or scars on the face. Clothes I couldn't see much of, except for the dark knot of a tie against his white shirt.

Something else, too: there was no sexual interest in his eyes. None at all, yet he didn't break his gaze.

Come on, you need a first arrest of the night. Get him over here and bust him.

I walked a few paces, tried to swing my hips a little. Turned to make eye contact again, sending him an overtly questioning look.

The man pulled into traffic and away.

What was that all about? Lost his nerve, maybe. Dammit.

I paced another five minutes before, at last, a car slid to the curb on my side of the street, a Chevy sedan about fifteen years past its prime. It had, I noticed, Arkansas plates.

I walked to the curb and bent slightly from the waist, looking in through the rolled-down window. The driver who looked back was white, with thick, tawny hair that fell over the top of his squarish black-rim eyeglasses. He was thin in build, save for the beginnings of softness at his middle, and his large hands, on the wheel, were freckled from sun exposure.

Disheartened, I glanced toward the backseat. A half-folded map was trying to accordion out across the top of a duffel bag, and a fishing rod was propped diagonally from the floor on one side to the rear-window shelf on the other, on which rested a well-worn Houston Astros cap. I knew it.

It was hard to imagine how this out-of-towner had gotten so lost he'd washed up on one of Minneapolis's most vice-prone boulevards, but he was here now, and I'd give him the directions he was pulling over for. *Well, Lieutenant, I didn't actually make any vice arrests, but I did help a rube find the Days Inn.*

The driver rolled down the passenger-side window, his eyes on mine, seemingly in anticipation of saying something, but then he didn't speak. The beat of silence stretched out between us, with expectation on both sides, before he finally said, 'Well, get in, sugar. Don't wait for me to ask you.'

If I live to be a hundred, I'll never have men figured out.

'Why don't you pull around the corner a minute,' I suggested, recovering from my misconception, 'and we can talk.' Going anywhere with a would-be trick is dangerous, and strictly forbidden.

The sedan trundled around the corner to a small parking lot, and I followed. The driver cut the engine, and I slid into the passenger seat.

'How you doing?' he said.

I shrugged, studying him from behind my mask of pallid makeup. His age was hard to judge. Mid-thirties, maybe. I'd read it off his driver's license when I made the bust.

'What's your name?' he asked.

'Sarah,' I said.

'Sarah,' he repeated. 'My name's Gareth. You can call me Gary. Most people do.'

The sound of the Ozarks in his voice was disarming, but I went forward with business. 'What's on your mind tonight, Gary?'

He didn't take the hint. 'I'm staying in town tonight, on my way up north, to do some fishing.'

'Yeah,' I said. 'I saw your pole in the back.'

He gave me a small smile. 'I designed that pole,' he said. 'That's what I do for a living. Well, I do a couple of things. That's one of them. You want a smoke?'

'No, thanks,' I told him.

'Well, I'm gonna have one,' he said.

Usually the men are nervous, and in a hurry. This man acted like we'd just sat down together at a lounge for cocktails. He was entirely at ease, rolling down his window to exhale with almost lordly pleasure. 'Yeah,' he said reflectively, 'I heard you've got some of the best fishing in America, up in your lake country. Is that true?'

'I don't fish,' I said lamely. I'd never had to make small talk with a john before. This really was not going well at all.

'Some friends told me I should come,' he went on. 'My wife died a few years ago. I haven't taken any vacation time since then.'

His eyelashes were black, much darker than the rest of his fair coloring would have indicated, when his gaze flicked downward as if he were shy about saying that last part. I wondered if he'd been with another woman in those years he'd referred to, or if he was trying to work up to making me the first. And I imagined myself standing before a judge someday, not long from now, and explaining that in a world full of men who beat up prostitutes, spent the milk money on sex, and brought diseases home to their wives, I had gone out on the streets on Hennepin County's behalf and caught a courteous, widowed fishing pole designer.

'Gary,' I said, straightening, 'are you ever going to ask me for sex?'

He blinked, but I thought I saw a flicker of amusement behind his thick glasses. 'Are all you Minnesotans in this big a hurry?' he asked.

'Well,' I said, 'I can't speak for all Minnesotans, especially since I come from out West, but in my case it has a lot to do with the fact that I'm a Hennepin County Sheriff's detective. And if you suggest some kind of sex-for-money deal, then I'm going to have to arrest you, and I'd really rather not do that if it's all the same to you. I'm guessing it is.'

Gary, who had come perilously close to dropping his cigarette from his mouth onto his lap, said, 'You're a cop?'

'On my good days,' I said, and opened the door to the Chevy and climbed out. Then I turned in the doorway. 'One last thing,' I said.

I'd been planning to leave him with an admonition to leave the working girls alone while in Minneapolis, but then I saw something I should have noticed before. His hand, resting on the steering wheel, had a warm tone from the sun even where it wasn't freckled. All except for

13

a slightly paler line on the ring finger. The tan line was too recent for the passage of time he'd been widowed. He'd been wearing the ring much longer. My glib words dried up in my throat. 'Never mind,' I said.

That should have been the end of it, but Gareth's voice caught up with me.

'Sarah,' he said.

I turned back.

'Be safe,' he said.

It was an unexpected kindness, and I merely nodded, not knowing what I might have said.

Perhaps five minutes of pacing my spot again let me recover my composure, even a little bit of bravado. That made two men I'd let slip through my net tonight. *The next guy so much as looks at my ass,* I thought, *I swear to God, I'm going to arrest him.*

The next car was a gleaming dove-gray sedan. Again a window rolled down, and I leaned over to look in. A middle-aged man sat behind the wheel, slender, balding, a little Mediterranean-looking, wearing a well-tailored suit.

'May I offer you a ride?' he asked.

'Why don't you pull around the corner,' I said, 'and we can talk for a minute, okay?'

Unlike Gary, this man had no interest in learning my name, although he told me I could call him Paul. The car's interior smelled new, and a sticker identified it as part of a rental fleet. Paul was from out of town.

'What's on your mind tonight, Paul?' I asked.

'I thought you might want to make a little deal,' he said. 'Do you like coke?'

I looked at him sidewise. Better and better, a soliciting bust with a side of narcotics possession. 'Who doesn't?' I said.

'I thought maybe with a few lines you could go down to fifty dollars for a half-and-half.'

Just what the world needs, a frugal john. 'Seventy-five.'

'That's fine.' Paul's heart wasn't in the negotiation.

'And I need to see the blow first.'

'It's right back there, in my briefcase,' he said, indicating the backseat with a slight wave of his hand. 'Do you have, ah, someplace we can go?'

Ignoring him, I rose to my knees and turned, pulling his slender briefcase onto the front seat with us. 'Is this thing locked?' I asked, but didn't wait before I pressed the release with my thumb. It snapped noisily, and I opened the case. There it was, such a world of trouble for this guy in such a little plastic bag.

Paul was unfazed by my coarse behavior. Paul was a man of the world. He knew that an expensive suit pays for itself in the long run, that business class is a rip-off, and that $75 hookers give their johns a hard time. As I snapped the briefcase shut, Paul restated his earlier question.

'So,' he asked, 'do you have somewhere that you take men?'

'I sure do,' I told him cheerfully, pulling my shield out of my leather coat.

* * *

It was after four in the morning when I left work, after staying late to cover for a co-worker whose child was sick. But even when I left, I wasn't tired, just hungry. I was thinking that if I knocked on the back door of a bakery, I might be able to buy something really fresh and warm from the oven.

It was on this errand, which took me toward the outskirts of the city, that I saw a woman refilling a *Star Tribune* rack. Impulse made me pull to the side of the road. Shiloh had taken care of our subscription to the *Strib*, and in his absence, I'd let it lapse.

The days of the newspaper boy, the kid on the bike, are largely over. The circulation driver was perhaps 30, with a pinched, makeupless face and short, flyaway hair. Her Toyota Starlet idled by the curb. The look she gave me as I approached was wary; she thought I was looking for a free paper before she closed the rack.

'Go ahead,' I told her. 'I'll buy one after you're finished.'

The woman set up the display copy in the window and let the door close with a slam. I stepped into the place she'd been, fishing for a pair of quarters.

'Is that a kid, at this hour?' she asked, behind me.

'Is what a kid?' I asked absently, feeding the coin slot.

'Yelling like that. You didn't hear it?'

She must have had ears like radar. Or maybe she had kids and there was such a thing as maternal intuition.

16

'I don't hear anything,' I said.

'Over there,' she said, pointing.

I looked. Empty street, streetlights, shuttered businesses. A running figure on the sidewalk, about 10 or 11 years old. A child in the street. At four-thirty in the morning.

I ran to intercept him.

Closing the distance between us, I raised my hands and gestured for the boy to stop. He was thin, and breathing like a fire horse. He had pale skin, but black hair that looked like it had been cut in the time-honored bowl method with household shears, and his shirt and pants were too big.

'What's wrong?' I said, dropping to my heels before him. 'Is someone hurting you?'

The boy released a torrent of words, but all in what was, to the best of my knowledge, a Slavic language. We stared at each other in mutual frustrated incomprehension. Then he twisted away from me and pointed back in the direction he'd come.

A drainage ditch ran through this small, light-industrial neighborhood; I could hear its full-throated sound, working overtime after the heavy recent rains. Where it went under the street, a fence of three tubular rails lined the sidewalk, ribcage-high on an adult. Near it, on the sidewalk, were stiff forms of metal that resolved themselves, on a closer look, into bikes heeled over on their side. Two bikes. One kid.

The boy was right behind me as I ran over for a closer look. Just before the drainage ditch went under the street, it dropped a surprisingly good distance into a wider pool bounded by cement walls to prevent overflow onto the street in rains like the kind we'd been having. In drier weather, we'd probably have been looking down into some mud and marshy grass, through which ran a sedate creek. Not now. This early morning, the rains had created a catchpool that roiled irregularly, turbulently.

'Did somebody fall?' To illustrate, I made walking fingers with one hand toward the railing, rising slightly to illustrate climbing, and then I imitated a plunge down.

The kid nodded and said something I didn't understand.

The newspaper driver had arrived behind us. 'Call 911,' I said, swinging a leg over the railing. 'Tell them a kid fell in. Take this boy with you and keep him calm.' I didn't wait for her to acknowledge my request, climbing down to dangle from the lowest railing, with my feet swinging above the surface of the water.

All this, from the kid pointing to the water to my instructions to the newspaper driver to my climb over the fence, took maybe ninety seconds. But it was long enough for me to think of last fall and 14-year-old Ellie Bernhardt. I'd jumped into the Mississippi River after her and briefly made myself famous around the department for it, particularly because I wasn't a very strong swimmer.

I wish I could say that when I flashed back on Ellie Bernhardt I was thinking something ironic, like, *Why does this stuff always happen to me?* But I wasn't. I was simply thinking, *God, don't*

18

let me drown. Then I let go.

This water was warmer than I remembered the waters of the Mississippi, but still cool. And turbulent, pulling in varying directions, but not hard. I felt the tugging most strongly low down, toward my calves and feet, in the direction of the underpass, where the water was being drawn under the street.

Diving down, I opened my eyes, to see nothing before me but a brown-gray wall. I felt around in the direction the water was flowing, toward the street. It stood to reason that anything heavy that had fallen into the water would have gotten pulled in that direction. But my fingers brushed nothing, and my lungs began to burn. Air never seems to last as long as it should in these situations. It didn't help that my heart was probably slamming away at 140 beats a minute. I rose and broke the surface, panting. As I did so, something bumped my foot.

I inhaled fast and made a jackknife dive, feeling ahead of me again. This time, something brushed against my hand, not solid, more like cloth. It was animated by water, so that it rippled against my hand. When I caught it in my hand and pulled, I felt a corresponding resistance. It wasn't just an old shirt that had ended up in a canal. Someone was in it.

Surfacing was one thing, but it was harder to pull the child up. The thin body had no buoyancy and was weighed down by sodden clothes and waterlogged shoes. Wet black hair broke the surface first, shining and plastered against pale skin. I rolled him over so that his face was raised toward the still-dark sky.

In the rescue textbooks it looks so simple; the diagrams are so clean and neat. The boy and I were illustrating something else: the messiness of real life. I was trying to get a feel for whether he was breathing, if his rib cage was rising and falling under my encircling arm. Theoretically, I should have been able to tell, but I couldn't. I looked hopefully up toward the railing for the Toyota woman, but she wasn't there. Just concrete wall on every side, at least five feet of it above the water level. There was no purchase, no handholds that I could see. The boy's weight kept pushing me under, my legs working hard, treading water, wanting support where there wasn't any.

Just then, a face appeared at the railing. He was a stranger, but the sight of his face filled me with relief.

He was quite young, perhaps 23 or 24, and Asian, his face sculpted in hard, clean lines, his eyes thoughtful. He'd shaved almost all his head, except for a patch like a trapezoidal Mohawk near the front; it should have looked silly but didn't. I couldn't see what he was wearing, a uniform or civilian clothes, but I didn't need to. Some people show up in difficult times, and it doesn't matter that you've never met them before. You see their faces and immediately know they've come to help. He was one of those.

'How you guys doing down there?' he asked.

'Not good.'

He nodded, quite calm. 'Okay,' he said, looking at the water thoughtfully as if this were a physics problem in a textbook. 'I'm going see if I can't drop a backboard.'

That's what he did. When I'd gotten the boy onto the board, I watched his chest and stomach, wrapped in the wet embrace of a sodden red T-shirt. It fell as I watched, rose again. He was breathing. My mind was eased by the sight, like my body felt newly light at being shed of the boy's weight in the water.

When I was up on the street again, I could see that the rescuer wore the dark-blue jumpsuit of a paramedic. His partner, younger yet and blond, was taking care of the boy. The Asian medic glanced over at them, sized up the situation as under control, and sat on his heels next to me.

'I'm all right,' I said.

'I know,' he told me.

There we were: a tall, courteous kid with a postmodern hair-cut and a half-drowned county detective.

'Sarah Pribek,' I said, holding out my hand. 'Hennepin County Sheriff's Department.'

He shook my hand. 'Nate Shigawa,' he said.

'Pleased to meet you,' I said.

From behind him came a high, thin cry. The newspaper driver had returned, and she wasn't alone. With her was the boy who'd raised the alarm about his fallen brother and a woman in an inexpensive print dress and long black hair tucked back in a headscarf. The woman was looking around — not at her son, whom the young EMT was attending to, but everywhere else. Into the back of the ambulance, on the nearby ground, at Shigawa and me. She spoke rapidly in the same Slavic tongue as her son.

When her sharp, urgent inquiries earned her only blank looks, she ran to the bikes. She pointed at one of them, then to the boy who stood by the Toyota, dry and unharmed. Then she picked up the second bike and pointed to the boy on the stretcher. Then she thumped the handlebars of the second bike, as if to indicate a rider there.

Shigawa and I looked at each other, having the same terrible realization: *this woman has three children*.

We both went to the railing, to look down at the water rolling below, unbroken by anything that resembled a hand or a foot or a scrap of material. It had been too long. Far too long.

'I'll go,' I said. 'I've already been in.'

'No, don't do that,' said Shigawa's partner, coming to join us. His name tag identified him as Schiller.

'Somebody's got to,' I said.

'In a couple of hours it'll be daywatch,' Schiller said. 'The county can send some divers out. They're trained for this.' Schiller was clearly a newly minted EMT, and I'd seen the expression on his face before, a hard fixed look that young rookie cops affect when they don't want the world to see that the job hasn't made them jaded and world-weary yet.

I shook my head. 'No. This can't wait.'

'Why can't it?' Schiller asked, his face empty with incomprehension.

I did not want to put my body back in that opaque, dirty water, did not want to get it in my ears and eyes again. But I had to. In my mind was the image of a child's body under that brackish water, scudding along the bottom of the canal, perhaps sucked against some natural barrier or manmade screen, hair floating, maybe rolling over and over like a log for hours. I couldn't imagine leaving him or her there, like a piece of trash, while we went off for dry clothes and breakfast. I tried to find the words to express that to Schiller and couldn't. But I didn't have to.

'If you don't understand why, she can't explain it to you,' Shigawa said.

There was a beat of silence as Schiller looked away from me, to his partner, registering the minor betrayal. 'You don't have to take an attitude about it, Nate,' he said, and walked away.

I swung a leg over the railing again.

'I'll be right up here,' Shigawa said.

'I know,' I said. 'See you soon.'

★ ★ ★

In the end, we had the whole 911 experience, a fire engine and an MPD cruiser joining the ambulance at the scene. The MPD officers were Roz, a sergeant in her fifties with short sandy hair, a former K-9 handler rumored to have no less than eight dogs at home. She was acting as the field training officer for a rookie, Lockhart, who looked like a teenage girl in a police officer's uniform.

Beyond the emergency personnel was a

semicircle of neighborhood people. Maybe the noise had woken them, or perhaps they'd already been starting their day when they heard the commotion. It was after five now, the sky turning a pale electric blue.

The kind of people who show up at accident scenes are often derided as morbid sightseers, but more than once they've supported my faith that people essentially want to help each other. One woman, seeing my drenched clothes, went to retrieve a long-sleeved thermal shirt and sweatpants that belonged to her husband; I gratefully accepted them and awkwardly changed in the crew space of the fire engine at the curb, taking an extra moment afterward to sit and draw strength from the dry warmth and unfamiliar musk of the clothes before emerging again to see the aftermath of the terrible little tragedy.

I found the body about where I expected to. The intensity of the spring runoff had created a vertical nest of branches and twigs up against the opening where the canal went under the street. The barrier had caught all kinds of things in its embrace, beer cans and scraps of tarpaulin, the plastic rings that hold six-packs together. And amid all of that, the soft flesh of a little boy.

'You need to get looked at,' Shigawa said now, by my side. 'Why don't you ride back in with us?'

'No,' I said. 'I'm all right.'

'There are infections you can get,' Shigawa said. 'You should see a doctor.'

'No,' I said flatly. I disliked sounding

24

argumentative, but I couldn't tell Shigawa the reason behind my refusal. Everyone's afraid of something, and in my case, it's going to the doctor.

'Actually,' a new voice intervened, 'we're going to need Detective Pribek for a statement. That'll be downtown.'

It was Roz. I didn't know her well, but felt very grateful to her just then. 'She's right,' I said to Shigawa. To Roz, I said, 'I have to drive my own car. It's around here somewhere, and that way you won't have to bring me back afterward.'

'That'll be okay,' Roz said. 'Lockhart, why don't you ride downtown with Detective Pribek?'

★   ★   ★

There'd really been no need for it, but I'd sensed that sending Lockhart with me had been Roz's casual way of laying a comforting hand on my shoulder after the morning's events. At the precinct, no one was available to take a statement right away, so Lockhart left me at an unoccupied desk to wait. There, lulled by the familiar sound of the dispatch radio and swaddled in a strange man's clothes, I rested my head on my folded arms and slept.

2

The three brothers were Croatian. They'd been in America about eight days, living with their parents in the crowded home of their assimilated aunt, uncle, and cousins, who'd been in Minneapolis over a year. The boys still weren't totally on Central Time, and they often woke when their father and uncle got up at four to go to their jobs at a snack-foods plant.

The brothers were also enamored of their cousins' bicycles, which they had just learned to ride. That morning, awake and adventurous as kids of that age often are, they went out for a ride after their father went to work, even though they'd been forbidden to take the bikes out without supervision.

It was the boy perched on the handlebars that had gone over the railing when his brother lost his balance and let the bike wobble. That same brother, the oldest, had jumped into the water after him. He'd survived the rescue attempt; it was the younger brother, small and thin, who'd been sucked down to die.

The parents had insisted on coming downtown the day after the accident to thank me. They were accompanied by their relatives, who spoke fractured but passable English; I was accompanied by our department spokeswoman, who seemed as uncomfortable as I was. It was an encounter that was linguistically awkward and terribly sad, and I wished they hadn't bothered.

I hadn't been back at my desk long when my lieutenant stopped by, on his way out.

'Detective Pribek,' he said. 'How are you.'

William Prewitt, in his mid-fifties, had a way of asking questions that often didn't sound like questions.

'Good, thanks,' I said. 'And you?'

'Fine,' he said briskly. 'I might have something for you to run down. A small thing.'

'Sure,' I said. 'What is it?'

'We've been hearing some rumors, just a few whispers, about someone practicing medicine without a license,' he told me.

'Sounds like a job for the State Board of Medicine to me,' I said.

'This isn't a simple licensure issue, like a doctor forgetting to send in the renewal paperwork,' Prewitt corrected me. 'We're not at all sure this guy is really a doctor. He's probably just passing himself off as one. He's also possibly operating out of a public housing building somewhere.'

'That's daring,' I said. 'Has this guy botched anything and dumped someone on the ER doorstep?'

'Not that I've heard,' Prewitt said. 'But we really don't know very much. It's just a subtle, persistent rumor. There may be nothing to it.'

There were two ways that statement could be interpreted. It could mean, *This case is probably a dead end, so I'm kicking it down to my youngest and least-experienced investigator, the one who's already under a cloud around the department.* Or he could be saying, *This is a tricky case with few leads, one that needs to be handled carefully. Show me your stuff, Pribek.*

'What do you want me to do?' I asked.

'Just ask around, check out the story with your informants,' Prewitt told me.

'Sure,' I said. 'I can do that.'

He left with a little tilt of his chin that said, *Carry on.*

I slid open my lowest desk drawer and found an envelope toward the back. Inside it was a motley assortment of pieces of paper, the names and phone numbers of my informants. Now I shuffled through them, thinking of where to start. Prewitt hadn't said anything to suggest the unlicensed doctor was urgent. Nor had he even sounded hopeful that I was going to find anything. For that very reason, I wanted to start working on this right away. I was going to find this guy, and faster than Prewitt expected, too. I was going to show him my stuff.

Someone cleared her throat before me. 'Sarah?'

It was Tyesha, one of our nonuniformed support staff, standing in front of my desk. She was five-two and still thin at 30 despite having three children. She greeted people at the front desk, answered the phone, and generally directed traffic.

'What's up?' I said.

'There's a young woman here who wants to talk about her brother being missing,' Tyesha said.

'Has she filed a report?' I asked.

'She says she has, but that it's a little more complicated than that,' Tyesha explained. 'She'd like to talk to someone about it.'

'Okay,' I said. 'Send her back.'

Tyesha returned a moment later with a woman even shorter than she, about five-one, with a fragile, slender build. She wore what I took for office clothes, a shimmering lavender silk shirt over black trousers and low-heeled black shoes. She had long blond hair, blue eyes, milk-white skin. 'This is Detective Sarah Pribek,' Tyesha said. 'Sarah, this is . . . ' She stopped, in the manner of someone who's either forgotten a name or how to pronounce it. 'I'm sorry,' she said to the visitor.

'Don't be,' the young woman said. 'It's Marlinchen.'

'Nice to meet you, Marlinchen,' I said. 'Please, have a seat.'

She did, and Tyesha left us together.

'Spell your name for me, will you?' I asked her.

The young woman reached for the yellow sticky pad on my desk and turned it around to face her. Taking a pen from her backpack, she wrote quickly, then pulled off the top sheet.

Marlinchen Hennessy, it said. She'd added her phone number underneath.

'Is this a Swedish name?' I asked.

''Marlinchen' is German,' she said. 'Technically, it's pronounced Mar-*leen*-chen, but everyone gives it an Americanized pronunciation: Mar-*lin*-chen.' It had the sound of a speech she'd given many times before. 'The last name, Hennessy, is Irish, of course. My brothers all have traditional

29

Celtic names. My twin brother's name is Aidan.'
Her voice dropped a little lower. 'He's the one
I'm here about.'

'Tell me about that,' I said. 'You said that you
filed a report already?'

Marlinchen Hennessy nodded. 'I reported
Aidan missing in Georgia. That's where he's
been living for the past five years. He — '

I held up a hand to stop her. 'Wait. He lives in
Georgia and that's where he's missing from, but
you want Hennepin County to look into it?'

She nodded quickly. 'Aidan's from here, and
has connections here. He could be headed back
this way, and I thought that might make it
pertinent to you, here in Hennepin County.'

I frowned. ' 'Headed back this way'? In other
words, you think he's traveling of his own
volition?'

'That's what they think down in Georgia,'
Marlinchen said.

'If that's true,' I said, 'then there's nothing to
investigate. Adults are free to move about
without checking in with relatives.'

'Aidan's not 18 yet,' she said quietly.

'But you said he's your twin,' I said.

'I'm 17,' she said.

I hoped my surprise didn't show on my face.
I'd taken her for 20, 21. 'Okay,' I said, thinking,
'this raises another issue entirely. What are your
parents doing about all this?'

'My mother is dead,' Marlinchen told me.

'I'm sorry,' I said. Then, just as she was about
to speak again, I asked, 'How long ago?'

'Ten years,' she said.

'I'm sorry,' I said, then realized I'd just said that a moment earlier.

Marlinchen Hennessy moved on. 'My father is Hugh Hennessy, the writer.' She looked for recognition in my face. 'He wrote *The Channel?*' she prompted.

'That sounds familiar,' I said, 'but we're getting off the point. Where is your father today?'

'Why do you ask?' she said.

'What I'm wondering is why he's sent his 17-year-old daughter to deal with the Sheriff's Department instead of coming himself,' I explained.

'He doesn't know about Aidan,' Marlinchen said quickly. 'He's up north, in a cabin he owns near Tait Lake. It's kind of remote, and it doesn't have a phone.'

Her eyes had an odd glitter to them. It looked like alarm, but I didn't understand its source.

'Dad goes there to write,' she said. 'When his work isn't going well, he needs lots of quiet and solitude. But he didn't start going up there until I was old enough to take care of my three younger brothers. He's very responsible.'

She'd veered off into a defense of her father's parenting methods, for no reason I could ascertain. I tried to bring her back on course.

'But there's someone who can go get him, right?' I said. 'A neighbor, a ranger, somebody like that? I'm just saying that this is something Aidan's father should know about.'

That remark didn't quite have the calming effect I'd planned.

'I don't understand why there's this emphasis

on my father!' Marlinchen said, her voice rising. 'He's not a policeman. *He's* not going to find Aidan. That's the job of the police, and they're not doing anything as far as I can tell!'

I tapped the end of a pencil against my desk. 'If this is the quality of cooperation you're giving the police in Georgia,' I said, 'it's hard for me to imagine what they *could* do for you.'

'I shouldn't have come,' Marlinchen said quickly, jumping to her feet.

'Wait,' I said placatingly, but she was already nearly running for the exit. Everyone working around me stopped to watch her flight.

'*Wait,*' I said more loudly, standing. But she was gone.

'She's fleeing the interview! She's fleeing the interview!' a deputy said, mimicking Frances McDormand's broad Minnesotan accent in *Fargo.* The other deputies laughed.

'Thanks,' I said. 'If you enjoyed the show, my monkey will be around shortly with a tin cup.'

★   ★   ★

With no way to follow up on that resounding success, I drove to South Minneapolis to talk to my first informant about Prewitt's medical-fraud case.

When Shiloh had gotten accepted to the FBI Academy and quit the MPD, he'd had a kind of fire sale, giving me some useful phone numbers, from his contacts with federal agencies to street-level informants. Like Lydia Neely, who he knew from his early career in Narcotics. Lydia had been arrested while driving over the county line with a lot of British Columbian marijuana in the trunk of her car. Several officers had been in on the bust, as is typical of Narcotics cases, but it was Shiloh who'd taken an interest in Lydia's situation. He was the one who'd found out that she had no priors and was muling for a boyfriend who subscribed to the theory that women are less likely to be stopped by drug agents. Had someone not informed on Lydia, the boyfriend would have been right.

Shiloh, with his typical concern for the unfortunate, had gone out of his way to intercede for Lydia and to keep her out of prison. She'd done some time in the workhouse, and checked in with a probation officer afterward. She'd also become Shiloh's informant, and when he left the MPD, I'd inherited her name and number.

I hadn't seen Lydia in some time, mostly because she wasn't the most useful informant anymore. She'd gotten a good job in a South Minneapolis salon, and the new and better boyfriend she'd found had recently become a husband. That sort of rehabilitation was the point of the intervention Shiloh had made, but it also meant that she didn't associate with criminals much anymore, and so she didn't get to hear interesting things. It's a truth the public doesn't want to hear: good citizens often don't make for good informants, and good informants are necessary to police work.

But I had to start somewhere in my search for Prewitt's unlicensed doctor, and Lydia still lived close to the ground.

Her job made it particularly convenient for me to stop by. For obvious reasons, I didn't identify myself as a cop when visiting informants. It was useful, for that reason, to be a female investigator visiting a women's salon; it raised no antennae among bystanders. More good fortune: she was working in a narrow back room of shampooing stations when I arrived, with no one close enough to overhear us.

'Hey, Detective Pribek,' Lydia said. Hard plastic clattered as she rinsed a set of curlers with a jet of water from the hose, her brown hands moving in the sink.

'Sarah,' I corrected her.

'You want a cup of coffee?' she asked me.

'No, thanks,' I said. Her courtesy made me uncomfortable, because I didn't feel I'd built any personal rapport with her; rather, I sensed she tolerated me because she'd liked Shiloh. 'I'm not going to take up too much of your time,' I went on. 'I just need to know if you've heard about something.'

When I explained my errand, something flickered in Lydia's eyes.

'You know who I'm talking about?' I prompted.

'Not by name,' Lydia said. 'You hear him whispered about, but that's all.'

'So what's his story?' I asked. 'Is he even a doctor, or is he an unemployed vet, or what?'

Lydia shook her head. 'Sorry, I don't know any of those things.' Then she added, 'I think Ghislaine knows him.'

34

'Oh,' I said. 'I didn't know you knew her.'

Ghislaine Morris had been another of Shiloh's informants. He had given me her number, too, but I hadn't had much opportunity to deal with her.

'She was my roommate,' Lydia said. 'Before the bust.' She meant her own arrest for transporting.

'All right,' I said. 'I'll talk to Ghislaine.'

Lydia slid a clear plastic bin of rollers into a cabinet above the line of shampoo bowls and closed the door. I moved into the doorway but didn't leave.

'How's married life?' I asked.

'Good,' Lydia said.

'You like it?' I added lamely. *She just said as much, stupid*, I told myself.

'Yeah,' she said.

'Well, I'll let you get back to work,' I said.

But she spoke as I turned away. 'Detective Pribek,' she said, hesitant.

I turned back.

'I noticed . . . I don't mean to pry, but I noticed that you don't wear your wedding ring anymore.'

'Oh,' I said. Self-consciously I touched my ring finger. 'I'm doing a detail on the street that doesn't allow me to wear a wedding band.' I didn't say the words *prostitution decoy*, but Lydia probably got the picture.

Maybe she sensed even more than that. 'Shiloh's okay, isn't he?' she said.

Had she read the papers? Did she know about Blue Earth? Her dark eyes gave me no clue.

35

'I'll tell him you asked about him,' I said, evading her question, 'the next time I see him.'

★   ★   ★

The next time I see him. I hadn't been back to Wisconsin since the visit I'd made shortly after Shiloh was sent there. We were separated by more than simple geographical distance. Blue Earth lay between us. My trip West to meet his family lay between us. Things that were too difficult to speak about. Even in the good times, Shiloh could be unnervingly quiet; for my part, I was never good at putting feelings into words. I suppose it was inevitable that in hard times we'd fallen back on old ways. We'd fallen silent.

3

A small storm moved across Hennepin County that night, toward Wisconsin. I slept through the thunder, yet woke abruptly before daylight. A brief moment of disorientation — *Where's Shiloh?* — and then things came together in my mind, and I realized that the telephone was ringing.

'Hello,' I said, my voice rusty with sleep.

'It's me.'

'What the hell, Gen?' My voice had become stronger, but also more irritable. 'It's five — '

'I know what time it is in Minneapolis. This is important.'

The note of dismay in her voice brought me from awake to alert. 'What is it?' I asked.

'You know this is the last thing I wanted to have happen — '

'Just tell me.'

'I think they're investigating you for Royce Stewart's murder,' Genevieve said.

Relief warmed me. 'Oh, that,' I said. 'I've known that for a while, but don't worry; I think it's dead in the water. Nobody from Blue Earth's been up here since they interviewed me six months ago.'

'Six *months?*' Gen's voice, very clear despite the fact that she was halfway around the world, carried a distinct note of disbelief. 'You've known about this for six months and you never told me?'

'Don't be mad, but I knew before you even left for France,' I said. 'I was tipped, but I didn't tell you, because I knew you'd react just this way. Overreact, I mean.'

'Who tipped you?' Curiosity briefly diluted her alarm.

'Christian Kilander,' I said. 'You know him; he hears everything.'

'Has he told you anything lately?' she said.

'What do you mean, 'lately'?'

'A man came to Doug and Deb's house asking questions. He was there yesterday, Deb said.'

'Yesterday?' I sat up in bed, sheets sliding away.

Deborah and Doug Lowe were Gen's sister and brother-in-law. Gen had lived with them at their farmhouse in Mankato after her daughter's death, and it was to their place that we'd returned, late at night, after Stewart's death. Naturally, they'd be of interest to an investigator.

'I asked Deb his name, but she couldn't remember.' She listened for a response. 'Are you there?'

'I'm here,' I said. 'Look, everything will be fine. They can't put Stewart's death on me. I didn't kill him.'

'That's faulty logic and you know it,' she said.

'Let me handle it,' I said. 'Promise me you won't worry.'

'I can't promise that. This is — '

'Gen,' I said, 'I'm really not going to discuss this anymore.'

The silence on the other end of the line suggested something repressed, a sigh or a sharp

38

word. Finally she yielded. 'You sound hoarse,' she said. 'You're not getting a cold, are you?'

'I'm never sick,' I told her. 'I'm probably hoarse because I just woke — oh, wait.'

I was thinking back to a day ago, the time I'd spent shivering in the cool early-morning air, soaking wet.

'What?' Gen prompted.

I explained to her about the boys and drainage canal.

When I was finished, she chided me. 'What is it with you? You're like a dog. Always this headfirst impulse to rescue people.'

I smiled, because she sounded like the older sister and teacher she'd been in the days of our partnership. I, too, fell into my role. 'Not true,' I said. 'I went in feetfirst.'

'Go back to sleep,' Genevieve said gently. 'Call me sometime when you've got a day off.'

'I will,' I said.

★ ★ ★

That evening I made a very convincing streetwalker, wan and surly. My throat felt raw and wet, and I knew Gen's words, *You're not getting a cold, are you?* were true. But my sullenness seemed to have an aphrodisiac effect on the men on the street. I would have beaten my record for busts in one night if I hadn't taken a half-hour break for a prearranged meeting with Ghislaine Morris.

On the way there, I tried to recall what it was that Shiloh had said about her. I did remember that he'd hesitated before handing off Ghislaine's number.

'I don't really talk to her much anymore,' Shiloh had said, sorting through the cardboard box of his things, long legs kicked up on the coffee table.

'Why not?' I said. 'Is she not useful?'

'No, Gish is a sponge,' Shiloh said. 'She hears everything.'

'So what's the story?' I'd said.

He'd shrugged. 'No story. Something about her just bothers me. I don't know what, exactly.'

I'd pressed him to elaborate, but he wouldn't, and when Shiloh doesn't want to talk about something, it's over.

So I'd met with Ghislaine personally, a month or two later — I don't know what I expected, but it wasn't who'd showed up.

Ghislaine Morris was 22, not thin, but not fat either. She had a sweet, open face and full hips. Her blond hair was cropped in a short, boyish style, and her brown eyes were friendly. She was pushing a stroller, with a then six-month-old baby in it. He had curly brown hair and cinnamon skin and huge eyes that took in the world like documentary cameras.

Over an inexpensive meal, Ghislaine told me about her life, about Shadrick's father, who was 'no longer in our lives,' and about her parents in Dearborn, Michigan, who'd kicked her out of the house when they'd found out she was pregnant with a child whose father was black, so that Ghislaine had to come to Minnesota to stay with a friend. She had a shoplifting bust on her

40

record, but had gotten probation. She told me she wanted to go back to school as soon as she could.

It was a meeting that I'd left rather confused. I had no earthly idea what it was that Shiloh saw in her that he didn't like. Shiloh was a preacher's son; if he had a flaw, it was his judgmental streak. Maybe he couldn't overcome a Puritan's disapproval of single motherhood at such a young age. For my part, I'd found her chatter infectious and her devotion to her son palpable. If her ambitions to go back to school and 'make something' of herself were somewhat generic, who was I to judge?

Tonight, she was late to our meeting at an unassuming little diner. I ordered a mug of herbal tea and sucked on a eucalyptus cough drop. My throat had started to stiffen up when I swallowed.

'Holy shit,' Ghislaine said when she arrived, pushing Shadrick in his stroller. 'I didn't even recognize you.'

She settled into the booth across from me, her eyes widening guilelessly. 'So this is what you look like when you're undercover?' I'd already warned her on the phone about my vice-detail look.

'*Undercover*'s a strong word,' I said. 'This is just soliciting busts. It's not a complicated sting operation.'

'Wow,' she said, and opened the menu.

The waitress, approaching on crepe-soled shoes, set a mug of tea down in front of me. 'You ready, sugar?' she asked Ghislaine.

41

'I'd like a cheeseburger with curly fries, and a strawberry milk shake,' Ghislaine said, folding up the menu and handing it to the waitress.

'We've got booster seats, if you want one for him,' the waitress told Ghislaine.

'No, that's okay,' Ghislaine said.

'He's a handsome little guy.'

'He sure is,' Ghislaine agreed.

As if he knew he was being discussed, Shad squealed, a surprisingly loud sound. Ghislaine leaned out of the booth and put her hands on the sides of his face, on his cheeks. 'That's *right*, you've got a fan club, don't you!' she said cheerfully.

The waitress disappeared into the kitchen. I cleared my throat, and Ghislaine straightened up. 'So what's up?' she asked, turning to business.

'Like I told you on the phone,' I said, 'I need some information.'

'Really?' Ghislaine said. 'How much?' She was asking how much it was worth.

'Let's wait and see if you know anything,' I said. 'We've been hearing some things about a guy who's practicing medicine without a license,' I said. 'Out of a private residence, maybe in one of the projects.'

Ghislaine's expression turned sour. 'Oh, him,' she said. 'Cisco.'

Jackpot. That was fairly easy, I thought. I'd only had to ask two informants.

'Cisco who?' I said.

'I don't remember his last name,' Ghislaine said.

'You've seen him?' I asked her.

The waitress reappeared at our side, setting down the burger and fries, then a long tulip-shaped glass of strawberry milk shake and the extra in the silver tumbler. A curly fry fell from the plate.

'Anything else?' she said.

'No,' I said for both of us. The waitress moved off.

'You've been to see this guy?' I asked Ghislaine. 'In a professional capacity?'

Ghislaine picked up the fallen french fry and leaned out of the booth, handing it down to Shadrick.

'By *professional*, you mean *medical*?' she said. 'Yeah, I did. I had this thing that wouldn't go away. In my lungs, like bronchitis.'

I was curious. 'Why not just go see a doctor?'

Ghislaine shrugged. 'I heard he was good,' she said.

I heard he was good. That was something people said about someone they were looking at for an elective surgery, not someone working for cash under the table. But I let it slide. 'Did he help with your bronchitis?'

'I don't know,' Ghislaine said. 'It went away. But I wouldn't go back and see him again.'

'Why? Did he seem incompetent?'

She shook her head.

'Was his behavior toward you inappropriate?'

She shrugged unhelpfully. 'I don't know, I just didn't like him.'

'Why not?' I asked.

'I just didn't. Are you going to bust him?'

Ghislaine applied her rosebud mouth to her straw.

'If this guy's doing what people say he's been doing, then yes, we will,' I said. 'Where does he live?'

'You know where the towers are, right?' She named a main thoroughfare in South Minneapolis, referring to a pair of public housing buildings that stood there.

'Sure, I know them,' I said. 'What's the apartment number?'

'I forget,' Ghislaine said. 'But he lives on the very top floor. You just get off the elevator and it's the second door down on that side of the hall.'

'Top floor of which building?'

'The one closest to the street,' she said.

'You're sure?'

She nodded.

'Don't I need to call first?'

Ghislaine shook her head, drank a little more of her milk shake. 'He's drop-in, all hours,' she said. 'This guy's an agoraphobic or something, never goes out.'

'Thanks,' I said. I laid several bills on the table. 'That should cover the tab, and the help.'

4

Lust may never sleep, but Sunday night is a slow night in the sex trade, too slow to waste a detective on a prostitution-decoy sting. It left me free to pursue 'Cisco.' I even had an excuse to see him: my cold was in full bloom. I was coughing incessantly, congested and sniffling.

Now my problem was this: Cisco might take one look at me and see, if not an undercover cop, a middle-class individual who didn't need to seek doctoring in a housing project late at night. His clientele probably ran to people with little money and few options in medical care — the poor and disenfranchised, illegal immigrants, maybe criminals.

Maybe hookers, too.

That's how I ended up, on a Sunday night, wriggling into my vice-decoy clothes: this time, a shiny, sleeveless pink top and tight calf-length black pants. After applying the usual makeup, I looked at the mirror, at my artificially pale face, and felt a chill of anxiety down my spine.

A SWAT veteran had lectured my Sheriff's academy class about on-the-job nerves. *When you feel fear, try to determine its source,* he'd said. *Sometimes it's not coming from where you think it is, and sometimes if you know what the fear is really about, you can defuse it.*

Was I afraid of Cisco because he was, supposedly, a doctor?

My medical phobia was a specific one. I wasn't afraid of paramedics, and I gave blood when the blood bank set up shop downtown, in a reassuring nonmedical setting. But I hated *going to the doctor:* that powerlessness as you waited behind the closed door, with the overhead light bouncing off the instruments and the creepy anatomical posters hanging on the wall. Down to the second, I could identify the worst part: the moment when you heard the door handle start to turn.

But Cisco's as-yet-unseen apartment wasn't that place. According to Prewitt, Cisco probably wasn't even a real doctor. To us, he was a suspect.

Was *that* in itself frightening? This was undercover work, which is always potentially dangerous.

I nodded, as if someone were here to share my revelation. I'd located the source of my nerves: I was afraid of the unknown Cisco, of being alone with him in his apartment. Maybe I should ask for some kind of backup.

All Prewitt asked you to do was check this guy out, I reminded myself. *You don't even have to identify yourself. You're just going to go over there and see what's what. You want help for that?*

What I was doing needed to be done. Whoever Cisco was — a med-school washout or a con artist faking it from having worked in a medical office — he was clearly fooling enough people to have a small clientele, which meant he was bleeding money off the poor and uneducated

46

just when they were at their most vulnerable. If he hadn't screwed up badly enough to cause permanent injury or death yet, well, it was probably just a matter of time. This guy needed to be taken off the playing field, and Prewitt had trusted me to get the job started. I couldn't go back to my lieutenant now and tell him I wanted backup to go see a suspect armed only with a stethoscope.

★   ★   ★

The elevator in the north tower took a long time to come. There were no lighted numbers above the doors to mark its progress downward, and I whistled quietly as I waited. Such behaviors were Method acting for cops, keeping the nerves at bay.

A faint *ping* sounded, but for a moment nothing happened. A long moment. Then the single-panel door slid to the side. I stepped into the car and pressed number 26, for the top floor. After a moment the door slid shut, and again, nothing happened.

I pressed the 26 again. The car lurched upward. From above me, the other side of the elevator's roof, came an odd groaning sound I'd never heard an elevator make, and underneath that sound, a squeak of cables working: *screek, screek, screek*. Inside the car, there were lighted numbers to allow passengers to watch their progress. For an inordinately long time the 2 stayed lit. Then 3. More rumbling from above; 4 . . . 5 . . . 6 . . .

If I'd known it was going to take this long, I'd have brought something to read, I thought. The mental complaint was bravado. I rode elevators all the time at work, but this one was bothering me.

At 26, the car lurched to a halt. But for a moment, nothing happened. The door stayed closed.

'Come on,' I said under my breath. The elevator's balky performance seemed like a bad omen for my whole visit here.

The door slid open and I stepped out into the hallway, walked down to the second door, and knocked.

What if Ghislaine misremembered which apartment this guy lives in? I thought, in the wait that followed.

The door opened about two inches, just to the end of a security chain. A slice of masculine face appeared in the gap, but about two feet lower than where I expected it. When I understood why, I found myself momentarily at a loss for words.

'Can I help you?' the man said, finally.

'Are you' — I coughed to clear phlegm from my throat — 'Cisco? Ghislaine Morris gave me your name. I need to get looked at.'

Cisco closed the door in my face. Behind the wall the chain scraped, and the door swung wide. As he let me in, Cisco rolled backward in his wheelchair to give me space.

Height was hard to gauge, but he was a long, lean form in the chair, dressed in a dark-gray sweatshirt that revealed a little bit of white from

48

the collar of the T-shirt he wore underneath. The same white T-shirt peeked out from under the sweatshirt at his hips, over his dark-blue workman's trousers. His feet were bare. He had a lean face, with black hair that brushed his shoulders, feathery at the ends.

He certainly wasn't hiding what he did. Beyond him, I saw low shelves lined with texts on medicine and anatomy. On the wall was a framed diploma, and where most people would have put the couch stood a long table lined with a sheet of tissue paper. It looked almost like a doctor's examining table, except that it was lower, reflecting the level from which Cisco had to approach the world. The table was positioned just under a hanging light fixture. At the foot of the table was a chest, like a footlocker, and a little beyond that was a two-drawer filing cabinet.

'What's troubling you?' Cisco said.

'I have a bad cold,' I said, 'or the flu.'

'Mmm,' Cisco said noncommittally.

'How much do you charge?' I asked him.

'Let's not get to that just yet,' Cisco said. 'Most colds run their course within a week,' he said, 'even without any kind of treatment. I'm not sure why you're seeking help.'

Maybe this guy had the most sensitively tuned radar for cops I'd ever run across. Still, it was hard to be scared of him, given the situation. Unless he had a gun tucked under that fringe of T-shirt.

I sniffled again. 'I'm never sick. That's why this is tripping me out. I want to be sure nothing's behind it.'

49

'Did your friend Ghislaine suggest I could prescribe something for you, something stronger than over-the-counter meds?' Cisco asked.

'No,' I said honestly.

'Because I can't,' Cisco went on. 'I expect Ghislaine didn't pass along what I told her when she came to see me, so I'm going to tell you what I tell everyone. I don't know what brought you to me in a city full of doctors' offices; I don't ask people that,' Cisco continued. 'But this is not the ideal situation in which to get your medical care. If you have another option, you should seriously think about taking it.'

If he thinks that little speech is a disclaimer that'll protect him from criminal charges, he's got another thing coming.

'Understood. How much do you charge?' I said flatly.

'To look at you?' he said. 'Forty.'

That's all? I thought. It surprised me that he'd put himself at risk by doing something this illegal, and then charge relatively little for it. On the other hand, his clientele probably didn't have much money to spare.

'Do you want me to look at you?' he asked.

'I didn't come this far to just go away,' I told him, thinking of Prewitt.

'All right,' Cisco said. 'I take the money up front. Why don't you set it on my bookshelf over there, then take your shirt off and get on my exam table. I'll be with you in a minute.' He rolled backward, turning the wheelchair toward his kitchen.

The money first. Cisco might be reasonably

50

priced, but he certainly wasn't naive. I laid two twenties on the top of the bookshelf as I'd been directed. Water ran in Cisco's kitchen. He was at the sink, his back turned to me.

It was the first moment I'd had to regain my mental footing. The fact that he was a paraplegic had thrown me, but only momentarily. It was his behavior that I continued to find unusual. Normally, criminals, particularly con artists, are hyperalert when meeting strangers. They hide it well, but you can sense it, a kind of power-line hum that radiates off them. But Cisco didn't seem so much alert as aware. He wasn't nervous, and he wasn't drunk or on anything, either. He was simply *relaxed*, and that was the thing that didn't add up.

I turned to study the living room. Virtually nowhere were any personal touches. I drifted over to look at the framed diploma on the wall.

C. Agustin Ruiz, the name read. Above it, in larger letters, were the words *Columbia University, College of Physicians and Surgeons*.

'Holy shit,' I said, unable to censor myself in time. The heavy paper clearly marked the certificate as nothing you could make with a home-computer word-processing program. This guy was bona fide.

'Something wrong?' Cisco said.

'That's a good school, isn't it?' I asked.

He turned to see me looking at his diploma. 'Most people would say so,' he said. 'Didn't I tell you to take off your shirt?'

I pulled my shiny pink sleeveless top over my head and sat down on the table, feeling

51

self-conscious in a black half-cup bra. With my hands at my sides, resting on the edge of the exam table, I noticed something about the material underneath. It was cloth-covered, rounded, and cream-colored.

'Is this a *massage table*?' I asked Cisco, who'd come near to take a few objects from his footlocker.

'You must have made a wrong turn on the way to Cedars-Sinai,' he said dryly.

Some bedside manner, I thought. But he was right.

Cisco rolled to the side of the exam table and turned on the overhead light with an in-line switch in the cord. A stethoscope was draped around his neck, a blood pressure cuff in his lap. He held a yellow legal pad on his lap.

'Are you going to take notes?' I asked.

'All doctors do,' Cisco said. 'What's your name?'

I tensed. Cisco noticed it. 'We can do this AA style, if you like,' he said. 'First name and last initial.'

'Sarah P.,' I said.

'What do you do for a living?' he asked.

I gave him a dry stare ringed heavily with black eyeliner.

Cisco licked his teeth speculatively. 'Right,' he said. 'Are you taking any medications currently?'

'No,' I said.

'Do you use?'

'Use what?' I knew what he meant, but felt like giving him a hard time, like Sarah P. the hooker would have.

'Drugs.'

'No,' I said.

'Date of your last menstrual period?'

'I don't remember,' I said, 'but I'm regular.'

'Any chance you could be pregnant now?'

'If I were, could you fix it for me?' I asked.

'We're going in circles. Do you think you might be pregnant?'

I shook my head. When he didn't move on, I said, 'No. I'm sure.'

'Okay,' Cisco said. 'Let's get started.'

He laid the cool surface of the stethoscope against my sternum. He nodded. 'Breathe deeply for me,' he said. I did, closing my eyes. 'Again.'

A shredding sound made me open my eyes. Cisco was unwrapping the blood-pressure cuff.

'You've got all the equipment,' I said.

'Not nearly what I'd like to have,' he said.

Obediently I held out my arm, and he pumped air into the cuff, then let it hiss out, watching his stethoscope.

'Hundred and four over seventy,' Cisco noted. 'Nice.'

He'd surprised me. On my rare visits to doctors, I'd always had high readings. White-coat hypertension, they called it, blood pressure that was only high in medical settings.

But Cisco's place was different. He acted like a doctor, and this was an exam, yet I was clearly in someone's home. There was a faint scent of cooking in the air, instead of that disturbing antiseptic smell of a doctor's office.

He took my temperature, read the thermometer in silence, and shook it out. He looked in

53

each ear with an otoscope, felt the glands at the side of my neck.

'When did you first notice the symptoms?' he asked.

'Two days ago.'

'Any reason to think you might be immuno-suppressed?'

'No,' I said.

'Are you prone to ear infections?'

'No.'

'Are either of your ears bothering you?'

'No,' I said again.

Cisco rolled backward slightly. 'You can put your shirt back on,' he said, giving the shiny pink thing the honor of being called a shirt, something I wouldn't have done. I pulled the top over my head, straightened my hair with my fingers.

'Here's the deal,' he said. 'You seem to be a person in good health, with a bad cold. It's not the end of the world. Get plenty of fluids and rest, take some vitamin C, and treat the symptoms with some over-the-counter remedies.'

'All right.'

'There is one other thing.' Cisco's tone had changed, sharpening my attention. 'I'm not real happy with the way your left ear looks. We usually see infections in children, not adults, and you say it's not bothering you, so I'm not going to worry about it too much. But if it starts to hurt you, go to a clinic. You may need antibiotics, and I can't prescribe for you.'

'Okay,' I said.

He rolled back a few paces and retrieved

something else from his chest. A red leaflet, which he came back to hand to me. It was an informational pamphlet from a walk-in sexual health clinic.

'I'm not making judgments here,' Cisco said. 'But if you're trading sex for money or drugs, then you need to get tested for HIV and other diseases. And if you test negative for everything, you need to talk to someone about how you can stay negative.'

The skin on my face felt warm and sensitized, the way it sometimes does when someone is kind to me for no good reason. I took the flyer.

'By the way, in answer to your earlier question,' he said, 'I don't do abortions.'

'Did that offend you?' I asked.

'No,' Cisco said. He did not elaborate.

I was free to go, but now that the hard part was over, my curiosity was rising. I said, 'So, you went to medical school and everything?'

'Yes,' he said. He was putting away his instruments in the chest.

'But you don't have a license?'

'I used to,' he said.

'What happened?'

'That's a longer story than we probably have time for,' Cisco said, his tone measured. He was at his filing cabinet now, tearing the top sheet of paper off his legal pad, finding a place for it in the top drawer.

Dear God, the man kept *files*. When I made my report to Prewitt and we got a warrant, an extensive search wasn't going to be necessary. Cisco was carefully documenting and organizing everything we needed to hang him.

Cisco rolled forward to collect the two twenties from the bookcase. When he didn't take it anywhere, I understood that he didn't want to put the money away while I was in his apartment, so I wouldn't see where his stash was. He was careful.

'You know,' I said, 'forty dollars doesn't seem like a lot of money.'

'I don't plan to get rich doing this.'

'Then why do it at all?' I asked.

'I fill a need,' Cisco said. 'Believe it or not, people do fall through the cracks of the health-care system. Some don't have insurance. Some are illegal immigrants. They're intimidated by ERs, the crowds and the waits and tension there. I provide a service.'

'And, of course, they pay you,' I pointed out, playing devil's advocate.

'I'm part of what the World Bank calls the informal economy,' Cisco said. 'It's accepted practice in many countries.'

'But you said you don't have the equipment you'd like,' I pointed out.

'You'd be surprised what's available from medical-supply houses,' he said. 'No drugs, of course. But I've been able to get much of what I need for my practice here, which is mostly minor injuries, burns, things like that. I'm also able to give reassurance to people with small problems, like yours. And when people have more serious problems, I'm an early-warning system. When people come to me with symptoms that trouble me, or conditions that are beyond my capacity to treat, I tell them in no uncertain terms to get to

56

a clinic or hospital.'

'About how many patients do you find yourself sending away to a real doctor?' I said.

The warmth died away from Cisco's dark eyes. 'I am a real doctor,' he said.

'I didn't mean — ' I said.

But it was too late; I'd said the wrong thing. 'I think we're finished here,' Cisco said, rolling backward to put a little more space between us. 'Good night, Sarah.'

⋆　⋆　⋆

Shiloh and I rented the first floor of an older two-story house. It afforded more privacy than you'd expect, because behind it, on the other side of a barbed-wire fence, was an open field and then the railroad tracks on their raised man-made berm. I pulled into the narrow driveway alongside the house and went in through the back door. The outer screen door gave way grudgingly, creaking. It was stiff, in need of maintenance I hadn't yet given it.

The place had been Shiloh's before it had been mine, and it was still largely his personality that was imprinted throughout the gently shabby interior. Probably a number of women would have made their own mark by now, but I wasn't one of them. I'd always felt a certain peace among Shiloh's eclectic paperback books and weathered furniture.

I flicked the kitchen light on and set my shoulder bag on the cluttered kitchen table, pushing aside a stack of unread mail and the legal pad on which I'd been trying to compose a letter to Shiloh. I was much more physically tired than the evening's work accounted for, but I understood why. The visit to Cisco's had been wearying. Genevieve, a veteran interrogator, had taught me that lying is hard on the body: it speeds the heart and demands more oxygen for the bloodstream.

I went into the bathroom, reached for the faucet handle in the bathtub, and turned on the hot water. Then, on impulse, I put the stopper in the drain rather than starting a shower. Sitting on the edge of the tub, I watched the water begin to pool.

The last piece of advice my mother ever gave me was not to take baths in motel rooms, because you never know who's been using the bathtubs or how well they've been cleaned. Strange advice, but we were in a motel at the time.

It was ovarian cancer that had claimed my mother: swift, silent, deceptively painless in its early stages. After treatments at our local hospital in rural New Mexico were unsuccessful, my mother had sought treatment at a research university in Texas. My father had approved of the idea. *They'll fix you up*, he'd said glibly, in denial to the end. He did not come along, but sent me to accompany her.

When my mother went in for her exploratory surgery, I waited in the oncologist's office, drinking a Dr Pepper and looking through the glossy four-color books Dr. Schwartz kept out for visitors and their families. At nine, I didn't read as well as I should have, but if the book had a lot of pictures, I would have my nose buried in it, looking studious and rapt to the world outside. That's what I was doing when Dr. Schwartz returned a half hour later.

Still in his surgical scrubs, he walked past me into his inner office, picked up the phone on his desk, and dialed. At nine, I had the preternaturally good hearing that many children do, and both ends of the conversation were audible to me.

'Sandeep, it's me,' he said. 'If you want to move your schedule up a little bit, you can. I'm already done with the exploratory I had at eleven-thirty.'

'*That was quick.*'

'Unfortunately, yes,' my mother's doctor said. 'Totally metastasized. When I saw how far it had gone, I just closed up. We were out of there way ahead of schedule.'

Dr. Schwartz made another phone call immediately after that one, and this time, I immediately recognized the voice on the other end.

'I think it's time you drove out here,' Dr. Schwartz said, lighting a cigarette. 'I'd like to talk to you in person.'

'*You can talk to me now, Doctor,*' my father said. '*Is my wife not in shape to travel by herself?*'

'Actually, you should be prepared to stay here awhile,' Dr. Schwartz said.

A long pause. '*You're not telling me Rose's case is terminal, are you?*'

Dr. Schwartz looked up to see me looking at him. He took the phone away from his face. 'Sarah, sweetie,' he said, 'why don't you run down the hall and get yourself something to drink?'

'I still have half of the Dr Pepper you bought me,' I said, pointing.

'Then can you get me a diet something? Coke or Sprite, doesn't matter.'

In the hall, I'd asked a tall black orderly what *terminal* meant. He'd said, 'I dunno, kid.' I'd been young enough to believe him.

A gurgling noise interrupted my thoughts. The water in the tub had reached the drainplate. I shut it off and hunted under the sink for a jar of bath salts, poured a generous amount into the steaming water, and got in. As I did, I thought for no reason of Marlinchen Hennessy, my visitor of four days ago.

The association seemed to come from nowhere, but it couldn't have. Did the bath salts — cleanly herbal instead of cloyingly floral — bring up a scent she'd been wearing? No, that wasn't it.

Marlinchen had told me about her mother's premature death; I had just been remembering my mother. There was the link. She'd said her mother had died ten years ago, which would have made her seven at the time.

I had mishandled Marlinchen Hennessy. Some of that was undoubtedly due to the way she'd looked. My first impression of Marlinchen Hennessy had been of a young woman of perhaps 21, and even after she'd told me she was

17, I hadn't really internalized it. I'd spoken to her as bluntly as I would have to an adult, forgetting that even adults are sometimes shaken up by a cop's natural directness.

Certainly, Marlinchen hadn't helped her own case with her evasions and defensiveness. But I'd been a cop long enough to know that sometimes people need help the most when they appear to deserve it the least. Ultimately, Marlinchen had made it clear that the burden of finding her brother had fallen on her, and had reached out to me for help, and I'd run her off.

Perhaps there was something I could do to remedy that. If nothing else, Hennepin County didn't pay me to look the other way when one of its citizens behaved strangely, rushing away rather than answering seemingly harmless questions.

5

The deputy in Georgia who'd taken the missing-persons report on Aidan had a slight smoker's rasp riding over his thick, interrogative accent. 'You have some information about Aidan Hennessy for me?' he asked.

'No,' I told Deputy Fredericks. 'I was hoping it was the other way around. I hardly know anything.'

I hadn't contacted Marlinchen Hennessy yet, deciding to get a little background information first, just to get my footing. Which was why I was squeezing this phone call in before my regular duties at work.

'Hennessy's from your area,' Fredericks said. 'That's why you're calling?'

'Yeah,' I said. 'Let me tell you about it.' I ran quickly through the scant information Marlinchen Hennessy shared with me, finishing by saying, 'When I said I was going to have to talk to her father, she became distraught and left.'

'If she could have hung up on you, she probably would have,' Fredericks said, laughter in his voice. 'That's what she did to me.'

'There's more to the story?' I said.

'Some,' he said. 'I didn't know the kid, Aidan, but I know the guy he was living with. Pete Benjamin. His family's been here forever. I guess Aidan had been living with him for five years. Anyway, he's obviously a runaway.'

62

'How do you figure that?' I asked him.

'His things were gone,' Fredericks said. 'And he was a good-size boy, about six feet. Worked on the farm. I don't think anyone would mark him as someone to mess with.'

'When did Benjamin report the kid missing?' I asked.

'He didn't,' Fredericks said. 'I didn't find out about this until just recently, when Miss Hennessy called me. Nearly the first thing I asked Pete was why he hadn't come to talk to someone about this. He said he'd called the father, Hugh, right away. Hugh Hennessy said that the kid would probably show up at home in Minneapolis, and Pete shouldn't worry about it.'

'That's pretty casual,' I remarked.

'Well, I guess the boy had done it before. Got a Greyhound all the way back to Minnesota, trying to go home.'

'Well, if Aidan got on a bus this time around, or even hitchhiked, he'd be here by now,' I said.

'Is that a joke?' Fredericks asked me.

'What do you mean?'

'Aidan Hennessy ran away six months ago.'

'Six *months*?' I echoed.

'I guess Miss Hennessy didn't tell you that,' Fredericks said.

'You're saying Hugh Hennessy never filed a report or called you guys?' I said, wanting to be sure about it.

'Yeah. Our first contact from the Hennessys came from the daughter, two weeks ago. And when I asked to talk with the father, I got the same song and dance that you did: he's up north, he can't be reached. I told Miss Hennessy to get on that, contacting him.

'Then, a few days later, I get another call from Miss Hennessy, wanting to know what progress has been made. I turn it around, ask *her* what progress has been made on getting her father to call me. She gets upset and hangs up on me.'

'And that's everything, to date?' I asked.

'Well, I filed a report, and I sent his picture out, but I've heard nothing. I've got to tell you, for a teenage runaway, he's keeping a real low profile. If he were arrested, even if he were using a false name, the fingerprint card would pretty much tell us it was him.'

'You have fingerprints on him?' I said, frowning. 'Was he arrested down there?'

'Nothing like that. Miss Hennessy didn't tell you about her brother's hand?'

'No,' I said.

'Her brother is missing a finger on his left hand. The card would have only nine prints on it.'

'I didn't know that,' I said. 'But then, our conversation wasn't exactly a long-ranging one.'

'She's a funny one, isn't she?' Fredericks said. 'I guess she started looking for a detective up in the Cities to listen to her story, and you got elected. Did you explain to her about jurisdictional lines?'

'Yeah,' I said. 'But you know what's interesting to me in all this?'

'The father?' Fredericks said.

'Yeah,' I said. 'He knew his son was missing and told his friend he'd take care of it, but then he never did anything. And then the daughter, Marlinchen, is willing to nag us about finding her brother, but she won't bother her old man up at his cabin. And when I pressed her about it, it upset her to the point that she walked out on me.'

'It is odd,' Fredericks said. 'If you find out anything up there I should know about, give me a call.'

'I will,' I told him.

★ ★ ★

The deputy I reached at a sheriff's substation in Cook County, near Tait Lake, identified himself as Begans. He sounded quite young.

'So what can we help you with?' Begans asked.

'I'm trying to get in touch with a man who's got a cabin up there,' I said. 'I'm told there's no phone, and he's holed up writing a book.'

'Nice work if you can get it,' Begans said. 'What's the name?'

'Hugh Hennessy,' I said. 'I need to talk to him about a missing-persons case. Don't scare him, just ask him to get in touch at his earliest convenience.'

'His . . . earliest . . . convenience,' Begans said slowly, obviously writing it down. 'Okay, whereabouts is the cabin?'

'I don't know,' I admitted.

'Well, *that's* going to slow things down,' Begans said, sounding bemused.

'I know, I'm sorry,' I said. 'I don't have a lot of information.'

'You know, we've got a guy here who's three weeks from retirement,' Begans said. 'He knows everything about this area, after thirty-five years here. Let me ask him about Hennessy.'

'That'd be great,' I said.

After we'd signed off, I went into the kitchen to make tea. The cold symptoms were abating, just as Cisco had suggested they would. In another day, I thought, I'd probably feel good enough to crave coffee again. The prospect made me feel better.

I was leaning against the counter in the break room, waiting for the microwave to finish nuking the water for my tea, when a quiet voice in my mind said, apropos of nothing, *Isn't it possible that you're sending that nice kid Begans on a wild-goose chase for nothing? Isn't there a big assumption here you haven't checked yet?*

What if Hugh Hennessy were in Minneapolis and simply refusing to become involved in his oldest son's situation?

With the lemon tea steeping on my desk, I dug Marlinchen Hennessy's phone number out of my desk and dialed it.

'Hello?' A boy's voice, adolescent.

'Is Hugh Hennessy there?' I asked.

'No, I'm sorry,' the boy said.

'Is he going to be in later tonight?'

'No, he's out of town.' He did not offer to take a message. 'This is Liam, can I help you with something?' he asked.

'No, I don't think so,' I said. 'I think I'd better call back later.'

66

The story that Hugh Hennessy was out of town was cohering. So far.

★ ★ ★

While I'd been on the phone with Fredericks, or perhaps Begans, two young men were knocking over a liquor store in Eden Prairie. I caught the call and drove down there to talk to the clerk and the sole customer who'd witnessed the holdup. The details were sketchy: the two guys were probably white, wearing nylon stockings that flattened and obfuscated facial features. I took notes, left my card, and asked the witnesses to call me if they remembered anything else.

As I drove back to the city, the sun was playing hide-and-seek with us behind galleons of cloud, deep gray on the bottom, white at the edges. I was nearly at the parking ramp the detectives used, when a red light stopped me. Just then, two men emerged from the overhang of the Government Center. Normally, I would have ignored them: two men in suits, a common sight downtown. But one of them was familiar to me. At six-five, he stood out in a crowd, and his gait was distinct: long and confident strides, but not hurried ones, as if to say, *I'm going to rule the world, but all in good time.*

I knew Christian Kilander both as a county prosecutor and a regular player in pickup basketball games. We'd always been friendly but never close, and he'd surprised me when he'd broken ranks with the system we both served to warn me that I was the primary suspect in the

Royce Stewart investigation. Immediately after Gen's warning phone call, I'd wanted to seek him out, ask if he'd heard anything. I hadn't done so because the last thing I needed was for anyone, even Kilander, to know that I was concerned about the Royce Stewart case.

Maybe I wasn't being honest with myself, either. I hadn't sought Kilander's help for another, simpler reason. Since our meeting beside the fountain last December, we hadn't spoken, except briefly as part of an investigation. When we crossed paths downtown, he only nodded where he would have greeted me before, and I had the uncomfortable feeling that he was avoiding a tainted colleague in the same way that a fastidious man would avoid a mud puddle on the sidewalk.

Now Kilander's companion turned slightly, looking west, and I realized I'd seen him before. He was six feet, with brown hair graying at the temples, somewhere in his mid-thirties. Then I knew: unless I was very mistaken, he was the man I'd seen watching me from behind the wheel of his car, when I was doing my prostitution-decoy operation.

Then the light changed, and I was pushed ahead with the end-of-day traffic. In my rearview mirror, Kilander and his new colleague crossed their intersection, and I lost sight of them.

★ ★ ★

Back at my desk, I was writing up a quick report when the phone rang.

68

'I have some news for you,' Begans said.

'Okay,' I told him. 'Shoot.'

'Well, Bob knew where Hugh Hennessy's cabin was, and then we had some business up there anyway, kids target-shooting where they're not supposed to. We drove up and knocked on the door.'

'And?' Begans seemed to want to be asked.

'There's nobody there. Nobody's been there for a while. Locked up tight. The water's shut off.'

'No kidding?' But I'd been coming to suspect it: that Hugh Hennessy, not Aidan, was the real X in the equation.

'Yes. Is that what you needed to know?' Begans asked.

'It is,' I told him, shifting the receiver to my other ear; my left was sore from having the phone pressed to it. 'I appreciate how quickly you got to it. Wish Bob a happy retirement for me.'

Begans chuckled. 'Oh, he'll hate it. In three weeks he'll be so sick of fishing he'll be here asking for his old job back.'

After we'd hung up, I thought about what I'd learned. Aidan Hennessy, I'd reflected, wasn't Hennepin County's problem. But if Hugh Hennessy, a county resident, was missing, that sure as hell was our business, wasn't it?

I could easily get the Hennessys' address, but going to the house wouldn't be productive. I didn't believe that Hugh was there, simply refusing to be a part of the search for his missing son. The boy, Liam, had told me that Hugh wasn't there, and he'd done so without me identifying myself, which meant that *He's out of town* was the answer the Hennessy children were giving all callers.

Did the kids really believe Hugh was at his cabin? Or were they lying?

The key person here was Marlinchen. She was the only person in the equation who'd sought help. For that very reason, paradoxically, I wasn't going to call Marlinchen Hennessy again today, nor visit the house. Lawyers, at least in the courtroom, never ask a question they don't know the answer to. It was a useful tenet in interview situations overall. I needed to know at least some of the answers before I confronted Marlinchen. If not, she could feed me any story she liked, and I wouldn't know the difference.

Then I realized something else. My left ear was still hurting, and it wasn't the outer shell, sore from having a receiver pressed against it. This was more of a throb, deeper, in the ear canal itself. It was actually fairly painful.

I'm not real happy with the way your left ear looks, Cisco had said. Oh, great. Who'd have predicted this guy would be a real, competent physician?

I'd have to write my report on Cisco soon. I wasn't going to feel sorry for him. I didn't know how he'd gotten into whatever desperate situation made him see patients in a public high-rise, but he was clearly a highly intelligent person. He was smart enough to know that if he wanted to break the law, he'd go to jail like anyone else.

Still, I wondered how long a sentence he'd get.

6

Two days later, the pain in my ear was worse, but I kept it in abeyance with aspirin. The cold had passed, I told myself, so this would pass too. I tried to ignore the fact that Cisco had suggested otherwise, warning that I might need an antibiotic prescription.

Stop worrying about his goddamned advice, I thought. *This will go away on its own, most things do. Doctors can't admit that, because if they did, they'd be out of a job.*

But the day after that, my ear was refusing to be ignored. The aspirin I'd taken had worn off in the night, and when I woke, my eardrum pulsed like a second, painful heartbeat. I lifted myself to a sitting position very slowly. I didn't want to cause even the smallest rise in blood pressure that might make the throbbing worse.

When I was ready, I went to the bathroom. My face was a study in contrast, pale with spots of high, febrile color. I swallowed the last three aspirin and pitched the bottle into the trash. *Come on, this is probably the worst of it. One more day and you'll turn a corner*, I told myself.

I took a fifteen-minute shower with the door and window tightly closed, inhaling steam. After that, and a cup of tea and two slices of toast, the aspirin started to kick in. I felt marginally better, good enough to get dressed and go out.

I suppose some people would think it strange that someone with a blistering earache and a fever wouldn't call in sick, but in fact, I went in early. I didn't want to sit around the house with nothing to think about but how much my ear hurt and how long it might take to heal if I kept refusing to see a doctor. I wanted the distraction of work, and if my shift was still hours away, then Hugh Hennessy could easily fill those hours.

'Sarah.' Tyesha looked up in mild surprise from her desk. 'I was just about to call you. Prewitt wanted you to come in a little early today. Not *this* early, though. Around three-thirty, he said.'

'That's fine.' I tucked a strand of hair behind my good ear. 'Did he say why?'

Tyesha shook her head. 'Sorry, he didn't.'

No one else commented on my presence downtown at midday. I didn't socialize, just drank tea and looked at the official data on Hugh Hennessy. He had never been arrested locally, nor sued. He did have a moving violation from two years ago, an illegal U-turn, and had mailed in the fine without incident. Nothing there.

911 Recap, where they can look up calls dating back for years, was my last stop, and required an in-person visit.

The Hennessys lived in the western reaches of Hennepin County, on the shore of the big lake, Minnetonka. *Nice work if you can get it*, as Deputy Begans would have said. Much of outlying Hennepin County had become built up and suburban, but there was still quiet, privacy, land, and history to be bought on the shores of Lake Minnetonka. Some of the county's richest citizens lived on its inlets and bays.

Even as I gave the clerk the Hennessys' address, I was thinking it wouldn't yield anything. I believed there was probably something wrong at the Hennessy home, but I doubted it was the kind of *wrong* that sent the police out to their quiet lakeside address. It would be, instead, a quiet, simmering distress that even the neighbors didn't know about.

'We sent an ambulance out there three weeks ago,' the young clerk told me.

'You did?' I said, startled. It never pays to assume. 'What for?'

He read from the brief narrative. 'Possible brain attack, male 43 years old, collapsed and nonresponsive,' he read. 'He went to HCMC.'

'And then what?' I asked.

'That's all I know,' he said.

'Did you find any other calls to that address?'

'No,' he said. 'Just the one.'

'Thanks for your help,' I said. Then I added, 'Brain attack?' The terminology wasn't familiar.

'In other words, stroke.'

★　★　★

At Hennepin County Medical Center, a white-haired man was at the patient-information desk. I gave him Hugh Hennessy's name, and he tapped at his computer keyboard.

73

'Not here,' the man said.

'Was he discharged, or . . . ' I didn't want to use the word *died*. 'What was the resolution of his treatment here?'

'I don't have that information,' he said. 'You'd need to go to Medical Records.'

The elevator I rode down in was outsized, made to handle wheelchairs and stretchers. At the records office, a young red-haired woman was behind the computer. I laid my shield on the counter for her to see. 'I need to know where a patient named Hugh Hennessy went from here,' I said.

'Sorry,' she said. 'Badge or no badge, I can't give out patient information without a subpoena.'

'They brought him in on a stroke,' I said. 'If he died here, I need to know that.'

She shook her head, wordlessly apologizing.

I sighed, or tried to. My lungs felt as though they'd shrunk to a child's size, and I couldn't get a full breath.

Maybe I sounded more exasperated than I realized, or looked more pathetic. The clerk's hands tapped against her keyboard. I took it for a dismissal — she was getting back to work, from what I could see — but she said, 'You know, Park Christian is an excellent rehab facility for stroke patients.' Her smile was guileless.

'Is it?' I said, realizing what she was really telling me. 'Thank you very much.'

Park Christian Hospital was outside Minneapolis proper, in a pleasantly verdant setting that must have been comforting to the relatives of the

74

frail and stricken. Behind a set of automatic double doors, a rush of cold, conditioned air greeted me. Instantly, after the heat of the summer day and a long ride out there, I felt chills begin. But the pain in my ear was under control, held down by aspirin, and that was what mattered.

'Can I help you?' the receptionist said.

'I'd like to see Hugh Hennessy,' I said. Too late I realized I should have brought some sort of prop with me: flowers, a card. 'I'm a friend of the family.'

I expected a runaround. *You're not on the visitors' list*, or some similar refusal. Instead the woman said, 'I'll have Freddy take you back.'

I almost said, *You will?* I'd just wanted to confirm where Hugh Hennessy was; now I actually had to face the man, with no excuse for being there. 'Are you sure I won't be disrupting a routine, or anything? I could come later,' I offered.

A door beside the desk swung open and a man appeared.

He was young, but with an older man's mien. His face was soft and pouchy, his blond hair cut in a short, square style that few guys in their twenties would have chosen. His name tag read, *Freddy*. He looked at me. 'Are you here to see Hugh Hennessy?'

'That'd be me,' I admitted.

He gestured to the door, for me to follow him. 'It's too bad you didn't get here a little earlier,' Freddy said. 'You just missed his daughter.'

'Marlinchen was here?'

'A very pretty girl,' he commented, and I heard no lechery in it. 'She's been here quite often.'

We walked back through a hallway, then through a glassed-in breezeway to another wing. Outside the glass I could see open space, lawn and pathways, and beyond that a deep pond.

'Is Mr. Hennessy alert?' I asked. 'Is he verbal?'

'Alert? I think he's aware,' Freddy said. 'Verbal, no. He has expressive aphasia. That means that we think he understands a lot of what's going on around him, but when he tries to speak, it doesn't make much sense.'

'Is that the extent of the damage?' I asked.

Freddy shook his head. 'He's in a wheelchair right now, for weakness on the right side of his body, but we're working on that. And some neglect.'

'Neglect?'

'Where someone loses awareness of one side of the body, and one side of their surroundings.'

'I see.' For a moment I'd thought Freddy was telling me Hugh had been improperly cared for, elsewhere.

We stopped outside a door. 'This is his room,' Freddy said.

Inside, the air was still and quiet. The room held two low beds, but Hugh Hennessy wasn't in either of them. He sat in a wheelchair by the window, chin on chest, eyes closed.

'Is something wrong?' I asked, worried.

Freddy smiled at my alarm. 'It's all right. He's just fallen asleep.'

He was slender of build, his hair light brown,

76

cut sharply across the forehead in the style of a man who doesn't put much stock in his looks. I wasn't prepared for him to look so young, even in the ravages of poor health. The air-conditioning gave me another chill, and I wondered why they kept it so cold where old and infirm people were.

Freddy tipped his head to one side. 'Are you feeling all right?' he asked.

'Sure,' I said. 'Why?'

'You look a little off-color,' he said.

'It was hot outside,' I said, as if that explained everything.

Hugh Hennessy's eyelids fluttered, and his pale eyes half opened. I couldn't tell if he was awake, or saw me, but guilt stabbed me, as though he'd caught me in his room under false pretenses.

'Actually,' I told Freddy, 'I'm not feeling so great. I'm going to get some air.'

'That's fine,' he said gently. 'Come back when you're feeling better.'

★   ★   ★

The hospital's parking lot had an *Entry Only* arrow at one end and an *Exit Only* arrow at the other. Following the prescribed direction, I had to make a right turn onto a side street to get back to the road I'd taken to the hospital. That's why I saw the slight form of Marlinchen Hennessy, waiting on a bus bench.

I stopped the Nova and called from the window.

77

'Remember me?' I said.

She looked up, startled.

'I was just driving by and I recognized you,' I said. 'Where are you going?'

'Home,' she said.

'Want a lift?'

'My house is a ways from here,' she said, still wary.

'That's okay,' I said. 'It's a nice day for a drive.'

A criminal, someone with experience of the cops, would have known it was too coincidental to be true, a detective driving by and innocently offering a ride. But Marlinchen was young, and when I looked over my shoulder, feigning worry about another car approaching, she felt guilty.

'Come on if you're coming,' I urged.

Marlinchen picked up her backpack and ran out to me. She jumped into the passenger side and slammed the door. I accelerated and we were on our way. *Gotcha*, I thought. She wasn't going to be fleeing *this* interview, not at 65 miles an hour.

It was a sad day that I had to take pleasure in cornering a teenage girl as though she were a hardened perp, but you take your victories where you can get them.

'Roll down the window if you want,' I said. I was still alternating between too hot and too cold; it wouldn't make much difference to me. Marlinchen rolled her window halfway down.

'Were you coming from school?' I said. 'I didn't think there were any out in this area.'

'No, I get out of school at noon,' she said. 'I'm

a senior, and all my graduation requirements were satisfied, so I took an abbreviated schedule.'

'That must be nice,' I said.

'I'm enjoying it.' Her tone sounded a little more relaxed and confident.

'So what brought you out to this area?'

'I was at the hospital,' Marlinchen said briefly.

'Really? Why?' *I'm giving you a chance here. Tell me the truth.*

'I volunteer there, when I can,' she said. She wasn't looking at me.

Too bad, Marlinchen. There goes your no-hitter. 'That's nice of you,' I said. 'Convenient, too. Gives you a chance to visit your father.'

For a moment, the only sound was the Nova's rumbling engine. Then I heard Marlinchen sniffling. She laid her head against the door frame of the Nova, and her shoulders shook.

Suddenly it didn't seem so funny to me that I'd been reduced to entrapping a teenage girl with her own evasions. I had pursued Hugh's whereabouts as though it were just an intellectual exercise, not thinking of the human feelings underneath.

I spoke as gently as possible. 'Your father's had a stroke, your mother's dead, you're the oldest in the family, and your twin brother's whereabouts are unknown,' I said. 'That's a lot of trouble to deal with, and usually the last thing I'd do is pile on, but I can't help you if you keep lying to me.'

Marlinchen didn't answer. She cried for a while as we got off the 394 and onto the secondary roads that threaded the wetlands around the big lake, where bait stores and diners ceded to houses set back from the road. I began to realize just how far Marlinchen had ridden on a bus to see me down at the detective division.

'I'm going to need specific directions pretty soon,' I said, relieved to have something normal to say.

'Oh,' Marlinchen said. Her voice was wet, but she seemed more composed as she straightened in her seat and began to direct me.

The Hennessys lived on a little peninsula that ran out into the lake, at the end of an unmarked dirt road. I'd expected a writer to live in something opulent, but the Hennessy house, while big, was unpretentious. It was two stories, with an exterior of weather-beaten wood. Tall lilac trees, still in bloom, crowded the front door, and dark purple irises irregularly cropped up around a crooked stone path. The grass in front clearly hadn't been mowed recently. A smaller building stood off to the side, perhaps a carriage house in the home's early-twentieth-century life. A willow fountained over its far side.

The dirt driveway ran alongside the house, and as I pulled up in the Nova, I realized the back of the house, facing the lake, was its true 'front.' Here was a broad, covered back porch, with French double doors. A high window on the second story looked out over the lake, with a trellis of ornamental grapevines crawling up alongside it. A wide, grassy slope led down to the lake, where an apron of rocks ran along the water's edge, holding off the erosion process. A single tree stood halfway to the water's edge, several creamy blossoms among its dark, glossy leaves.

I killed the Nova's engine. I could leave now, but it would undermine everything I'd done since calling Marlinchen over to get in my car. Her willingness to lie was well established. If I put off this conversation until tomorrow, she'd have time to massage the facts to her liking, in readiness for our next meeting.

'So,' I said. 'Tell me.'

'Where should I start?'

'With your father's stroke,' I said. 'That was three weeks ago, is that right?'

She nodded.

'Why cover it up?' I asked.

'Dad's a writer,' she said. 'He's famous. It would have gotten into the news.'

'Is that a problem?' I said. 'He's sick. It's not a scandal.'

Marlinchen pressed her lips together, thinking. 'I wanted to protect his privacy,' she said.

'You told me he was up north finishing a novel, Marlinchen,' I pointed out. 'I'm not a member of the media, and you were asking for my help, and you still lied to me. That's a little more than protecting your dad's privacy.'

She dropped her head. 'I don't want my brothers to go to foster homes,' she said softly. 'In a few weeks I'll be 18, and then I can be their guardian. But if Family Services finds out about Dad before then, they'd split us up.'

'That's a pretty drastic expectation,' I told her. 'Social workers don't go around looking for families to break up. They take the whole situation into account. It's very possible that if you're getting along okay with the younger kids, they'd probably just want you to have a temporary guardian until you turn 18.'

'That's not necessary.'

'It's not a big deal,' I assured her. 'You'll call on an adult relative to step in until your dad's better.'

'There isn't anyone,' she said. Reading the skepticism on my face, she went on. 'My mother had a sister, but she's dead. All my grandparents are dead except for my grandmother on my mother's side. She's in an assisted-living facility in Berlin. She speaks mostly German.'

'Okay, I'd rule her out,' I agreed, pausing to think. 'Listen, can I come in?'

Marlinchen led me up the back steps, onto the porch, and in through a pair of French doors. The Hennessy home was as graceful inside as out: good pine wood, a rough-beamed ceiling, and eclectic touches everywhere. We were in a family room, the modernity of a wide-screen TV offsetting the shabby-elegant furniture, a nubby throw blanket thrown over a velvety couch. Beyond, I could see the kitchen. There was plenty of space to work; pots and pans overhung a center-island butcher block.

'Would you like something to drink?' Marlinchen led me toward the kitchen, moving with the assurance people have in their longtime homes.

'Ice water is fine.'

Marlinchen fixed me a tall glass, and iced tea for herself. I wandered into the kitchen behind

82

her and looked around. My request to come inside hadn't been an idle one; as a social worker would have, I'd wanted to see evidence of how the kids were living, whether the house was clean, what they were eating. From my perspective, they were keeping better house than a lot of bachelor cops I knew. The kitchen was as clean as the family room we'd come through. A faint smell of cooking hung in the air, and there were vegetable peelings in the drain trap, suggesting a healthy diet. The houseplants I'd seen were green and healthy; they were being watered.

Marlinchen said, 'Detective Pribek, can we talk about Aidan?'

'Sure,' I said. 'But Aidan's nearly 18, and on the road by choice. When he does turn 18, which you've said is a few weeks away, it'll be no one's business but his own where he is. If he doesn't want his family to know his whereabouts, well, you may not like it, but that's his choice.'

Marlinchen slipped into one of the chairs against the kitchen counter. 'He's my brother,' she said. 'I have to know that he's all right.'

I remained standing; I didn't want to get mired in this situation. 'I'm sorry,' I said. 'I understand that you're afraid for him. But with a runaway who's been gone as long as Aidan has, there's just not much the police can do. You're solidly in private-investigator territory here. I can recommend several to you, competent people who, for a fee, will make finding your brother their job.'

'What kind of a fee?' she asked.

'Depends,' I said. 'Somebody good will charge you at least a hundred dollars an hour.'

She winced.

'I know it sounds like a lot,' I said. 'But I wouldn't bargain-hunt in this case. If you don't get somebody good, it'll take longer to find Aidan. You'll end up paying one way or another. And,' I added, 'it's not unheard-of for unethical investigators to set their rates low to get people in the door, then drag their heels and pad their hours. You don't end up saving money at all.'

'I see.' Marlinchen was starting to look lost. 'How many hours do you think it would take for them to find him?'

'I really wouldn't feel comfortable estimating,' I said. 'They could find him with three phone calls. Or it could take weeks.'

'I see,' she said again. Obviously, she wasn't feeling any better about the situation, and it wasn't hard to guess why.

'It's money, isn't it?' I said.

The Hennessys lived in a wealthy enclave on the lake; I'd assumed that not only was Marlinchen capably handling the household affairs but that, in doing so, she was drawing on a comfortable sum of her father's savings. At least, I had until just now.

'I know we look in good shape financially,' Marlinchen said. 'But I only have access to Dad's checking account; he gave me his ATM number. But for everything else, I need to be his conservator, and I can't do that until I turn 18. Even then, there might be some delays. He has aphasia; it's a speech and comprehension

84

disorder. Dad needs to recover enough that an officer of the court can see that he understands what's being said to him, and that the mark he's making really represents his desire to make me a conservator.'

She sounded surprisingly knowledgeable. 'Does your father have a lawyer who's helping you with this?' I asked.

Marlinchen nodded. 'I don't know that I'd call Mr. DeRose 'Dad's lawyer,' but he helped with some things when Mother died, and when I called him, he was willing to do the conservatorship work on contingency. I can pay him once I get access to the accounts.'

I hoped DeRose was someone ethical; this slender, tentative 17-year-old with a wealthy father would look like a slot machine on two feet to a lawyer who wasn't.

But with Marlinchen's very next words, I had to reconsider the *wealthy father* part.

'Even then,' Marlinchen went on, 'there's just Dad's passbook savings to tap, and each of us has a college-savings trust. But that's not a lot of money. A lot of what Dad earned went to paying off this house. Which is fine, but we can't eat the house and the great view,' she said, gesturing toward the lake. Then she amended her words. 'Things aren't *that* bad, yet, but there's certainly not money for a hundred-dollar-an-hour investigator for an open-ended period of time. That's why I was hoping that someone on the police here would find Aidan's case had enough merit to take it on.'

I was starting to feel like those old-time

aviators who took off from New York for the West Coast on a cloudy day, got turned around in a fog bank, and ended up committed to a trip to Europe. I'd wanted to help Marlinchen, but I'd also wanted it to be short and simple. And for a moment, it had seemed like it was going to be: I'd found Hugh Hennessy and determined that his daughter's reasons for covering up his absence, while misguided, weren't criminal. I'd thought, then, that I could simply reassure Marlinchen that Aidan was probably okay, recommend a competent private investigator, and forget the whole thing. I'd thought I could sum up the Hennessy affair in three words: *Not My Problem*.

Instead I found that Marlinchen was alone with a houseful of younger siblings with no adult relatives to call on, and despite her father's literary successes, without a comfortable supply of money. Now I was summing up the Hennessys in four words: *No End in Sight*.

And my goddamn ear was starting to hurt again. The aspirin was wearing off, and the pain was beginning to ramp up from its dull, medicated ache toward the sharp throb I'd woken up with the last two mornings. It was driving nobler feelings from my mind.

'I wish it were just a matter of merit,' I said. 'But Hennepin County pays me to investigate cases where the law has been broken within its borders. That's not the situation here. Look, I'll talk to the PIs I know, see if one of them won't take you pro bono. Maybe — '

A rustling from beyond us, the front of the

house, made Marlinchen look up. Three boys, loaded down with backpacks, trooped into the kitchen. Their idle conversation stopped short when they saw me with their sister.

None was blond like Marlinchen; they had Hugh's brown hair. The youngest boy's was quite shaggy, but other than that, they looked well groomed and clean, and obviously healthy.

Marlinchen slid from the stool. 'Guys, this is Detective Sarah Pribek,' she said. 'I spoke to her the other day, about Aidan. You remember I said I was going into the city to do that.'

One of the boys, a muscular kid in a sleeveless T-shirt, spoke. 'I thought that — '

'We can talk about it later,' Marlinchen said. She carried on with introductions. 'Sarah, this is Liam, he's 16,' the tallest boy, thin, with longish, slightly darker hair and wire-rim glasses, 'and Colm, he's 14,' the well-built boy who'd spoken, 'and the little guy is Donal, 11.' Donal was the shaggy-haired one; underneath the mop his face was unformed, like children's often are.

'It's nice to meet you all,' I said, 'but I really should get going. I've got to be at work.' To Marlinchen I said, 'I'll make those phone calls I mentioned, tonight or tomorrow, and get back to you with a referral.'

It wasn't going to be an easy sell, I thought, but maybe I could catch one of the PIs I knew in a generous mood.

Marlinchen nodded. 'Let me walk you out,' she said.

Outside on the deck, she turned earnest again. 'Detective Pribek, you're not going to report us, right?' she asked. 'To Family Services?'

'I'm legally required to, Marlinchen,' I said.

Her shoulders dropped infinitesimally, and she looked away from me, toward the lake.

I didn't know why she felt the way she did, as if she and her brothers were being sentenced to an orphanage of times past, with high Gothic gates and meals of thin gruel. But suddenly I saw myself through her eyes and didn't like what I saw. I'd come in here and seen evidence of her careful housekeeping and her cooking and the obvious love she had for her younger brothers, and sorry, it wasn't good enough and I'm reporting you to the county and by the way, I don't care where your brother is. You want to find him, pay up.

'Look,' I said, relenting, 'maybe I could help you out a little with Aidan.'

'Really?' she said.

'You said you've only got school until noon, right? Why don't I come out tomorrow around one, and we can talk about this some more.'

To say that Marlinchen Hennessy smiled didn't quite do it justice. Throughout our short acquaintance, she'd never made more than a small smile of greeting. I wasn't prepared for the sight of her natural happiness; it was brilliant as the first fire-blossom of a lit match. The thought of getting more involved with the Hennessys wasn't entirely appealing, but it was touching to see how much an offer of help meant to Marlinchen.

I gave her my card. 'Both cell and pager are on there,' I said. 'In case you have a schedule conflict, or something.'

'I won't,' she said.

★   ★   ★

As soon as I was back in the car, I groped in my shoulder bag for the aspirin bottle. It wasn't there.

It's in the trash can in your bathroom, genius, where you threw it this morning after taking the last of the aspirin. You were going to pick up some more, remember?

The readout on my cell phone said it was 3:45. Even without a stop at a convenience store, I'd be late for work.

I backed the Nova around in a three-quarter circle and accelerated down the Hennessys' long driveway. Someone at work would have a couple of painkillers I could score.

7

'Lieutenant Prewitt is looking for you,' Tyesha said, as soon as I came in.

'I'm only five minutes — oh, *hell*.' I'd forgotten all about Prewitt's request that I come in early. 'Is he in his office?'

He was, but we didn't stay there. When I entered, Prewitt rose from behind his desk. 'Detective Pribek,' he said. 'Come on down to the conference room.'

'Sure,' I said.

He didn't mention that I was thirty-five minutes late for whatever this appointment was, but obviously he knew it. It was too late for me to ask for another five minutes to score some aspirin off a co-worker.

'I'm really just making introductions here,' Prewitt said, and opened the door to our conference room. As we entered, the man sitting at the long table inside got to his feet.

My surprise distracted me from the pain in my ear. It was the stranger who I'd seen twice now: first watching me on my vice detail, then with Kilander on the street corner. Up close, he had a lean, tired face, yet a fairly young one too, despite the threads of gray at his temples. I didn't revise my estimate of his age: about 35.

'Detective Sarah Pribek,' Prewitt said, 'this is Gray Diaz, from the Faribault County district attorney's office.'

Faribault County. Blue Earth.

Diaz came out from around his chair and offered me his hand. 'Detective Pribek,' he said.

'Pleased to meet you,' I said.

He let go of my hand and nodded to Prewitt. 'Thanks, Will,' he said. Prewitt withdrew.

'Please, have a seat,' Diaz said.

We did. I hoped, but doubted, that I looked better than I felt.

'Are you a prosecutor?' I asked.

'I'm a DA's investigator,' Diaz said. 'I've been with Faribault County for about six weeks.'

'Do you like it down there?' I asked.

'Well, it's fairly quiet,' Diaz said. 'That's why I started reading some old files.'

A little drop of sweat crawled between my shoulder blades, down toward the small of my back.

Diaz set a thick manila folder on the table before him. 'This is a case that was forwarded to our office about three months ago, before I came on board. It was a joint investigation by the Sheriff's and Fire departments,' he said.

'Royce Stewart,' I said. There was no point in waiting for him to say the name.

'Yes,' he said, and there might have been a faint note of surprise in his voice at my forthrightness. 'The file definitely caught my attention. Naturally, given your familiarity with the people and events in the case, I wanted to talk to you.' He tapped a fingernail against the file. 'I thought we could start by just reviewing the known facts. You can correct me if you think I've got anything wrong.'

91

Diaz opened his file and ran down Royce Stewart's life in the dry, telegrammatic fragments of an official record.

'Royce Stewart was 25 years old at the time of his death,' he began. 'Lived most of his life in Faribault County, arrests and convictions there for indecent exposure and lewd conduct; a juvenile arrest for looking in the windows of a woman's home late at night, charges dropped. At 24, he moved to the Twin Cities, where he had a conviction for DWI, and much more significant, was arrested and charged with the rape and murder of Kamareia Brown, the daughter of Detective Genevieve Brown of the Hennepin County Sheriff's Department. Your partner.' Diaz paused, sipping from a glass of water at his side. 'The case was dismissed for technical reasons, and Stewart returned to Blue Earth.

'In October, firefighters are called out to the property on which Stewart lived. The outbuilding that he lived in is ablaze, and his body is found in it the next day.' Diaz turned a page, although I was sure the details of the case were already locked into his memory. 'A little over eight hours after the fire, former MPD detective Michael Shiloh turns himself in to police in Mason City, Iowa, and confesses to Stewart's murder. The strange thing is that Shiloh asserts he killed Stewart a week earlier, by running him down in a stolen truck on the highway outside Blue Earth.

'An investigation bears out the fact that Shiloh stole the truck, but rather than running Stewart down, he was in a one-vehicle wreck due to ice

92

on the road. In the accident, he sustained a serious head injury that confused his memories and impaired his judgment. Fearing arrest for his 'crime,' he traveled south on foot, avoiding contact with other people, and finally, in Mason City, Iowa, turned himself in. His belief that he killed Stewart, according to a psychologist, was due partly to the head injury and partly to his persistent prior visualization of carrying out the crime. Michael Shiloh did not contest the charge of auto theft and is currently incarcerated in Wisconsin.' Diaz drank a little more water. 'It's quite a story.'

'You said you wanted me to point out anything incorrect in your file,' I said. 'There are two things you didn't include.'

Diaz lifted a courteous eyebrow. 'Please.'

'Shiloh didn't *fail* to kill Shorty, he decided not to. Even if it was at the last minute.'

Diaz nodded, seeming to take it seriously. 'And you know this how?'

'Shiloh told me,' I said.

'I should point out that nobody can independently verify that,' Diaz said. 'You're depending on your husband's word.'

I wasn't. Royce Stewart had told me so. Just before he died.

'But that's immaterial to the subject at hand, which is Stewart's death,' Diaz said. 'There wasn't a lot of doubt in investigators' minds that Stewart's place was deliberately set on fire, or that he was already dead when the place burned. The file wasn't set aside for lack of evidence that a crime had been committed. The problem was lack of evidence pointing to an identifiable suspect. As soon as I read this file, I thought my colleagues had been too hasty in dismissing the obvious person.'

I stayed quiet.

'They'd discounted a man who'd already admitted to going to Blue Earth intending to kill Royce Stewart. Who wasn't alibied the night Royce Stewart died.'

'*Shiloh* is your suspect?' I asked him.

'Your husband is definitely a person of interest,' Diaz said.

Person of interest is to *suspect* what *tropical storm* is to *hurricane*.

'That's impossible,' I said. 'The evidence rules him out.'

Notwithstanding that I knew for a fact Shiloh hadn't killed Stewart, I was also familiar with all the evidence that had told investigators he couldn't have done so. Shiloh's injuries, the wrecked truck, the seven-day gap between his aborted attempt to kill Stewart and Stewart's actual death . . . all these things supported the assertion that Shiloh had not had anything to do with Stewart's murder.

'Are you sure?' Diaz said. 'There was a nine-hour window between Stewart's murder and Shiloh's appearance in Mason City. That's ample time to travel less than a hundred miles.'

'On foot?' I said.

'No, by car or truck. Just because no one has come forward to say they picked him up hitchhiking doesn't mean no one did.'

'There may be a nine-hour window that night,'

I said, 'but there's also a seven-day window between Shiloh's try at running Royce Stewart down and the time that he showed up in Mason City. It's hard to make a case that — ' I fell silent, understanding something.

'You were saying?' Diaz prompted.

I didn't answer right away. This man was playing a game, and while I should have known better, I'd started playing it with him. 'Have you spoken to Shiloh yet, at the prison?' I asked.

Diaz said, 'I'm not prepared to share all the details of the investigation right now.'

'You haven't,' I said, 'because Shiloh isn't your *person of interest*. I am. You're deflecting my attention by pretending that Shiloh is your suspect. You want me to jump to his defense and argue the points of the case with you, until I give up some detail I couldn't have known unless I killed Shorty.' That had been Stewart's nick-name, codified on the vanity license plate of his car. 'That's the second detail you left out of your story. You left out any reference to me being in the area and talking to Stewart the night he died. If you talked to the people at the bar, you know I was there,' I said. 'That makes me an obvious suspect. But instead of approaching me directly, you're pretending you want to talk to me as a 'fellow investigator.''

This was a tactic that even worked on street criminals. When talking to a suspect with priors, sometimes detectives will ask him to speculate on how a crime might have been carried out, what he might have done if he had committed the act. If it works, the criminal will drop his guard and spill a critical detail that he shouldn't have known.

'Let me answer the question you're not asking,' I said. 'I did not kill Royce Stewart. I was down there, in Blue Earth. I was at the bar. I spoke to him. But I didn't kill him.'

'Detective Pribek,' Diaz said, 'I'm not here to offend you. I'm here to do a job.'

He was right; I'd spoken more freely than I'd intended. The pain in my ear was fraying my nerves.

'I'm sorry,' I said. 'I know that. I've had a cold, and my ear is really bothering me. Can you give me a minute to get some aspirin?'

'Actually,' Diaz said, 'I'd like us to keep going with this now that we're on a roll.'

Another key point in interrogation: once things start heating up, don't give your suspect time to regroup.

'Let's talk about the night you went to Blue Earth,' Diaz said. 'What led you to go there?'

'I had come to understand that Shiloh had stolen and wrecked the truck on the highway. I recognized his motives, that he wanted to run Shorty down, but I knew he'd failed, because Royce Stewart was alive. In fact, Stewart was the suspect in the theft of the truck, because his fingerprints placed him at the scene of the accident. What I didn't understand was what happened to Shiloh after the wreck.'

'So you went down there.'

'To talk to Shorty, yes.' My ear was pulsing steadily with my heartbeat, which was going a little faster than usual.

96

'How did you know he would be at the bar?' Diaz asked.

'I didn't know for — *Ow! God.*'

Now it had done something new. There had been a popping sensation, followed by a crackle of something like static. I'd heard people talk about their ears popping during the ascent and descent of airplanes, but I didn't think this was the same thing. Instead I imagined blisters had risen on my eardrum like bubbles, and one of them bursting.

'Your ear?' Diaz asked.

'Yeah,' I said, rubbing the outer shell ineffectually.

'We'll try to wrap this up fairly quickly,' Diaz assured me. 'You were saying?'

'I was saying that I didn't know for sure he'd be at the bar, but I'd heard he spent a lot of time there.'

'And luckily for you, he was,' Diaz commented. 'What did you discuss with him?'

'I wanted to know what he knew about Shiloh's disappearance,' I said. 'He refused to talk to me.'

'And then what did you do?' Diaz asked.

'I drove partway home,' I said. 'My partner, Genevieve, was living in Mankato with her sister and brother-in-law, and I knew I could sleep there.'

In second grade we'd studied the ear. I tried not to remember the illustration of the eardrum, tried not to imagine my own as a swollen, dark-pink balloon of fluid, getting more distended by the hour.

'You didn't go to Stewart's house before you left Blue Earth?'

This was a potential trap. So far I'd been telling the truth, albeit with omissions. I hadn't needed to lie. This was where I had to step off the trail.

'No,' I said. 'I didn't.'

'Minneapolis to Blue Earth is nearly a three-hour drive,' Diaz said. 'So you drove all that way, found Stewart at the bar, and when he refused to talk about your husband, you just got back in the car and left? Seems to me like you gave up kind of easily.'

My ear crackled again, making a rushing noise like static. 'Shorty told me he knew, and I quote, 'jack shit.' I couldn't prove otherwise. There wasn't a lot I could do after that.'

'So that's your story: you drove to Blue Earth, saw Shorty briefly at the bar, and drove to Mankato?' Diaz said.

'That's what happened,' I said.

Most of what I had told Diaz was true. The lie was one of omission. I'd left out Genevieve, who'd followed me to Blue Earth, coming and going unseen like a malevolent shadow.

Diaz shook his head, as though disappointed in a pupil who isn't performing up to par. He shuffled papers back into his manila file. 'I suppose that's all, for now.'

When I stood, a red-gray haze swam up in my vision and my ear throbbed a little harder.

'Oh, I forgot one thing,' Diaz said. 'Is there any reason why someone would have seen you and your car outside Stewart's home on the night in question?' Diaz asked.

I was still standing motionless, trying to get my vision to clear. Diaz's question did not help. *Get a grip. Breathe.*

'I'm not the only person who looks like me or drives a 1970 Nova,' I said.

The reddish haze receded and the colors of the world broke through again.

'I see,' Diaz said. 'Thank you for your help, Detective Pribek.'

★ ★ ★

It's an investigator's classic, the is-there-any-reason question. It implied there was an eyewitness, but didn't actually claim it outright. The interview subject was supposed to fall into the trap and start making facile, blustering excuses, thus confirming what the investigator had only suspected.

Knowing it was a tactic didn't stop it from being scary as hell. *If Diaz had more evidence, he'd have come out with it*, I told myself in the restroom, where I'd just downed two Advil and splashed cold water on my face, being careful not to get any in my ear.

When I lifted my head to see my reflection in the mirror, my pale face shone from sweat and water. The strands of hair closest to my face were damp. Other than my work clothes and shoulder holster, I looked like a nineteenth-century consumptive in a charity-hospital ward. I stared at my own image and came to grips with the worst realization I'd had all day: I needed to visit a doctor's office.

Aviation experts will tell you that you're safer in the air than you are on the ground. Statistics confirm this. But in any airport lounge you'll see some poor soul sitting in one of the plastic chairs, elbows on knees, hands hanging loose, feet planted, head down. It's a nearly prayerful position, as though he or she is about to do the most dangerous thing imaginable. And in the mind of an aerophobe, they are.

Phobias are like that. It doesn't matter that the fear is irrational. Sometimes the mind's danger instinct just kicks in for no reason, and it won't shut off in the face of comforting statistics or personal affirmations. For me, the equivalent of an airport lounge is the waiting room of a doctor's office. At five minutes before 5 P.M., I went into a walk-in medical clinic, checked in, and assumed the position. My limbs felt heavy and strengthless, like I had water in my fuel line. To my left, a heavyset man in workman's clothes, a paint-speckled cell phone at his hip, watched traffic through the window.

The door that led into the inner offices swung open. 'Washington?' the nurse said.

The housepainter rose from the chairs and ambled toward the door. I sighed, reprieved.

I looked out the window. On the radio, newscasters had been talking about heavy weather coming, and through the plate glass, I could see the yellowish clouds on the horizon. It was still a ways off.

The door opened again. 'Pribek?' the nurse said.

I didn't lift my head, looking up instead through the hair that had slid forward across my face. She couldn't tell I was looking at her.

For God's sake, what are you doing? Get up.

'Sarah Pribek?' the nurse said.

I got to my feet, weak-legged. I still didn't make eye contact with the nurse as I turned to the exit door, the one to the outside world. I stepped on the rubber mat, and the door slid pneumatically open. My knees felt as though they would give out underneath me. I was half expecting some apprehension attempt, as if the nurse would say *That's her!* and reinforcements would rush out to wrestle me back inside.

But nothing happened, and I was out into the rays of the late-afternoon sun. My legs regained some of their strength and I began to walk faster, reaching my car.

I lasted two hours at home, heating towels in the dryer and holding them to my ear. Then I had an idea.

8

'This is a different look for you,' Cisco said.

I'd changed into my oldest jeans, faded almost to velvet, and Shiloh's blue-and-orange-striped pullover, and a pair of basketball shoes over thick socks. Cisco was inventorying me through the crack of the door that the chain allowed, and no sooner had he spoken than he seemed to realize that this was not a time for levity. 'Are you all right?' he asked.

'No,' I said. 'Can I come in?'

The same drill: Cisco shut the door, undid the chain, and rolled back in his wheelchair to let me in. Then he said, 'What's wrong?'

'My ear is killing me,' I told him. 'It started hurting a few days ago, like you said, and hasn't stopped. The thing is, I'm not sure it was just the cold that did it. I was in a drainage canal last week, I mean over my head. The water was runoff water. It was probably dirty.'

I was rambling, so afraid he'd send me away without treating me that I was throwing every extraneous bit of information I could at him. 'Can you look at it?' I finished.

'Go ahead and get on the examining table,' he said.

I did as he said, while he retrieved my notes from his filing cabinet, washed his hands, and took out his equipment. I don't know why Cisco's place didn't scare me the way the clinic had, but here I felt, if not relaxed, at least in control of my fear.

Like before, Cisco took my blood pressure. 'You're a little elevated,' he said. He put a finger on my wrist, finding the radial pulse, and made a note on his yellow pad, then took an otoscope from his footlocker. 'Which ear?' he asked.

'The left,' I said.

When he put the small, square end of the instrument into my ear, I jumped a little and flinched. 'Easy,' he said.

I closed my eyes and tried to relax. His breathing fluttered the loose hairs on my shoulder.

Cisco withdrew the tube and rolled back a little way, and I could see the change that had come over his face. 'I seem to remember telling you to go to a clinic if your ear started bothering you,' he said.

'I know.'

'Please tell me why you didn't do that.'

'I hoped it would just go away on its own,' I said lamely.

'Well, it hasn't,' Cisco said. 'At this stage, your eardrum needs to be lanced.'

'You can do that here, right?' I was so far gone with the pain of the infection itself that the prospect of having my eardrum stabbed with a needle didn't really sink in.

'I'm trained for it,' he said slowly, 'but I'm not ideally equipped here.'

I leaned down and dug in my shoulder bag. 'This is three hundred dollars,' I said. I'd stopped by the ATM on my way over. I laid the money on the shelf where I'd put the forty dollars the other night.

'Money's not the issue,' Cisco said. 'You need to go to an office for this.'

'I can't,' I said.

Cisco tapped a fingertip impatiently on the handrim of his wheelchair. 'Why on earth not?'

'I don't like those kinds of places,' I said. 'I get . . . I get scared.'

'Why?'

'I don't know,' I said. Fear was making me inarticulate. 'Please help me with this,' I finished. 'I can't go anywhere else.'

He would say no; he had his principles, just as he'd told me the other night. But there was something new in his eyes. Maybe compassion.

'This is going to hurt,' Cisco said. It was a concession.

'I've got that covered,' I said. Reaching back into the bag, I pulled out the bottle of whiskey I'd bought on the way over.

Cisco lowered his head slightly to rub the bridge of his nose with two fingers. 'Jesus,' he said. Then he sighed. 'Do you want a glass?'

'No,' I said.

'Then get some of that in you,' Cisco said. 'Plenty of it. I'll get ready.'

He rolled away from me; I drank. I closed my eyes and heard his movements as he readied for the procedure. From somewhere beyond the walls I thought I heard a dog bark. A big dog, from the timbre of the sound. That wasn't right, was it? A dog, here? I drank again, deeply.

'So,' Cisco said, his back turned to me, 'while

104

we wait, why don't you tell me how you decided to jump into a drainage canal.'

'I went in after a couple of kids who fell into the water.'

'I thought the hooker with the heart of gold was only in the movies.'

'I'm not a hooker,' I told him.

It was important for me to make that distinction, I guess, because I'd already shown him my real self. I didn't like the idea of being caught between identities, half-and-half. 'I'm not,' I said again, when he didn't answer.

'Duly noted,' he said lightly. I didn't know whether he believed me.

When I felt I'd drank enough, I lay down carefully on the massage table. I closed my eyes and the room spun a little. I opened them again. Again I found myself looking at his med-school diploma. *C. Agustin Ruiz*. Not *F*, for *Francisco*, as I would have expected. That was odd.

Cisco rolled close to me. He'd tied a dark-blue bandanna around most of his hair, and gathered the rest up in a small ponytail on his neck, like a surgeon might put his hair under a cap. He held a towel in his hands. 'How are you feeling?' he asked me.

'Preoperative,' I said.

Cisco laughed, a low, pleasant sound. 'You don't sound as slurry as I'd like. Have a little more.'

Obedient as a child, I drank, both hands on the bottle.

'What happened to the kids you pulled out of the drainage canal?' Cisco asked.

'You don't really believe I did that,' I said. It was getting easier to say what was on my mind; there was no two-second delay between thought and words. 'It's okay, I don't care that you're humoring me. The answer is, the older brother lived. The younger one didn't.'

Cisco turned sober. 'I heard something about that on the radio,' he said. He believed me.

'Is your full name Cisco?' I asked, speaking on the random thought.

'No.'

'What is it, then?'

'Cicero,' he said. 'A simple-enough name, but some people find the extra syllable unmanageable.'

'I like it,' I said.

'My father loved the classics. My brother's name is Ulises.' He paused. 'I think you might be ready to do this. No, relax. I need to clean your ear first.'

The cleaning wasn't painful, but I flinched at the wet pressure in an unaccustomed place. To distract me, Cicero made one-sided conversation, the way doctors do.

'You're lucky, in a way,' he said. 'Ten years ago, only an otolaryngologist would know how to do this. They started teaching it again when viruses and bacteria became so antibiotic-resistant, in the nineties. We started seeing more and more kids with infections that wouldn't respond to antimicrobial treatment.'

There was something in his voice that I hadn't heard in a while, a quiet deliberateness that reminded me of the grandparents of the Indian kids I'd known in New Mexico.

He withdrew. My ear felt damp and cool.

'Go ahead and lie down,' he instructed. I did, exposing the left ear to him.

'Close your eyes. I'm going to turn on another light.' He pulled the angled neck of a lamp down close to my head. It must have had a high-wattage bulb, maybe halogen, because I could feel the heat on the side of my cheek and neck. He took my face in his long fingers.

'Lift your head up,' Cicero told me. I obeyed, and he spread the towel underneath my head. I lay back down. In the corner of my eye I saw him pick something up. A needle. It seemed quite long, sinister in the lamplight.

'Two things,' Cicero said. 'I don't have an aspirator, so after I do this, turn your head to the side so it can drain onto the towel. Second: this is going to hurt.'

'You said that already,' I said, sounding drunk to myself at last. 'You don't have to dwell on it.'

'But I need you to keep quiet when I do this,' he explained. 'I don't want any cops coming here.'

Too late, I thought, and the laughter I tried to suppress made a high, giddy sound. Cicero looked at me quizzically, and I tried to get myself under control and failed. 'No,' I said, still laughing. 'I don't think I can promise that *at all*.'

'If you're having second thoughts, we can still get you to an ER.'

My laughter dried up at the prospect.

'All right, then,' Cicero said. 'Turn your head a little.'

I did what he said, closed my eyes.

He laid his free hand over my mouth. 'Be very still,' he said.

When the needle struck I was glad I hadn't promised not to scream. The pain sliced right through the alcohol haze. I felt Cicero's hands turning my head, because I'd forgotten his instructions to do so, and then hot liquid splashed down my ear, onto the towel.

'Oh, God,' I whispered. My eyes were still closed. 'Oh, *God*.' Now that I was on my side, my knees were trying to inch toward my chest, toward the fetal position.

'Keep your head down, that's it.' Cicero whispered encouragement to me, taking my hand.

'I'm going to be sick,' I told him.

'Breathe,' he instructed.

I tried to obey. One deep breath, and then another. 'I want to sit up,' I said, thinking it would alleviate the nausea.

He let me, and as soon as I was upright, the nausea did begin to subside. A few more deep breaths dispelled it to the point that I knew I could keep it under control.

'Better?' Cicero asked.

'Yeah,' I said.

'You want the bathroom?'

I was expecting a small, closetlike space, and so was surprised by the dimensions of the bathroom. Of course: it had to accommodate Cicero's wheelchair. There was a tubular railing along the wall and inside the shower, where a benchlike seat extended out from the tiled wall. I didn't turn on the bathroom light, imagining it would seem blinding. Instead I washed up by the minimal light that came in from the hallway.

A single towel hung by the sink, no washcloth. I opened the tap and ran a thin stream of water into the basin. I dampened the side of my face with water from my fingers, rubbed them against the bar of soap and then against my neck, raising a thin foam on the wet skin. I put my fingers under the stream of water again and rinsed as well as I could, but couldn't keep a trickle of water from escaping down the neckline of my sweater. I pressed the thick material of my shirt against my skin, blotting away the water.

When I came out, Cicero was cleaning up his exam table. I watched him, not sure what to say.

'I feel pretty good,' I lied.

But he was looking at me speculatively, in a way that sharpened my attention.

'What?' I said.

'You're in no shape to be driving anywhere,' he said.

'I know,' I said quickly. The pain had felt sobering, but that was a misperception; I was drunk.

'You need to sleep awhile,' Cicero said.

'What, on your exam table?' I said.

Cicero sighed, reaching up to pull off the bandanna and release the little ponytail. 'No,' he said slowly.

'What, then?'

'Look,' he said, 'this is not an offer I'd usually make, but I think I'm going to have you sleep in my bedroom.'

'Really?' I sensed he wasn't terribly comfortable with the idea; I wasn't, either. But I knew he was right. I couldn't drive until I'd fully sobered.

He was already rolling toward the bedroom, and I turned to follow. He opened the bedroom door and flicked on the light.

A narrow single bed was covered with a cinnamon-brown counterpane, a black-and-white Ansel Adams print of Yosemite on the wall. A set of hand weights, probably twenty pounds each, were half hidden under the bed. Along the wall ran a low and narrow table, almost a shelf, covered with family photos. Some of the pictures were quite old, in black-and-white.

'This is nice,' I said.

'Out there is my office,' Cicero said. 'In here is my home.'

I walked in behind him. To our immediate right was a sliding closet door. It was mirrored, showing us the reflections of a drunk, lost cop and an altruistic criminal. Quickly I looked away.

'Why don't you turn on the desk lamp,' Cicero suggested. 'It doesn't throw a lot of light, so you can sleep with it on if you like. And if you want to shut it off later, you can reach it from the bed, unlike the wall switch.'

I walked over to the desk and did as he'd recommended. Cicero turned off the brighter overhead fixture, and we were immersed in a low, golden light.

'You can close the blinds on the window, too, if you like. But we're twenty-six stories up. No one's going to peek in. I sleep with them open,' he said.

When he began to back out of the room, I turned and said, 'What about you?'

'What about me?'

'You're not going to try to sleep on the exam table, are you?'

Cicero laughed. 'No, don't worry,' he said. 'I keep late hours.'

'But — '

'If it gets that late, and I need to go to bed, I'll wake you and kick you out. I'm not Mother Teresa.'

When he was gone, I stripped down to the sweater and my underwear and wondered: Was it right to get *in* the bed? That seemed so personal, but I didn't want to wake up in an hour, on top of the covers, because I was cold.

I slipped experimentally between the comforter and the blanket, a compromise that made sense to my alcohol-and-exhaustion-clouded mind, and turned off the lamp.

An indeterminate time later I awoke in darkness. Where the hell was I? I heard masculine, adult voices from behind a door and the sound filled me with a dread I didn't understand. My heart jumped up from its slow sleeping rhythm.

Then two words became distinguishable: *pecho* and *fiebre*. I recognized the voice of Cicero Ruiz, and heard a baby's hoarse cough. I closed my eyes and slept again.

★ ★ ★

When I raised my head again from sleep, I sensed that hours had passed. Something had wakened me, though, and I looked around and saw the low form of Cicero in very dim, flickering light. He was placing a lighted candle on the table of family photos; there was another candle already on the table, flame still and steady.

'What — ' I said.

'The storm came in,' he said. 'The power's out. I was afraid you'd wake up in a strange place in the dark and not be able to find your way around.'

I sat up, facing him and the end of the bed. 'Oh,' I said, and rubbed at my face. 'What time is it?'

'Nearly two,' he said.

'I'm sorry,' I said. 'You should have got me up.'

'Well, you're awake now. Have you slept enough?'

'Yes,' I said. 'I feel a lot better. Can I use your bathroom again?'

Cicero held out the candle. I threw back the comforter and slid down the bed, climbing over the low footboard at the end. Too late it occurred to me to be self-conscious about being half dressed. But Cicero had seen it all before. He was a doctor. I took the candle from him.

In the bathroom, I found toothpaste in Cicero's medicine chest. I rubbed some on my tongue and spread it across my teeth and gums, then spit and rinsed my mouth out. I splashed water on my face afterward. The makeshift ritual made me feel like a normal human being again. It helped that my left ear felt better. It was sore, but sore in a way that was far preferable to the pulsing, sharp pain of this afternoon. I chanced looking in the mirror. I'd expected to be bloodshot, but my eyes were surprisingly clear.

I took the candle back into the bedroom. The way Cicero watched me walk was familiar.

'You're giving me your field sobriety test, aren't you?' I said.

'I want to be sure you're okay to drive,' he said. 'Sit down and talk to me for a moment. I'm going to tell you two important things.'

I sat on the edge of the bed, and he rolled closer.

'First, I want to see you again in forty-eight hours, to check that your ear is healing properly.'

I nodded assent.

He picked up a slip of paper. 'The second thing: this is a prescription for an antibiotic. It's likely your body can lick this without penicillin, but it'll do so faster with help.'

'I thought you didn't prescribe,' I said.

'The pad was brought to me by a patient,' Cicero said. 'I didn't even want to know where she got it. I don't use it. But I'm making an exception.' He paused, underscoring that this was serious business. 'This prescription comes with conditions. First: you tell no one I have a prescription pad here. I never tell people, myself.'

'I won't,' I said.

'Second, a prescription for antibiotics shouldn't raise a red flag for the pharmacist. Antibiotics aren't commonly sought in prescription fraud.'

'You're saying there's a chance that, if I go fill

this, I could get busted?'

'A very small chance. Usually people who try to fake prescriptions get caught because they don't know how to write scrips. Doctors and pharmacists communicate with each other in a language all their own. It's not easy to fake. Obviously, there's nothing wrong with the way this one is written, except that the license number I wrote is completely invalid,' he said. 'If they do bust you, they'll probably go in the back, call the police, and then stall you until the cops arrive.'

What a sordid little story it would make: Hennepin County detective caught scamming prescription drugs.

'So if it takes more than ten minutes for them to find your prescription, if they say they can't track it down, just leave,' Cicero told me. 'But this is the second condition: if you do get caught, this doesn't come back on me.' He held out the prescription, but just a little, bargaining. 'I have enough problems. I do not need to get arrested. If you give me your word you won't give me up, that's good enough for me.'

'I give you my word,' I said.

He gave me the slip of paper.

'Why, though?' I asked him. 'Why do you trust me?'

'I don't know,' he said. 'I just do.'

A silence settled between us. The candlelight flickering on the family photos made the table look like an altar to the spirits of Cicero's ancestors, although at least one of the prints was recent: it was Cicero at what must have been his

114

med-school graduation. His smile looked genuine, not the tense rictus some people produce
when faced with a camera and a demand to
smile. He was easily half a head taller than the
people surrounding him.

Half a head taller. He was standing. He was
able-bodied.

'How tall were you?' I asked without thinking.

'Were?' he repeated.

Heat immediately rose to my face. 'I'm sorry,'
I said. 'I meant — '

'Six feet,' Cicero said. 'The tallest man in my
family, ever.'

'I didn't mean — '

'It's all right,' he said.

My embarrassment began to recede slightly,
but still I looked down at my bare feet. 'I should
go.'

'Sarah,' he said, 'are you afraid to touch me?'

It was true, we were sitting close together, and
I had been careful not to let our limbs touch.

'Of course not,' I said. 'You examined me, for
God's sake.'

'That was me touching you,' he said. 'That's
not the same thing. Does it disturb you that I'm
paralyzed?'

'I'm married,' I said.

'I see,' Cicero said quietly. 'You wear no
wedding ring and are free to stay out until two in
the morning, but when I make an overture to
you, suddenly you're married.'

'My husband is in prison,' I said.

He didn't believe me; I could see that.

'He got sent up for auto theft,' I said. 'He's in

prison in Wisconsin.'

Cicero's expression didn't change, but at last he said, 'Then I suppose you should go.'

'It's not because you're paralyzed,' I said. I don't know why it was important to me to establish that. I leaned forward and laid a hand on his thigh. It was stupid, a chickenshit half measure.

'I can't feel that, Sarah,' Cicero said. 'You don't have to do anything to prove to me that you're open-minded. But if you're going to touch me, do it somewhere I can feel it.' He reached over and took my hand. 'Let me show you something,' he said.

With his other hand, he pulled up his shirt. 'A lot of people think a paraplegic's body has one sharp line between sensation and no sensation, like the line that divides light and dark on the moon,' he said. 'But it's more like the way twilight falls on the earth.'

He placed my hand high on his rib cage. 'Here, I can feel everything.' He slid his hand and mine, underneath it, a little lower. 'Down here, only temperature, but not pressure. Down here,' a little lower still, 'full dark.'

Keeping eye contact, I laid my left hand on the other side of his rib cage, and Cicero put his hands on my hips, pulling me toward him. There was nowhere to go but onto the wheelchair, and cautiously I put my knees on each side of his thighs, on the edges of the seat, so I was kneeling in front of him.

He had no insecurity about having to tip his face upward to kiss a woman, and when he did it, he went deep almost immediately, probing with his tongue. It shocked me; that kind of deep, invasive kiss from a virtual stranger was disturbing and exciting and I felt something roll over deep in my stomach, like nerves, except warmer.

Our dim reflection in the mirrored closet doors showed man, woman, and chair; a sexual tableau I'd never expected to be a part of. Men had taken me into their homes before, and into their beds. But in climbing onto Cicero's wheelchair, I was being taken into the very center of his life, almost his body. It made me wonder if Cicero Ruiz had a special insight into how it felt to be penetrated.

★   ★   ★

The third time I woke up, the flames of the candles were almost completely recessed in deep pits of wax. It no longer mattered; the sky was lightening to predawn blue beyond the window, just starting to illuminate the bedroom. Cicero slept so close to me that I could feel the warmth of his skin. It was reassuring until I saw Shiloh's old shirt hanging off the back of Cicero's wheelchair, and I felt something cold in my stomach, like I was looking at a map and nothing was familiar.

I slipped out of bed and put my clothes on as quietly as possible, picked up the prescription, and turned the knob of the bedroom door in that time-honored, half-speed way people do when they are sneaking into, or out of, bedrooms.

Cicero didn't even open his eyes when he spoke, and his voice was rusty with sleep.

'It's just a little sympathy between humans, Sarah,' he said. 'Don't let it ruin your week.'

9

After eight uninterrupted hours of sleep at home, I woke up in my warm, stifling bedroom wanting several things all at once: ice water; a hot, hot shower; and some kind of food I couldn't quite identify. I satisfied the first two needs first, lingering in the shower. It was amazing how much better my ear felt already. It wasn't even sore. It just had that pleasant, empty heaviness that sometimes replaces pain, the way your head feels after a particularly nasty headache rolls out, letting you free of its grip at last.

Dressed in a pair of cutoffs and a tank shirt against the hot weather, I went into the kitchen and looked over the lightly stocked refrigerator and cupboards. Nothing appealed to me. Whatever this odd craving was, it wasn't the usual impulse-eating suspects: caffeine, sugar, salt, or red meat. I went out the back entryway, into the yard.

Last night's storm had left the skies clean, with just a few white clouds left over in the west. The sun was high in the sky, but the overhanging elms filtered out all but a few of its rays. My neighbor's underfed Siamese cat prowled through the overgrown grass of our narrow, untended backyard, stopped, assessed me as no threat, and went on. I, also, went on, to the basement door and down into the cobwebbed dimness.

Down here was what Shiloh called the 'Armageddon food,' canned things only to be eaten in case of natural disaster, riot, martial law, or nuclear attack. I'd always thought the kind of food that kept well in emergencies — ready-to-eat, low-sodium soups and powdered milk and fruit in syrup — was too depressing to be eaten as the world fell apart. 'We need liquor down here,' I'd said. 'A few bottles of whiskey and some jars of chocolate sauce.'

Shiloh, sitting on his heels in the dimness, surveying the shelves, had dryly agreed. *Oh, sure*, he'd said. *Maybe we should put a bed down here, too. As the world goes up in flames outside, we can give ourselves over to every kind of perversion.* And then he'd given me that look, the one that reminded me that few people have as deep a pleasure in wickedness as the once devout, like Shiloh, a preacher's son.

Goddammit. While it was impossible to forget that I was living alone, that my husband was in prison in another state, every once in a while it hit me afresh that, *hey, it's Shiloh who isn't here anymore.* And today of all days I did not want to be thinking those kinds of thoughts.

Fortunately, I was almost immediately distracted. As I moved for the stairs with a jar of applesauce and a can of pears in my hands, I tripped in the poorly lit surroundings. The culprit, on the floor, was an old and battered toolbox that I knew held tools we didn't use on a weekly or even monthly basis, unlike the wrench and pliers. But I knew without opening it that it held something else, too: an unregistered .25

with cheap silver plating.

Genevieve's sister, Deb, had given it to me, what seemed like a hundred years ago. She'd come by it innocently enough; it was a relic from her days of living in a bad East St. Louis neighborhood. She was overdue to get rid of it, and I'd promised her I'd take care of that. But immediately after that, Shiloh's disappearance and our subsequent troubles had wiped my promise from my mind. I'd stashed the cheap little gun in the basement, and here it had remained. Given the suspicion I'd been under in the Royce Stewart case, I'd felt I couldn't simply take it to work and give it to our evidence techs for disposal. That was truer than ever now, with Gray Diaz in town.

I nudged the toolbox away from the base of the stairs with my foot, deciding I'd deal with the .25 soon, but not today.

Upstairs again, I ate the whole can of pears with a little grated cheddar cheese on top of it, and was a quarter of the way into the jar of applesauce when I heard a knock at my door.

The curtains on the windowed top half of the door were sheer, and through them I could see a full, broad masculine form. I pulled back the curtain and saw Detective Van Noord, to whom I'd made my apologies yesterday before fleeing work.

I opened the door. 'What's going on?'

'Prewitt sent me,' he said. 'To see if you were here. We couldn't get ahold of you.'

'It's my day off,' I said. 'Is something going on?'

121

I meant a public-safety emergency, all hands needed. But the afternoon outside was quiet, no sirens in the distance.

'No, nothing like that,' Van Noord said. 'But you left so abruptly yesterday, in the middle of your shift, that Prewitt was worried. He asked me to check on the situation.'

'I was sick,' I said blankly. 'I told you that yesterday.'

'I know, and I told him, but he still asked me to check on you, and then we couldn't reach you, not on your cell or your pager — '

'Why didn't you call here?' I asked again.

'We did, and kept getting a busy signal.'

'The phone's off the hook,' I said, remembering only now the decision I'd made very early that morning. 'I'm sorry, I didn't mean to worry anyone.'

But it still didn't make any sense, Prewitt sending Van Noord here. 'Are you shorthanded?' I asked. 'I'm feeling a lot better today. I could come in.'

'Oh, no, no,' he said, waving off the suggestion. 'You stay home, take care of that ear. But you might want to keep your cell on. Just so we can get in touch if we need you,' he advised.

'Sure,' I agreed.

When he was gone, I went into the kitchen and put the phone receiver back on its cradle. Then I poured myself a glass of water and washed down the first dose of antibiotics. I'd bought them just after leaving Cicero's, at a 24-hour pharmacy, waiting at the counter with a nonchalance so forced it would have clearly broadcast my paranoia to anyone who'd truly been paying attention.

The world had gone crazy, I thought. I was scamming prescription drugs. Lieutenant Prewitt was sending his detectives around to check on sick personnel. The sanest person I'd dealt with in the last forty-eight hours was Cicero Ruiz.

Cicero. Now, there was a problem.

In the brief time that I'd known Cicero Ruiz, I'd seen him not only give an examination and dispense medical advice, but also perform something that qualified as minor surgery. Then he'd revealed himself to be in possession of a prescription pad and willing to write a prescription; I had only his word that he was making a solitary exception in my case. Cicero had incriminated himself as readily and thoroughly as if I'd written a script for him to follow. But I couldn't turn him in, not now. It was as simple as this: I'd given him my word.

He'd extracted that promise from me only in relation to the illegal prescription and the prospect that I'd get caught with it. But in principle, I'd promised something much larger. *I do not need to get arrested*, Cicero had said. I'd promised I wouldn't get him in trouble with the law.

Even if I hadn't made that promise, would I be on more solid ground right now? The greater issue was my own behavior. I hadn't faked an ear infection. That had been genuine, and I'd accepted medical care from Cicero for it, which had to be the ethical equivalent of buying stolen goods from a fence or placing a bet with an illegal bookmaker. Then I'd participated in a prescription fraud. And just for good measure, I'd become sexually involved with a suspect.

Whatever happened, I couldn't turn him in now. I'd crossed too many lines.

10

'I feel really bad,' I said.

I was standing on the Hennessys' doorstep. Marlinchen had answered my knock, tinier than I remembered in faded jeans and what looked like a child's T-shirt with a pencil-line dark-blue heart at the center. She'd listened with guarded patience as I'd explained about the illness that had made me a little more than twenty-four hours late in keeping our appointment.

Only late yesterday had I remembered it, my promise to drive out and talk with Marlinchen again. What made me feel worse was that when I'd checked the messages on my cell phone, there'd been nothing from her. She'd written me off as an adult who'd dismissed her and her problems as insignificant.

'I thought you'd changed your mind,' Marlinchen told me. 'You made a point of saying that Aidan was way out of your jurisdiction.'

'I wouldn't just stand you up,' I said. 'Can I come in now, or is this a bad time?'

'It's fine,' Marlinchen said, stepping aside to let me into their entryway. 'But I thought you worked in the afternoon and evening.'

'I do, but this is my day off,' I said. 'And anyway, I'm rotating back onto day shifts soon.'

Marlinchen led me back toward the kitchen and family room where we'd been earlier. Nowhere in the house could I hear activity, but there was a live feel in the air, and I knew the boys were around.

The kitchen, in fact, was occupied, but not by anyone cooking or eating. Instead, Donal sat in a chair that was elevated by an encyclopedia volume under each leg. He had a beach towel wrapped around his chest and shoulders. A pair of shears lay on a nearby counter, and a small corona of light-brown hair lay on the floor around the chair legs.

'Donal, you remember Detective Pribek,' Marlinchen said, picking up the shears.

'Hello,' Donal said.

'Hey,' I said. On second inspection, he looked younger than 11, his face still soft and pale with childhood.

To Marlinchen, I said, 'Maybe I should wait until you're done with Donal's haircut before we get into . . . what we talked about the other day.'

But she disagreed. 'All my brothers know the situation,' she said. 'We can discuss it now.'

'All right,' I said. 'Let me start with a broad question: Why wasn't Aidan living at home?'

Marlinchen finger-combed Donal's hair until a half inch stuck out at the ends, then cut. 'Dad is a widower. He was raising five small children. That was just too many,' she said. 'Aidan was the oldest, and the best suited to adapt to life away from home.'

'I thought Aidan was your twin,' I said.

Marlinchen smiled. 'I make that mistake a lot, calling Aidan 'the oldest.' I don't know why I do that, he was only born fifty-seven minutes before me.' She smoothed Donal's hair down over his ear, then took up another thick strand and trimmed the end. 'It's ironic, too, because Aidan was held back to repeat the fourth grade, so after that, a lot of people assumed he was younger than me.'

That didn't really tell me anything; I tried to get back on track. 'That was the only reason Aidan was sent away?' I reiterated. 'Your father just had too many kids?'

'Do you have children, Detective Pribek?' Marlinchen asked. Her voice had that faint shimmer of patronization that mothers have when asking single friends this question.

'No,' I admitted.

'Of course, I don't either,' she said, 'but I know it's very, very difficult raising five kids on your own. Dad tried, but he just had his hands too full, with his teaching and his writing. He also had pretty severe pain sometimes, from a degenerative disk. There were episodes where it was almost disabling.' More hair fell. 'Later, he developed an ulcer, I think from the pressure of working and raising a family on his own.'

'Mmm,' I said, noncommittal. 'When was the last time you heard from Aidan?'

'We don't really hear from him,' Marlinchen said. Her eyes were down, on her work. 'The last I saw him was when he left for Illinois.' Another tiny sheaf of light-brown hair fluttered to the floor.

'Illinois?' I said.

'Before he went to Georgia, he lived with our aunt, Brigitte, outside of Rockford, Illinois,' Marlinchen explained. 'He would have stayed there, but Aunt Brigitte died five months later, and that was when Pete Benjamin offered to let Aidan live on his farm.'

'How did your aunt die?' I asked.

'A car accident,' Marlinchen said.

'How did your father and Pete Benjamin know each other?' I said.

'They grew up in Atlanta together,' she said. 'Pete inherited a lot of land and went to farm it. Dad went to college, and the rest was history.' She paused to concentrate, lining up hair. 'I think Dad thought Aidan would learn a lot from living on a farm. Dad left college at 19 and traveled through America, and he worked a lot of manual jobs, like farm labor. He said he learned more about life working on the road than in any classroom.'

Marlinchen tugged at the hair on either side of Donal's ears. 'Does this look even to you, Detective Pribek?'

I studied her handiwork. 'Yeah,' I said. 'I think it does.'

Marlinchen pulled back the beach towel. 'Off you go, sport,' she said.

'Finally,' Donal said. 'Can I have a Popsicle?'

'I guess that'd be all right,' Marlinchen said.

As Donal raided the refrigerator and left, I asked, 'Do you know anything about Aidan's friends in Georgia, his interests, where he might have gone?'

Marlinchen shook her head. 'I wish I did. Maybe Mr. Benjamin can help you with that.'

'That's a good point,' I said. 'I'll need his phone number. And I could use a picture of Aidan.'

Upstairs, the first doorway was Marlinchen's. Inside, she almost immediately folded her legs underneath her and sank to a cross-legged position beside the bed. Reaching underneath the dust ruffle, she pulled out a wooden box and opened the lid. 'This'll take me just a minute,' she said.

While Marlinchen riffled through her box, I looked around at her bedroom. It was orderly and clean; I wouldn't have expected otherwise. The twin bed was neatly made, covered in cream-colored eyelet. Her desk faced the window, likewise painted cream, and at its edge a pen with an old-fashioned ostrich-feather plume stood at the ready. It was charming, but the real work undoubtedly was done on the laptop that sat, jarringly modern, at the desk's center.

'Do you write?' I asked her. 'I mean, outside of school?'

Marlinchen shook her head, still looking down into the box. 'Liam does,' she said.

Atop the dresser were two photos in frames. One was a snapshot of Marlinchen among classmates on what looked like a class trip to a Twins game, another of Marlinchen and her three younger brothers on the bank of a creek. For the bedroom of a middle-class teenage girl, it was a surprisingly small amount of sentimentalia. In doing missing-persons work, I'd been in a few adolescent girls' rooms, and I'd seen displays that made me wish I owned stock in Kodak: dates, proms, class trips, sleepovers, all memorialized in pictures.

'Here,' Marlinchen's voice interrupted me, 'while you're looking at photos, here's one of Aidan.'

The Polaroid showed a boy of perhaps 11, standing next to a tire swing, which dangled from the willow I'd seen on the far side of the house. The boy in the photo clearly was going to be tall, taller than Hugh Hennessy, I thought. And, though the detail didn't leap out, when you looked at the hand on the rope, you could see the nub of dark pink flesh where the smallest finger should have been. Otherwise, Aidan Hennessy was pleasant-looking, serious in expression, blond and blue-eyed like his sister.

'Listen,' I said, 'do you have a photo of Aidan that's more recent?' I said.

'No,' she said. 'Is that a problem?'

'Yes,' I said. 'The years between 12 and 17 are important ones. Kids change a lot. Hair gets darker, and faces change shape as they lose baby fat. Or sometimes kids gain weight. And they pierce and bleach and dye, too.'

'I don't think Aidan would do that,' she said. 'Besides, he won't be hard to identify. You really can't miss the hand,' she said.

'No, I suppose not,' I said. 'How'd that happen, anyway?'

'A dog,' Marlinchen said. 'He was bitten.'

'Ouch,' I said. 'How old was he?'

'Three, maybe four,' Marlinchen said. 'I really don't remember it, except he was in the hospital a long time, and when they brought him back, I was scared of him, because of his hand. I started

130

crying, and wouldn't play with him.'

'Really?' I said. But maybe it wasn't so strange, that a little girl would be so rattled by her brother's frightening injury. 'Tell me something else: How did you find out Aidan had run away from the farm in Georgia?'

Marlinchen nodded. 'Oh, that. E-mail,' she said. 'After Dad had his stroke, for a few days I spent a lot of time in here, looking through all his papers and financial records and so on. I read his e-mails on the computer, and at the bottom of the list were the old ones. You know, the ones you don't delete?'

'You have his password?'

'No, the password automatically comes up when he logs in, as asterisks, you know?'

I nodded.

'So I just had to hit Return.' Marlinchen untucked a leg that had been crossed under her other thigh. 'I wasn't reading all the messages, but this one said, 'Re: Aidan,' so it caught my eye. I opened it and I saw Pete's message to my dad, and under that, my dad's original message to him.'

A farmer with e-mail? Well, why not?

'The messages were both about Aidan having run away. I guess there was a miscommunication about who'd report it to the police. I was afraid that neither one had, so I called Deputy Fredericks in Georgia.'

According to what Fredericks had told me, the communication between Pete Benjamin and Hugh Hennessy had been quite clear: that Hugh would deal with Aidan's having bolted from the farm. But I didn't want to get into that issue at the moment. I said, 'Marlinchen, Deputy Fredericks told me that Aidan had run away to Minnesota once before.'

Marlinchen nodded.

'Your father sent him back, is that right?' I asked.

She nodded again, looking down at the floor.

'Did anything in particular cause Aidan to run away?' I asked.

She shook her head.

'Are you sure?' I pressed her.

'He was homesick. He came here and Dad sent him back. That's all.' She chewed her lower lip. 'Detective Pribek, what I said earlier, about not knowing anything about Aidan's day-to-day life, or hearing from him . . . I know it might sound strange, that Aidan was sent away, and we've had so little contact with him, but after Mother died . . . it changes so many things in the dynamics of a family. It's hard for people to understand, and I don't think I explain it very well.'

'It's not so hard to understand as you might think,' I said. 'My mother died when I was young, and later my father sent me to Minnesota at 13, to live with a great-aunt I'd never even met before. It sounds severe, but in the end it was for the best.'

'Then you understand,' Marlinchen said, her voice almost relieved. 'I knew there was a reason why I felt like you could help.'

'I'm not in a position to do that much,' I cautioned her. 'I'm just going to do some things over the phone and on the computer that'll go faster for me than they would for you. I can't travel to Illinois or Georgia.'

'I know,' Marlinchen said quickly. 'Anything you can do, I appreciate.'

'Then,' I said, 'I need to talk to your brothers.'

★   ★   ★

It was Colm who'd been watching TV in the family room earlier; when I returned he was still there, lounging on the couch in T-shirt and sweatpants.

'Hey,' he said, not making eye contact.

The big TV screen showed an outdoor gun range with a glimpse of East Coast greenery in the background. Young men and women in blue shirts rolled to their feet, raised weapons, and fired rapidly at the black outlines of targets.

'It's a special about Quantico,' Colm said. 'That's where they train FBI agents.'

'I know,' I said, watching. For a moment it transfixed me, all the youth and righteousness and promise that the trainees seemed to embody, standing on a vista where the best of their professional lives was just about to open up before them, and my heart felt briefly leaden at the sight.

Then I shook my head, clearing away the reverie, and said to Colm, 'Maybe you could turn off the TV for a couple of minutes. I just need to ask you a few questions about your brother.'

Colm rolled off the couch to switch off the

133

television, and I took a seat, flipping open my notebook. 'When was the last time you had contact with Aidan?' I asked.

'When he left,' Colm said, taking a seat at the other end of the couch.

'Nothing since? Letters, phone calls?'

Colm shook his head, chewed at the corner of a fingernail.

'Based on what you know about him, can you guess at where he might have gone when he ran away?'

Colm shook his head again.

'Can you tell me anything about why it was Aidan who was sent away?' I asked. 'As opposed to both the twins, or one of the younger kids.'

Colm shrugged. 'I don't know.'

'You can't speculate at all?'

'I was nine,' he said. 'Nobody told me anything.'

'Thanks,' I said, flipping the notebook closed.

'That's it?' Colm said, startled.

'That's it,' I affirmed, getting up.

'You didn't even write anything down,' Colm said.

'I don't usually write down things like 'I don't know' and 'I was nine,'' I said.

Colm looked a little sheepish.

'There's not a lot you can tell me if you haven't seen or heard from him,' I explained.

He turned the television back on. The agents-in-training were now learning to break down and clean their guns. I wondered if the field of law enforcement held an appeal for Colm Hennessy, like it did for many boys his age.

'They do really good weapons training at Quantico,' I offered.

Colm's light-blue eyes flicked to me again. 'What kind of gun do you use?'

'A .40 caliber Smith & Wesson.'

'Isn't that a lot of gun for a woman to handle?' Colm asked.

'Excuse me?' I said, though I'd heard him clearly.

He shrugged. 'It's a big gun.'

It was on the tip of my tongue to tell him that I'd been the second-best shooter in my Sheriff's academy class, but it was probably beneath the dignity of a county detective to get into a verbal pissing match with a boy half her age. So I bit my tongue and asked, 'Are you interested in shooting?'

'Not really,' Colm said. 'Dad hates guns. He won't have one in the house, not even for hunting.' He shrugged. 'Doesn't matter. I'm more into close-quarters fighting.'

'With what,' I asked, 'a television remote?' Something in his dismissive tone had pushed me over the edge.

Colm really looked at me for the first time, as if he'd been bitten by something that he didn't think had a mouth. His lips tightened with embarrassment, and finally he said, 'No, I have a heavy bag. And weights, out in the far garage.'

★ ★ ★

Upstairs, I found Liam Hennessy at the computer in his father's study. There, he told me essentially the same thing Colm had, just in more words. Liam, too, hadn't heard from or written to Aidan since his older brother left for Illinois, and he too felt that Aidan had been sent away from home only because their father was struggling to raise five kids.

'It seems odd to me, though,' I said, 'that Aidan didn't come home for summers, or on holidays.'

Liam looked at the computer screen, blue light reflecting off his glasses, as though the answer could be found there. 'Summer is an important time on a farm,' he said, 'so it's unlikely that Pete could have spared him then. As for holidays, I guess Dad felt that Aidan really needed to settle in at Pete's, and think of that as his home.'

'For five years? That's an awful long ban on visits home.'

Liam nodded slowly. It was clear he was uncomfortable. 'I wish I could tell you more,' he said, 'but I was young at the time. No one really explained it to me.'

'Okay,' I said. 'If you think of anything else . . . '

'I'll let you know,' he said hastily.

I got to my feet. Liam had lifted his long-fingered hands back to the keyboard, as if eager to escape again into whatever he'd been writing when I interrupted him, and I realized for the first time that it might not be homework that absorbed him. Liam, Marlinchen had said, was the aspiring writer among the kids.

On the way out, I paused at the doorway. 'What happened to your carpet here?' The edge, where it met the carpeting of the hall, was rough-edged and fraying, as if the person who'd laid it had hacked it off carelessly with a utility knife.

'Dad happened to it,' Liam said, a flicker of amusement on his face. 'He put down the carpet in here himself. It's like that all around the edges. We're used to it.'

It was true; the whole perimeter of the room looked the same as the doorway, rough-edged.

'Don't take this the wrong way,' I said, 'but was your father drinking when he was on this home-improvement kick?'

It wasn't as light a question as my tone implied. Whenever there's trouble in a family, it's good to know which way the alcohol is flowing, if at all.

Liam smiled, untroubled by my inquiry. 'I wouldn't know,' he said. 'I mean, Dad put down the carpet a long time ago, before my time. But I do know that he never drank much, and he quit a few years back. Just for general health reasons. It was never a problem.'

★   ★   ★

Marlinchen walked me out to my car, after I'd finished. 'Were the boys helpful?' she asked.

'Yes, they were,' I said. The truth was that they hadn't said anything useful, but neither had they seemed deliberately obstructionist. I'd spoken to Donal last, just to be thorough, but he scarcely remembered his older brother, and I'd only spent about three minutes with him.

A white cat emerged from the grass and went to Marlinchen, winding a figure eight around her ankles, pushing its trapezoidal head against Marlinchen's shins.

'Friend of yours?' I said.

'Snowball,' she affirmed. 'Our cat. I hardly ever see her in the daytime anymore. She gets around.' She sat on her heels to run one hand over the cat's arched spine, then straightened.

'Well, she's got plenty of room for that,' I said, looking around. The Hennessys and their neighbors had lots of open space between lots.

I also noticed again the freestanding outbuilding that I'd taken for a nineteenth-century carriage house; it was what Colm must have meant by 'the far garage,' where he had his exercise equipment. Closer to Marlinchen and me was the lone tree on the bank of the lake. In this area, sugar maples were everywhere, as were smaller spruces and hardy little pines. Lilacs seemed to be the flowering tree of choice; some were still in bloom. This tree was none of them. It was obviously ornamental, deliberately planted in its solitary spot. I didn't think I'd ever seen one like it before, though its few flowers, cream-colored and orchidaceous, were vaguely familiar.

'What kind of tree is that?' I asked.

'It's a magnolia,' Marlinchen said.

'Really? I didn't know they'd grow this far north,' I commented.

Marlinchen's face was turned from me, looking toward the tree. 'It was here when a real-estate agent showed our parents this place. It's what convinced my mother that this house was The One.' I could hear a smile in Marlinchen's voice. 'She and Dad met in Georgia. She thought it was fate.'

11

Young. I was young. I was too young to remember much of anything.

That was the refrain I was getting from the Hennessy children, and to be fair, it was probably true. I was overdue for an adult perspective on the Hennessy situation, and with Hugh incapacitated and his wife dead, there wasn't one.

Hugh Hennessy, though, wasn't just any citizen. He was a successful writer. At least some of the details of his life must have been chronicled, and would be available to me. For that, I needed the University of Minnesota library.

I started with a Web search on Hugh's name. It told me that he had written three books, with more than a few years between publication of each. All three were considered to be largely semiautobiographical. The first, *Twilight*, was an indictment of his parents' slowly withering marriage in suburban Atlanta. The second, *The Channel*, was a story about his ancestors in New Orleans, named for the Irish Channel section of that city. *The Channel* was the book that had sounded vaguely familiar to me when Marlinchen had mentioned it, and now I understood why; it had been his most popular work, praised by many critics as warm without being sentimental, unflinching about American prejudice without resorting to self-pity.

Hennessy's third book, *A Rainbow at Night*, was widely perceived as a fictionalization of the Hennessy marriage, which had ended with the death of Hennessy's wife at age 31. The title came from the protagonist's thought, verbalized close to the end of the book, that he had once had 'a dream of love that was beautiful but ultimately impossible, like a rainbow at night.'

A photo surfaced among the reviews that the Web search turned up. In it I saw a younger incarnation of the invalid I'd seen sleeping at Park Christian Hospital. He was a slight man with thin sandy hair and eyes that looked a pale blue, and his expression was, if not pinched, not quite at ease. His publisher's Web site also posted his author bio, clearly from the back of *Rainbow*.

> *With his first novel,* Twilight, *published at age 25, Hugh Hennessy told America a cautionary tale about the perils of assimilation and upward mobility set in his own suburban Atlanta. His follow-up novel,* The Channel, *about his Irish forebears, was both praised by critics and beloved by millions of readers, and adapted into a major motion picture. Hennessy has been a guest professor and writer-in-residence at several American colleges. He lives with his four children in Minneapolis, Minnesota.*

I was wrong, though, in expecting to find interviews with Hennessy among the search results. A common phrase in news stories and reviews was something like: 'Hennessy, who prefers to let his writing speak for itself . . .' Here and there was a reference to 'a 1987 interview,' or 'a 1989 interview.' Hugh had given his last interview, as far as I could tell, in 1990. There were, however, references to longer magazine profiles, and these I found in the stacks.

The longest piece, 'A Rainbow in Shadow,' was written for *The New York Times Magazine* by a former *Pioneer Press* reporter named Patrick Healy, to coincide with the publication of *A Rainbow at Night*. I started with his work, and followed up with two other pieces that had run in national magazines.

This is the story that emerged.

Hugh Hennessy was born in 1962, into a comfortable Atlanta suburb. His father was a cardiac surgeon who'd played football in college and had hunted and fished regularly in later life. His mother never worked outside the home. If it was a bad marriage, as Hugh was later to imply in *Twilight*, it wasn't the sort of bad marriage that brought cops to the front doorstep. Neither was Hugh troubled as an adolescent, at least in any way that police and available academic records showed. Hugh excelled at all his studies. While his slight stature kept him off the football team, he'd been an aggressive wrestler, posting a good record in his weight class.

Emory University granted Hugh a partial academic scholarship, despite his parents' comfortable finances. It was at Emory that Hugh Hennessy met the two people who would be his most constant companions. One was J. D. Campion, a part-Lakota literature student from South Dakota. The other was a beautiful German-born folklore and anthropology major, Elisabeth Hannelore Baumann.

The three were inseparable during their first two years at school. After that, Campion and Hennessy dropped out, much to the displeasure of Hennessy's parents. J. D. and Hugh planned to travel America, like young literary lions of an earlier generation had done.

Literally on the eve of their departure, Hennessy married Elisabeth Baumann. Both were 19, and their haste gave rise to rumors of a pregnancy, but those whisperings eventually proved unfounded. Apparently, the wedding had its roots in an urgency that was emotional, not biological. She stayed in school, a simple silver ring on her finger, her stomach flat. Hennessy embarked on a journey of self-discovery in sweat with Campion.

They refined taconite on the Range. They harvested hard red winter wheat in South Dakota. They worked in the shipyards of Duluth, once an outlaw border town. They traveled south to see the New Orleans where Hennessy's great-grandparents had arrived in America, and stayed to work on the docks and be arrested in a brawl that cleared out a working-class bar there. They were either gathering fodder for their future writings, if you wanted to be charitable, or creating a legend, if you wanted to be cynical.

The New Orleans mug shots ran along with Healy's story. Campion, dark and thin, was appropriately resigned and surly in his, but Hennessy was smiling.

Smiling. I couldn't figure that out for a minute, but then I realized: well-bred, middle-class Hugh Hennessy had been told all his life to smile when he was having his picture taken. For his booking photo, he did it automatically.

Somewhere in that interim period, Hennessy began work on *Twilight*, the fictionalization of his parents' middle-class life in Atlanta. In time, he felt strongly enough about its potential that he'd come home to Atlanta to ready it for publication. Elisabeth, who had finished her degree, supported her husband as he finished his novel at white heat, sending it off to agents at age 24. In due time, *Twilight* was purchased, published, and hailed as a singular achievement.

As friends of Hennessy's parents recalled (both were dead by the writing of Healy's piece), the book had a chilling effect between parents and son. That was no surprise. What did seem to surprise Hennessy was the way his book was received in his hometown.

'*Twilight* was perceived, or perhaps misperceived, as a sweeping condemnation of the mores and priorities of the New South,' wrote Healy. 'Reviews of the book were distinctly cooler in the Southern press. One can extrapolate how it might have been viewed among Hennessy's associates and neighbors in Atlanta. Taking a no-prophet-is-received-in-his-homeland stance, Hennessy found the most pointedly Northern home he could have adopted: Minnesota.'

Minneapolis was a new chapter in the

Hennessys' life. As money from *Twilight* began to roll in, Elisabeth quit working to become a graduate student. The couple bought a house on Lake Minnetonka, and Hugh began working on his second book.

Again using fictional characters that clearly sprouted off his family tree, *The Channel* portrayed people with lives that were 'as alternately sunny and stormy as the world of *Twilight* is airless.' The immigrants Aidan and Maeve Hennessy had several children, and all their stories were touched on, but as a writer, Hugh Hennessy seemed most taken with the lives of his two great-uncles, who were minor figures in the New Orleans underworld of their day. Their finest — or worst — hour came when they were implicated in a daring series of truck-hijackings for which they were never arrested. If Hugh ever questioned the ethics of their lifestyle, or whether they had had alternatives to a life of theft and violence, it wasn't an issue raised in *The Channel*. Indulging a writer's fancy for artifacts from the fictional world, he bought a pair of restored revolvers of the kind his great-uncles had used; they appeared in a photograph of Hugh's study that accompanied one magazine profile.

The Channel cemented Hugh's reputation as a writer of merit. It was that rare piece of modern fiction that is both praised by the highest stratum of critics and read on subways and beaches. *The Channel* went to the top of the bestseller lists and stayed there for weeks.

If you could pick one word to describe the

world of the Hennessys back then, *fertile* would have been a good choice. Their family, their wealth, and their esteem were all growing in the Northern soil of Minnesota. Hugh and Elisabeth were celebrated in their adopted city, and Hugh stressed in interviews that they weren't going anywhere. This was what he'd always wanted, he said: a little land, roots, and the kind of big family he would have liked to have grown up in.

The 'family' part was certainly coming together. Elisabeth was close to delivering her fourth child in five years; she and Hugh already had three-year-old twins and a toddler, Liam. Funds weren't a problem. If *Twilight* had brought in respectable money, *The Channel* brought in a lot more, and Hugh was in demand as a lecturer at Twin Cities schools. He and Elisabeth entertained often; J. D. Campion was a frequent guest at their home. As a poet, he'd been enjoying a lesser success, but his volume of poetry, *Turning Shadow*, had won awards. It was both literate and in places vividly erotic, and for a while, it was the perfect book to peek sexily out of a college sophomore's backpack at the coffeehouse. Magazine writers made much of the literary friendship: the rootless, restless poet and the happily married scribe of family and heritage complemented each other in the public eye.

Then, shortly after the birth of Colm Hennessy, the parties stopped. So did the interviews. Rather abruptly, the Hennessys closed their doors to public life.

To the world, it seemed as though the

Hennessys had simply become deeply committed to raising a family. But if this were the case, the Hennessys were taking things to extremes. Campion, too, was suddenly excised from their lives. For years, he stayed away from Minnesota.

There were whispers of a falling out between Hugh and J. D., rumors that a longtime rivalry for Elisabeth's affections had finally boiled over, scalding the friendship beyond repair. There was a one-sentence reference, in Healy's story, to Campion's short-lived relationship with Elisabeth's younger sister, Brigitte, but Healy left it to the reader to draw the inference that Brigitte had been a failed substitute for her older sister in Campion's affections.

Others suggested the pernicious rivalry was professional, as Campion had never attained the heights his friend had. But the speculation remained speculation. Healy had been unable to reach the often-traveling Campion for an interview, and Hennessy had not cooperated with the story. Neither side of the split was told.

If Hugh wanted privacy, he got it. As years passed without a follow-up to *The Channel*, the world moved on. Even the Twin Cities media largely forgot about him, until the day it was reported that Elisabeth Hennessy's lifeless body had been found in the waters of Lake Minnetonka. She had left behind five children, the youngest only eleven months old.

For several years before her death, Elisabeth had been notably reclusive. Her husband taught at local colleges, but Elisabeth stayed at home, rarely going out or seeing friends. Perhaps this was simply consistent with having five children under the age of 10. If something darker, like postpartum depression, lay beneath it, there hadn't been enough evidence for the papers to even speculate. Coverage focused solely on tragedy striking at one of America's most respected writers on family ties, love, and loyalty.

Five years later, Hugh Hennessy had published his long-awaited third novel. *A Rainbow at Night* focused on the union of two passionate young people who had chosen, out of step with their modern world, to marry early and rear children immediately. It chronicled the trials and joys of such a young union, and then the narrator's struggle to make sense of the unexpected loss of his soulmate. It was well reviewed, and Hugh Hennessy was briefly in the public eye again. Then, once more, he faded from view.

Even the best of the profiles left questions unanswered. Had one of America's famous literary friendships been a longtime, unacknowledged love triangle that had poisoned its principals? Had Hugh Hennessy pushed his wife into having too many children, and ignored the warning signs of postpartum depression? These were issues that Healy and his peers couldn't explicitly raise. There was no one to address them. Hennessy was uncooperative, Campion in parts unknown, Elisabeth dead.

★ ★ ★

On my way home from the university, it had occurred to me that I was reaching the end of the second day since my eardrum lancing; I was due at Cicero's for the follow-up exam he'd requested. I was tempted to skip it. My ear hadn't hurt at all today, and the last thing I needed was to prolong my involvement with Cicero Ruiz, who I'd last seen while attempting to slip out of his bedroom unnoticed.

But I also recalled how he'd helped me when I'd needed it rather desperately. The least I could do was respect his professional judgment. He probably wouldn't want to mention the events of my last visit any more than I would. Neither of us would mention it; everything would be fine.

In my last visit to Cicero's, I'd been in too much pain with my ear to think about the slow, creaky elevator ride up to his apartment. This evening I noticed it anew: the shrieking cable beyond the ceiling, the flickering light, the slow progress from lighted number to lighted number. I told myself to quit being paranoid. It was slow; that didn't mean —

Above the roof, I heard a crunching noise, and the car came to an abrupt halt. The number 14 had been lit for a moment, perhaps more than a minute. I wanted to believe that someone on floor 14 had called the elevator, but I knew that wasn't true. By my estimation, I was in between floors 14 and 15, and I wasn't going to be getting any farther for a while.

'Perfect,' I said.

* * *

When I finally arrived on the 26th floor, I saw Cicero immediately, sitting in the open door of his apartment, talking with a young black woman who stood outside the closed door of the apartment across the hall. She was about 21 or 22, striking in a two-piece outfit of bronze and gold, a sleeveless shirt and wide-legged pants over low-heeled boots. She held her keys in one hand and a take-out bag in the other, seemingly home late from an office job. As I approached, she looked at me, expectant.

Cicero made the introduction. 'Sarah, this is Soleil, my neighbor,' he said. 'Soleil, this is Sarah.'

'Hey,' I said.

'Good to meet you,' Soleil said. 'I better be going,' she told Cicero, and unlocked her door.

Cicero put his hands on the wheels of his chair and backed up through his doorway, but he was slow enough doing it that I heard an odd sound behind me as Soleil went into her apartment. It sounded like claws ticking speedily across linoleum. I turned to see that in fact a big, fireplug-bodied black-and-tan dog had rushed to greet Soleil, and she'd gone down to sit on her heels, where he licked her face in the kind of reunion ecstasy that only dogs can feel. 'That's my bwoy,' she said, giving the last word a Caribbean twist.

Cicero closed his door, shutting out the spectacle.

'That was a dog,' I said.

'Yes, it was.'

'Not just any dog,' I said. 'That was a Rottweiler.'

'Indeed it was. Fidelio, by name.' Cicero rolled closer to the center of his living room.

'Dogs are allowed in this building?' I asked.

'No,' Cicero said. 'You disapprove?'

'No, no,' I said quickly. 'I like dogs. I'm just surprised she's getting away with it. It's hard to hide a dog that size. He must need to be walked and everything.'

Cicero nodded. 'And eventually she'll get caught. But not because of me or anyone on this floor. Fidelio's well behaved, and this is a live-and-let-live place,' Cicero said. 'The only thing I had to tell her is, he can't come in here.'

'Why not?'

'Sanitary reasons. No dogs in the exam room.'

'Of course,' I said, and then we fell into a moment of silence. I took out my billfold. 'So,' I said, 'how much for tonight's visit?'

'Forty,' Cicero said. 'I'll be right with you.'

He rolled over to his kitchen sink. I took out two twenties and laid them on the shelf, stood awkwardly in Cicero's living room, wishing he kept more personal items out on display so I could pretend to study them. Anything to sandbag against the memory of intimacy that threatened like a silent wall of water. Cicero was doing an excellent job of not showing any sign that he remembered that we'd slept together two nights ago. I was having a little more difficulty with that. Maybe what Shiloh didn't know wouldn't hurt him, but that was a facile, easy excuse and it gave me no comfort.

151

I drew a deep, steadying breath. Cicero, washing up at his kitchen sink, misinterpreted it.

'Don't be nervous,' he said, over the sound of running water. 'I expect this to be painless.'

'That's what doctors always say,' I told him.

'No, we say, 'This won't hurt a bit,'' he corrected me.

I laughed. 'Sorry I'm late, by the way. I got stuck in your elevator.'

I'd intended to entertain him with the story of how the emergency phone hadn't worked and I'd been rescued by a pair of teenage residents with a pry bar, who'd forced open a gap about the size of a doghouse door, and how I'd lowered myself awkwardly down to the fourteenth-floor hallway. But Cicero turned so sharply, the words died on my lips.

'You did?' he said.

'What's wrong?' I said. 'It was just an inconvenience.'

Cicero shook his head and rolled back into the living room. 'That elevator's a goddamned menace,' he said vehemently. 'You're the third person I've heard about that's been trapped.' He rummaged in his supply chest, shook down a thermometer. 'Okay, put this under your tongue.'

'I don't have a temperature.'

'Sarah, quit doing my job for me.' There was a bit of iron in his voice now. Meekly, I complied.

Cicero took his time inspecting my ear. Then he took the thermometer from my mouth. He read it silently. When he spoke it was to ask me questions about symptoms I'd had in the past two days: dizziness, pain, difficulty or anomalies in my hearing? I told him no to all those inquiries, and that yes, I'd been taking my antibiotics.

He put the thermometer and the otoscope away.

'Well, your temperature is 98.6, your ear looks very nice, and you sound like you're doing quite well,' he said. 'You heal fast.' He took out his legal pad and wrote again.

'What are you writing?' I asked.

'Just notes,' he said. 'Even though you're reportedly 'never sick,' you may need to come see me again someday, given your aversion to traditional doctors.'

'I hope not to,' I said. 'No offense.'

'Still, do you mind if I ask a few questions, like a medical history, in case I see you again?'

Something about the idea made me nervous; Cicero saw it. 'They're just for my private use,' he said. 'No one else will see them.'

What the hell, all he would ask about was my health history, which was extremely uneventful. And he was right: I might need to see him again someday. 'All right,' I said.

The first questions were easy.

'Last name?'

'Pribek.' I spelled it for him.

'Age?'

'Twenty-nine.'

'Known allergies?'

'None,' I said.

'Are your parents living?'

I shook my head again.

'What were the causes of death?' he asked me.

'My father had a heart attack a few years ago. My mother — ' I swallowed. 'My mother died of ovarian cancer.'

'Were you a child?'

'At one time, sure, we all were,' I said, trying to make a joke of it.

'I mean, when your mother died, were you a child?' He wouldn't let me evade it.

'I was nine.' My throat felt stiff, and I wasn't sure why. I'd told this to other people before.

'Siblings?' Cicero asked quietly.

'One brother, he's dead,' I said, and quickly added, 'An accident, not related to any health concerns.' Buddy had died in a helicopter crash in the Army, and I didn't want to answer any more questions about him.

'What about your husband, how long has he been in prison?'

'Five months,' I said. Quickly I lowered my head. 'Sorry, I think I've got something in my eye,' I said, rubbing wetness away.

'Are you in contact with him at all?'

'No,' I said.

My head was in my hands now. We were both still trying to pretend: Cicero was pretending to take a medical history, and I was pretending I wasn't crying.

'But you've got plenty of friends in the Cities you can talk to?'

I didn't say anything.

'Oh,' Cicero said.

'You do an interesting medical history,' I said, my voice wet.

It's hard for people in wheelchairs to enfold

people, so Cicero reached across the space between us to rub between my bowed shoulder blades and stroke my hair. 'Okay,' he said softly. 'Okay.'

★   ★   ★

I'd like to say that he initiated the sex, afterward. But I did.

I rarely cry, and it seems like bad form to do it in front of a virtual stranger. But with Cicero it was different. He'd already seen me sick, phobic, irrational, drunk, and in pain. There weren't a lot of barriers left to fall. Then, when the brief spasm of sadness had passed, I'd wanted to do this with him.

'I'm sorry,' I said aloud, lying wedged against Cicero in his single bed, my cheek against his bare shoulder.

'What for?' he asked.

'Being a basket case every time you've seen me, I guess,' I said. 'I'm surprised you even like me.'

'How do you know I like you?' Cicero asked me lightly.

'I don't think you'd sleep with someone you didn't like,' I told him seriously. 'Am I wrong about that?'

'No,' Cicero said. 'You're not wrong.'

'Why don't you have a girlfriend?' I asked him. 'Is it because you're agoraphobic?'

Cicero raised himself up on his elbows, looking at me quizzically. 'Where'd you get the idea I was agoraphobic?'

'Ghislaine,' I said. Everything I'd seen since meeting him had supported what she'd said.

'Ghislaine,' he said. 'Of course.'

'You really don't like her,' I said, sitting up. 'What's the story there? By the way, she's not a friend of mine. I barely know her.'

'I barely know her either,' Cicero said. 'She doesn't know much about me either; I'm not agoraphobic. But to answer your question, Ghislaine is the person who brought me the prescription pad.'

I was only briefly surprised. Cicero had referred to the person who'd brought him the pad as 'she.' *I didn't even want to know where she got it.*

Cicero went on. 'She came to visit me. Brought her cute little kid with her, told me how hard it was, raising a son on her own. His father's not around anymore, she says, and there's no support from her parents in Dearborn.'

'That part I know,' I said.

'Ghislaine said she hated going to the public clinic and being treated like a second-class citizen, so here she was. I said, 'Glad to help, what can I do for you?' She tells me she thinks there's a lump in her breast, can I check for her? And she takes off her shirt. I do what she asks. And I'm very careful about it, I don't want to miss anything. I don't feel a thing and tell her so. I tell her she's young and breast cancer isn't too great a risk at her age, but to please keep examining monthly and stay vigilant.'

'You felt comfortable with that? You didn't

156

send her elsewhere for a test?'

'I really am a doctor,' he reminded me. 'I'm as competent here as I would be in an office. Any doctor would have told her the same thing. Particularly in the age of HMOs, not one doctor in a hundred would have ordered a mammogram based on what she reported and I felt.'

'Sorry,' I said.

'It's okay. Besides, you haven't heard the whole thing yet. She cheered up and agreed she was probably overreacting. Then she put her shirt back on and said that she had something for me.'

'Here it comes,' I said.

'Right. The prescription pad. She was sweet as saccharine. She told me she wanted me to have it, because she knew I could do a lot of good with it, for my patients. Then she asked me to write her a scrip for Valium.'

'Are you kidding?' But I knew he wasn't.

'It all made sense then. She never thought there was a lump in her breast. She decided she'd soften me up by showing me her goods, and I'd be willing to do anything for her. I don't know if she wanted the Valium for herself, or more likely, if she had a boyfriend who could turn around and sell it. I didn't want to know.'

'You told her no, obviously,' I said. The reason for Ghislaine's small scowl in the diner, when the subject of 'Cisco' had first come up, was now quite clear.

'I told her no, I wasn't going to get into the scrip-writing business, not even to help my

157

patients, much less to start perpetrating prescription fraud. So she asked for the pad back. Again, I said no. I wasn't going to use it, but I saw no reason she should have it.' Cicero paused, remembering. 'Then she asked me what would happen if she told the cops about me. I said, 'The same thing that would happen if I told the cops you stole a prescription pad, so let's both pretend this never happened.' She got up and said, 'Fine, keep it.' I was still worried about her threat to turn me in, so I told her she could take her forty dollars back. She did.'

'Jesus,' I said.

'When she picked up the money, she asked if I'd always been a paraplegic. I said no. She said, 'I guess that's why you can afford to let forty dollars walk out the door. Since you don't have working equipment, you're not paying for sex anymore.''

I winced. When people can quote verbatim like that, it's usually because the words in question had ricocheted around inside the psyche like the fragments of a hollow-point bullet.

'Hey, don't look like that,' Cicero said. 'She was ignorant.'

The truth was that I'd been nearly as naive as Ghislaine, shocked when Cicero had taken my hand and guided it down to where I could feel him stiffening under my touch. Later, he'd explained to me about reflex erections.

'Ignorant is excusable,' I said. 'Spiteful is something else.'

'She probably doesn't feel very good about

herself,' Cicero said. 'Unkind people often don't.'

'You're so charitable,' I said.

'What's wrong with that?' he asked.

I looked out the window at the city below. 'We don't live in a world that rewards that anymore,' I said. 'If it ever did.'

12

My first day back on daytime shifts was about as unproductive as I'd expected. I reported for work with shadows under my eyes and helped my body clock to readjust with a lot of coffee. On my lunch break, I went to Family Services and made the required minors-at-risk report on the Hennessys. I didn't allow myself to feel as though I was letting Marlinchen down. The system was there to help kids like her; my report was part of that.

The most significant job of the day was a robbery. I took the call and interviewed witnesses. The details were familiar: two young white guys with nylon-stocking masks taking down a convenience store at gunpoint, quite similar to the robbery I'd investigated last week. *We love patterns*, I imagined telling the anonymous young gunmen, consolidating the two reports into one folder. *Don't quit while you're ahead; just keep on doing it like you're doing it. We'll meet someday.*

My phone rang, and I picked it up with my mind still half on the young robbers.

'Ms. Pribek?' The voice was clearly coming across long-distance wires. 'This is Pete Benjamin.'

'Mr. Benjamin,' I said. Hugh Hennessy's friend, who'd taken Aidan in. 'Thank you for calling back.'

'I've already spoken to the authorities here, Ms. Pribek,' said Benjamin. 'I'd be happy to tell you what I told Mr. Fredericks: Aidan didn't disappear. He left of his own accord, which is unfortunate but not terribly unusual. There's a long history of young people striking out on their own when they tire of the life a farm provides. And Aidan, unlike many young people, didn't even have family ties to keep him here.'

When he fell silent, I asked him a question. 'But specifically, what do you think led Aidan to leave when he did?'

'Well, as I said, the rural lifestyle is very unsatisfying to young people.'

'Other than that, I mean,' I said.

There was a beat of silence. 'I'm not sure why there has to be an 'other than that.''

'Let me put it this way: Did you talk to Aidan about what was going on in his life?' I asked.

'Aidan and I spoke daily,' Benjamin said.

I let the silence underline the evasiveness of his answer.

'I was not Aidan's father. But if something were troubling him, I think I would have known,' Benjamin said.

'If I can ask,' I said, 'why did you agree to take on Hugh Hennessy's oldest son? It seems like a huge burden, even for a friend of the family.'

'Well,' Benjamin said, 'Hugh and I went way back. Our families knew each other, and we grew up in the same neighborhood in Atlanta.' He paused. 'I've had a lifelong interest in literature, so I guess you could also say I'm an admirer of Hugh's work as well as an old friend.'

'So you were a frequent visitor at Hugh's home, a familiar figure to Aidan?' I asked.

Another beat of silence. 'Not really. Hugh and I were quite close in younger years, but he lived up north as an adult, and I inherited the farm and went home to work it. We really didn't see each other as adults.' He anticipated my follow-up question. 'Largely, I think Hugh thought of me to take in Aidan, and I agreed to do it, because I have a sizable farm and no one to help with it. Hugh was struggling to raise five children on his own; I had none. It seemed like an imbalance easily fixed. Hugh also sent money for Aidan's needs: school clothes and so on.'

'Did Hugh pay for room and board?' I asked.

'No, I thought in light of the help Aidan would be to me, that wasn't necessary.' He cleared his throat. 'I should point out that the chores I asked of Aidan weren't excessive. I was careful to give him time for his homework and such socializing as he wanted to do, which wasn't much.'

'Right,' I said. 'On Hugh's end, do you know what motivated him to send Aidan away?'

'He was raising five children on his own,' said Benjamin. 'I think it was terribly difficult for him. You know, Deputy Fredericks didn't get into such personal detail during our talks.'

'We all have different ways of approaching the job,' I said, beginning to sketch on the pad on my desk. 'Aidan ran away before,' I said. 'Tell me about that.'

Benjamin cleared his throat. 'That happened early on,' he said. 'I think it's not an uncommon reaction for children who've just been sent to live someplace new. They run away, because they don't think two or more steps ahead. They simply think that if they can physically reach their old home, everything will be fine. The idea seems to be, 'If I can get home, they'll keep me.' Aidan seemed to feel the same.'

'But he was sent back?'

'Yes.'

'Did Aidan try to run away again?' I asked. 'Before this last time?'

'No,' Benjamin said. 'No, after he came back from Minnesota, he settled in here. Our relationship wasn't close, but it was cordial. If you've called hoping to find out about some fight or a watershed event that caused Aidan to run away, there simply wasn't one.'

My sketch had turned into a winding highway. After Pete Benjamin and I hung up, I added a gesture of a walking figure in the distance, at the roadside, but beyond that I didn't know what to add. A city skyline ahead? An ocean and sunset? A prison?

From the official data banks I had access to, I'd learned that Aidan Hennessy had never been arrested, not even on a curfew violation or another of the 'youth status offenses' that carry no penalty but would have identified him as a runaway and dumped him into the juvenile-services system.

That meant one of a couple of things. One, Aidan Hennessy was the rare runaway who was working and keeping himself alive without breaking the law at all. Two, he was keeping himself fed through the usual street crimes that runaways fall into, but was smart and lucky and hadn't yet been arrested. Three, he was living off a woman.

Four, he was dead. For Marlinchen's sake, that was a prospect I didn't want to consider.

★ ★ ★

Before I left that day, I went to see Prewitt. It had taken a while, but I'd finally realized what it meant when Van Noord had told me I should keep my cell or pager on, so people knew where I was.

He was in conversation with a Fish and Wildlife officer when I came around, but he'd seen me standing outside his doorway.

'Come in, Detective Pribek,' Prewitt said, as the Fish and Wildlife man exited. 'I didn't expect to see you today. What's on your mind.'

'I wanted to apologize for the other day, when I had my phone off the hook,' I said, moving to stand just inside the doorway. 'I had an ear infection; you know that, right?'

'Of course,' he said. 'You're better today, I hope.'

'Yes, I am,' I said. Then, uncomfortably, I went on. 'Lieutenant, when you sent Detective Van Noord by my house, was that about Gray Diaz?'

I was hoping he would be puzzled, and say, *No, of course not.*

'Yes,' he said.

So much for hopes.

'I didn't check your personnel records, but you're known for never taking sick leave,' Prewitt

164

said. 'Then Gray Diaz comes in to talk to you about your involvement in the death of Royce Stewart, and you come out looking ashen, tell Van Noord you're sick, and leave. The next day you can't be reached.' He let the words sink in. 'It didn't look very good; you can see that, can't you?'

'You really thought I'd left town?' I said.

'I simply wanted your whereabouts confirmed,' he said mildly. 'Bear in mind, Pribek, you have not been charged with anything, and until you are charged or indicted, your status here will remain unaffected. Nobody's suggested any kind of leave for you.'

'I know that,' I said.

'What I'm suggesting is that if nobody around here is talking about Gray Diaz's investigation, maybe you shouldn't be the first to bring it up,' he said.

'I haven't,' I said.

'On the contrary, you just walked into my office and mentioned it. I didn't come to you,' he said. 'About my decision to send Van Noord to your house: I was mildly troubled by a state of affairs, I acted on it, I satisfied my curiosity. That was the end of it, as far as I was concerned.'

'I didn't mean to question your judgment, but I need to say one thing. I am not going to sneak out of town in the middle of the night,' I said. 'No, what I'm really trying to say is something else.' I swallowed. 'I did not kill Royce Stewart.'

'I can't tell you how happy I am to hear that,' Prewitt said blandly. 'Is there anything else?'

'No,' I said. I had a little tremor in my chest

from how bluntly I'd just spoken.

'I'll see you tomorrow, then.'

At the door, I paused and turned back. 'There is one other thing,' I said. 'That unlicensed physician you asked me to look into? I've checked with my informants, and I haven't been able to track it to a source.' My voice was very casual. 'I really don't think there's anything to it.'

13

Last year, after his accident in Blue Earth, my husband had been missing for seven days. I'd exhausted my professional knowledge of missing-persons work in looking for him. I'd traveled and spoken to his family. Furthermore, as his wife, I'd had full access to Shiloh's accounts, his papers, his home. None of it had made any difference. It was as if he'd simply been erased.

With Aidan Hennessy, I was in the opposite situation. He should have been easy as hell to find. Aidan was an underage runaway, not a fugitive. The longer he spent on the road, the more likely it should have been that he'd be arrested for vagrancy or petty theft. He simply shouldn't have been this hard to find.

Yet I'd spent three days working the various law-enforcement databases I had access to, and none of it was helping. Deputy Fredericks had e-mailed me Aidan's last school-yearbook photo, but that didn't count as an advance. Unless Aidan Hennessy fell into a drainage canal someplace near where I just happened to be, I didn't think I was going to find him.

It was that frustration that drove me backward, on my next day off, to the elementary school where all the Hennessy children had received their early education, and which Donal still attended.

Marlinchen had mentioned her fifth-grade teacher, Mrs. Hansen, in a brief phone conversation we'd had earlier that morning. Hansen had taught both Marlinchen and Aidan, although not in the same year, because Aidan had been held back to repeat the fourth grade. By my calculations, that made her the last teacher in Minnesota to be familiar with Aidan Hennessy, and the one most likely to remember him.

The school didn't look impressive, given the relative wealth of the neighborhood it was in. It was an assortment of one-story red-brick buildings. Children swarmed around the play structures in the yard; it was their lunch recess.

On her lunch break, Mrs. Hansen was grading papers in her classroom. I stepped inside and immediately felt like a giantess as I walked up through the low desks toward the larger one where Mrs. Hansen sat. She was full-breasted for a woman otherwise slightly built — I gauged her at about five-one — and wore glasses on a gold chain over her off-white shell sweater. Her blond hair was shoulder-length, cut in a flattering way close around the face. Only by looking closely could you see she was nearing 50.

'Can I help you?' Hansen said.

'I hope so,' I said. 'My name is Sarah Pribek. I'm a detective, and I wanted to talk to you about a runaway I'm looking for.' I laid Marlinchen's old photo of Aidan on her desk.

Hansen took the photo and raised her eyebrows, then furrowed them in a slightly exaggerated show of scrutiny. 'Oh, my goodness,

168

yes,' she said. 'Aidan Hennessy. His little brother Donal might have been one of my students last year, but he went to Ms. Campbell instead.' She frowned. 'Aidan had a sister, too. I taught her the year before. They were . . . ' Then she broke off.

'They were supposed to advance to your class together,' I finished for her. 'They're twins, but he was held back a year. You're not revealing anything the family didn't share with me.'

She nodded affirmation. 'That's correct. What was the girl's name, again? Something unusual.'

'Marlinchen,' I said.

'He and his sister would be in high school now, correct?'

'She is,' I said. 'He's been a runaway for six months.'

'Oh, my,' Hansen said. 'That's too bad.' She exaggerated her facial expressions, like adults who deal with the young often do, but the feeling underneath seemed genuine.

'You liked him?'

'Yes, I did,' she said. 'A sweet boy. Not a lot of self-confidence. Didn't raise his hand or volunteer answers.' Then she seemed to realign herself behind the desk, as for a formal Q and A with me. 'I don't know how much I can help you. He was my student some time ago. Five years.'

There was no place for me to sit. In nearly every other situation, a person with a desk has a chair on the other side for visitors. Not so with schoolteachers. I leaned back against the nearest student desk and immediately thought better of it as it began to slide away from my weight.

'He's been living out of state for those five years,' I told her. 'You're the last teacher in this district who would have taught him. I'm just curious about what you remember.'

Hansen frowned apologetically. 'Not very much,' she said. 'Aidan stands out in my memory mostly because of that missing finger. I used to see it whenever he was writing at his desk, and it always gave me a little bit of a turn.'

'You must remember something more,' I encouraged her. 'You said you liked him.'

Hansen played with the glasses on her chain. 'Sometimes you get a' — she waffled a hand in the air — 'a feeling from students. Aidan seemed old beyond his years, but that might have been because he was older than his classmates, at least when I had him. And taller.' She paused, thinking. 'But he seemed ill at ease sometimes, uncomfortable around adults.'

'Do you know why?' I asked.

'He wasn't the ablest of students; often that erodes children's self-esteem, particularly in front of grown-ups, who kids see as authority figures who judge them on classroom achievements.' She paused. 'Aidan seemed more at ease on the playground. He was athletic and confident.'

'Did he get into fights?' I asked.

Hansen smiled. 'Yes, he did. Aidan was very protective of his sister and two younger brothers. Particularly the one who was bookish.'

'Liam,' I said.

'Yes, Liam. He was a mark for bullies. Aidan crossed paths with some of them.' She paused. 'I should say that Aidan probably fought on his own behalf, too; he wasn't a saint. But he wasn't . . . I don't remember him as hostile. I find it impossible to like the bullies, and I liked Aidan.'

I nodded. 'Were there behavior problems beyond fighting?'

She considered. 'He didn't always do his homework.'

'He'd forget?' I asked.

Hansen shook her head. 'I think he just couldn't grasp some of the material,' she said. 'As I said, he wasn't the best of students.'

'Neither was I,' I said, smiling wryly. 'Thanks for your time.'

★ ★ ★

After work, I drove out to the Hennessy house. Marlinchen was out front when I arrived, standing astride a bicycle. She waved when she heard me approach.

I wasn't a connoisseur of bicycles, but hers was lovely: a frame painted in a metallic-tangerine color, narrow tires for speed, and drop handlebars mounted upside down, so that they curved back like ram's horns. The effect was ruined only by a pair of bulging saddlebags, one on each side of the front wheel, making the bike look like a racing Thoroughbred pressed into packhorse duty.

'Hi,' Marlinchen said. 'I just got back from the store.' The color in her cheeks was high but healthy, and there was a sheen of sweat on her face.

171

'You know,' I told her, 'the way you have those handlebars mounted may look sexy, but you're not going to feel so good when the end of one of them is embedded in your kidney after an accident.'

Marlinchen made a little face at me. 'Don't be such a cop,' she said. 'Did you know that a lot of bike messengers don't even have brakes on their rides anymore?'

My first thought was, *Cool*. But I kept my disapproving look in place, saying instead, 'That's their problem. If I were you, I'd go to wherever you get this bike worked on and have the handlebars turned back around.'

'I work on it myself,' she said, sitting on her heels to unload one of the saddlebags. 'Taking it to the shop is expensive, and Dad's useless with tools.' She set a white plastic grocery bag on the ground, then crossed to the other saddlebag.

'So you took the handlebars off, disconnected and reconnected the brakes, and everything?'

A flicker of sadness crossed her face. 'Aidan and I did the handlebars together,' she said. 'Just before he left.' She picked up the grocery bags.

'That's why I'm here,' I said. 'I wanted to bring you up to date on Aidan. There's not much new,' I added hastily, 'but I'd like to talk about some things.'

I followed her inside and to the kitchen, where she set the groceries on the counter. 'Want to go on the back porch?' Marlinchen asked. 'It's nice out.'

It was a pleasantly crisp day, with recent rains having cleared all the humidity out of the air.

Somewhere a power mower droned, and dandelion and cottonwood fluff rode the breezes.

'I have something for you,' I said, and took out the photo of Aidan I'd printed from my e-mail, handing it across the wooden picnic table.

'Oh, my God,' Marlinchen said. She took the piece of paper from me by the edges, as though it might break. 'You were right. He does look different.'

In the photo, Aidan's face had gained some adult length of bone and thinned a bit; the main difference between this Aidan and the 11-year-old was that this one had hair pulled back, out of sight, suggesting length.

'Where did you get this?' she said.

'It wasn't great detective work,' I told her. 'It's a yearbook photo, that's all.'

But I wanted to have a picture of her brother before her while we talked. It would remind her what this whole thing was about.

'I haven't learned much,' I said. 'I've talked to Deputy Fredericks and Pete Benjamin, and done what I can, but I've been kind of hobbled.'

'Because of the distance involved and the jurisdictional lines,' Marlinchen said.

'Partly,' I agreed, 'but there are other problems, closer to home.'

'Like what?'

'The question I keep coming back to,' I said, 'is why Aidan was sent away in the first place.'

Marlinchen shifted her weight. 'It was an arrangement of convenience,' she said. 'Dad just had his hands too full.'

'So you've said,' I told her. 'So has Colm. And

173

Liam. You're all in agreement on this. *Perfectly* in agreement, as if you'd discussed it in advance.'

Marlinchen looked down, at a fingernail slightly discolored by grease from her bicycle chain. 'Couldn't that mean,' she said stiffly, 'that it's the truth?'

'Is it?' I said. 'Did you know the author bio for *A Rainbow at Night* says that your father has four children?'

She knew, instantly, what I was talking about. 'It says he lives *in Minnesota* with his four children,' she said quickly. 'That's technically true.' She meant that Aidan had been sent away by the time of *Rainbow*'s publication.

'It still makes it sound like your father has only four kids,' I said.

'Dad doesn't even write those things,' Marlinchen said. 'Somebody at his publisher does.'

'Based on information from who?' I said.

An outboard engine hummed on the lake in a bouncing rhythm, as though it were bucking waves.

'You and your brothers all say that you haven't seen Aidan in five years,' I went on. 'Not a phone call, not a letter, not a visit home for the holidays. That's not an arrangement of convenience. That's banishment, Marlinchen. Aidan hasn't just been erased from your father's bio. He's been erased from your lives.'

Marlinchen's color was still high, and I didn't think it was left over from the exertion of her ride. 'You're making way too much of this,' she said. 'Fostering out children used to be a common tradition. Your own father did it, you said.'

'My father was a truck driver. He was on the road the better part of the year. It's not a comparable situation,' I said. 'Did Aidan do something? Was there some reason your father thought he needed to be isolated in Illinois, and then Georgia?'

'No,' she said softly. 'He didn't do anything.' The sudden quietness of her voice was like barometric pressure dropping.

'What about your father, then?' I said. 'If this wasn't about Aidan, was it something to do with him?'

'No,' Marlinchen said, even more quietly.

'Okay, I get it,' I said. 'Everybody loves everybody, and then suddenly Aidan's sent away permanently to live with virtual strangers. Yeah, that makes perfect sense.'

'I don't understand what you're getting at,' Marlinchen said, her voice rising at last. 'You're not supposed to be psychoanalyzing my family, you're supposed to be finding Aidan. Instead you haven't done anything except find a yearbook photo and cast slights on my brother's character and my father's!'

I sat back slightly. As long as I'd known her, Marlinchen had been almost achingly polite. Now the Marlinchen who was emerging from that shell wasn't the one I'd expected: an imperious princess, giving orders to a member of the servant class.

'You know what?' I said. 'I've done about as well as anyone could with the constraints you've

175

put on me. You want to feed me half-truths and pretend it won't impede my search for Aidan. You're half interested in finding Aidan and half interested in protecting your father's image. You've got one foot on each horse, and you're trying to pretend they're running in the same direction.'

I'd expected her anger to completely boil over, but that wasn't what happened. Some women, particularly small ones, learn to wield exquisite courtesy like a weapon. Suddenly, she seemed to draw on a reservoir of poise. When she spoke, I heard a thousand closed doors in her voice.

'I know you've done everything you can, Detective Pribek, and spent more time than you can afford,' she said. 'I'm sure my father will want to thank you, when he's fully recovered.'

'Marlinchen, I'm not saying that — '

'I'm sorry,' she said, 'I really have to put the groceries away.'

Then she was gone, the French doors closing firmly behind her.

14

Marlinchen was the last person I should have come off second best to in an interview situation; she was just a kid. But she outclassed me; that was the problem. For all that I wore the authority of a county detective, I was still keenly aware of my rough edges when the job took me into the graceful homes and worlds of middle- and upper-class citizens, especially those like Marlinchen, who wore the intellect she'd inherited from her father as comfortably as she might have worn family jewels. She was the princess, in her shabby-elegant old castle on a shining lake, and I, a civil servant, was the commoner, feeling obligated to help her for reasons I didn't fully understand.

A lot of cops profess a special concern and protectiveness for the young. Asked to explain, they'll tell you, 'Cops are moms and dads, too.' That wasn't true with me. I alone among my peers in the detective division was childless. If anything, I was too close to my own youth. When Colm had made his dig at women and guns, I'd made my bitchy remark about the TV remote. When Marlinchen had attacked me on the issue of my professional abilities, I'd given it back to her, and twice as hard. I was acting less like a surrogate parent than an insulted sibling.

At 29, though I tried to cover up for it, I often felt raw and unfinished inside, psychologically colt-legged and wrong-footed. It was still too easy for me to reach out and touch the feelings of adolescence.

When I was 13, my mother's aunt, Virginia, a waitress-bartender with long gray-streaked hair and my mother's eyes, picked me up at the Greyhound station in Minneapolis. We'd driven three and a half hours to the Iron Range town in which she lived. Much of the year that followed was a blur.

I slept poorly and had bad dreams, all of which were set in my native New Mexico, the details of which were lost to me on waking. Memory, overall, was a problem that year; I was so forgetful that after a teacher conference, Ginny agreed to have me tested by the school psychologist, to see if something was seriously wrong.

The results were apparently inconclusive, but my memory did not immediately improve. I racked up several detentions for incomplete homework, not because I refused to do the assignments, but because I'd forgotten to bring home the textbook or write down the page and question numbers. I left the lunches I packed at home in the refrigerator. This was during the growth spurt that eventually took me to five-eleven, and the hunger pangs I experienced when I forgot to bring lunch to school crossed the line from unpleasant to painful. Once, after only having two sticks of chewing gum on lunch break, I grayed out in PE and ended up in the nurse's office.

My father called twice a week to start,

dropping back to once a week by mid-autumn. I used the word *fine* a lot. In early December, he asked if the weather was bothering me.

I'd experienced snow in the mountains of New Mexico, but nothing could have prepared me for what happened in northern Minnesota in January: the full-dark skies before even five in the evening, the warlike rollout of snowplows on the streets after every fresh snow, the eerie abandoned streets of a minus-thirty-degree morning. One day, wrapping myself in a scarf to walk home from school after detention in subzero weather, I commented to a janitor on the possibility of snow later.

'Have to warm up for that,' the janitor said, looking out at the clear sky. It was the first time I'd heard that it could be too cold to allow precipitation. Late that night, I'd looked out my window to where an ice-colored moon glowed in the airless reaches of the sky, and wondered how I had ever come to live in a place where it could get too cold to snow.

More than anything, it was basketball that turned things around, in my freshman year of high school. I didn't have any feeling for the sport, other than having thrown a ball at a dilapidated netless hoop a few times in New Mexico. But Ginny suggested that I try out, and I was too apathetic to refuse her anything, so I did.

I never try to explain to people what basketball was to me; it'd come out sounding like inspirational sports-movie clichés. It wasn't just that it was my first experience of being part of a larger unit, an understanding that I'd bring to cop work. It was as simple as this: after a year of numbness, in which I'd had no adolescent hungers, basketball gave me something to want. Halfway through the season, I started showing up early for practice, doing box jumps to strengthen my calf muscles and shuttle drills for agility, running after school for stamina. As I did, I'd felt a tension ease in my chest that had been there so long I hadn't even recognized it.

'I was worried about you last year,' Ginny told me.

'I know,' I'd said. 'I'm okay.'

⋆　⋆　⋆

It remained my habit to this day, taking my anxieties to the gym. Glad for the old T-shirt and shorts I kept in the trunk of the Nova, I went there now. But after I'd changed in the women's locker room and gone upstairs, I stopped in the doorway of the cardio room, seeing a familiar form. Gray Diaz was running on the treadmill at a pretty good clip. I felt a reaction flush under my skin, but he was looking down at the machine's readout. He hadn't seen me yet.

I turned and went down the stairs. It didn't matter, I told myself. I'd go out for a run tomorrow morning, when it was cool.

'You shouldn't let him chase you off.'

A voice as low-timbred as a radio announcer's stopped me by the locker-room door. I turned and looked around. There was nobody that Deputy Stone could have been talking to but me.

Jason Stone was 26, tall, and handsome. He had a smooth, low voice, and fluttered some pulses among the unmarried women in the department. He had recently been cleared of wrongdoing in an excessive-force complaint.

'I'm sorry?' I said.

'Gray Diaz,' Stone said. 'I know who he is. Don't let him get to you.'

The correct response, if there was one, wouldn't come to me.

'Detective Pribek . . . may I call you Sarah?' he asked, solicitous. 'I just wanted to tell you that a lot of us are behind you,' he said.

'Behind me on what?' I said.

'What you did in Blue Earth,' he said.

'I didn't do anything in Blue Earth,' I said. 'Whatever you heard, you heard wrong.'

'Royce Stewart needed to take a dirt nap,' he said. His voice sounded extremely reasonable. 'That a guy like Diaz would try to come up here and further his career on it, at your expense — Sarah, that's reprehensible to a lot of us.'

'I don't think you heard me,' I said. 'I didn't do anything in Blue Earth.'

'I know,' Stone said, his expression saying we both knew better. 'Keep your head up.'

I stayed in the shower and the locker room as long as possible, and then left as quickly as I could. I'd had enough of running into co-workers for one night.

That wasn't, though, how it worked out.

I drove to Surdyk's, a liquor store in the East Hennepin district, where I aimlessly cruised the aisles until I decided on a marked-down

Australian cabernet. It was when I was walking back through the parking lot that Christian Kilander stepped out between two parked cars and into my path.

'Detective Pribek,' he said, recovering smoothly from the surprise.

It occurred to me that I'd never seen him off duty before, not like this. He wore good suits to work, and tank shirts and shorts to the basketball courts, but tonight he was wearing slightly faded jeans and a cream-colored shirt.

'How have you been?' I said awkwardly.

'Pretty well, thanks,' he said. 'And you?'

'Fine,' I said. 'You know, I saw you the other day.'

'You did?' he said.

'With Gray Diaz.'

I didn't know exactly why I was bringing it up. Perhaps it stung just a little, imagining Kilander to be friendly with this man who'd come to the Cities to nail me for something I didn't do.

'I know him,' Kilander acknowledged.

'He's a friend of yours?' I asked.

Kilander held up a palm. 'I don't think I want to be in this conversation.' He started moving away from the gleaming black hindquarter of his BMW and toward the store.

'What?' I said blankly. '*Chris.*'

He turned, or half turned, to face me.

'You can't seriously think I was working up to asking for inside information. Do you?' I demanded.

He said nothing.

'For God's sake, I didn't seek *you* out last

winter. It was you who came to *me*, to tell me I was a suspect.'

'Yes, I did.' Kilander's eyes, so often amused and ironic, were serious. 'And I expected you to deny being the person responsible for Stewart's death. You never did.' He turned away.

'I didn't think I had to,' I said, to his retreating form.

* * *

Back in my car, I sat for a moment, looking out at the post-sunset sky. I'd been trying to ask Kilander how he knew Diaz, that was all. I wouldn't have asked for inside information. Would I?

I realized that I couldn't say for sure. I was more afraid of Gray Diaz than I had been letting on, even to myself.

How could Kilander think I was guilty of Royce Stewart's murder? Jason Stone was one thing, but Kilander's words had hurt.

Go home, Sarah. Have a glass of wine, go to sleep early.

Instead I rummaged in my bag for my cell phone, dialed 411.

'What listing, please?'

'Cicero Ruiz.'

Get real. He's a reclusive guy deeply involved in a highly illegal activity. He's not going to have a listed phone number.

'I have a C. Ruiz,' the operator said.

Unlikely. 'Go ahead, give it to me,' I said.

I would call and stumble through a conversation with a stranger in my rusty Spanish. *Lo siento.* Sorry to bother you.

Cicero picked up on the third ring.

'It's me,' I said.

'Sarah,' he said. 'How are you?'

'I'm all right,' I said. 'I'm not sick. My ear is fine.'

'That's good,' he said.

'And I . . . I can't sleep with you again,' I said. 'Because of my husband.'

'You called to tell me that?' Cicero asked.

'No,' I said.

'What, then?'

'Can I come see you anyway?' I said.

Through the open window I could see Venus just starting to pierce the fading light of the sky.

'I can't think why not,' Cicero said.

15

An hour later I was standing on the roof of Cicero's building, looking up at the light-bleached sky over Minneapolis; only a few constellations were distinguishable. The real astronomy lay twenty-six stories below: the industrial-tangerine grid of city streets, the ascension and declination of the world most of us knew.

Behind me, Cicero lay on his back on a blanket we'd brought up, arms crossed behind his head in the traditional stargazer's position, wine in a chipped eight-ounce glass within arm's reach. His wheelchair nowhere in sight, he looked very much able-bodied, like a hiker at rest.

He was a very discreet person, Cicero. After our brief exchange on the phone, he hadn't asked me anything more about why I wouldn't sleep with him again. Which was good, because I wasn't sure I could explain it. I'd crossed a line, both in personal morals and professional ethics, and that couldn't just be erased. But I think my desire to go back over to the right side of that line was rooted in my unease with how easily I'd crossed it in the first place. Sometimes I wondered if there were a hidden moral flaw inside me, one that had driven me into the line of work I did, where right and wrong were so clearly delineated.

But when I'd arrived, Cicero had merely looked over the Australian wine I'd brought and asked me how I was. I'd said I was fine, and he'd said he was fine, and then a small discomfort had descended on the conversation. Cicero broke the silence by asking me if I wanted to go up on the roof.

I'd thought it was a joke, but he'd explained how it was possible. We'd parked his wheelchair and set the brake at the foot of the emergency stairwell that led to the roof. When Cicero was seated on the lowest stair, I'd taken his lower legs just under the knee, and Cicero had raised his upper body off the stairs, weight on the heels of his hands. His method wasn't, I saw, unlike the triceps exercise I sometimes did at the gym, lowering myself from a weight bench. But Cicero was ascending, going up the stairs literally on his arms. Supporting his legs and following, I was still assuming less than a third of his body weight. It couldn't have been easy, and I understood then the importance of the hand weights I'd seen under his bed.

'That wasn't pretty, and it was slow,' Cicero had said when we were up, 'but it got the job done.'

I'd poured wine into the mismatched glasses I'd carried up in advance, along with the blanket.

'You know what the most difficult part was?' he asked.

'What?' I said.

'Letting a woman help me with it,' he said. 'With the guys down the hall, it's different.'

186

'You've done this before?'

'Several times,' he said, accepting the wine. 'I need fresh air every once in a while.'

Now, standing at the rooftop's edge, cupping my wine in my hands, I thought about that. Wouldn't it simply be easier for Cicero to get in the elevator and go downstairs and outside for air? 'Cicero,' I began, 'I know what you said the other night, but *are* you agoraphobic? It's no big deal to me if you are.'

He laughed. 'No, I'm really not agoraphobic.'

'Then why don't you ever go out?' As soon as I'd said them, I regretted the words. 'I mean, you don't have to tell me — '

'No, it's okay. I have no secrets.' Cicero unfolded one arm to indicate the unoccupied part of the blanket. 'Come sit down. It's a story that's going to take me a little time to tell.'

I walked over and sat cross-legged on the edge of the blanket.

'It has to do with how I became paralyzed,' Cicero said. 'I was injured in a mine collapse.'

'You went down as part of a rescue crew?' I asked. It seemed odd to me that medical personnel — not EMTs or paramedics but actual doctors — would be sent into harm's way.

But Cicero shook his head. 'I was working down there,' he said.

'As a *miner*?' I said.

Cicero nodded. 'It was after I lost my license to practice medicine.'

Every time I thought I had a handle on this man's situation, I learned something new. The idea of Cicero being in a mine disaster was so unexpected that I set aside my curiosity about how he'd lost his medical license, which so far he'd only alluded to. That could wait. 'Tell me,' I said.

'This is going to take me a minute to explain,' he said, and lifted himself up onto his elbows, to drink a little wine. 'I grew up in Colorado, in a mining area. My father had worked in the mines, this five-foot-seven-inch guy, covered in coal dust, reading a paperback copy of the *Iliad* on his lunch break. I was getting back to my roots, you could call it.'

'You worked with your old man?' I interrupted.

Cicero shook his head. 'My parents were both gone by then. When I came back, I got hired at a small, family-owned, nonunion operation, working the very last of a played-out coal seam. I wasn't real popular for my first couple of months.' Cicero seemed amused by the memory. 'On my first day, the crew foreman, Silas, asked me what I'd been doing before getting hired there. I told him the truth, that I was a doctor. Looking back, I don't think he believed me. I'm pretty sure he thought I was giving him a hard time. He just said, 'Well, it's my job to keep you from killing yourself or anyone else until you get tired of banging your head on the ceiling and go looking for some other work.''

'Nice guy,' I said.

'He *was* a good guy,' Cicero corrected me. 'Silas was younger than a lot of his crew, but he'd been down in the mines since he was 18, and he knew his shit. I paid attention to him, and after a couple of months, I pretty much knew what I was doing. Silas started talking to me other than to say things like 'Don't stand there.' We'd eat lunch together and talk.' Cicero paused, drank some wine. 'We were both kind of nervous about the safety situation. To put it mildly, small nonunion mines tend not to be the safety leaders in the field. But when it actually happened, it surprised me, how quietly it started.'

'What started?' I asked.

'What the industry calls an ignition accident,' Cicero said. 'Down in a mine, you hear roof falls a lot, and blasts, so the noise I heard that day didn't bother me. It sounded like business as usual to me. The first I knew anything was wrong was when I felt the air reverse direction.'

I tilted my head, signaling incomprehension.

'Mines need to breathe, just like people,' he explained. 'Ventilation systems ensure that excess blackdamp — that's methane — is carried away from where miners are working and fresh air is carried in. In some mines, like ours, the fans create a wind of seven or eight miles an hour. That's significant enough that you can feel it, but you're used to it. You don't notice it until it stops. It feels like the air has actually reversed direction. If you know what it means, it's not a good feeling. Silas felt it the same time I did, and we looked at each other.

'That's when we heard men yelling, and we stopped working and traveled to the scene. At the site, I saw that there were two men down, injured. There'd been a roof fall, which had caused a spark, which caused a small explosion. A fire was burning, but no one was dead. The foreman in that section saw Silas and me come out from behind a crosscut. He wanted Silas there, but when he saw me, I was still a new guy to him. 'Not you,' he said to me. 'Get out of here.' But Silas said, 'You want him here. He's a doctor.''

Far below, a siren wailed; involuntarily I looked to the roof's edge. It was the sound of my work; I was Pavlovian that way.

'To understand what happened next,' Cicero said, not noticing my moment of inattention, 'you've got to understand a little about mine accidents. Often, the first ignition doesn't kill anyone. But it does start a fire, and it also compromises the ventilation system. When the ventilation system stops working, methane builds up. It's the subsequent explosions that kill people.

'There's time to evacuate, but the problem is, not everyone does. Some miners travel toward the blast, instead of away, to render aid. That's the ethic down there, to help each other. I don't know if I stayed at the scene because I thought I had really become a miner, or because I was still a doctor, but for whichever reason, I was still at the face when the second explosion happened.' He stopped to reach over to the wine bottle again, poured a little more, drank.

'I was thrown, and when my vision cleared, I saw that the remaining guys were starting to evacuate,' he said. 'They knew the situation was out of control. They wanted to get me out, but I couldn't move my legs. The men said they'd send down rescue guys with a backboard, and if the paramedics were afraid to come down in a mine, they'd bring the backboard themselves.

'But the situation was still volatile, with a threat of more ignitions. I could hear the rescue personnel, up above where I was. Their superiors were saying they had to pull out. The rescuers radioed back that they still had a man down there to bring up, but they were overruled. I heard their noises growing fainter, and then they were gone.'

Cicero's knuckles seemed a little paler as he held the glass, the only sign of emotion.

'I was okay at first. I thought, *Silas will make them come back for me*, but then I saw Silas. He was dead. That was when it became real to me, that I could die down there.' He paused. 'I was okay while my lamp held out. That was about thirty hours.'

'*Thirty?*' I said, amazed. 'How long were you down there?'

'Sixty-one hours.' Cicero drained the rest of the wine. 'About half that was in total blackness. Around that time, my imagination ran away with me. I was completely paranoid. I was sure that the paramedics had been lying when they'd said they were coming back. It was too dangerous; the company would just seal off that part of the mine and tell my brother that I'd been one of those who'd died instantly.'

He'd finished his wine, and was supine again.

'Of course, it didn't happen that way. They came back,' Cicero said. 'In the hospital, I told

191

myself over and over that my spinal cord was in shock, that I'd walk again. It took a while to accept that I wouldn't. I did that in rehab, the hardest part of which was getting the bill afterward. The mine declared bankruptcy after the accident, and we all lost our medical coverage.'

'Typical,' I said.

'There's a lawsuit, on behalf of everyone injured, and I'm part of it. But it's being dragged out in court. Meanwhile, my medical debts can charitably be described as 'massive,' and I now have a preexisting condition that insurers won't cover.'

'But you're in good health, aren't you?' I interrupted.

'Right now, yes,' Cicero said. 'But being a paraplegic, even a healthy one, isn't cheap. And it makes you vulnerable to other health problems down the road. Those problems can be headed off with preventive care and physical therapy — '

'Which an insurer won't pay for, because it's part of a preexisting condition,' I finished for him.

'Exactly. Right now, I have some basic medical assistance for the indigent. If I got a job, I wouldn't be eligible for it any longer, and then my noncovered health-care costs would subsume a large part of any income I'd make. I'm in that rare situation where getting employment would actually drag me down, not lift me up.'

I'd expected a story along these lines, but hadn't anticipated how completely he was trapped.

'Other than medicine, from which I am barred,' Cicero said, 'there's nothing I'm equipped to do that would bring home anything close to what I need to survive without adequate health insurance. And if I did find work, there is one hospital, two clinics, and a number of medical professionals with claims to my future earnings. Right now, I'm referring my creditors to the legal precedent of *Blood v. Turnip*.'

I said the necessary, inadequate thing. 'There's got to be some way to get around the rules. Somebody's got to see that the situation's ridiculous. This isn't supposed to happen.'

Cicero laughed. 'No, it's not,' he said. 'It's the result of a daisy chain of misfortunes. If only I weren't banned from the only profession in which I can make a viable income. If only I hadn't chosen that particular mine to work at. And so on.

'Everyone does see it's ridiculous. Finding a way around it is a different story. The medical social worker at the rehab clinic in Colorado decided I should come to Minneapolis, because my brother Ulises was here. Once here, I was assigned a caseworker who was 23 and stumped. She got me disability checks, and that was it. It's not her fault. The system isn't set up to handle individual circumstances. Nobody is authorized to change the rules or interpret the subtleties. Everybody would *like* to help you, but no one actually *can*.'

'That can't just be the end of it,' I said, turning my palms up, fingers splayed.

Cicero surveyed me. 'You don't cohere

sometimes,' he said. 'You seem so world-weary on the surface, but under the surface you have these veins of naive faith in the system.' He shrugged. 'But I've told you a good deal more than I thought I would, and I still didn't answer your original question.'

'What original question?' I honestly couldn't remember.

'Exactly,' Cicero said. 'I was telling you about the mine accident. What I might not have made clear was that I spent sixty-one hours lying in a space with dimensions only slightly more generous than a grave.' He paused. 'Since then, I have a very hard time with enclosed spaces. I'm not agoraphobic, I'm claustrophobic. It's why I rarely go out.'

'The elevator,' I said, understanding.

'That goddamned elevator,' he agreed. 'I'm not afraid of a six-minute descent; it'd be hard, but I could do it. But if I got trapped, I'm not sure if I could take it.' There was shame in his averted gaze. 'God knows it's stupid.'

'Fears are irrational,' I said. 'I'm living proof of that.'

Cicero didn't respond, tipping his head back to observe the lights of a plane. MSP was to the south of us, and the jetliners climbed across the city's airspace with assembly-line regularity. In twenty hours, their passengers could be any-where in the world. Down here was Cicero, whose world had become so small that, for him, ascending one flight of stairs to see the night sky was a journey.

'But if you stay in all the time,' I said, 'how are

194

you getting food, groceries?'

'From my patients,' Cicero explained. 'I'm not a strictly cash business; I trade in favors and services, too.'

'What about meeting people?' I said.

'They come to me,' Cicero said. 'Dripping blood or coughing, but I take them as they come.'

'Women, I mean.'

'Ah, yes, women,' Cicero said. 'Who wouldn't want to date an insolvent paraplegic?'

'Cicero,' I reproved him.

'Sarah,' he said, 'don't make a project out of me.' His tone said the subject was off-limits. I dropped my gaze, accepting his rebuke.

'Things were better when I first came to Minneapolis,' he said. 'Ulises had a ground-floor apartment — no elevator needed — and I had a van. Nothing great, but it had hand controls, and it ran.' He paused. 'I've still got the van, downstairs, but I might as well sell it. It's not doing me any good now, and one of the kids down the hall has to go down once a week and start it, so it doesn't just die of neglect.'

This part of his story raised an obvious question. 'Cicero,' I said, 'where's your brother now? You said they sent you here to live with him.'

Cicero's dark eyes seemed more sober than they had been only a moment ago. 'I did live with him,' he confirmed. 'That's a story for another time.'

'I thought you had no secrets,' I reminded him.

195

'I don't,' Cicero said. 'But it's probably not a story you want to hear on top of the one I just told.'

'Is he dead?' I persisted.

'Yes,' Cicero said. 'He's dead.'

I shook my head, eyes lowered. 'Jesus,' I said.

'Don't look like that,' he said.

'Jesus, Cicero.'

'Don't feel sorry for me, Sarah,' Cicero said.

'I don't,' I said. I'm not sure if I was lying.

16

There were three of us in Judge Henderson's chambers: the judge himself, a graying-haired black man who said little; Lorraine, a social worker; and me.

'It's not a typical situation,' Lorraine was saying. 'I was at the house, and it's all as Detective Pribek described it. The home is clean, the children are attending school. There are no small children in the home. The youngest is 11, with the others at 14, 16, and 17. The daughter was very forthcoming and cooperative when I made the visit.'

'And the father?' Judge Henderson asked. His voice was low and pleasant, like the rumble of thunder on a distant horizon.

Lorraine leaned forward. 'He's recuperating slowly. He was moved from acute care at HCMC to a convalescent home, and he's expected to make a fairly good recovery, with the most serious problem being a lingering speech disorder. The daughter is seeking conservatorship.'

The judge nodded. 'Through a lawyer, I trust.'

'Certainly,' Lorraine said.

I glanced up at the Roman numerals on the face of the judge's clock. It was three-thirty in the afternoon. So far, I wasn't sure why I was there. I'd thought that they needed me to talk about what I knew of the Hennessy family

197

situation, since I was the one who'd made the child-at-risk report. But thus far I hadn't been asked a single question.

'Well, it seems you've been thorough, as always.' Judge Henderson leaned back in his chair, so far that the top of his balding head nearly disappeared into a glossy green plant on his bookcase. 'Detective Pribek, this is where you come in.'

Lorraine turned to me also. 'We have a pilot program, for situations in which minors seeking emancipation are paired up with suitable adults to supervise them for a probationary period. It's only being done, of course, in cases where the minor is considered a good candidate and they have no adult relatives who can fill such a role.'

'You want me to be a guardian to the Hennessy children?' I said.

'Not quite a guardian, more like a watchful eye,' Lorraine said.

'I have no background in social work,' I reminded her.

'But you are a responsible law-enforcement professional, and you seem to have had more contact with these kids than anyone else.' She paused. 'Marlinchen Hennessy is an extraordinarily good candidate for guardianship, and she's only weeks away from her eighteenth birthday. We're not comfortable leaving the children on their own for that amount of time, but sending the children into foster care seems, well, ludicrous.'

Hedging, I said, 'I'm not sure Marlinchen would agree to it.' I was thinking of how we'd

198

left things between us.

'In fact, when I made my home visit, the oldest daughter spoke highly of you,' Lorraine said.

'Only daughter,' I corrected her. Marlinchen Hennessy had no sisters.

Lorraine smiled, and I realized I'd stepped into a trap, revealing myself as someone who'd invested time and energy into knowing this young family. I sighed.

'I'm not totally opposed to stepping in,' I said, 'but I think there's a larger problem here. Marlinchen is pursuing guardianship of her younger siblings *and* conservatorship of her father, at the same time. Don't you think that's a bit much?'

Lorraine bit her lip. It was the judge who spoke. 'Detective Pribek,' he said, 'the family is still the sacred and essential unit in American life. Before we in the judicial branch split one up, we need to have damn good reason. If there were other relatives, even a close friend of the family, who could step in here, I'd go that route. But there isn't. In this situation, I feel that this is the best I can do for the family.'

'What is it I'd be doing?' I asked, yielding.

'Just keep an eye on them,' Lorraine said. 'Ensure that the laundry is getting done and they're not having cold cereal every night for dinner. You certainly don't need to be living with them, but spend some time out there.' She paused. 'I should also mention that you get a stipend for this.'

'But it won't be a factor in your retirement

199

planning,' Judge Henderson added dryly, and I surprised myself by laughing with him.

'So,' Lorraine said, 'are you willing?'

What they were asking was far afield of the work I did for Hennepin County. I had no children; I hadn't even grown up with younger siblings. But I realized something: it was too late to say I wasn't involved. Our last meeting notwithstanding, I liked Marlinchen Hennessy. And if I spent more time with her, I might be able to finish what I'd started: locating Aidan Hennessy.

'All right,' I said. 'I'll do it.'

★ ★ ★

They hadn't told me, but Marlinchen Hennessy had been in another room all the while. After I'd agreed to supervise the Hennessy kids, Lorraine had brought her in and explained the situation to her. Marlinchen, not surprisingly, had assented.

We'd gone back downstairs in the elevator together, where I'd told her that after I was done with work, I'd drive her home, and we'd explain the situation to her brothers. Marlinchen had nodded, quickly agreeable, otherwise quiet. I'd left her at a small table in the second-story plaza of the Pillsbury Center, drinking a Coke and doing homework.

Clearly, I thought on my way back to work, Marlinchen still saw me as an authority figure. If I was going to spend the next few weeks looking in regularly on her and her brothers, I at least wanted her to loosen up a little.

What I needed was to spend some time with Marlinchen in which I wasn't probing into uncomfortable family affairs, time in which neither of us brought up Hugh, or Aidan, or family finances, or jurisdictional lines. What we needed was to do something totally different. Something fun.

When I got to the detective division, I told Van Noord I was going to leave a little early.

*   *   *

'We're going to get arrested,' Marlinchen said flatly.

At six, the day's light was just starting to mellow. Marlinchen and I were on a county road outside the Cities, near the St. Croix River. I'd pulled the Nova over to the side so she and I could switch places.

Marlinchen had been fine a little earlier, when, in an empty church parking lot, I'd taught her the basics of driving. She'd made a 15-mile-per-hour circuit around the pavement, braking, learning to reverse. 'This isn't that hard,' she'd said, pleasure growing along with confidence.

Now it was a different story.

'Do I have to do this on a highway?' she said, her voice taking on a wheedling quality. 'Shouldn't I start out on a 25-mile-per-hour street somewhere?'

'Those kinds of streets have cross traffic, four-way intersections, and kids on wobbly bikes,' I told her. 'Here you've got nothing but clear, straight road.'

A flatbed truck roared past us at 75 miles per hour. Seeing that, Marlinchen eyed me reproachfully.

'You're running a household without even being able to drive to the store,' I said. It was an argument I'd made earlier, when I'd first suggested a driving lesson to her. 'You need to learn this.'

'What if I'm not going fast enough for the traffic?' she asked.

'They'll pass,' I said. 'Country drivers love to pass; it breaks up the monotony.' To forestall any further argument, I got out of the car. Halfway around the front fender, I saw Marlinchen reluctantly climb out as well.

'With great effort,' I said dryly, when we'd traded places, 'unwrap one of your hands and put down the parking brake, like you did before. Good. Now, with your foot on the brake, put the car in drive. *Your right foot*. Do *not* drive two-footed.'

Marlinchen pulled to the shoulder and stopped there, looking around. A few seconds passed, then a few more. There wasn't a single vehicle in either direction. I didn't know what she was looking for.

Was I pushing her too hard? I'd wanted her to loosen up for once, and do something fun, but Marlinchen didn't seem to be enjoying herself at all.

'We're the only car in sight,' I pointed out. 'Conditions are not going to get any better.'

Marlinchen took her foot off the brake and

pulled onto the road. The speedometer needle rose with painful slowness to 30. Then to 35. Finally to 45.

I said, 'The speed limit's 55.'

'I know,' Marlinchen said.

'Which means much of the traffic is going 65,' I explained. 'Speed up.'

The engine noise pitched upward, and the speedometer needle began to creep forward again. When it got to 60, Marlinchen looked visibly relieved at being able to ease up on the accelerator.

'Feeling okay?' I said.

'Yes,' she said, sounding surprised. Her hands relaxed on the wheel. 'Where are we going?' she asked.

'No destination,' I said. 'This road runs a long way. Just get comfortable with driving.'

In the right-side mirror, a vehicle appeared. It looked the size of a fly, but that was changing fast. The fly resolved into a big Ford pickup, gaining on us fast.

'Look in your rearview mirror,' I said.

She did. Instantly, her hands tensed on the wheel again.

'No problem,' I assured her. 'He's going to pass us.'

'What do I need to do?' Marlinchen asked me.

'Nothing. He'll do it all. Watch what he does.'

The truck caught up with us and tailgated for about twenty seconds. Marlinchen looked in the mirror at him for about nineteen of those seconds.

'Don't spend all your time looking at him,' I

said. 'Be looking ahead. That's where you're going.'

The truck, having asked us to speed up and getting no response, dropped back a polite distance. Then its big black nose dipped slightly out toward the center line, looking ahead, where there was no oncoming traffic in sight, just broken yellow lines. The driver swung out easily into the opposing lane, sped past us at about 90 mph, and cut back in.

'Wow,' Marlinchen said.

'See?' I said. 'No big deal. If there was any opposing traffic, you might have wanted to ease off the accelerator a little, just to make sure he could get back in safely. Or, once he was ahead of you, you could flash your lights. That means you're letting him cut back in.'

'There's a code of conduct?' Marlinchen said. 'Cool.'

We drove another ten minutes. Then a vehicle came into view ahead of us. A goldenrod machine, a tractor. We were gaining fast, and it was soon clear that the farmer was driving about 20 mph.

'Pass him,' I said.

'What?'

'Pass him. This guy's crawling. We'll be stuck behind him forever if you don't.'

'I can't,' she said.

'Yes you can. This car's got some power. It'll do it. But once you start, don't try to pull out. Indecision gets people hurt.'

We fell in behind the tractor. I looked ahead to ensure there was no one coming.

'You're clear,' I said. 'Go.'

The engine throbbed as Marlinchen swung into the opposite lane. The rpm needle jumped, and the speedometer began climbing: 70, 75, 80. There was that interminable moment, the one where you feel like you'll never draw clear of whatever you're passing, no matter how slow it was going a minute ago. We crawled forward. On the horizon, a small white blur appeared. An approaching vehicle.

Marlinchen did what I'd half known she would. The engine noise dropped to a low hum, the rpm falling. She wanted to cut back in.

'No!' I told her sharply. 'You're committed, remember?'

The rpm noise pitched higher again, and the speedometer climbed to 90. Then 95. We cleared the front end of the tractor. Marlinchen kept the accelerator down; 100 miles per hour. She glanced back to the tractor.

'You're clear,' I said. 'Get back over.'

With visible relief, she did. A moment later, a white pickup whizzed past us. It hadn't even been close, really.

'Oh, wow,' Marlinchen said. She took a deep breath and let it out. Then she looked in her rearview and waved gaily back at the tractor's driver, as though he'd done her a great favor. 'That was kind of fun.'

' 'Fun' is not a familiar feeling to you, is it?' I asked her. 'Do you want to pull over and put your head between your knees until it passes?'

'Oh, shut up,' Marlinchen said, and broke into

a high string of giggles at her own boldness. I laughed, too.

'You think you're a real badass now, don't you?' I said. 'That was nothing. When I was your age — '

'Here it comes,' she said good-naturedly.

' — my friend Garnet Pike and I were learning to do a fishtail 180, also known as a bootlegger's turn.'

'I don't know what either of those things are,' she said.

'It's a 180-degree turn you do using the parking brake while cranking the wheel around hard. You can't do it with a lot of the cars they make today, with high centers of gravity. Garnet had read about it and wanted to try. So she talked me into borrowing my aunt's car, a sedan with a good engine, and we went out to the airport.'

'The *airport?*' Marlinchen said.

'You're thinking of MSP. This was just a rural airport, one runway, no tower. And in the evening, when we went, no one was taking off or landing.' I backpedaled slightly. 'I'm not saying we should have done it. It *was* trespassing.'

'In other words, don't try this at home,' she said.

'Right. Anyway, the runway was the perfect spot to practice, both long and wide, with nothing to hit. After two false starts, Garnet got up her nerve and did it. And back then, whatever Garnet did, I felt I had to do,' I said. 'So we switched places, and I did.'

For a moment I was back there, hearing the

sound of my own giddy, relieved laughter, seeing the little scented pine tree rocking crazily from Aunt Ginny's rearview mirror. To this day, it's what I think of when I smell that synthetic pine scent.

'Let me guess,' Marlinchen said. 'You want to teach it to me.'

I shook my head. 'No, I know you're not ready for that. But I'll do a demonstration for you.'

'No, thank you,' she said firmly. 'I'd toss my cookies.'

'No you wouldn't,' I said. 'It'd be over before you knew it. In fact — '

'Look, a Dairy Queen!' Marlinchen interrupted, excited by a red-roofed shack on the roadside. 'Can we stop?'

'You're driving the car,' I said.

* * *

A short while later, we were sitting at a shaded spot overlooking the St. Croix River. Marlinchen had driven us there while I held her large, semiliquid ice-cream confection and my own order of onion rings. Ahead, the sun was shining on the river, but behind us, iron-colored clouds were piling up in the west. The contrast was so stark it almost looked like the thunderheads had been added into the scene with a moviemaker's computer graphics.

'Going to be some weather tonight,' I said. 'A storm, maybe hail.'

Marlinchen spooned up some of her ice cream. 'The big storms used to scare me when I was a kid,' she said. 'One of my first memories is of lightning striking the house. I didn't see it, I just remember the noise, and how scared my mother was. For years after that, any loud noises scared me,' she said.

'It was that bad?'

'I don't think I would have been affected by it so badly if my mother hadn't been,' Marlinchen said. 'She came into my room, crying, and told me 'Lightning struck the house' and put me straight to bed. I started crying, because she seemed so upset. I thought she meant that lightning was going to strike the house again and again. She slept in the bed with me that night.'

Elisabeth Hennessy had drowned under suspicious circumstances, with whispers of suicide surrounding her death. Her daughter's memory made me wonder if Marlinchen's mother had been troubled throughout her young life, if a highly tuned nervous system had turned the excitement of Minnesota's summer thunderstorms into terrifying psychodramas.

'Is something wrong?' Marlinchen asked me.

'No,' I said. I couldn't think of a tactful way to ask whether Elisabeth Hennessy had been fearful or neurotic, so I filed away the issue for another time.

'How old were you when your mother died?' Marlinchen asked me.

I hoped my surprise didn't show on my face. She was something of a mind reader. Not spot-on, but close. 'I was nine,' I said. 'Almost ten.'

Marlinchen paused with her plastic spoon

halfway to her mouth. 'The other day, I thought you said you came to Minnesota when you were 13,' she remarked. 'What happened in between?'

I'd told the story of my migration to Minnesota to a number of people, and none had asked that specific question. Until now.

'I told you my dad was a truck driver, right?' I said. 'He was on the road a lot. But until I was 13, my older brother, Buddy, lived at home. Then he joined the army and moved away, so I would have been living alone. That was mostly why. But also . . . ' I hesitated.

'What?'

'That summer, I think, a girl went missing. She was about my age, and in a small town, things like that cause a real panic.' A waterbird swept low over the river. 'I haven't thought about that for years.'

'Why not?'

'It was a long time ago. I was young.' I shrugged. 'Anyway, that might have had an influence on my father's feelings. Besides that, I was becoming a teenager. My father probably thought I needed a feminine influence.'

'I see,' Marlinchen said dryly. 'So it was your aunt's feminine influence that led you to break into airports and practice stunt driving?'

'Right,' I agreed. 'Ginny was the mellowest aunt ever. She worked evenings and weekends at a bar and grill, and she mostly let me do my own thing. Want one of these?' I held out the onion rings, and she took one.

'Thanks. So is your aunt still up on the Range?' she asked.

'No, she died when I was 19, of a stroke. Not like your dad,' I added quickly, seeing Marlinchen's little twitch of reaction. 'Hers was down in the brain stem, where a lot of the body's autonomic functions are. If there's such a thing as a good location to have a stroke, that's not it.'

After a few minutes, when Marlinchen had finished her ice cream, I got to my feet. 'Come on,' I said, 'let's head out.'

We walked down to the car together in silence. This time, I got behind the wheel, and at the end of the dirt lane we'd followed to our vantage point, I turned north instead of south onto the road.

'Aren't we going the wrong way?' Marlinchen said as we continued to accelerate.

'Yes,' I told her. Then I hauled up on the parking brake and turned the wheel hard. The Nova slewed in a 180, back wheels drifting briefly onto the shoulder, and then we were heading west, picking up speed again.

'See?' I said. 'That didn't hurt a bit, did it?'

17

Another gas-station mini-mart was hit; it was clearly the same two perpetrators. *Welcome back, guys,* I thought.

After taking initial witness reports, I reviewed security video from the first two stores, hoping that by watching tape from the day before the robberies, I might recognize these guys without their stocking masks, casing the place.

When I got off work, I was thinking that it might be a good night to go out to the lake in time for dinner. Marlinchen's cooking was probably better than mine. I rode the elevator down to the parking garage.

'Detective Pribek!'

I turned to see Gray Diaz approaching along a lane of parked vehicles. He wasn't alone. The man behind him was in his early fifties, tall, and slender, dressed in simple plainclothes: shirtsleeves and trousers, no tie. His eyes were gray behind wire-rim glasses. He too was familiar, but I couldn't quite place him.

'I'm glad we caught you before you left for the day,' Diaz said. He was holding a piece of paper in his hands. 'You know Gil Hennig, correct?'

'Yes,' I said, recognition kicking in. Hennig was a Bureau of Criminal Apprehension technician. I'd seen him at crime scenes, brushing fingerprint dust onto doorways, making casts of footprints, never drawing attention to himself.

'What can I do for you guys?' I said, feeling the little flutter of anxiety in my stomach that Diaz caused.

'Gil came down with me to get your car,' Diaz said. He held up the piece of paper. It was a warrant. 'You're welcome to look this over.'

I took the warrant from his hand and scanned it. It allowed testing for hair, fiber, prints, and blood. The work would be done at the BCA's crime lab. Hennepin County had its own laboratory, but this wasn't a Hennepin County case, and the BCA did testing for smaller jurisdictions, like the one Diaz served.

'If there's anything you need from the car, why don't you get it now?' Diaz suggested. 'The warrant covers contents of the car, but we'll be flexible. Officer Hennig will just need to watch, and he'll need to briefly inspect whatever you remove.'

'I don't need anything,' I said. There were tire tools in the trunk, the first-aid kit, and a few other emergency items. Cassettes in the glove compartment, and two $50 bills for towing in case of breakdown. I had no doubt the money would still be there when the Nova was returned to me.

Hennig spoke. 'I'll need the key, then.'

My fingers were clumsy. After perhaps sixty seconds, a period that seemed much longer with the two men watching me, I scraped the Nova's key between the tight double coils of the key ring and out to freedom.

Hennig walked over to my car, not needing me to point it out for him. In a moment, a tow truck had pulled in behind it, and they were hooking it up.

'I know this is an inconvenience,' Gray Diaz said. 'Can I give you a ride somewhere?'

'No,' I said. 'Thanks.'

'Really,' Diaz said. 'It's no trouble.'

I shook my head. 'I have a friend who's just about to get off work,' I said. 'I'll get a ride from her.'

'Are you sure?' Diaz said as we started walking toward the elevators, the direction from which I'd come.

'Positive,' I said.

Back upstairs, I disappeared into the women's room. I wasn't sure exactly where Diaz had gone, but I didn't want him to see me standing around, obviously without a friend I intended to hit up for a ride.

The restroom was unoccupied. I rested my haunches against the counter in silence.

Shorty had never been in my car, but of course Diaz couldn't know that. He knew that Stewart had been at the Sportsman bar, where I'd spoken to him, and shortly thereafter had been dead in his burning house. For all Diaz knew, Shorty could have been in my car in the interim, either alive as a passenger, or dead in the trunk. I could have killed him elsewhere and transported the body back to his house to burn it in a weak cover-up attempt.

The problem was, while Shorty hadn't been in my car, his blood had been. I'd been at the scene and even knelt beside him as he bled out, trying to persuade him to tell me a story that would otherwise have died with him. Stewart had told me what I needed to know, and all the while his warm blood had soaked into my clothes. Later, when Gen and I had gotten to her sister's farmhouse, we'd washed our bloody clothes in the basement machine, and carefully gone over the porch and house, making sure no trace of Blue Earth had followed us there to implicate us. The next day, I'd gone to a carwash and given the Nova the most thorough cleaning, washing, and vacuuming it had ever suffered at my hands.

That didn't mean, though, that Henning and his peers wouldn't find anything. Many criminals attempted such cleanups, but good technicians still found what was left behind. Evidence could survive a long time under the right circumstances. It was entirely possible that technicians could find blood in the car and identify it as Shorty's.

There was a rustling noise, of motion, in one of the bathroom stalls. The door opened and Roz, the MPD sergeant, came out. She stopped short and looked at me with frank surprise. I must have been looking at her the same way. There's not a lot of reason for sitting or standing around a restroom in silent inactivity for ten minutes, and that's what we'd just caught each other doing.

'What's up?' I said lamely. I noticed that her eyes seemed red-rimmed.

'Ah, I'm not even supposed to be here,' she said. 'I had to put Rosco down today.'

'Rosco?' I said.

'My first K-9 partner,' she said.

'Oh, hell,' I said. 'That's awful.'

'Yeah, well, it was for the best. He could hardly eat anymore. I fixed him ground steak the day before yesterday and he just looked at it, didn't touch it. I knew it was time.' She waved a hand in the air. 'I thought there was something I could be doing down here, to get my mind off it, but there's nothing.' She sighed. 'What about you?'

'Looking for a ride home,' I said. 'I don't have a car.'

Roz didn't comment on the fact that I was 'looking for a ride home' by standing around alone in a restroom. She said, 'I might as well give you a lift.'

We went down to the garage in silence. Then, behind the wheel, she said, 'You want to get a drink instead?'

★ ★ ★

'Okay, okay. No, wait,' I heard my own voice saying. 'Okay, I've been pissed on four times, but I've only been thrown up on once. I'm very proud of that.'

'You've been pissed on *four times*?' Roz demanded, over the bar noise.

'One of those times deserves a, what do you call it, an asterisk,' I clarified, my hands wrapped around an empty highball glass. 'This suspect was strapped down to a stretcher by EMTs, he'd been hurt in a fight in a biker bar. None of us

215

even saw how he managed to whip it out, much less aim for my leg. He was like a *ventriloquist* with that stuff.'

Roz and I had initially wanted to go someplace dark and quiet, but had chosen a lively urban-professional bar instead, because we didn't want to run into fellow cops, and the Friday-night happy-hour food would be better.

We drank to Rosco, and over the next few hours drank nearly enough to toast her other seven dogs. When the chips and seven-layer dip the bartender had set out wasn't enough, we split a basket of seasoned potato wedges.

She asked about Gen. I asked how her trainee, Lockhart, was coming along. She told me she'd never believed that bullshit about me being involved in some murder down in Blue Earth. I told her I'd never credited the rumors about her being a lesbian. Roz told me she was a lesbian. I bought the next two rounds.

After a blurry length of time, Roz told me the story of Rosco's finest hour.

'So we're all out in the sticks, searching for this dangerous escaped convict — this is four-thirty or so in the morning, and it's still pretty dark. Rosco's got a scent, and he runs until he stops at this tree. Then he doubles back, and runs around the tree again. He's all excited.

'We think this guy's up the tree, so everyone runs over and points their weapons and flashlights up at the branches. But there's no one there. Rosco's still circling the tree, barking at me, and I can't figure what he wants. The BCA guys are getting kind of pissed, like Rosco's

216

screwing up. They want me to pull him back onto the trail, and I have to tell them: you don't *lead* these dogs, you follow them. Then Rosco jumps up with his front paws on the tree and barks again, like to say, *I've done my job, now you take over, stupid.*' Roz peered at me, owlish from drink. 'You know what it was?'

'The guy was hiding in the tree?'

'That's right. *In the tree,*' Roz said, squeezing my arm for emphasis. 'He'd climbed up into the branches to look around, and the tree was dead and the trunk hollowed out, and when he was climbing back down, he either slipped or he decided to hide in there.' She sipped at her beer. 'He couldn't get back out, and just about froze to death in the night. He was unconscious. But they thawed him out and put him on trial, and sent him to prison for life.'

'A happy ending,' I said.

'Yeah,' Roz said. 'What time is it?'

'Little after nine,' I said.

'I don't think I can drive,' Roz said.

' 'Kay,' I told her.

'Dammit, this whole thing was supposed to be me giving you a ride home,' Roz insisted.

' 'S all right,' I told her.

In the end, Roz's girlfriend, Amy, ended up taking a cab downtown in order to drive her home. Amy assured me it was no trouble to give me a lift, too. She didn't recognize the address I gave her. But Roz did.

'You live in a *housing project?*' she said, incredulous.

217

18

A loose-limbed teenage boy ambled by in the hallway of the 26th floor of the north tower. His eyes met mine and flicked away; he went on to the apartment at the end of the hall. I was in front of 2605, where I'd knocked on the door, but gotten no answer. I tried again.

Then Cicero opened the door, wet-haired, a towel held half-crumpled in one hand. His shirt was damp where he'd obviously pulled it on hastily, without adequately drying the skin underneath.

'Is this a bad time?' I said.

'No, no,' he said. 'Come on in.'

Inside, a smell of Ivory soap and steam had drifted into his living room. I said, 'Sorry, I'm empty-handed tonight.'

'You don't have to bring me anything to come over here,' Cicero said. 'But am I right in guessing that while you didn't bring a bottle this time, you haven't been abstaining tonight? I thought I detected a semiliquid s in your — '

A knock on the door interrupted him. Cicero rolled to the door and opened it partway.

'I burned my arm,' a female voice said.

Cicero rolled back, and his patient entered. She was a thin white woman with lank brown hair, dressed in a disjointed ensemble of spaghetti-strapped satin camisole over

218

sweatpants, and she held a wet paper towel to her arm.

'How'd this happen, Darlene?' Cicero asked.

'Cooking,' she said, and looked at me. But I saw her eyes, and knew from her pinpoint pupils that drugs were probably at the root of whatever kitchen accident she'd had.

Cicero turned to me. 'Sarah, would you mind waiting in the other room?'

I nodded agreement and withdrew into his bedroom. If I knew him, this would take longer than just cleaning the burn and putting a topical salve on it; I doubted he'd missed her contracted pupils any more than I had, and he would probably follow treatment with advice on where to seek drug-dependency counseling.

The blinds of the window were up, as always, and the lights of Minneapolis lay below; I went over to look down. Cicero's voice and Darlene's were faint through the bedroom door. Other than that, nothing. It was surprising how thick the walls of this building were. There were people around us, but I heard none of their activities. Other than hearing Fidelio bark once, my visits here had been like coming to someplace high atop a mountain. Normally, it was peaceful. Tonight, it was unnerving.

Roz had been a great distraction, as had the noise and crowd of the bar and the war stories we'd told each other. But now the question I'd been pushing from my mind came back to me, unappeased. What would happen if the BCA found Stewart's blood in my car?

To be questioned as a primary suspect in

Royce Stewart's death had been painful. To see the distrust in the faces of some of my colleagues, and the perverse approval in the eyes of others — that had been distressing. But ultimately, I'd always had an escape clause where Shorty was concerned. I'd always known that if I were arrested or indicted, Genevieve would come back and tell the truth. I'd still be a conspirator in Shorty's death, but not an accused murderer.

Now an unhappy possibility had arisen. Was it possible that Genevieve's confession wouldn't be enough? If all the physical evidence pointed to me, and so did all the witness testimony from Blue Earth, would a grand jury weigh Gen's unlikely claim of guilt against the preponderance of evidence, and send me to trial instead? Once that happened, there would be very little to keep a jury from convicting me.

When I'd first been questioned by detectives from Faribault County, lying to protect Genevieve had seemed natural and right. Now I wondered if I hadn't dug for myself a deeper hole than I'd ever realized.

The bedroom door opened, and I turned from the window.

'Hey,' Cicero said from the doorway, 'sorry about that.'

'It's your job,' I said.

'Are you hungry?'

I realized that I was. 'How did you know that?'

'Med school,' Cicero said. 'We're taught to catch malnutrition early. What did you have for dinner?'

'Four whiskey sours, three beers, and half a basket of potato wedges,' I admitted.

'If there's a more balanced meal than that, I haven't heard of it,' Cicero said. 'Let me make you some coffee and see what I've got in the way of food.'

I frowned. He was far from rich; I wasn't even sure he was solvent. 'You shouldn't waste your food on me,' I said.

'Enjoy it and it won't be a waste,' Cicero said.

He fixed me a tomato-and-avocado sandwich with a cup of coffee; we went back into his bedroom while I ate.

After I was mostly done, Cicero asked, 'So, why were we drinking tonight?'

'Why is it that doctors always say *we* when they mean *you*?' I asked him.

'It suggests empathy,' Cicero said. 'You weren't celebrating, were you?'

'No,' I said.

'What's wrong?'

'Nothing, really.' I lifted the mug of coffee as if it would protect me from his curiosity.

'Like hell. What's wrong?'

I licked a drop of tomato-stained mayonnaise from my finger. 'That was a really good sandwich,' I said.

'Thank you. What's wrong?'

I sighed. 'It's complicated,' I said. 'It has to do with what my husband went to prison for, and . . . I just thought I was doing the right thing, and now I'm not so sure. Maybe you can understand that. What am I saying, of course you can.' I gave him a knowing look. 'That's how you

221

lost your license, isn't it? Assisted suicide. You helped a terminally ill patient to die, right?'

Cicero lifted an eyebrow. 'How do you know that?'

'It wasn't hard to figure out,' I said. 'Compassion. It's your fatal flaw.'

'Sexual misconduct,' he said.

'What?' I asked.

'I lost my license for sexual misconduct with a patient.'

'You're joking,' I said.

'Sarah,' he reproved me, 'why on earth would I make a joke about something like that?'

Chastised, I took refuge in my coffee once again. I drank, then spoke more carefully. 'But it was a misunderstanding, right?' I said. 'A false accusation?'

'No,' Cicero said. 'It was sexual misconduct, period.'

I wanted to say, *That's not possible.*

'She came into the ER one night on a suicide attempt,' Cicero said. 'She was tiny, barely five feet tall, with waist-length blond hair. I could see that the suicide attempt was ambivalent. She'd cut her wrists, but only shallowly. I got her admitted to the crisis unit, and during the process, she told me her story.

'She was British, had come to New York at 16 to study ballet. There was a rift in her family: her mother was dead, and she didn't talk much anymore to her father and sister. She'd wanted to start a new life in the States, but things didn't go well. She'd started to struggle with her

222

weight, which meant anorexia and amphetamines, and then alcohol and downers to cope with all the stress. She had a series of boyfriends, none of whom treated her well, and when her career evaporated, she'd married the worst of them, a man with a more serious drug problem than she had. She had two babies in quick succession, and quit drugs for her children's sake, but her husband never did, nor was he faithful. One day she woke up and realized she was trapped in a strange city and a loveless marriage, with two small children and no viable skills. That was when she decided her kids would be better off without her.

'She was obviously troubled, but to me it seemed that something in her was struggling to survive, suicidal ideation or not. I was hopeful about her case, but after I got her a bed in the psych ward, I didn't hear anything about her again.

'She never forgot me, though. One night, about six months later, she left me three phone messages at the ER. I called her and found out that she was in crisis again. Her husband, who'd been a needle user, had told her he was HIV positive and didn't think he could support her or the kids anymore, then took some cash and the car and left. She hadn't heard from him in two days. She couldn't come in to the ER, because she had no car and no one to watch her babies, but she badly needed someone to talk to, in person, not over a crisis line. She asked if I could come over.'

Cicero rubbed his temple, remembering. 'I

can remember to the minute how long I had before I got off work. Forty-two minutes; there was a digital clock hanging in the corner. I looked at it and told her I'd be there soon.'

It wasn't right that I was feeling angry at this woman. My anger should have been focused on Cicero. I could see how he must have appeared to her: tall, competent, caring, handsome, and sworn to first do no harm. But instead I felt a spark of anger at the unknown, needy, grasping woman who I knew was about to drag Cicero into a trap that would cost him his job, his license, and eventually his legs.

'On the way over,' Cicero went on, 'I'd been thinking about what I would tell her: that she had to get tested for HIV, places where she could get help taking care of her children. But she didn't want to talk about her problems when I got there. She was composed, making tea in her kitchen in this long white nightgown. She didn't seem crazy, and she didn't seem suicidal. If she had, everything would have gone differently.'

I felt a little chill when Cicero said the word *suicidal*, realizing where this story might be going.

'She told me about her childhood, ballet, and England. In the middle of this reminiscing, she said it was ironic that she'd married her husband in order to stay in America after her visa expired. Now all she wanted was to be in London again, and she was afraid that was never going to happen. She said she felt like her life was over at age 22.'

The building's air-conditioning kicked in,

224

noisy in the silence between his words.

'It seemed very, very natural,' Cicero said, 'to put my arms around her and hold her.'

He said no more, bringing the curtain down on the first act of a two-act story.

'She could have been HIV positive,' I reminded him, as if the danger hadn't long passed, one way or another.

'I knew that,' Cicero said. 'Did you ever read *Hamlet*?'

'Once,' I said.

'Did you notice the oddly sexual imagery in Ophelia's burial, how the queen compares a bridal bed to a grave?'

'What are you saying?'

'That sometimes proximity to death can be erotic. She was Ophelia to me. I wanted to lie down in her grave and bring her back to life.'

'So I was right the first time,' I said. 'It was compassion.'

'If you can be compassionate and selfish at the same time,' Cicero said. 'If she needed to feel alive, I needed that, too. In those days, sometimes I'd leave work so numb from what I'd been doing all night that I felt like a walking dead man. That was before I realized how lucky I was just to be walking.' He said this very simply, without self-pity. 'I was 34 then. I told myself the same lie a lot of ER staff tell themselves: I didn't have time for a relationship, that no woman would tolerate the crazy hours or understand the stress I was under. Other women in the ER did, and I hooked up with a few of them, but those were just friendly trysts. Relief sex, we called it sometimes. And I had some one-night stands with women I met in bars. Underneath it all, I was probably pretty goddamned lonely, although I couldn't have seen it back then.'

I was sitting on the floor; now I slid closer to him so that I could take his hand. Cicero let me, but he said, 'Don't feel sorry for me. I deserved everything that happened next. Her sister came over from Manchester and helped her file a lawsuit against the hospital. In the hearings, a lot of things came out that I hadn't known. Since her suicide attempt, this woman had been seeing a psychiatrist, and had been diagnosed with borderline personality disorder. She had a terrible time with men, couldn't trust them, but at the same time had been known to fixate on men she barely knew, as potential lovers and saviors. She'd been transferred to a female psychiatrist after transference had caused problems with a male therapist.'

'You didn't know any of that,' I said.

Cicero's expression told me I should have known better. 'The mentally ill cannot be expected to identify themselves as ill.'

'I just meant, it seems like an awfully harsh punishment for what you did.'

' "Into whatever houses I enter, I will go into them for the benefit of the sick," ' Cicero said. 'It's part of the Oath.'

I looked down into my empty coffee cup. 'Is it guilt, then, that makes you keep seeing patients under these circumstances?' I indicated the small and underequipped exam room that lay beyond his bedroom door.

Cicero considered that. 'Not really,' he said. 'It's selfishness, almost. You know how some dogs — herding dogs, rescue dogs — are bred to work? Even when they're raised as house pets, they wake up in the morning and look at a human to say, *How can I help?* It's bred into them. Some people are that way, too. I have to do what I'm trained for. I'm a working breed.' He lifted a shoulder in something that wasn't quite a shrug. 'I can't change now. I am what I am.'

★ ★ ★

I caught the last bus home, sometime after midnight. As I got on, a young woman got off at the back exit. Just as she did, our eyes met. Ghislaine, for once without Shadrick, eyed me quite curiously for a long moment before she dropped down the back steps and through the doors.

19

It's a detective's prerogative to use a car from the motor pool, and it didn't raise any eyebrows at work when I began using one. If word had spread that the BCA had my car for testing, no one referred to it, even implicitly, in my presence. Meanwhile, I used the motor pool car not only for work but to drive out in the evenings and visit the Hennessys.

Kids adapt to the whims and dictates of adults the way the rest of us adapt to changes in the weather. The Hennessy boys accepted my new role in their lives with a shrug. I checked the details that Lorraine had mentioned; it was clear that the laundry was getting done, and the house was as clean as anyone could reasonably expect with four young people living in it. The Hennessy home wasn't meant to look aseptically neat, anyway; that was part of its charm. It was an old house, and everywhere were testaments that this was a longtime family home. There were nicks in the shabby-elegant pine furniture, and along an upstairs hallway, there were dots and dashes of bleach, a Morse-code tale of someone's haphazard attempt to scrub out stains. From the length of the pattern, I didn't think it was Kool-Aid. Blood, maybe, from a nosebleed or some childhood mishap.

But on a day-to-day basis, the kids kept the house fairly tidy. It was soon plain to me that

228

these kids had been self-directed from an early age; Hugh hadn't been a micromanager as a parent for a long time, perhaps never. Other kids might have fallen apart after what had happened to Hugh; the Hennessy kids had taken the reins of their lives also automatically.

The absent Aidan was still on my mind. But by now I was familiar with Marlinchen's ready defenses. If I was going to make any more progress on the subject of her brother, I'd have to approach the issue a lot more carefully than I had last time. For now, I was letting it lie.

I did speak to her around ten o'clock one evening, when I'd stayed later than usual, because she was standing alone on the back porch, her slight figure a dispirited silhouette. She was looking out into the darkness of her nearest neighbor's land. There was absolutely nothing of interest out there, but she seemed troubled.

'Is something wrong?' I asked, slipping through the French doors from the family room out onto the deck.

Marlinchen turned. 'No, not really. It's Snowball,' she said.

'Your cat?'

'She's never out this late,' Marlinchen said. 'She always comes in around eight-thirty or nine. Like clockwork.'

'I wouldn't assume the worst,' I said. 'A friend once told me about a cat she'd owned that liked to ramble. Turns out the cat had a double life. Another family was feeding it and giving it water; they had pictures of the cat in their home.'

Marlinchen smiled but said nothing.

'Snowball might have gone into someone's home or garage and got locked in,' I went on. 'She'll turn up tomorrow.'

'I'm sure you're right,' she said.

'Are you really feeling okay?' I said. 'You seem a little down.'

'Just tired, I guess,' she said, and a muscle twitched in her cheek as if she were trying to suppress a yawn.

I nodded. 'What do you hear about your father?'

A strand of hair slipped loose from her high ponytail, and Marlinchen wiped it away from her face. 'He's in physical therapy,' she said. 'He's walking with a quad cane now. That's a cane with four little feet on it, for greater stability.'

'Like training wheels that don't roll?'

'Right,' she said. 'After that, he moves on to a regular cane, and then walking on his own.'

'That sounds like good progress,' I said.

'It is,' she said, 'physically.'

'Physically?' I asked, thinking that she meant Hugh's spirits were low.

'His verbal skills aren't getting much better,' she said. 'They think he understands a lot of what's going on around him — which is good for chances of getting the conservatorship — but he can't really speak or write. It's all garbled. He confuses *me* with *you*, or *he* with *she*,' Marlinchen explained. She looked over at me as if expecting some kind of response. Then she said, 'Aphasia is the worst thing that can happen to a writer.' Hearing her own words, Marlinchen

230

quickly clarified them. 'It's not about the money. We'll get by, even if he never writes again. But writing is the core of who Dad is,' she said. 'If he gets everything else back, but can't write again . . . it's the worst thing the stroke could have taken.'

There wasn't much that I could say that wouldn't be false comfort. 'Give it time,' I said.

★   ★   ★

You never get a car back from the crime lab quite how you turned it over. I'd heard this before, but hadn't understood it until I picked up the Nova at the Hennepin County impound facility, which was where the BCA sent it after testing. A chemical odor clung to the car's interior. When the early-evening light hit the Nova's windows, revealing a faint purple-white haze, I realized what it was. Superglue. They'd fumed for prints with it.

Diaz had to know that hoping for fingerprints after more than six months — in a vehicle that had been in use all that time — was an investigator's version of a Hail Mary pass. But he'd been damned thorough. That faint purple-white haze on the glass never came off.

Sarah, don't whine. Not even to yourself.

And then I looked down, and saw something that wiped petty concerns about the condition of my car from my mind. A square of carpet had been cut out of the floor.

They'd found blood. To inspect the carpeting was one thing, but to remove some for further

231

testing meant they'd found something they were fairly sure was blood.

While I drove home, I engaged in a mostly pointless exercise, trying to estimate how long it might take the BCA to do the lab work. More often than not, the testing process took weeks. Then again, it was possible that Diaz had some stroke with the BCA, and they'd expedite these tests. I couldn't count on having all that long.

* * *

Even though I would have preferred to go straight home, I stopped by the Hennessys' instead. I arrived to find Liam apparently digging under the willow tree, leaning into his work with a spade. Yet his clothes, a white shirt and gray pants, were clearly what he'd worn to school, not consistent with gardening. There was a sealed plastic trash bag near his feet.

I walked across the grass to Liam's side. It was warm enough out that I felt the five-degree drop in temperature as the shadow of the willow tree fell across my face, then my body. 'What is that?' I asked him. There was something in the trash bag; it was rounded but shapeless, as though it held an unbaked loaf of bread. Color wasn't discernible through the pellucid green plastic.

Liam stopped working, raised a shoulder diffidently as if trying to decide how to phrase something. 'It used to be Snowball,' he said finally.

'Oh, hell,' I said. 'What happened?' Now that I knew what I was looking at, I could see that the

232

color the bag masked was red: a murky, greenish red, like blood in a parking-lot oil puddle.

'Something got to her,' Liam said. 'We don't know what. She was ripped up pretty badly.'

'Where did you find her?'

Liam pointed. 'Down at the end of the driveway, off to the side.' He leaned into the spade handle again and forced more upturned black soil out of the hole he was making. 'I said I'd bury her. I didn't want Marlinchen looking at it anymore. I thought she was going to be sick this morning.'

I felt a small sting of guilt; it was me who'd glibly told Marlinchen that Snowball would be home safe in the morning.

'It bothers me, too,' Liam said. 'I can't think of any animal around here that would do this.'

He was looking at me as if for comment, and I realized that he was calling on me as an expert in violent death, even that of pets.

'There are some natural predators around here,' I said, thinking. 'Coyote, fox, black bear.'

Liam was skeptical. 'I never see anything like that. We don't even see the tracks.'

'Generally, animals like that stay away from humans,' I said. 'But as rural areas get more built up, they do come into human settlements to look for food. People have spotted them around here.'

'I suppose,' Liam said.

20

My next trip to the gym was more successful. I didn't run into Diaz, or my unwanted supporter, Jason Stone, either. I bought groceries after and, on the way home, was stopped at a traffic light when something caught my attention. A lone figure was climbing up a concrete staircase that led to a pedestrian-and-bike overpass over the freeway. Except he wasn't really climbing.

Popular culture writes off drinking to excess as a rite of passage among the young, but there's something painful to watch about someone who has drunk himself into complete incapacitation. The boy — he looked underage in his hoodie, loose jeans, and running shoes — was literally crawling up the stairs toward the bridge on his hands and knees. At the halfway landing, he stopped and lay down to rest. Or he'd passed out.

A horn sounded behind me. The light had turned green, and I was holding everybody up. I pulled away, into the intersection.

The last I saw of the young man was that, as if galvanized by the sound of the horn, he had started crawling again.

A rectangular pattern, across the interstate and back along a side road, brought me to the corresponding staircase on the other side of the pedestrian walkway. I didn't go up to intercept the kid. He'd be safe crossing the highway; the overpass was bounded on each side by a high chain-link fence. Even if he rose to his feet and walked, there was no way he could topple over into traffic.

In time he appeared at the top of the stairs, staggering, but nonetheless on his legs. He looked down at the steps as though they were an obstacle course, then wisely decided to descend on hands and knees, just like he'd gone up. I got out of the car and climbed up the stairs to meet him.

His body, viewed from above, was even more slender up close, and his hair looked a little too blond to be true. When he looked up from my running shoes to my face, that suspicion was confirmed: his features were clearly Asian. Hmong possibly, or Vietnamese.

I saw something else, too. He wasn't just under 21; he was clearly under 18.

'Are you all right?' I said. 'Can you hear me?'

His eyes focused in on my face. 'Oh no,' he said in a tone of resigned dread. 'Oh no. Police.'

How do they always know? I thought. I was wearing nothing remotely official: mid-calf-length leggings, a T-shirt, and a hooded jacket.

'Can you stand up?' I asked.

'I don' want to go to juvie,' he said in the same tone. There was no accent in his voice, marking him clearly as second-generation American.

'I'm not arresting you,' I said.

'I hate it at juvie,' he moaned.

'One, I doubt you've ever been,' I said, hooking a hand around his upper arm and pulling. 'Two, you're not under arrest. Stand up.'

'No, no, no,' he said, refusing to yield to my pressure. He wasn't heavy, but I couldn't get him up without his cooperation.

'Kid,' I told him, 'you've got something in your sleeve that might someday be a bicep. There's got to be enough muscle in your quadriceps to get you on your feet.'

'I don' want to go to juvie,' he said, still droning lifelessly.

'*Up*,' I said.

When we got to my car, I put him in the backseat. He was only five-eight or so, and thin, but it'd still be safer there in case he got squirrelly on the ride to wherever we were going. Sometimes drunks who couldn't even get coordinated enough to walk properly suddenly recovered enough to become violent. I fastened the seat belt around him.

As I got behind the wheel, he said once again, 'I don't want to go in, I don't want to go to juvie,' and fell bonelessly sideways to lie down, head to hipbone, on the backseat.

'Kid,' I said, 'how many police officers have you seen that patrol while wearing workout clothes and driving an old car that smells like superglue fumes?'

His lips dropped slightly apart. Too many concepts at once; I'd blown his mind.

'Let me ask you something easier,' I said. 'What's your name?'

'Special K.'

Of course. 'No, your government name,' I said.

'Kelvin,' he said.

236

'Okay, Kelvin, where do you live?'

The address he slurred was becoming very familiar. I started the car, pulled away from the curb.

'It smells funny in here,' he said, ending with a slushy word that could have been *Officer*.

'Yeah, that's the superglue I mentioned.'

'Is making me sick,' he said, and he didn't sound good.

'Do you think alcohol might have something to do with that?'

'*Real* sick,' he said.

'Kelvin,' I said, glancing in the rearview mirror, 'if you throw up in my car, I'm going to ask the prosecutor for special circumstances.'

★ ★ ★

Special K, cowed by the thought of a vomiting-in-an-official-vehicle enhancement to whatever charge he believed he was facing, kept it together until we arrived at the towers.

I helped him out of the car, but as soon as I let go, he stumbled and nearly fell, sinking to his knees. He looked up, squinting, at the south tower.

'Home?' he asked, blinking.

'I told you that I wasn't arresting you,' I reminded him.

'Oh good,' Kelvin said. Then his gaze clouded, his attention focused inward like a newscaster receiving breaking news through his earpiece, and he doubled over to vomit on my running shoes.

'You broke my streak,' I said.

An older sister, almost heartbreakingly beautiful in a cheap sateen robe, took in the sight of Kelvin with a disapproving thinning of the lips that told me this wasn't the first time he'd been delivered home in such a state. 'Thank you,' she whispered, and then, looking at my shoes, 'Sorry.'

When I was outside again, my eyes strayed involuntarily upward, at the north tower.

Oh, why not? You're here already.

In the confines of the little elevator, the odor of the vomit I'd mostly scraped off my shoes was unmistakable. I couldn't go visiting like this. On the 26th floor, I detoured back from the elevator to the stairs, and took my shoes off on the landing, behind the stairwell door. There was no worry that they would tempt thieves. I took off my socks as well. There's a dignity to bare feet that stocking feet just don't have.

When Cicero answered the door, I said, 'I was just in the neighborhood. I'll leave if I'm interrupting something.'

'Where are your shoes?'

'They're in the stairwell,' I said.

'I see,' Cicero said, as though this were completely reasonable. 'Every time I consider asking you more about your personal life, something like this happens, and I realize how much more fascinating it is not to know.' He rolled backward in the doorway, admitting me.

I declined anything to eat, but Cicero made us both tea, and we went into his bedroom.

'Who's this?' I said.

'Who?' Cicero asked.

I was looking at the photos on the low bookcase in his bedroom. 'Him,' I said, tapping what looked like the oldest of the photos, in weathered black-and-white.

It was a young man on a horse. The man, a teenage boy, really, wore a broad-brimmed hat and what might have been his nicest clothes, dark trousers and a cream-colored collarless shirt. The horse was beautiful: obviously nearly as young as the boy, with a dark-brown or black coat that gleamed even in an old photo, neck arched with impatience at being reined in long enough for the photo to be taken.

'That's my grandfather,' Cicero said. 'In Guatemala.'

'How old is he, in the photo?'

'Eighteen,' Cicero said. 'I never knew him; he died not long after I was born. But I'm told that he loved that horse. Back then, a fast horse was your five-liter. I guess it wasn't really his, it was the family's. But he thought of the horse as his, until one day he came home to find his father had sold it to pay for his sister's wedding dress.'

'No shit?' I said, amused.

'Oh, yes. He was just beside himself,' Cicero said. 'At least, that's how the story goes.'

'Were you born there?' I asked.

'In Guatemala? No,' Cicero said. 'Here in America. My parents wouldn't even let Ulises and me learn Spanish until we were well grounded in English.'

'You know,' I said, 'we were going to get back to the story of your brother, and we never did.'

239

Cicero picked up an unrelated photo on his bookcase, one in which he seemed to be hiking with a female friend, and set it back down. 'There's not much to tell,' he said.

His pointless action with the photo told me differently, and I waited for the rest.

'Ulises moved here with a girlfriend,' Cicero went on. 'She quit him eventually, but he liked it here, so he stayed. They sent me up here to live with him about four years ago, after rehab, and he died a year after that.'

It wasn't the end; in fact, it was a prologue.

'Ulises was a baker,' Cicero said. 'He had screwy hours, starting work at two in the morning, at a little bakery in St. Paul.'

Immediately I knew the story Cicero was going to tell.

'The neighborhood wasn't the best. There was some drug activity there,' Cicero said. 'One night, as Ulises was going to work, there was an APB in Ramsey County for a drug suspect who'd taken a shot at some cops. Ulises drove a car similar to the one they were looking for. A couple of plainclothes Narcotics officers saw him parking behind the bakery and they braced him as he got out of the car.'

'And they shot him,' I said. You didn't have to be a cop to have heard about it.

Cicero nodded. 'They said afterward that he ignored commands to raise his hands and reached for a weapon instead. Both of them opened fire. They hit him seven times and killed him.'

'I remember,' I said. 'It was awful.'

240

'I believe them when they say he was reaching into his jacket. Ulises was probably reaching for his wallet. They were in street clothes, in a bad neighborhood, at two in the morning, pointing guns at him. Ulises probably thought he was being robbed. There was even a newspaper columnist who floated that theory, but the police never lent it any credence at all.'

Oh, yes they did, I thought, *just never in public forums.* I remembered the days of heated debate that had gone on in locker rooms and shooting ranges, anywhere cops talked among themselves.

'They also suggested, early on, that Ulises had ignored their commands because his English wasn't good enough. They had to back down from that idea. English was his first language, just like it was mine, and everyone who knew him knew that.' He paused. 'Naturally, the review board found no fault with the officers. They went back to work, and a week or so later, I had to move up here.'

'I'm so sorry,' I said.

'Don't be,' Cicero said. 'It's not your fault.'

'Cicero,' I said, 'I probably should tell you something.'

My lie of omission — about being a cop — no longer rested lightly on my shoulders. I looked over at the photos, found the one of a younger Cicero and his brother. There was something lighter in Ulises's expression. A physician's seriousness informed Cicero's face, even at rest; Ulises looked more easygoing.

'I'm right here,' Cicero said patiently.

241

Come on, Sarah, it's not that hard. Three little words: I'm a cop.

Then we both heard it, the muffled shrill sound that was my cell phone ringing in the depths of my shoulder bag. I turned from the photos on the table, shot Cicero an apologetic look, and dug the phone from the bag.

'Sarah?' It was Marlinchen. 'I'm sorry to bother you, but — '

'What is it?' I asked, antenna up.

'I think someone's outside the house. Liam heard noises earlier, when he went out to take a break from studying, and I just heard something outside the bathroom window while I was brushing my teeth. They don't sound like animal noises to me.'

I could easily have told her to call the police in her area, but noises outside a house weren't likely to be a top priority, and ten at night wasn't a peak time for staffing at most smaller departments. The Hennessys would likely get a ten-minute visit, sometime in the next two hours. I couldn't leave it at that. The Hennessy kids were my responsibility.

'I'll come over,' I said.

★ ★ ★

Despite her disclaimer — *They don't sound like animal noises to me* — I thought that Marlinchen had probably heard whatever had killed Snowball. If it had hunted on their grounds before, there was no reason it wouldn't come back. But it was quite dark as I got close to

242

the Hennessy home, and I didn't blame Marlinchen for being afraid.

She met me at the door, Colm and Liam not far behind her. 'Thank you for coming out,' she said quickly.

'You're welcome. I'm going to make a quick check of the house, then the grounds,' I told her.

'The house?' Marlinchen said, startled. 'The noises were outside.'

'Are you sure all the doors have been locked all night long?'

'I think . . . I guess . . . ,' Marlinchen tried to answer, but she wasn't quite sure, and her two brothers remained silent.

'Better to check,' I said. 'Where's Donal, by the way?'

'Sleeping,' Marlinchen said. 'I sent him to bed a half hour ago.'

I checked on him first, and his chest rose and fell evenly in the light that spilled across his bed when I opened the door. Moving inside, I checked the closets as quietly as possible, and under both the beds. Nothing.

I went through the darkened upstairs rooms, then the downstairs. A door in the kitchen led down to a basement, and I shone my flashlight into its shadowy corners. There was some old furniture stored down there, and two mattresses. A smell of dust and concrete hung in the air. It wasn't orderly, but I found nothing that suggested a recent intruder.

When I'd finished with the house, I went out into the garage, where Hugh's Suburban stood. There was no one hiding under it, and the

243

closets held only canned food and camping equipment, and a few dusty old bottles of wine.

Outside, I went to the broad back porch and dropped to my hands and knees, looking between a wide gap in the boards through which a human might easily have squeezed. Underneath was nothing but an expanse of dust and small nondescript rocks. I walked out to the fence line on either side of the house, poked around the bushes at the property's edge, looked under the small wooden dock at the lake's edge. No broken branches, no footprints to be seen. The only thing that was out of place was the little rise of overturned-and-smoothed soil near the willow tree, the resting place of the late Snowball.

Last, I went to the detached garage. The door was unlocked. Stepping inside, I pointed the flashlight beam into the darkness, and jumped.

'Son of a bitch,' I whispered. At first glance, it had looked like a body hanging from the rafters: a heavy bag. To the right of it was a weight bench. Colm's gym, as the other kids called it.

The rest of the building was taken up by a car, an early-eighties BMW. Underneath a layer of dust, the paint seemed to be a deep bottle green. Its windows were likewise filmed with dust, like a corpse's eyes, and all four tires were flat. It wasn't damaged in any other way, but it had clearly been years since it was driven. I pointed the flashlight at a window, and the beam pierced the light layer of dust to show nothing out of the ordinary: pale-brown leather seats, all empty. Spiders had gotten inside, their webs threaded across the bars of the headrests and dangled loosely from the ceiling handgrips.

'Everything looks fine,' I told Marlinchen when she answered my knock at the door. 'I think you probably heard an animal of some kind.'

Marlinchen looked sheepish. 'Maybe what happened to Snowball has me on edge,' she said.

'That's understandable,' I told her. 'In fact, I was thinking I might as well just stay out here with you guys tonight.'

'Really?' she said. 'That's not necessary, honest.'

I'd expected that this would startle her, and said, 'Well, it is late, and it's a long drive back . . . '

'Oh,' Marlinchen said, falling back immediately into her good manners. 'I understand. I didn't mean — '

'It's okay,' I said. 'Look, I need to ask you another favor, if I'm going to stay out here all night. Can I run my shoes through your washing machine?'

The washer and dryer were both in the garage where Hugh kept his Suburban. I threw in both my Nikes and my socks, poured in detergent, and set the temperature control to the hot-water setting. As the first cycle started with a muted sound of rushing water, I crossed to the cabinet I'd checked out before, the one where the old wine lived.

Back in the house, the family room was unlit, the TV off. The kids had gone upstairs, and the whole downstairs was dark, except for the

245

kitchen. I walked over and set the wine bottle down.

Footsteps told me Marlinchen was coming down the stairs. 'Sarah? I was just on my way to bed. One thing I need to tell you — '

'Come down a second,' I said, interrupting her. 'I need to ask you something, too.'

Marlinchen leaned out a little, over the stairway railing. I tilted the wine for her to see. 'I found this in your garage. Liam said your father doesn't drink anymore; I think it must be left over.' In fact, the year on the bottle was about eight years past. 'There's no sense in letting it go to vinegar. Do you mind?'

'I don't see why not,' she said. 'Listen — '

'Good,' I said. 'Come join me.' I fished a corkscrew from a drawer.

'You mean, drink some?' Marlinchen's voice, from the stairs, sounded both scandalized and tantalized.

I took down two oversized goblets from a high shelf. 'Sure,' I said. 'I wouldn't make a habit of it, but you're running a whole household. I think a glass of wine isn't out of order.'

Outside the kitchen window, all was inky black, except for the lights of a pleasure boat drifting on the lake. I killed the main kitchen light, so that two overhead recessed lamps isolated the counter in a long pool of illumination, and pulled the cork from the wine. I didn't say anything more to Marlinchen. She was intrigued. She'd come.

I can't say I felt totally comfortable with what I was doing. But I wanted to speak freely to

246

Marlinchen, and for her to speak as freely to me, and from what I'd seen, her armature wasn't going to come down unaided.

When I sat down at the counter, I heard her footsteps again, descending. She slipped onto the stool next to mine, and I poured until her glass was nearly full. Her eyes widened.

'Don't worry,' I said. 'That's not so much, for wine.' I pushed the glass over to her. 'If anyone ever tries to serve you that much vodka, question their motives.'

We drank. Marlinchen winced.

'I know,' I said, 'but stick with it. Its charms will become more apparent as time goes by.' I held up my own glass, watching the way the light pierced the ruby liquid. 'One of the Puritans, like Cotton or Increase Mather, said this great thing about wine. He called it 'a good creature of God.''

'That's lovely,' said Marlinchen.

Shiloh had told me that, Shiloh with his love-hate relationship with the Christian faith and his eclectic but vast knowledge of its followers and teachings.

'The thing I was trying to say earlier,' Marlinchen said, 'is that you can't close the door in Dad's bedroom. The knob is virtually useless. People have been known to get stuck in there.'

'That's probably not hard to fix,' I said.

'I know, but Dad's hopeless about things like that,' Marlinchen said. 'Not only is he hopeless with tools, I mean, he's fundamentally incapable of caring about stuff like that. He'd rather just keep the door cracked all the time.' She smiled, rueful.

'To each his own.' I poured myself a splash more wine. 'If memory serves,' I said, 'you should be studying for final exams right about now, right?'

Marlinchen nodded.

'You never mentioned,' I said, 'where you've applied to college and if you've been accepted anywhere yet.'

'Actually,' she said, 'I'm putting school off for a while. I mean, I'm not Liam. It's not like my grades are that great.'

'They'd probably be a lot better if you hadn't been running a household of five,' I pointed out.

Marlinchen paused with the wineglass close to her lips. 'These are extenuating circumstances, with Dad in the hospital — '

'Bullshit,' I said. 'You're balancing a checkbook, keeping a house clean, planning meals, cooking them, doing the grocery shopping. These are not things you learn to do in a matter of weeks. I have a feeling you've been doing them a lot longer than your old man's been in the hospital, and even if your father makes a full recovery, things aren't going to change much.'

She hesitated before speaking. 'Family is important to me,' she said.

'That's fine,' I said, pouring her more wine, 'but Donal is 11 years old. By the time he's 18 and ready to move out, you'll be 24. Are you going to put off college until then?'

'College isn't for everyone,' she said. 'I bet you didn't go.'

'I went for a year,' I said.

'See?'

'But it was long enough for me to find out I didn't want what it had to offer,' I said. 'You should find out too, before you're too old for the dorms and Jell-O shots and all the things that make college more than just school,' I said. 'Even right now there are things you should be doing with your high school years that you're not. Like dating, or just going to the movies with friends.'

Marlinchen drank, mostly to stall for time. She was thinking up verbal evasive maneuvers. 'You're a friend,' she said after a second, her voice sweet. 'You want to go to the movies sometime?'

'I'm not the sort of friend you should have at your age,' I said.

Marlinchen looked pleased, and I realized I'd stepped into a trap. 'That raises an interesting point,' she said. 'You're out here, late at night, with a bunch of kids you hardly know. Why aren't *you* out dating, Detective Pribek?'

'Because I'm — ' I broke off. I really didn't want to explain Shiloh to her.

Marlinchen saw my discomfort, and her newfound audacity drained away. 'I didn't mean to pry,' she said gently. 'If you're gay, Sarah, I'm totally all right with that.'

She was so sincere that I felt absurdly touched, but now I had to correct her misperception. 'Well, gay people date, too,' I pointed out. 'But what I was going to say was 'Because I'm married.''

Marlinchen's mouth fell open slightly, in

249

shock. 'But . . . where's your husband?' she finished.

'Wisconsin,' I said.

'You're separated?'

'Sort of,' I said.

Marlinchen wasn't dense; she heard that I didn't want to talk about it anymore. She played with the stem of her wineglass instead. 'That's too bad,' she said, and then nearly let the glass slip from her fingers.

'Careful,' I said, steadying it. 'Let me weigh that down for you.' I poured again.

'You're right,' she said. 'The charm does become appear . . . apparent.'

'Stick with me, kid,' I said. 'I'll take you places.' *Like Hazelden.*

But I noted the high color in Marlinchen's cheeks, and judged that she was ready for the direction I wanted to take the conversation. With a hundred-pound nondrinker, it didn't take long.

'Since I've been out here, visiting you kids,' I said, 'you haven't mentioned Aidan to me. Not once.'

She spoke quickly. 'I am sorry about the way I talked to you, the day that — '

I shook my head. 'That's not what I mean,' I told her. 'I'm not angry about what you said, but the question I asked you that day still stands.' I paused, watching her face. She undoubtedly remembered what we'd been talking about, but I reminded her anyway. 'Kids don't get sent away from their families for no reason,' I said. 'Good reasons, bad reasons . . . there's always something.'

True to form, she didn't answer.

'I get the feeling that there's something else you'd like to tell me,' I said. 'Do you trust me, Marlinchen?'

'Oh, yes,' she said. 'It's just that Aidan is a painful issue.'

'Sometimes, in my line of work,' I said, 'I tell people they have to make their pain worse for a while on the way to making it better, or they'll go on dealing with the same low-grade pain indefinitely.'

Marlinchen looked straight ahead, staring out into the blackness beyond the kitchen windows. She wasn't ready to make the pain worse. I'd tried.

'Finish your wine,' I said, 'and let's go to bed.'

★   ★   ★

I very nearly shut myself into Hugh Hennessy's bedroom before I remembered the loose knob. Leaving the door cracked, I felt a little frisson of anxiety. It was so dark and quiet out here, I felt like I had stepped into a Gothic novel, complete with trick doors that trapped you behind them. In bed, I missed the small city noises that would have helped me sleep.

Because I'd left the door open, nothing alerted me that someone else was in the bedroom until I heard movement. I rolled over quickly, judged from the shape of the shadow that it was Marlinchen, and relaxed. She was barefoot, dressed only in a camisole and boxer shorts.

'What is it?' I said.

'I want to talk about Aidan,' she said.

Finally.

Marlinchen came closer, to sit on the floor by the bed.

'I didn't say anything against Aidan being sent away. I thought it was for the best.' She drew in a shuddery breath. 'I was afraid of what would happen if Aidan stayed.'

'Why were you afraid?' I asked.

'He was beating Aidan,' she said. 'Toward the end. But it started a long time before that.'

'Tell me,' I said.

21

Marlinchen Hennessy was her father's little girl; she was bright and verbal, and her father loved to read to her and teach her new words and listen to what she was learning in school. No sound had been sweeter to her own ears than the nickname of 'Marli' that only Daddy used, and it hadn't been until she was perhaps 10 that she'd realized that Daddy wasn't six feet tall, but only five-foot-eight.

Aidan, quiet as his twin sister was talkative, gravitated to their pensive, withdrawn mother. Like an astronomer, he studied her silences and her moods. When she seemed saddest, she'd draw him up into her lap and hold him, stroke his golden hair, kiss his maimed hand. Sometimes they'd sit together under the magnolia tree and look out at the waters of the lake. When he thought it would make her feel better, he'd bring the baby down to her, first Colm, whose weight had bowed Aidan's small back, then later baby Donal. That was close, of course, to the end.

All the children had been stricken by their mother's sudden death, but none more than Aidan. After the funeral, he'd lain under the magnolia tree and wept without restraint. Daddy had finally looked out the window and seen Aidan there, and his lips had narrowed to a thin line, and he'd opened the door and gone down the back steps and stood at Aidan's side. Marli, watching from her bedroom window, hadn't been able to hear his words, but Aidan wasn't responding. Then Daddy had bent down and pulled Aidan to his feet, and when he saw Aidan was still crying, slapped his face.

Marli forgot her shock in a day or two. She was young.

She was busy, too. There was so much to learn. Daddy gave her a footstool so she could reach the table where she changed Donal's diapers. She dressed the baby in the morning and put him down for his naps and to bed in the evening. In the weeks after Mother's death, there were babysitters, but soon they faded away. 'It's our home,' Daddy said. 'We'll take care of it, like we'll take care of each other.'

Marlinchen liked that idea. She thought of it as she poured cereal into bowls for her brothers and made their school lunches and washed up the dishes. She was not yet eight years old.

Marlinchen worried about her father constantly. She'd heard him talking to someone on the phone about having an ulcer. That was new, in addition to the back pain that came and went, and Marlinchen knew that stress aggravated it. With Mother gone, Daddy had to do the shopping for six now, and drive them to school and buy them their clothes and school supplies.

Daddy used to kiss the top of her head and say, 'What would I do without you?' He sampled the dinners she started cooking at eight years old, her first recipes, and proclaimed every one of them 'superb,' even the ones she knew she'd messed up. He came to stand in the doorway sometimes when she was reading bedtime stories to Colm and Donal. She'd always pretend she didn't see him, keeping her pride in his approval to herself.

There were other compensations: a little extra spending money. A white kitten on her birthday. Marlinchen was the first girl in her class to have pierced ears, with permission from Daddy, who said she was mature enough for them at nine.

Lost in the unconscious narcissism of childhood, she didn't realize for a long time that Daddy never really made eye contact with Aidan much, or spoke directly to him. If Marli was around, that's who he talked to. When Marlinchen did begin to notice this, she thought it was because Aidan was so quiet all the time, and self-sufficient. Not like Colm and Liam, who got scraped knees and had arguments that needed to be refereed, or Donal, who needed everything. Aidan never required much of anything.

Then, one midwinter day, he got sick.

It wasn't serious. Shouldn't have been, at least. It was a flu, one of those things that runs around schools in wintertime. Aidan caught it, but kept going to school until a teacher sent him home.

When Marli got home that day, she went to his room to see how he was doing. He was very sleepy. When she touched his cheek, it was like a furnace covered by a thin layer of muscle and skin. She took his temperature with the little thermometer from the bathroom. What it showed her made her run to her father's study.

Daddy was working on a lecture he was giving at Augsberg College. She found him deep into his writing.

'Daddy?'

'Hi, honey,' he'd said, not stopping his work.

'I think Aidan's really sick,' she said.

'It's the flu,' Daddy said. 'Bed rest is the only thing you can do for it.'

'I think he needs a doctor,' Marlinchen said. 'His temperature is 104.'

'Really?' Daddy said. 'Better give him a couple of ibuprofen, then. That'll take the fever down.' He was still typing.

Marlinchen swallowed. 'I really think he needs a doctor, Daddy.'

Daddy had stopped typing, but he hadn't turned around. 'Did you hear me? Give him the ibuprofen,' he said. His voice had become sharp. 'I'm giving this lecture tomorrow. I don't have time for this shit.'

'All right,' she said faintly.

Marlinchen had seen a movie where people saved a man with a high fever. She made Aidan wash the ibuprofen down with a big glass of ice water, and then another, and she ran him a very cold bath and made him get in it. In an hour, his temperature registered at 100, and she knew he'd be okay.

Daddy came out of his study three hours later. 'I'm sorry, Marli,' he said.

Relief warmed her.

'I shouldn't have said that four-letter word in front of you,' he said. 'That's a bad word, I know.' He pressed $20 into her hand. 'How

256

about ordering pizza tonight, so you don't have to cook?'

Daddy's back had been hurting of late, Marlinchen decided later. That was probably behind his short temper.

Another year passed, and another. She was taking on more and more responsibility around the house. Despite the fact that he wasn't teaching, Daddy seemed busier than ever, staying behind his study door for long hours, working on the new book. Outside, the other kids looked to her not only for meals but for homework help, reprimands, discipline.

All except for Aidan. He was a help. He watched Colm and Donal — Liam was already well into his love affair with books — when she needed to study, playing catch with them or taking them for rambles along the lake. And Aidan was her friend in a way the other boys weren't. They shared jokes and secrets, and when Daddy went to bed early with pain in his back, sometimes they'd stay up together and watch forbidden R-rated movies on cable.

Aidan alone among her brothers could be described as tall. And when they were both 11, her brother had a growth spurt. One day, while the family was assembling around the dinner table, she'd noticed Aidan standing at the open refrigerator door, his maimed hand resting casually on the side of the appliance, looking in. It hit her suddenly how tall he was, how his arms were beginning to take on that smooth ripple of muscle that men had. He looked older than 11.

And then Marlinchen noticed her father. He

was looking at Aidan, too, and his blue eyes were oddly narrow. He didn't say anything. In fact, he was quiet all that night.

Dad had been quiet a lot of late. Marlinchen began to suspect his writing wasn't going well, and she knew his ulcer was acting up. He spoke tersely and was short-tempered. It was around that time that the Photo Incident occurred. Marlinchen always thought of it like that, like some historical event that would be capitalized in a history textbook.

Daddy had put Marlinchen in charge of the family photos from long ago; she enjoyed making albums. She'd given Aidan a photo that was too big for an album, an eight-by-ten of their mother holding him in her lap under the magnolia tree. Aidan had never done much to decorate his half of his and Liam's room, but he bought a frame for the picture and hung it up next to his certificate for being the fastest miler in his grade at school.

It had been up for two days when Dad, passing the older boys' room on his way out, saw it.

'That photo doesn't belong to you,' he'd said to Aidan, 'and I don't like seeing it in that cheap drugstore frame.'

'The photo's mine,' Aidan had insisted. 'Marlinchen gave it to me.'

Dad had simply walked over and picked up the photo and the frame.

'That's mine,' Aidan repeated.

Dad pulled the photo free of the velvety backing. 'You can have the frame,' he said. 'I

258

believe you when you say you bought it. The photo isn't yours.'

'Yes, it is,' Aidan said, one last time, but Dad had ignored him, walked away.

The next day was the anniversary of their mother's death. They always went to put flowers on her grave on that day, every year. It was a family tradition.

This day, when Aidan went to the garage with everyone else, Dad had laid his hand on the car door when Aidan reached for the handle, and shook his head. 'You're staying home,' he said.

'What?' Aidan's throat had worked, as if he'd misheard.

'You know, you've been doing poorly in school again this year,' he'd said. 'Your teacher suggested I restrict you from outings and family trips until your work improves. I think she's right.'

Marlinchen's eyes had been trained on her twin brother's face. She knew how much their mother's memory meant to him. Aidan had waited, as if Dad would relent. Then, color flooding his cheeks, he'd gone back to the house.

It wasn't for two days that Dad realized what Aidan had done with his time alone in the house. That afternoon, Dad came out of his studio and down the hall to find Aidan laboring over his homework.

'Where is it?' he'd demanded.

'Where is what?' Aidan asked.

Aidan had taken the photo from his father's study, and wherever he'd hidden it, Dad couldn't find it. He'd torn Aidan's half of the bedroom apart, he'd searched the bathroom and old hiding places around the house, but without luck. He refused to ask Aidan again where the photo was, but his black mood hung like a cloud over the house. Aidan said little, his face closed, but Marlinchen was deeply frightened.

'Can't you just give the photo back?' Marlinchen said.

'No,' Aidan told her. 'It's not here anymore.'

'You're provoking him.'

'He took something that was mine,' Aidan said. His voice was changing, and for a moment she heard a man's timbre, his future voice.

'If you just give it back, things will be all right,' she had said.

Marlinchen had better grades than Aidan. She helped him with his schoolwork. But now he was looking at her like he knew something she couldn't grasp.

'No, it won't,' he said. 'It's not about the picture.'

When the beatings started, Marlinchen and her younger brothers dealt with it by pretending that it wasn't happening. It wasn't that hard. Most of the hostilities were staged away from their eyes. When they heard something through the walls, Colm would turn up the volume on the TV set. Liam would put on the headphones of his Walkman and read. Marlinchen took Donal outside, to walk by the lake. Aidan himself never spoke of it in front of them, and he disguised the bruises from both them and his teachers.

The younger boys were changing; Marlinchen

260

saw it. They began pulling away from Aidan, as if afraid that the lightning that struck him regularly might strike one of them as well. Colm, who had once followed Aidan like a shadow, became rude and oppositional to him. At dinner he pointedly sat as far as possible from Aidan, echoing his father's opinions and ideas. Liam grew quiet and nervous, retreating into the stories he'd begun to write.

One day, in late spring, they were all outside, enjoying the first good weather. Colm was tossing a baseball around with Donal. Marlinchen was sitting at the outside table, finishing a book she needed to write a school report on. Aidan was working on Marlinchen's bike, the lovely metallic-orange one she'd just gotten and was still growing into. They'd taken the handlebars off and put them back on reversed, and Aidan was worried about the brake tension.

Colm made a long throw to Donal, who was standing near the deck stairs with his fielder's glove. The throw went wild and hit the porch railing about four feet from Aidan, who put a hand up to field it a second too late. The baseball ricocheted off the wooden railing into the kitchen window. Glass shattered.

They were all statues for a moment. They knew Dad was upstairs, and he would have heard.

'Shit,' Aidan said, getting up off his knees and walking toward the window. They all clustered around it, in time to see Dad enter the kitchen, observe the broken glass on the floor and the

261

baseball that had rolled to a stop by the refrigerator.

'Who did this?' he said, when he'd emerged onto the deck, his eyes taking them all in. There was silence for a moment, then Colm said, 'Aidan did.'

'What?' Marlinchen protested. '*Colm.*'

'Aidan did,' he insisted, nervy defiance on his face. Aidan, like her, was staring uncomprehending at Colm, who was looking only at their father.

Dad spoke to Aidan. 'Get upstairs,' he said. He didn't ask if what Colm said was true. Marlinchen knew that he wouldn't, not now and not upstairs.

'Colm,' she said when Aidan was gone, 'what did you do that for? It wasn't Aidan's fault.'

'How do you know?' Colm said mulishly. 'You were reading. You didn't see.' Then he went inside the house, retrieving his baseball.

Marlinchen watched him go, and as she did, she realized that there was a poison spreading through her family. What Colm did once, he would try again, because it had worked. Marlinchen was afraid of how things would change from there. But what happened next was far from what she'd expected.

It was perhaps a month later that their father called Marlinchen and Aidan into his study. 'I've been in touch with your aunt Brigitte, your mother's sister,' he said to both of them. 'She's generously offered to let Aidan live with her.'

Why? Marlinchen wanted to ask. They didn't even know Aunt Brigitte. She had never visited

262

Minnesota, and the family had never traveled to her home in Illinois.

Instead, she said, 'For how long?' Summer was here; that must be what her father had in mind, a summer away.

'We'll see,' her father said. He tapped a narrow folder on his desk with a Northwest Airlines logo. 'You leave as soon as school's out,' he told Aidan, who swallowed hard and left.

'*Dad*,' Marlinchen said softly, but she didn't know what else to say.

'Help him pack, would you?' her father said. 'Boys are hopeless at that sort of thing. And, honey' — he turned back from booting up the computer — 'tell your brothers, will you?'

Upstairs, Aidan required no help in packing, and he seemed to have already adjusted to the idea that had so shocked Marlinchen.

'Don't worry,' he said quietly, pulling out his suitcase. 'I'll be fine.'

'But we've never even *met* Aunt Brigitte,' Marlinchen protested.

'Yes, we did,' Aidan said. 'We were down there once, at her place in Illinois.'

Marlinchen gave him a quizzical look. 'I don't remember that,' she said. 'Besides, Dad doesn't even *like* her.'

'Then she's probably all right,' Aidan said bitterly.

'It's just for the summer, I bet.'

'Don't worry about it. I don't care where I live,' Aidan said.

'But — '

'Just drop it, okay?' Aidan said sharply. 'And

263

get your cat out of my suitcase.'

Marlinchen saw Snowball happily digging her claws into the clothes Aidan had laid in the open case. She got up from Liam's bed. 'Snowball isn't my cat; she belongs to all of us,' she said.

'No, she doesn't,' Aidan said. 'Snowball is your pet, and you're Dad's pet. Why don't you just leave me the fuck alone?'

Aidan had never thrown it in her face before, her special status with their father. Tears welled in Marlinchen's eyes.

'Linch,' Aidan said, relenting, but she fled, into the hallway, into her own room.

★ ★ ★

On the day of Aidan's early-morning flight, Marlinchen got up at 5 A.M. to make him pancakes. Her reflection in the blackness outside the kitchen window looked like the pinched face of an old woman whose hair had failed to go gray. Aidan ate only a third of what she'd made him.

She got up again at seven to make a second breakfast for the boys. Dad wasn't home yet. Liam cried at the breakfast table, and Donal followed suit. Colm's face was set and hard.

Marlinchen called Aidan a few times on the phone, until one day her father left the phone bill on her bed, with the Illinois calls outlined in yellow. She knew he didn't want money for the calls, and a cold feeling coalesced in her stomach. She started making the calls from pay phones, when she could, but opportunities were few and far between. Aidan told her he was all right, and that Aunt Brigitte was nice. After that there was little to say.

★ ★ ★

When school started, Hugh didn't bring Aidan home. Marlinchen started several times to ask her father why not, but the words froze in her throat. When Aunt Brigitte died in a car accident, and Aidan was sent farther south to live with an old friend of their father's, Marlinchen heard nothing about it until it was over and done with. When she finally found out, she understood that Aidan was never coming home. Their father was never going to change his mind.

I have to do something. I have to talk to him. I can't let Aidan live down there with someone we've never even met.

But she didn't say anything, not right away. If Marlinchen was afraid for Aidan, she was just as worried about her father. He'd been under pressure for so long, financial and otherwise. His back had flared up, and he was moodier than ever. Once, he'd said he'd had something important to tell her, and led her down to the magnolia tree to say it.

All the way down there, her heart had raced. What was he going to say? *I have cancer, I'm dying?* When they'd arrived, he'd been at a loss for words. He'd looked down at the ground and out at the lake, and finally told her about how much he'd loved her mother, how much he missed her, how important the kids were to him.

Still frightened, Marlinchen had hurried to say, *I understand, Daddy, we love you.* She hadn't understood what he meant by it. Was he still depressed over Mother's death? Could he be trying to tell her he was having suicidal thoughts? For nearly a month afterward, Marlinchen hadn't been able to sleep through the night. She'd gotten up at least once to creep down the hall and look into his bedroom, making sure he was all right, his chest rising and falling under the bedspread.

Not long afterward, something happened that changed everything.

At school one afternoon, during PE, she saw Aidan on the other side of the chain-link fence. He raised a single finger to his lips. When she left the campus that day, he fell into step beside her. The school-bus driver didn't notice as Aidan climbed aboard with everyone else.

For two days, Marlinchen hid him in the detached garage. She sneaked him food and brought him a blanket so he could sleep stretched out on the backseat of Dad's old, defunct BMW.

The second day, she told Liam. After dinner, they brought Aidan his food, and afterward, the three siblings sat and talked. Mostly Aidan spoke, telling them about Aunt Brigitte, who had been nice, but almost too sweet and clingy. He said Pete Benjamin was okay, but he was a total stranger, and after two weeks, Aidan had been too homesick and lonely for his siblings to stay any longer. He told them the story of his late-night escape, funding a bus ticket with money he'd saved from an allowance Aunt Brigitte had given him, of the night highway unfurling under the bus's headlights, of walking all day to Marlinchen's school. In the twilit world of the garage, the miseries of Aidan's life took on the character of adventures.

Then the door had opened, Colm in the breach. 'What's going on?' he'd said.

Three faces turned to him, and Colm's gaze came to rest on his oldest brother. For a moment he was startled, then his face hardened, and he said, 'I'm telling Dad.'

'Colm, no!' Marlinchen had jumped to her feet, but her younger brother was running for the house.

Their father was almost frighteningly still and quiet when he came to stand in the doorway, looking down at his estranged son, nodding as though he weren't surprised.

'Dad — ' Marlinchen began, trying to speak although her throat was turning to stone.

'It's okay, Marlinchen,' Hugh had said. 'I figured he'd turn up here.'

Then he'd addressed Aidan. 'You're going back in the morning,' their father had said. 'Until then, come up to the house. You can sleep on the couch downstairs tonight.'

Relief had filled Marlinchen; she'd expected much worse. That night, she'd made up a bed on the couch for her brother, and fell asleep instantly upon returning to bed. The tension of the last few days, of hiding Aidan, had taken its toll on her. Now it was over, and exhaustion claimed her.

But only an hour later, she'd awakened to muffled, familiar sounds of anger, from downstairs. Chest tight with apprehension, she crept downstairs.

It had never been this bad. Aidan sat on the kitchen floor, back against the refrigerator, his face bloody from the nose down. He was trying to stem the tide of a bleeding, broken nose, and his eyebrow was split. Her father was on his heels next to him, a handful of bloody hair in his fist, his face alien with anger.

He spoke close to Aidan's ear. Then he let go and stood.

With painful difficulty, Aidan got to his feet as well, and spit blood and saliva into his father's face.

Marlinchen felt a surge of raw fear at what would happen next, but her father only wiped his face and walked away.

Marlinchen stumbled back into the darkness when her father passed by, and he never saw her. For a moment, she sat with her arms wrapped around her knees in the darkness and fought back tears. From her low vantage point, she saw something she hadn't before. She looked into the forest of chair legs under the small breakfast table and saw shining eyes staring back at her. Donal. He was five years old. His face was blank with shock.

Immediately, she knew what had happened. Donal had sneaked downstairs for something he wasn't supposed to have, probably a piece of the lemon cake Marlinchen had made earlier. He'd hidden under the table when he'd thought he was going to be caught. He'd been under there the whole time. She didn't know what had sparked her father's rage at Aidan, but she knew Donal had seen everything.

It was at that moment that Marlinchen made her decision.

It was for the best that Aidan was leaving in the morning, that he lived a thousand miles away. Otherwise, things would only deteriorate. The younger boys would witness things like this, and worse, and God knew Aidan wouldn't be safe here, either. In Georgia he would. No matter what Pete Benjamin was like, he was better than this.

She came out from her hiding place, walked past Aidan, who had slipped back down into a sitting position, trying to stem the bleeding from his nose, and went to Donal.

'It's all right, baby,' she said, 'come on out.' Even though he was too big to be lifted up by someone her size, she managed it. Donal was limp and acquiescent in her arms. Marlinchen had expected tears, but he didn't cry.

The young are resilient, she decided as she tucked him into bed.

She did not go back downstairs to Aidan.

★　★　★

A Rainbow at Night was published later that year to reasonably good reviews, and Hugh did

269

lectures and signings. When he was on the road, he sent back postcards from every city, even if he'd only spent one night in a hotel room there. The following year, a movie studio optioned *The Channel*. From the proceeds, Hugh bought a cabin near Tait Lake, a place where he could get away and write, but first he took the whole family up there for a vacation. His ulcer and even his back pain seemed to improve. He seemed more at ease, talking and sometimes laughing at the dinner table. Following his lead, the boys were a little more relaxed as well. It was as if a corner had been turned.

Marlinchen never mentioned Aidan to her father again.

22

'You were a child,' I whispered, 'it wasn't your fault.'

After telling her story, Marlinchen had dissolved into quiet sobs and recriminations. 'If anything's happened to him,' she said, 'it's my fault. I stood by and let it happen. I didn't do anything.'

'There was nothing you could do,' I told her, patting her shaking shoulders awkwardly.

In time, she dried her tears and gathered her composure. 'I wanted to tell you,' she said, her voice steadier. 'But with something like this, the beatings . . . the first time it happens you look away and pray it's just a onetime thing. After that, it's like . . . if you didn't mention it yesterday, it's harder to think of mentioning it today, and even harder the next day, and finally you reach a point where everybody knows that everybody else knows, but to say it out loud would be like . . . '

'Like breaking all the windows,' I said.

'Yes,' she said, nodding. 'Like breaking all the windows.'

'What about Colm and Liam? Did the three of you discuss what you'd say when I asked why Aidan was sent away?'

She shook her head. 'I didn't have to tell them not to say anything. We never talk about it, even with each other.' Her pupils were wide in the darkness. 'Where do you think he is, Sarah? Really.'

'I just don't know,' I admitted. 'And it won't help to sit up at night theorizing about it. Go back to bed.'

But she said, 'When we were 11, and I was out walking on the ice of the lake . . . I forget why I was even doing that, but I fell through. I would have drowned if Aidan hadn't seen and come out after me.' Her voice quivered as if tears threatened again. 'We never told Dad what he'd done, so I wouldn't get in trouble for being out on the lake. But when Aidan needed my help . . . if Aidan has — '

'Don't think about it any more tonight,' I said. 'Let's both get some sleep.'

★ ★ ★

I doubt she slept. I know I didn't.

Marlinchen's story wasn't much of a surprise; I'd already started to suspect it. The problem was that there was a part of Aidan's story that I still didn't know, because Marlinchen herself didn't know it: Why was Aidan, alone, the lightning rod for his father's rage and resentment?

I supposed there was always the soap-opera answer. Aidan and Marlinchen were both blond, and in looks took after their lovely German mother. The other three boys looked like Hugh. The twins were the firstborn. Hugh and Elisabeth were two vertices of a literary love triangle. The third point, Campion, had been

272

frozen out of his friend Hugh's life several years after the twins were born. Conclusion: Campion was the twins' father. Somehow Hugh found out a few years later and had a falling-out with his old friend. Then Hugh had taken his feelings out on Aidan, Campion's bastard son. *Now for a word from our sponsor, Oxydol.*

Unfortunately, the paternity theory didn't really answer the question, it just rephrased it. 'Marli' had been a favorite of her father's, particularly after the death of her mother. If the Campion theory were true, the taint of his parentage hadn't stained her, just her twin. *Marlinchen have I loved, Aidan have I hated.* What was the rationale there?

It was these thoughts that kept me awake for a while, long enough to notice a sound outside Hugh's window: the wind shaking the grapevines on the trellis. Which was strange, because I was sleeping with the curtains open, and the treetops that were visible outside weren't moving at all.

I crept over to the window. The trellis shook again. Harder.

With nothing to change into, I'd been sleeping in my T-shirt and leggings. I yanked my hooded sweat jacket on, wishing for the shoes that were drying out in the Hennessy garage below, took my gun from my shoulder bag, and ran down the stairs.

The lean, shadowed figure was nearly up the vine-covered frame when I came around the side of the house. 'Stop right there!' I shouted up at him. 'I want you to climb back down, *slowly*, and when you get to the base of the trellis, stand facing it with your hands up on the frame and your feet about two feet back and spread apart.'

The figure — male and lean, that was all I could see on this moonless night — did as I instructed. In silhouette, I could just make out that long, loose hair was swaying as he descended. When he got to the bottom and laid his hands on the trellis frame at about the height of his head, I felt a little ripple of recognition go through me. Then the side of the house was flooded with electric light, removing all doubt.

Marlinchen stood in the doorway. It was she who'd tripped the floodlight. She was staring at the boy leaning against the side of the house. Staring at his left hand, the one missing its smallest finger.

'Aidan!'

'Stay where you are, Marlinchen,' I called to her.

She looked from me to her brother with growing incomprehension. 'Sarah, don't you understand? This is Aidan!'

If only it were that simple, I thought.

Maybe I should have handled it differently, but it was in my training: never cede control of a situation, not until you've satisfied yourself that things are all right. This situation surely wasn't, and although Aidan had obeyed my commands so far, he was taller and probably stronger than I was, and I wasn't easy about that.

By now the older boys were also outside. 'Aidan?' Liam said, disbelieving.

'The rest of you kids,' I said, nudging Aidan

274

back over to the wall, 'go back inside. I'll handle this.'

Only Colm obeyed me. Liam stayed where he was, as did Marlinchen.

I was patting Aidan down, feeling for suspicious objects. He didn't move, accepting my touch like a horse being shod. He was wearing a long-sleeved T-shirt, faded jeans, and a dirty hooded sweatshirt. In the side pocket I felt a narrow, hard object, about a finger's length, and carefully drew it out.

'What are you doing?' Marlinchen demanded again, close by my side. 'Stop it! That's *Aidan*.'

'One, please step back,' I told Marlinchen. 'Two, I *know* it's Aidan. He was breaking into your house carrying a switchblade knife.' I showed her.

Colm reappeared at my side. 'Do you need these?' he said, and my handcuffs gleamed in his hand. He looked pleased with himself for anticipating me.

I cleared my throat awkwardly. 'That won't be necessary,' I said. 'I'm not arresting your brother, I'm just taking him downtown for some questioning.'

Marlinchen was about to speak again, when Colm put his hand on her arm and tried to pull her away. 'Come on, Marlinchen,' he said. 'Let Sarah do her job.'

Marlinchen yanked her arm away and shot him a glare. Colm's attempt at authority melted away like a thin spring snow; he didn't try again. Liam hadn't obeyed my order to go back in the house, but at least he'd backed up to the open doorway. He was watching with a pained expression on his narrow face, as if he wanted to protest but didn't know what to say.

I'd been in this situation before. A good number of arrests you make as a patrol officer are in front of appalled family members, standing around in harsh porch lights or in messy living rooms, half-dressed, looking at you as if to say, *You can't do this, that's my husband. My daddy. My son. My brother.* It was never easy.

'Sarah — ' Marlinchen began, trying again.

'It's okay, Linch,' Aidan said, speaking for the first time. His voice was rusty, as if with disuse.

'Sarah, can't you just — '

'No,' I said, 'I can't. My first priority is keeping you and your family safe. I need to talk to your brother and find out what's what, and I can't do that here. I'm sorry.'

★ ★ ★

It's a hard lesson to learn: good and evil aren't like a game of cards. In cards, if you know that one player has three spades in their hand, then you can be assured that no one else at the table has more than one.

The mathematics of the human psyche are never that easy. Just because Hugh had proved himself a bad man, that didn't make Aidan a good one. I had only Aidan's word that his motives in climbing the trellis were innocent, and I wasn't sure I could believe him. Victims of violence were at a higher risk of becoming perpetrators of violence themselves, and Aidan, by Marlinchen's account, had been physically hurt and emotionally demoralized by his father.

Even if Hugh were safe in his rehab-center bed, the Hennessy kids weren't. By Marlinchen's account, they had enjoyed their father's favor, and after Aidan was unjustly sent away, they'd gone on with their lives. Couldn't he be more than a little angry about that?

I felt sorry for Aidan, but compassion was a luxury I could only afford in the abstract. Cops weren't taught to discriminate among predators who were wounded by life and those who were merely vicious. That was a distinction made somewhere down the line from us, by judges and juries.

'So,' I said, taking a chair opposite Aidan, in an interview room at Juvenile Justice. 'You're climbing up the trellis to your father's window, with a knife, at one in the morning after everyone's in bed asleep. It looks pretty bad on paper.' I leaned back, inviting him to speak. 'You don't have to answer any of my questions, but it might help your situation if you could ease my mind about your actions tonight.'

He hadn't said a word on the ride to the Juvenile Justice Center, not even to comment on the smell of superglue, as Kelvin had. I'd noticed his own scent, grass and dew, as if he'd been sleeping outdoors, and old sweat.

Now I had a chance to appraise him in good overhead light for the first time. The first thing my eyes went to was his maimed left hand; Aidan had laid it on the table as if daring me to ignore

277

it. Either the little finger had come off pretty cleanly at the joint, or perhaps a surgeon's instrument had evened out the damage. Still, there was something ugly about the dark pink skin of the stump, no matter how old the wound.

Beyond that, Aidan had made good on his early promise of height. At six feet, he'd easily outstripped his father, and I didn't think Colm or Liam would catch up, either. His long blond hair was stringy and unwashed, and his cheeks were precipitously hollow. A leather cord, some kind of necklace, disappeared under the collar of his T-shirt.

'I wanted to make sure Hugh wasn't home,' Aidan said. It was the first time I'd heard him speak since he'd said, *It's okay, Linch*, back at the house. 'I'd been around all day and some of the evening and I didn't see him. But his car was in the garage.'

'What do you mean, you were 'around'?' I said.

'I was watching the house,' Aidan said. 'I was waiting for Hugh to go out, so I could come in and see Linch and the boys. When I kept on not seeing him, I thought he might be out of town. But I couldn't be sure, so I kept out of sight, and later I tried to climb up to his bedroom, to make sure.'

'Well,' I said, 'the fact that you were lurking around outside the house for hours doesn't do much to defuse the fact that you climbed up the side of the house with a knife.' When Aidan didn't speak, I went on. 'In your covert surveillance of the house, who did you think I was?'

Aidan said, 'I didn't see you.'

'Really?' I said. 'I was there for over an hour before we all went to bed.'

'I wasn't around then,' Aidan said.

He didn't back down easily. I retraced my steps. 'So if you weren't around when I arrived, where were you?'

'Trying to find something to eat,' Aidan said.

'Where?' I repeated.

'A neighbor's garden,' Aidan said. 'They were growing some green peppers and carrots.'

He had to be starving. I thought of the vending machines in the correction officers' lunchroom, but I didn't want to break the rhythm of my questioning. About some things, Gray Diaz was right.

'Tell me about the switchblade,' I said.

'Protection,' Aidan said.

'From who?'

'I've been on the road,' Aidan said. 'Life out there can be dangerous. The knife was a good investment.'

His gaze was very even, unperturbed by my questioning. His eyes were the exact color of Marlinchen's.

'"Investment,"' I said. 'Interesting choice of words. You've been on your own for a long time. What have you been doing for money?'

'You mean, have I been jacking people?' Aidan asked. 'No.'

'When did you get into town?'

'This afternoon,' he said. 'I got a ride in Fergus Falls.'

'So,' I said, 'with all the time you've been away, what prompted you to come home? Why now?'

'I wanted to see my family,' he said, then quickly clarified, 'My sister and brothers, I mean.'

He hadn't needed to tell me how he felt about his father; I heard it every time Aidan called him *Hugh*, not *Father* or *Dad*.

'And maybe you wanted to tap your old man for money,' I suggested.

'No,' Aidan said, shaking his head for emphasis.

'What about Marlinchen's cat?'

'Snowball?' he said. 'What about her?'

I stayed quiet, waiting for him to betray nerves with some small gesture, or to fill an unbearable silence. But he did neither.

I paused, not sure whether there was anything else to throw at him. One thing came to mind.

'You know,' I said, 'since realizing your father wasn't at home, you've shown very little interest in where he actually is. Aren't you curious at all about that?'

Aidan Hennessy shrugged. 'Okay,' he said. 'Where is he?'

'Your father's in the hospital, recovering from a stroke,' I said.

Aidan's blue eyes flicked to mine. I'd surprised him at last, but there was no sign of concern in his gaze. Finally I said, 'Are you hungry?'

'I could eat,' he said.

The vending machines were poorly stocked. Behind the scratched plastic windows I saw a pillowy white bagel, jalapeño potato chips, pork rinds. The soda machine looked fully stocked, but sugar water was the last thing a hungry teenager needed on an empty stomach, when he wouldn't get anything substantial until morning.

I walked away, still holding a few quarters in the palm of my hand, to pace under the cold fluorescent lights.

I didn't like him climbing the trellis. I didn't like the switchblade knife in his possession. And most of all, I didn't like him hanging around outside the house at night, so soon after the ugly late-night death of Snowball. Marlinchen had quoted him as saying, years ago, *Snowball is your pet, and you're Dad's pet.*

If Aidan had come home full of anger, primed for a confrontation with his father, might he have taken out some of that anger on a smaller target? And wasn't there a chance, with his father safely out of his reach in a nursing home, that Aidan would deflect his anger again, onto his siblings?

I took out the switchblade that I'd confiscated from him, sprang the blade. Carefully, I looked for small traces of dried blood at the base of the blade and the haft, found nothing.

Doesn't mean he didn't clean it up really well.

Yet when I'd fired the question about Snowball at him without preamble or explanation, he'd responded exactly as he should have: *What about her?* Guileless confusion is one of

281

the hardest responses to fake. Moreover, I had no proof that, in climbing the trellis, Aidan hadn't been doing exactly what he'd said he was: checking to see if his father was home. I couldn't exactly blame him for that; the last time he'd come home unannounced, things had worked out pretty badly, to say the least.

I'd feel a lot more comfortable if I could leave him safely in the Juvenile Justice Center overnight. Then I could go home, get eight hours' sleep, and take another crack at talking to him in the morning. But I hadn't arrested Aidan, just taken him downtown for questioning. To keep him here, I needed to arrest him.

That was possible, of course: the switchblade was an illegal weapon. But according to my research, Aidan Hennessy had not yet been in trouble with the law. He had no criminal record. If I charged him with carrying an unlawful weapon, I'd stick him with one.

My head was starting to hurt. When Judge Henderson had given me the responsibility to look out for the Hennessys for a few weeks, neither of us had imagined that it would lead here, to making this kind of decision at the Juvenile Justice Center at three in the morning. Still, I'd taken on this burden; no setting it aside now. And while I had a responsibility to ensure that Marlinchen and her younger siblings stayed safe, didn't I have a tangential responsibility to Aidan, as well? He was one of the Hennessy kids, too.

When I got back to the interrogation room, Aidan looked at my empty hands, then to my face.

'I'm taking you home,' I said.

23

It did not come as a surprise that Marlinchen wasn't asleep when Aidan and I returned. She came out to wrap her arms around Aidan's neck and embrace him for a long moment, until I had to turn away from the intimacy of their reunion.

She fixed him a meal in the kitchen, two warm tuna sandwiches with melted cheddar cheese and an oversized glass of milk, and made up a bed for him on the sofa, where he fell into an exhausted sleep. Only when he was asleep did she turn her attention to me.

'Thank you,' she said. 'Thank you for bringing him back here.'

'We need to talk about that,' I told Marlinchen. 'Let's go upstairs.'

In Hugh's bedroom, I sat on the edge of the bed, and Marlinchen folded her legs gracefully to sit cross-legged on the floor. It was as though we'd rewound to an earlier point in the evening.

'Listen,' I told her, 'I know Aidan's your brother, and you've been carrying around a lot of guilt and a lot of anxiety where he's concerned. But do you really know that person down there?' I nodded toward the open door, signifying the stairway and the downstairs area that lay beyond it, where Aidan slept. 'It's like I said about the photo you showed me. Twelve to seventeen are some pretty important years. People change a lot, and Aidan's been spending those years in circumstances that we don't know a whole lot about.'

Marlinchen smiled at me, as though I were a child who didn't understand the real world. 'I don't have to know where he's been,' she said. 'He's all right.'

'How do you know?'

'I just know,' Marlinchen said. Her pupils, once again, were wide in the semidark. It made her look younger and more guileless than ever.

'I can't operate based on someone else's gut feelings,' I told her.

'What are you really saying?' she asked me.

'I'm going to spend a lot of time out here,' I said. I'd been thinking about it during the silent ride back here, with Aidan.

'That's what you've been doing,' she said, confused.

'More than I have,' I said. 'Even nights. I know that may seem strange to you kids; it does to me too. But the court gave me a responsibility for your safety. So until I feel better about this whole situation, I'm going to keep a close eye on things.'

Marlinchen smiled then, her natural and easy smile. 'That's all right,' she said. 'Really, I like having you here, Sarah. But — '

'I know. You think I'm worrying about nothing,' I said. 'Believe me, I hope I am.'

* * *

The next day, I was not at my best at work. There was a time when three hours of sleep

284

would have sufficed for me, but those days were gone. On the brighter side, not much of interest happened at work. The nylon-mask bandits had been quiet for a little while. Maybe they'd gotten day jobs or won the lottery.

Late in the day, my phone rang.

'Sarah, it's Chris Kilander,' the voice on the other end said.

'Kilander?' I said, straightening in my chair. We hadn't crossed paths since the evening we'd done it so uncomfortably in the parking lot of Surdyk's. 'What's going on?'

'I wondered if I could see you this evening,' he said.

'For what?'

'A little one-on-one,' he said. 'You're never at the courts anymore.'

Kilander been a power forward at Princeton. I was no one he'd look to for a challenging game of basketball. He wanted something else. The game was just a pretext.

'When?' I said.

★ ★ ★

Rain clouds were building overhead when I arrived at the courts, which were empty as I started stretching my quadriceps and hamstrings against the chain-link fence.

'Evening,' Kilander said, coming up behind me.

Although well muscled, his long legs looked quite pale in loose shorts, and I was reminded of the old days when slow-footed white guys

285

dominated professional basketball teams. I wasn't, however, deceived. He was going to be hard to beat.

'What are we playing to, twenty?' he said.

'Twenty's fine.'

Kilander threw the ball more at me than to me, a hard chest pass. 'Let's see what you've got,' he said.

The answer was *Not enough*. Kilander drove to the basket again and again. When he was up ten points to my six, he asked me, 'You played in high school, right? What were you, a guard?'

'Shooting guard first, then point guard,' I said, breathing hard.

'You play like a point guard. Conservative,' he said. Then he added, 'A high school point guard.'

'You play like a lawyer,' I said, still dribbling in place, watching him. 'I would have fouled you about four times by now if I weren't afraid you'd sue.'

'I won't sue,' Kilander said. 'I grant you amnesty in advance.'

I pivoted and tried to dive around him to the basket. He blocked me and got the ball. A moment later, I grabbed his shirt as he was going up to score, and later I threw an elbow when he was crowding me. He just laughed, then demonstrated his moral superiority not only by refusing to respond in kind but by suggesting we go to thirty points when he beat me 20–14. We did, which allowed him to beat me 30–22.

'Thank you,' he said, oddly seriously, when we were done.

'For what?' I asked, trying to catch my breath.

'For not giving up on an impossible battle,' he said.

'You're welcome,' I said, hearing the compliment in what some would have considered an insult. 'Thanks for not playing down to me.'

A sharp gust of wind swept across the court, forerunning rain. Kilander picked up his water bottle and walked over to the sidelines, taking a seat on a low stand of bleachers. I followed him, still holding the basketball. 'What's on your mind, Chris?' I asked.

'I want to say something,' Kilander said. 'What I said the other day, about you not denying you killed Royce Stewart? I was wrong. I've thought about it since then, and I know you didn't kill that man.'

'Thank you,' I said. Something felt lighter in my chest at his words. 'That means a lot to me.'

Kilander nodded casually. 'Listen, I don't know much about Diaz's investigation, and you know I couldn't tell you if I did. But I can tell you a few things about him, in general.' He paused to think. 'I wouldn't say I know the guy well, but we have an acquaintance in common, who's now on the bench in Rochester. Gray called me with some of the usual new-in-town questions: where's a good place to eat and so on.'

Several cyclists raced past the city courts, tires hissing on the pavement.

'Diaz is an intense guy,' Kilander said. 'He's University of Texas, a criminal justice major. Got his first gray hair in his junior year in college; that's where the nickname came from. He'd be working in the prosecutor's office in Dallas or Houston if it weren't for his father-in-law. His wife's from Blue Earth, and they moved back so she could be closer to her father, who's got a chronic heart condition.'

'That's too bad,' I said.

'In several ways. The condition's debilitating, but there's no prediction for life expectancy, not like the bad cancers. So Gray may be down there for the long haul, and he's not the kind of guy to stay challenged investigating the theft of farm equipment. In Faribault County, he probably feels like he's on a treadmill stuck on 'stroll.'' Kilander paused to set up his next words. 'For him, nailing a big-city cop would be fun. It's a challenge. Nothing personal.'

'Big-city cop?' I echoed. 'That's how he sees me?'

Kilander had discreetly left out the key word. *Corrupt big-city cop* was more likely how Diaz viewed me. I'd never been involved in departmental politics, and in fact I was the youngest and newest of the detective division. It was hard to realize others could see me so differently from how I saw myself.

I told Kilander, 'The other day, a deputy came up to me privately. He all but congratulated me for 'killing' Stewart.'

Kilander nodded but didn't speak.

'Chris . . . how many people do you think know about Diaz?'

'Well,' Kilander said, 'if a young uniformed deputy knows, what does that suggest to you?'

Oh, God. The first raindrops were starting to

288

fall, nearly as light as mist. 'Everyone,' I said.

Kilander moved a little closer. 'The young man who said that to you is a cretin,' he said. 'Sarah, other people will come to the same conclusion I have about you. Their instinct will tell them so; your conduct will, too. And when Diaz's investigation comes up short, your career will recover.'

I took a steadying breath. 'Thanks,' I said. 'I mean that.'

★   ★   ★

Only Liam was up when I reached the Hennessy house that night, studying late over a cup of decaffeinated coffee. I declined his offer to brew some for me. Instead we talked for a moment or two about Shakespeare; *Othello*, in particular, which he was writing a paper on.

Just before I left him, I asked, 'Did anything happen today? Anything strange, or uncomfortable?'

Liam caught the trend of my question. 'You mean, with Aidan?' he said. 'No.'

'After he's been gone so long, and everything that's happened, are you comfortable having him here?' I pursued.

'It's different now, having him back,' Liam said slowly. 'Uncomfortable? No.' He paused, as if thinking, but his next words were quite simple. 'I mean, he belongs here. He's our brother.'

24

For the next few days, I stayed close to the Hennessy kids, spending nights at their home. What surprised me was how easily they accepted my presence. I'd forgotten what it was like to be a teenager, how easily any adult in your life becomes Authority. Parents, teachers, principals, coaches: kids so easily ceded their privacy to them, and apparently, to the Hennessy kids, I was one such figure.

They went about their lives, and in what seemed good spirits, too. A week from Friday was the last day of school outright for Donal; Colm, Liam, and Marlinchen had one more week of final exams after that at their high school. In their activity, their chatter in the mornings before school, I heard both their anxiety about impending tests and their exhilaration at the prospect of freedom to come.

It was Aidan, though, whom I paid closest attention to. After his first night back, exhausted and disheveled from the road, he'd metamorphosed into someone who looked strikingly different. Once washed, his hair was as gold as Marlinchen's, and hung perfectly straight in a ponytail. In fact, if I'd been seeing him for the first time, that's what I would have noticed about him, the clean straight lines, like a kinetic sculpture, from the blond hair to the long legs. I never saw him without his hair pulled back in a ponytail, or without his necklace of tigereyes on a leather cord riding against the collar of his T-shirt.

The oldest Hennessy did nothing that troubled me; he also did nothing that particularly reassured me. He was unusually quiet for a teenage boy of his size; I rarely heard him enter a room, or leave it. He sneaked cigarettes sometimes behind the freestanding garage; other times I'd see him smoking under the magnolia tree. Once or twice I saw him looking at me, but what he was thinking, I couldn't tell. The second time I said, 'What?' but he merely shook his head and said, 'Nothing.'

On the job, my week was equally uneventful. The stocking-mask bandits knocked over their fourth business, this time a liquor store in St. Paul. I didn't have to do any investigating, but I got a heads-up call from a St. Paul detective, and I faxed my notes on the prior cases over to him.

Saturday dawned hot, and was expected to break temperature records. I slept until we were well into the heat, when there was a knock at the door and Marlinchen stuck her head in.

'Are you hungry?' she said. 'We're making waffles downstairs,' she said.

'I could eat,' I said.

Marlinchen nodded. 'I wanted to ask you for a favor, later in the day.'

I rolled onto my side. 'You want to ask later, or the favor is for later?' I asked.

'Dad's getting a lot better,' she said, ignoring my teasing, 'and I wanted to take everyone to see him. In the hospital.'

291

'Everyone?' I said. 'You guys won't all fit in my car.'

'I know,' Marlinchen said, 'but there's Dad's ride.'

The Suburban in the garage. I shook my head. 'No,' I said. 'I shouldn't be driving your father's SUV.'

'It'll be okay,' she said. 'It's insured through the end of August.'

'Well, if it's *insured*,' I said.

Marlinchen, missing the sarcasm, seemed happy. She came to sit on the end of the bed.

'It probably needs to be started up anyway,' I said, 'or pretty soon you won't be able to.' I thought of Cicero, the van he told me about that he sent the neighbor boys down to start up, and that thought led to another. 'Hey,' I said, 'what's the story with the BMW out in the detached garage?'

'Oh, that,' she said. 'It was Mom and Dad's a long time ago. It stopped running, and Dad put it away. He said he was going to fix it up someday, but he never did. I guess it has sentimental value. He absolutely will not sell it.'

'He was going to fix it up?' I said. 'I thought your father was worthless with tools.'

Marlinchen looked rueful. 'He is,' she said. 'But you know guys and their cars. It's a love thing.' She extended a hand to me. 'Anyway, get up, lazybones. The guys are downstairs burning all the waffles.'

I let her pull me up. 'Tell you what,' I said. 'I'll go to the hospital, but you can do the driving honors. You need to keep practicing.'

292

Typically, she hedged. 'I don't know,' she said. 'I've never driven the Suburban before.'

'You'd never driven my Nova before, either,' I pointed out. 'There's a first time for everything.'

★ ★ ★

'He's made a lot of progress in his physical therapy. Speech, not as much.'

Freddy, the serene male nurse I remembered from my first visit to the convalescent hospital, was leading us back to a visiting room in the rehab facility.

'He can hear you fine, so don't talk too loud. But it's best if you keep your statements open-ended and don't ask him any questions he'd feel obligated to try to answer. We're keeping the pressure off.'

The visiting room was pleasantly crowded with green plants and lit by wide glass windows. Near them, in a padded rocking chair with a quad cane at his side, was Hugh Hennessy.

Only Marlinchen seemed truly comfortable in this environment. She entered first, the rest of us following her. Freddy pulled up a chair by Hugh's rocker; Marlinchen stood on its other side. Colm, Liam, and Donal took a nearby couch, and Aidan and I stood, just beside the couch.

Moments earlier, in the parking lot of the hospital, the twins had shared a quick, quiet conversation.

'You can stay out here,' Marlinchen had told Aidan. She was holding a potted ivy grown along a frame in the shape of a heart; we'd stopped for it on the way over. 'Everyone will understand.'

The same thing had occurred to me; I'd thought it odd that the son who called his father *Hugh* was intent on accompanying his sister and brothers on this charitable visit.

'It's okay,' Aidan said. 'I'll go in.'

'Are you sure?' Marlinchen said, wanting, as always, to avoid unpleasantness of any kind.

'I'm not afraid to see him, Linch,' Aidan said, and the note of iron did a lot to explain his determination to be here, not to shy away from the man who'd exiled him years ago.

'That's not what I meant,' she'd said, looking down, sunlight flashing off one of her earrings. But they'd discussed it no further.

'Hi, Dad,' Marlinchen said now, brightly. 'We're all here. It's not just a visit, it's an invasion.'

Hugh, in his rocker, looked improved from the last time I'd seen him. His color was better, as was his posture. Marlinchen set the ivy at his side, and leaned over. 'Can you give me a kiss?'

Hugh leaned close to her, one hand steadying himself on the arm of the rocker, and obeyed. The doctors were right; he did understand what those around him were saying.

But he didn't, or couldn't, speak. Marlinchen carried the conversation, with Colm and Liam adding their comments sporadically. Hugh was clearly listening, but his voice came out as an unsteady rumble, or telegramlike half sentences that didn't make immediate sense. He seemed to understand he wasn't making sense, either, embarrassment lighting his blue eyes.

Something else: Hugh seemed focused only on Marlinchen and the three boys on the couch. After about five minutes, Freddy leaned over to speak to him. 'Mr. Hennessy, remember what we've been talking about, turning your head to scan the whole room?'

He was coaching his patient to compensate for the neglect, the tendency of some stroke patients to ignore stimuli from the side affected by the stroke. Hugh did as instructed. He turned his head, looking past the boys on the couch, and stopped. For the first time, he saw Aidan. A muscle jumped under his left eye. There was nothing impaired about his vision or his memory.

Marlinchen's smile became even more set. She seemed to realize what had happened, but said nothing to acknowledge Aidan's presence.

'I've been saving *The New York Review of Books* for you,' she told her father. 'I didn't throw any of them out. I'll read the better articles to you.'

Hugh's attention had not shifted. The muscles of his face were working, and a small bubble of saliva had appeared at the corner of his mouth. The sound he was making took shape. 'What is,' he said. 'What is. What is she. She is . . . '

Marlinchen shot me a nervous glance. 'Oh,' she said. 'Dad, this is Sarah Pribek. A friend of ours.'

But Hugh clearly wasn't looking at me. He was staring at Aidan, and I remembered what Marlinchen said, that Hugh was confusing his

295

pronouns. Hugh didn't mean to say *she*; he meant *he*. Hugh's blue eyes were narrow, and trained on his oldest son.

Beside me, Aidan shifted on his feet. 'Maybe I should take a little walk,' he said.

Marlinchen, forced to acknowledge what was happening, looked pained. 'I don't know,' she said.

On the couch, Colm seemed to have recused himself psychologically from the situation, examining a small callus on one of his weightlifter's hands. Liam looked from his father to his sister. His eyes were intent, but he said nothing.

I took the decision from Marlinchen's hands. 'Yeah, that might be a good idea,' I said. It was probably best that Hugh didn't have another stroke at the sight of his long-lost son.

Aidan slipped from the visiting room. After he left, Marlinchen carried on with her open-ended conversation, with Liam and Colm still helping at irregular intervals. Increasingly, I felt like an interloper, and after a moment I left the room, as Aidan had.

It was around one o'clock, with the iron heat of a June midday in full effect, but I wandered outside. The exit door was conveniently just beyond the visiting room, and I'd somehow wanted relief from the atmosphere of the nursing home: aseptic, yet cheerful; verdant with plants, yet somehow stale.

Once outside, I saw that Aidan had made the same decision. He was at a distance on the grounds, walking, and had drifted toward the only shade available, where willows overhung the shallow, reedy pond. The Canada geese that had been bathing there rose up and flew off at Aidan's approach. All but one, which was flopping awkwardly.

Aidan still hadn't noticed me following him. His attention was on the straggler goose. As it flailed forward into the sunlight, I saw a tiny flash of metal in its beak, and I realized what had happened. At one of the small lakes nearby, the bird had gotten a fishhook caught in its beak. It had flown here before settling down in this safe haven and trying to dislodge the hook, probably making things worse in the attempt.

Aidan, surprising me with his reflexes, snatched up the goose by its neck. The bird squalled with surprise. Its outstretched wings worked wildly, the tip of one scraping at Aidan's cheekbone and forehead while he worked at the goose's beak with his free hand. Aidan pulled his head back, out of reach of the bird's thrashing wings, and spoke to the goose, not loud enough for me to overhear. Then he withdrew his hand, and I saw light glint off the small crook of metal.

Aidan released the bird, which shook itself indignantly, then took to the air. It flew low at first, only a few feet over the turf, as if making a test flight to see that all systems were go. Then it banked higher and was out of sight. Aidan, after watching it disappear, moved toward the pond's edge. He cocked his arm and threw the fishhook out into the waters of the pond.

In a field full of cool, analytical thinkers, I'd always worked from instinct. In that moment, I

297

made up my mind about Aidan Hennessy.

It was such a small thing Aidan had done, removing the fishhook from the goose's beak, yet it spoke volumes. I didn't believe that Aidan had known that anyone was within view of him. He had acted naturally and without forethought to ease an animal's pain. I couldn't reconcile that image with the idea of him ripping up Marlinchen's cat.

Other people had tried to tell me. Marlinchen had been his staunchest defender, of course, but Liam had said it as well: *he's our brother.* And Mrs. Hansen, the grade-school teacher, had called Aidan a fighter but not a bully. I just hadn't been able to hear any of it. Gray Diaz's investigation, Prewitt's suspicion . . . it had all set me on edge, and the resulting paranoia had spread throughout my life, coloring how I'd viewed Aidan, making his unexpected return seem sinister.

When Aidan sat down in the shade of the willow, I went to join him.

'Hey,' I said, sitting with my knees drawn up, resting my forearms on them.

'Hey,' he said.

'Look,' I said, 'I should say something. I think we might have gotten off on the wrong foot.' *Come on, Sarah, you can do better than that.* 'I was too hard on you, the night you came home.'

Aidan looked over at me.

'Suspicion is a cop virtue,' I explained. 'It's my fallback position when I don't know what to think.'

'It's okay,' he said, taking out a pack of

298

cigarettes and starting to remove one. I suspected that he, like most smokers, fell back on cigarettes at awkward moments, not necessarily for the nicotine but just for the distraction of a simple physical activity. 'I mean, I can see how it might have looked to you.'

I nodded but said nothing else.

'I guess I should say, too . . . ' He paused, thinking. 'Well, Marlinchen says you've been looking out for them, since Hugh had his stroke.'

I shrugged. 'Mostly, it was my job.' I wasn't sure that was true, but it sounded good.

'Well, anyway, it's . . . ' Aidan tore up a handful of grass. 'I'm glad someone was there.' He slid the cigarette back in its pack.

'Quitting?' I asked him.

He shrugged. 'Marlinchen's on my case about it.'

That was Marlinchen, nothing if not forceful in her opinions. I plucked a dandelion globe. 'Can I ask you a question?' I said. 'It's another cop habit.'

'Go ahead,' he said.

'I know you don't have a criminal record,' I told him. 'That's kind of hard for a runaway to do, to survive without breaking the law. I don't mean to get in your business, but were you really law-abiding, or just lucky?'

'Mostly law-abiding,' Aidan said. 'There's always work off the books, if you know where to look for it. When I couldn't find jobs, I raided garbage bins behind stores. Panhandled. Made up stories about having a bus ticket stolen. That kind of thing,' he said.

'You never thought about contacting your dad for money?'

Aidan's eyes flicked toward the building, where Hugh was secreted behind the glare off the big plate-glass window. 'I didn't want anything from him,' he said. He didn't elaborate, not sure what I knew.

'It's okay,' I said carefully, knowing it was a sensitive area. 'Marlinchen told me about Hugh. About how things were before you were sent away.'

'It was a long time ago,' Aidan said, looking out at the waters of the pond. 'I try not to think about it.'

We were silent a moment. I decided not to push things further than we'd already gone, but Aidan surprised me by speaking again. 'You wanted to know, the other night, about why I decided to come home.' It was half a statement, half a question.

'Yeah,' I said, half responding, half prompting.

'There was no big thing that made me leave the farm in Georgia,' he said. 'Pete was okay, but he wasn't my family, and we never really warmed up to each other. I finally decided that the farm was his problem, not mine. So I split.'

'And you didn't want to come home, because of Hugh,' I said.

'Yeah,' Aidan said. 'I thought I'd go to California and start over. So I did. I made some friends, guys who'd watch my back if I watched theirs. Met some girls, had some times. But I didn't stay there, I came home because' — Aidan hesitated — 'it's not that easy to explain.'

'You don't have to tell me,' I said.

'It was just something that happened on the beach one night.' A wisp of dandelion fluff landed on Aidan's arm, and he brushed it away. 'When I said before that I was 'mostly' law-abiding, well, I was, but I did some drugs.' He looked at me, making sure I was okay with that before moving on. 'So one night, I was wired on crystal and sitting up smoking, because I knew I was never going to get to sleep. I don't know why, but at some point I started thinking about Minnesota, and all of a sudden I realized I didn't even remember what Donal looked like.' He shrugged. 'I don't know why it bothered me so much, but it did. And I realized that I'd been trying to tell myself that the people I'd met out in Cali were my new brothers and sisters, but that was bullshit. They weren't and never would be. Some people in your life you just can't substitute for. They aren't replaceable.'

In its low-key way, it was a story of extraordinary emotional largesse, but my radar for bullshit was quiet. I sensed he meant everything he said.

Then Aidan focused on something beyond me. I turned too, to see what it was. Marlinchen and her brothers were approaching. They were done visiting.

'Dad's making a lot of progress,' Marlinchen said, sounding pleased, when she reached us. 'He said my name. Well, the short version.'

Aidan said nothing.

'That's great,' I managed, a second or two belatedly.

25

'I talked to Gray Diaz,' Genevieve said, over the long-distance wires.

It was Sunday, and I had taken a little time for myself, going home to clean out the mailbox and check my messages. The house had that stillness that you feel after an absence, the once-wet dishrag hardened to a stiff fossil over the faucet, papers lying museumlike where I'd left them. Also awaiting me was a bag of tomatoes on the back step, the gift of my neighbor Mrs. Muzio, and a message on the machine. From Genevieve.

'Well, we knew he'd want to talk to you,' I told her. 'You're my ex-partner and the person I went to visit after my alleged crime.'

'That's not the point,' Genevieve said. 'Sarah, this guy really thinks you did it.'

'We knew that too, didn't we?'

'This is different,' she said. 'I was a cop for nearly twenty years. I spent those years listening to cops talk about their cases, their suspects, and their gut feelings. I know when they're just trying on theories for size, and I know when they've got religion. This guy has got religion, Sarah. He believes you killed Stewart.'

I hadn't told her about the Nova and the tests the BCA was running for Diaz. Certainly I couldn't say anything now; she'd only worry more.

'There's nothing you can do about it,' I said.

302

'I could come back.'

'No,' I said firmly. She meant *come back and confess*. This was exactly what I didn't want. 'Think about what you're offering to do. There'd be no turning back from it.'

She was quiet on the other end, and I knew she was internalizing the possibility of a life sentence. I pressed my advantage. 'We've come this far, Gen. Too far to panic and tear it all down with our own hands.'

My neighbor's scrawny Siamese cat stalked past the back door, looking for a handout. I stayed silent, letting my words sink in. Genevieve would see the logic in it. She'd always been logical, just as I'd always been intuitive.

Finally, Genevieve said, 'When all this is over, you're coming to see me, right?'

'Absolutely,' I said, relieved.

★　★　★

When we'd hung up, I got up from my place on the floor, went into the kitchen, and opened a can of tuna, scraping it onto an old, chipped plate.

The examination of the car was probably the worst of Diaz's investigation. What else was there for him to do, a search of the house? Diaz was a perceptive guy. Surely he'd recognize that I wasn't the sort of person to keep a diary, and if I did, I wouldn't write down explicitly incriminating things in it: *Dear Diary, I sure am glad I got away with killing Royce Stewart, and torching his place, too!* No, Diaz knew better.

I forced open the back screen door — it was really getting stiff — and set down the plate of tuna on the back step. From his prowls in the grass, the Siamese glared as though I were trying to poison him, but I knew he'd approach and eat after I was gone.

I didn't go back into the house, but down into the basement, instead, where the little .25, which Genevieve's sister had pressed on me, rested in the toolbox. I'd never used it; in fact, as far as I knew it had never been used in any crime. But I didn't feel comfortable having it around. Regardless of how unlikely it was that Diaz would get a warrant for the house, it was time for the little gun to go. The river would take it off my hands. One short walk out to the bridge, and the gun would scud gently along the riverbed until it got hung up on some natural impediment, to lie unseen and untouched for some small eternity.

It was when I was back in the house, watching the Siamese eat in that both dainty and ravenous way cats do, that I realized I knew somebody who needed the .25 a little more than the waters of the Mississippi.

★   ★   ★

The dinner hour was over, but the pleasant smell of cooking hung in the air of Cicero's hallway. The door at the end of the hall was open, and I waved at the shaven-headed boy standing in it as I approached. He made a half nod in return, chin thrust in the air.

I shifted the brown paper bag in my arms and

304

knocked at Cicero's door. No one answered.

Could he be sleeping? It was too early for that. I knocked again.

'Shorty looking for ya,' the boy in the doorway said to someone inside. I turned and saw the boy moving aside, heard Cicero making his goodbyes to the other people he'd been visiting inside the apartment.

'I don't think I've ever been called Shorty before,' I said when Cicero was at my side. He opened the door to his apartment, which was unlocked.

'It means 'girlfriend,'' he said.

'I know what it *means*,' I said, and left it at that. He couldn't have known why it gave me a little chill to be called that, Royce Stewart's nickname. 'Anyway,' I said, 'I brought you some things. From what you'd call the informal economy. You like tomatoes, right?'

'I love tomatoes,' Cicero said, his face slightly tipped to look down into the bag, 'and these still have that great smell. Of the leaves, I mean.'

It was one of my favorite things, too, the sharp spice of tomato leaves, so different from the sweetness of the fruit. 'I know,' I said.

Cicero went to put the bag on his kitchen counter. I used the time to dig into my shoulder bag. 'This is the other thing,' I said, pulling the .25 from the bag; its cheap silver plating gleamed in the lamplight. Earlier, I'd cleaned and oiled and test-fired it, ensuring that it was in working condition.

'Sarah, is that real?' Cicero had turned to look.

'It's real,' I said. 'It comes from — a kind of an

in-law,' I said. Genevieve was, after all, practically family to me.

'Is your husband's whole family involved in crime?' Cicero asked me, only half kidding.

I didn't answer him directly. 'This gun isn't registered to anyone that I know of, and if any crimes were committed with it, they were long ago and over state lines,' I said. 'I was going to get rid of it, but you need it more.'

'You think *I* need it?' Cicero said. I wasn't sure I'd ever seen him surprised before. There really was a first time for everything. 'What would I need a gun for?'

'You operate a cash business,' I told him, 'in a public housing building.'

'Thanks for the thought, but no,' Cicero said. 'I don't like guns.'

'You don't have to like it,' I said. 'But in a place like this — '

'In case you weren't aware,' Cicero interrupted, 'many people who live in public housing are working parents. Or senior citizens. The rate of church attendance — '

'I get your point,' I said, setting the gun down on the table, into a kind of psychological escrow between us. 'It doesn't really matter where you live. You keep cash in your home, and people know that. That's a risk in any neighborhood.'

'No,' Cicero said. 'People here look out for each other, and they respect what I do. I've helped many of them.' He saw that I was about to speak again and raised his hands. 'I understand the point you're making. I do. But I won't arm myself against my own patients.'

'You open your door to strangers, no questions asked,' I said.

'I open my door to people in need,' he said. 'The elderly, the indigent.'

'Can you honestly tell me you've never treated someone who was injured in the commission of a crime, or couldn't seek treatment in an ER because they were wanted by the authorities?'

'I don't ask those kind of questions,' he said.

'That's my point,' I said.

'I'm not worried about that,' Cicero said. 'I'm a very good judge of people.'

'Really?' I said. 'Did you know I'm a cop?'

The words seemed to hang in the air between us for a long time.

'You're serious, aren't you?' he said.

I nodded.

He believed me. Behind his dark eyes, all the evidence was aligning. 'When you first came here,' he said slowly, 'were you gathering information for an arrest?'

'Yes,' I said.

'The cold was a pretext.'

'Yes.'

'I see,' Cicero said. 'Get out of here.'

'What?' I said. There had been no change in his expression.

'You lied to me,' Cicero said. 'You came to me asking for help. I took you on faith, and you lied to me.'

The literal excuse was on the tip of my tongue, that he'd never asked outright what I did for a living, but it sounded small and weak to my own ears.

'I lied *for* you, too,' I said. 'I've sheltered you from arrest and prosecution.'

'Why?' Cicero said. 'Because you pity me?'

'No, of course not,' I said quickly. 'I just didn't think you deserved to be in prison.'

'In case you've been missing the subtle nuances, I'm already in a prison,' Cicero said. 'But catching subtle nuances isn't your strong point.'

This was something different, a shift in tone.

'You think you weren't lying to me because you never said outright that you weren't a cop,' he said. 'You tell yourself you're not having an affair because you don't sleep with me anymore.'

I felt as though I'd swallowed too much ice water. 'Cicero,' I began, but already I saw it was hopeless. 'Will you at least keep the gun?'

'No,' Cicero said.

I picked it up off the table, feeling heat crawling on my skin, under my face, on the back of my neck. He watched me.

At the door, I said, 'Cicero, is this about what happened to your brother?'

'Goodbye, Sarah,' he said.

26

Marlinchen surprised me when I came home that night by suggesting a glass of wine out under the magnolia tree. I was about to tell her that I didn't think it wise that she made a habit of wine at the end of the day, but she must have seen it coming, because she corrected me. 'I meant wine for you, and I'd have a ginger ale or something,' she said.

As we emerged from the French doors, I nearly collided with Aidan, who was out on the deck without the light on.

'What are you doing out here?' Marlinchen asked him.

'Just getting some air,' Aidan said.

'Oh,' Marlinchen said, accepting it. But I saw the narrow outline of his lighter in the front of his jeans, and I knew he'd been just about to sneak a cigarette. To cover his tracks, I spoke up.

'You know what I was noticing yesterday?' I said, looking up at the roofline. 'Your house.'

'Oh, God,' Marlinchen said, following my gaze. 'Does it need some kind of expensive repairs?'

'No,' I said. 'I was just thinking that whoever did the repairs, after the lightning strike, did a really good job. I've seen it from all angles, and I can't even identify the spot where it was repaired. Where exactly was it hit?'

It was Aidan who spoke. 'Lightning struck the

house?' he asked. 'When was this?'

'You must remember,' Marlinchen said, surprised. 'Back when we were kids. It was really loud.'

But there was no recognition on Aidan's face. 'It was that long ago?' he said. 'I mean, are you sure I was living here then?'

Marlinchen nodded. 'Oh, yes. This was before Colm was born. It was that night when Mother got so upset. She was crying, remember?' When it was clear that he didn't, she shook her head. 'Boys. You can sleep through anything.'

Just then, Colm's voice interrupted. 'Marlinchen!' His disembodied voice floated through the window.

Marlinchen made a little face, as if to apologize for the interruption. 'What?' she said loudly, leaning slightly toward the open window and her out-of-sight brother.

'We can't find Donal's, you know, his sign-up form!'

Whatever it was that Donal was registering for — a sports league or summer school — Marlinchen seemed to be familiar with it. 'Duty calls,' she said to us. 'I'll be right back.'

I stopped her. 'Wait,' I said. 'You didn't answer my question, about what part of the house was struck.'

Marlinchen paused, with her hand on the door. 'Sorry,' she said. 'After all this time, I can't remember.'

She went in. I turned back to Aidan.

'You know,' I said, 'if lightning really did strike

your house, you shouldn't have been able to sleep through it.'

'I believe you,' Aidan said. 'When I was living in Georgia, lightning hit a tree about a hundred yards from where I was working. That was loud enough to put the fear of God into me, and a hundred yards was a pretty safe distance.'

'Maybe you weren't at home that night,' I suggested. 'Could it have happened during the time that you were in the hospital?'

'The hospital?' Aidan echoed.

'When you lost your finger,' I explained. 'That would have been around the same time, according to what Marlinchen says.'

This did not clear up Aidan's confusion. 'I don't think I was ever in the hospital,' he said. 'I mean, it was just a finger. It's grisly, but there's not much you can do for an injury like that. Stop the bleeding, save the finger if you can, amputate if you can't. It's not like you'd need the ICU.'

'No,' I said, seeing that he was right. But hadn't Marlinchen said that Aidan had gone away for a time?

Quick footsteps announced Marlinchen's return, and she emerged onto the back deck. 'Ready?' she said to me.

We walked down to the magnolia tree, to sit in full view of the moonlit waters of the lake. Sitting cross-legged, I opened the wine bottle and poured some into a plastic cup. The first swallow burned a warm path down my throat.

'Other than his speech difficulties,' Marlinchen said, 'Dad was looking really good yesterday. Didn't you think so?'

311

'Sure,' I said, although I had little basis for comparison, other than the photos I'd seen of younger, healthier Hughs.

I swallowed more wine and lay back, the dark form of the last magnolia blossom nodding above me. For a while, we didn't speak. A bulky, graceful black shadow swept overhead, not far from the lake's banks. An owl, hunting by night.

Then Marlinchen said, 'Are you okay, Sarah?'

'Why wouldn't I be?' I asked.

'You seemed a little' — she wavered one hand in the air — 'a little off when you came in tonight.'

When I didn't say anything, she spoke again, and this time more carefully. 'You never talk about your husband,' she said. 'It's like he's dead, instead of in prison.'

A single magnolia petal fell from the tree and lay between us, creamy white at its wide end, smudged magenta at the inner tip.

'When we talked about Shiloh,' I said, 'I just said he was in Wisconsin. I don't remember telling you he was in prison.'

Even in the dimness I saw Marlinchen's face begin to stain its familiar pink.

'I was curious,' she said. 'I ran your name through a search engine.'

'Fair enough,' I said. 'But you also could have asked me. I would have told you.'

But my reference to Shiloh, that night, had been meant to deceive, I realized, and now I was ashamed of that. Unshaded, unadulterated truth was in short supply in the Hennessy household, and I hadn't really helped matters by adding half-truths of my own. Maybe somewhere in the moral calculus it had made a difference.

'I should have been up-front with you,' I said. 'I'm sorry.'

'It's all right,' she said.

'I guess I don't talk about him because I don't talk *with* him. He hasn't written to me for several months.'

'That's awful,' she said. 'Why not?'

I picked up the magnolia petal and stroked it with my thumb. Its texture was somewhere between velvet and candle wax. 'I remind Shiloh of things he'd rather forget,' I said. 'When I was looking for him, I found out something about him he didn't want me to know, and it opened up an old wound for him.'

'What did you find out?' Marlinchen said.

'That belongs to him,' I said. 'It's not mine to share.'

'So when he gets out, what'll you do?' she asked.

'I don't know,' I said.

Sharp surprise registered on her features. I'd given the wrong response.

'You think adults always know the answers?' I said.

'Well, no,' she admitted. 'It's just that . . . you seem so certain about everything.'

'No,' I said. 'Cops aren't really encouraged to second-guess themselves, but I make missteps all the time.' I was thinking about Cicero, and the little .25 now resting in the glove compartment of my car. 'You try to help people, and sometimes it seems they don't really want to be helped.'

Marlinchen nodded as if she knew what I was saying, although I doubted she really could. 'Have you ever thought about doing something else for a living?' she asked.

'No,' I said.

'Why not?'

'It's the only thing I'm trained for,' I said.

She wasn't satisfied. 'But why?'

'Why what?'

'It wasn't *always* the only thing you're trained for. At some point you made a decision to get trained for it. That's why you dropped out of college, right? To go into police work?'

I shook my head. 'No,' I said. 'When I left school, the last thing on my mind was becoming a cop.'

'What changed your mind?'

Those who go into law enforcement have a list of stock answers; generally, the same ones they give during the interview part of the application process: *I want to help people, every day there's a new challenge, I hate the thought of working at a desk.* I didn't use any of them.

'I don't know,' I said. 'Well, I do, but it's a long story. A long, boring story.'

I must have made it sound sufficiently boring, because Marlinchen didn't pursue it any further. After a few more minutes, by some silent agreement, we rose and headed up toward the house.

Much later, after the kids had gone to sleep and the house had quieted, I stood at Hugh

314

Hennessy's high window and looked down. I was still thinking about Marlinchen's sketchy tale of lightning striking the house and Aidan's inability to remember any such event.

Catholic by bloodline only, I had no religious training, but as a child I'd been haunted by something that the other kids had taken from their Sunday school teachings: that the world had been perfect, and then sin had entered it in a bolt of lightning. It was a metaphor, but for years I'd believed it literally.

Now I saw the Hennessy family in the same terms, unexpectedly and swiftly cursed. They'd been this Edenic little family, then lightning struck the house, then Aidan lost his finger to a brutal dog, then Elisabeth Hennessy drowned in the waters of the lake. Was it all simply bad luck?

Soon Marlinchen would be 18 and the guardian of her younger siblings, and my responsibilities here would be over. The best thing would be for me to ignore my feeling that something had gone very wrong with this family long before I was part of their lives. But I wasn't sure I could.

Marlinchen had asked me tonight why I chose to become a cop. She was right; it wasn't something I had drifted into. It was something I had chosen, part of what Genevieve called my headfirst impulse to help people.

Just before I slept that night, I heard the cry of a barred owl out over the lake. It sounded very like a human scream.

27

When I left Minnesota at 18, to claim a basketball scholarship at UNLV, I hadn't seen a future as a cop ahead of me. I wasn't looking too far ahead: just to more basketball and more schooling, in that order of importance. One thing I did feel fairly sure of was that I wouldn't live in Minnesota again. I'd grown up in New Mexico and thought myself a Westerner; going to school in Las Vegas was like going home, I'd told myself.

It wasn't. Vegas was sprawling and vivid and exciting, all in ways that couldn't involve an 18-year-old with little money and no car, who knew no one. Nor, that year, did I see much time in basketball games. I'd expected that, but still it made me restless. I went to my classes, trying and failing to be interested in the general-education, Western-civilization courses that make up a freshman's schedule. I didn't feel like a student. I didn't feel like an athlete. I didn't have any sense of a life coming together.

That was when I realized something I hadn't planned on: I was homesick for the Range. The shivering birches and white pines, the green grass and mine-scarred red dirt, the pit lakes as blue-green as semiprecious stones: somehow, when I hadn't been paying attention, it had gotten into my blood.

When my aunt Ginny had her stroke and died,

that summer, it destabilized me more than I realized at the time. In the fall I went back to school as normal, but nothing there made sense to me anymore. Within two weeks of the start of instruction, I wrote a letter to the coach and caught a Greyhound back to Minnesota, earnings from my summer job rolled up as traveler's checks in my duffel bag. I didn't know what I needed so badly, but somehow I was certain it lay back in Minnesota.

Drinking a cold, sweet Pepsi in a coffee shop across from the bus station in Duluth, I scanned the want ads. A taconite-mining company based in a small town was looking for a cleaning-and-maintenance trainee in their shop; it was one of the few entry-level positions in that kind of operation. On the opposite page from the job ads were 'housing to share' listings.

The three-bedroom house I moved into was already occupied by two women in their mid-twenties. Erin and Cheryl Anne were a nurse and a medical receptionist, respectively, and close friends. They'd lived in the rented house for over a year, losing their previous roommate to 'marriage and real life,' Cheryl Anne said. They were cordial and pleasant to me, and I to them, from the start.

That's where we got stuck, at cordiality. The passage of time and the fact that I paid a third of the rent did nothing to lessen the feeling that I'd moved into their long-established home. Sometimes, when the TV's blue light flickered over the living room, I joined them, but we rarely spoke. I never turned on the TV set on the occasions that

317

I was home alone. So, at the end of my first days on the job, hot Indian-summer days of late September, I'd walk down to the small and thinly stocked city library, to check out paperback thrillers.

When I think about those days, that's what I remember, the simplicity of it. Shopping for food not in the grocery store but in the drugstore, where the center aisle was full of cheap nonperishables: soft French bread so full of preservatives that it lasted for weeks, strawberry jam, 99-cent spaghetti and macaroni that stuck together no matter how carefully it was prepared. Evenings on the porch, drinking store-brand cola with ice cubes that tasted like the freezer, the last of the day's light dwindling in the west.

* * *

'What are you doing up there, Sadie?' my father asked, over the long-distance wires. 'Your aunt is gone, you've got no family there anymore.'

'I have friends here,' I said. 'I have a job.'

The job part was true, of course, but I had nothing that rose beyond friendly acquaintance-ships so far.

'I just don't understand it. You up and quit school for no reason that I can see, go live in a little town that isn't even where you grew up,' he said. 'You're not even taking night classes, are you?'

'No,' I said.

'Why would you want to live up there, in the middle of nowhere?'

318

'It was good enough — ' I started to say, then caught myself.

'Good enough for me to send you there when you were 13?' he said, finishing my thought. 'Is that what this is all about? You're angry?'

'No,' I said, 'no, I'm not. Look . . . ' I twisted the phone cord around my thumb. 'I'm just trying to have a life. To make a life, that's all.'

In the silence that followed I could almost hear him think that it wasn't much of a life, an industrial job and a rented room, but he couldn't say any more. I was 19, an adult.

'What about Christmas?' he asked. 'Wouldn't you like to come home then?'

New Mexico at Christmastime. Light glowing from the *farolitos* — sand-weighted brown paper bags with candles in them — and the sopaipillas and rich mole sauce of a traditional *Noche Buena* feast on Christmas Eve . . .

'Is Buddy coming home at Christmas, too?' I asked.

'Yes,' my father said. 'He's got a week of leave.'

I put another twist in the phone cord. 'I can't come,' I said.

'Why not? Surely you're not working?'

'The mine runs 365 days a year,' I said. 'It costs too much for them to shut the equipment down and then start it back up. And I was the most recent person hired. It's too early for me to ask for Christmas off.'

I wanted him to believe it, but he wasn't stupid. 'I haven't had you and your brother under the same roof for years,' my father said. 'Why is that, Sadie?' The bafflement in his voice

319

seemed, for all the world, to be genuine.

My thumb was turning red from having the phone cord wrapped so tightly around it. *You know why. I tried to tell you, and you wouldn't listen.*

'I'm sorry,' I said. 'I just can't come.'

★ ★ ★

January came, and with it the coldest weather of all. Night came so early that I walked home from work in darkness, and it was too cold and icy to go out after dinner. My chief entertainment became the paperback novels I checked out, several weeks' worth at a time, from the library on Saturday afternoon.

I should have realized something was wrong with my life when I strayed into the wrong section of the library, found a paperback of *Othello*, and immediately wanted to check it out.

After leaving school, I'd believed I'd never torture myself with anything an English teacher would approve of ever again. But then, standing amid the faint attic scent and educational posters of the public library, I felt a thrill of pleasure and nostalgia, remembering *Othello* as being the only Shakespeare I'd really liked. Something about the world Othello, Iago, and Cassio lived in, that world of martial duty and sometimes perverted honor, had spoken to me. At home on those coldest of nights, I read and reread *Othello*. The library had to send two overdue notices before I returned it.

If this were a movie, *Othello* would have

changed my life. I would have moved on to other Shakespeare plays, loved them too, and finally enrolled in community college. But it didn't work out that way. After *Othello*, I went back to the pulp novels I'd preferred before.

And then, in the spring, I found something else I liked to do.

★ ★ ★

In the maintenance shop, I worked with an Armenian-American girl, thick-waisted, dark-haired, pleasant-looking, easy to talk to. Her name was Silva, and she seemed to live for one thing: the dance at the VFW hall every Saturday night.

'You should come,' Silva said more than once, but I'd been noncommittal. Dances at the VFW hall sounded too much like bingo or pie suppers at a church to me, but one March night, I decided there was no harm in checking it out.

At nine-thirty, the scene at the VFW hall was surprisingly animated; people spilled out onto the steps along with light and music from inside. The high spirits of the crowd surprised me, but it didn't take long to learn the secret.

Technically, these dances were dry, meaning no alcohol was served. But, as is painfully typical of small-town life, the majority of the young people inside the hall were in some stage of intoxication. Bottles were passed around in the shadows of the parking lot, and if you weren't lucky enough to know someone who'd brought a bottle, there was Brent, a local entrepreneur who

321

parked his Buick LeSabre near the VFW hall and sold liquor from the trunk. Ill at ease, and feeling like an outsider, I quickly sought him out.

Alcohol hadn't been a part of my life since a few girls' nights out at UNLV. The single shot of whiskey hit me hard. Pleasurably hard. Not long after, a young man I didn't know asked me to dance, and I said yes. Silva, flushed with exertion and pleasure, brushed by and winked at me. I felt the world beginning to drift away, just a little. I liked it. Up until that moment, I hadn't realized how depriving and monastic an existence I'd created for myself. It was like a burden that I was only now letting slip from my shoulders.

That week I'd gotten my first pay adjustment, the one that marked the end of my initial six-month period at the mine. I felt newly rich, and in my current state of elation, I realized something: if making the world recede a little was pleasant, there was no reason not to make it recede even more. A *lot* more.

★ ★ ★

'Morning, Sarah. You want a ride?'

A bright Monday morning in early May. Kenny Olson had pulled up alongside me in his big Ford pickup truck, about a half mile from work. I clutched my purse closer to my ribs and ran around to the passenger side.

Kenny was one of the mine's security officers. Security mostly meant he kept hunters off company land, and chased away kids who came to cliff-jump and swim in the pit lakes. He was as good-natured as anyone I'd ever met, virtually never calling the police on trespassers, but merely sending them on their way. In addition to his security job, he was an every-other-weekend citizen jailer for the Sheriff's Department. When he wasn't doing that, he was hunting and fishing. Somehow, he and I had become friendly across the three-decade-plus divide between us.

'Thanks,' I said, scrambling in. 'Aren't you supposed to be at work already?' Kenny usually came on at the same time as the first shift of miners, the 7-to-3. Support staff, like me, came in an hour later, at eight.

'I told 'em I'd be late. Took Lorna to the doctor.'

'She's not sick, I hope?' I said.

'Oh no. The ear doctor. She's getting a hearing aid,' Kenny said, swinging wide through an intersection. 'Now she'll be able to hear all the stupid things I say. She's gonna lose all respect for me.'

I laughed. 'That'll never happen.' I set my bag between my feet. 'Hey, I've started saving up for a car.'

'You told me something like that,' Kenny said.

'Really?' I said, puzzled. 'When?'

We bounced over the entry to the employee lot, the bad shock absorbers on Kenny's truck intensifying the bump. Kenny didn't say anything as he steered the truck into a space at the end of a row. He didn't answer my question, and I thought maybe Kenny needed hearing aids

323

of his own, although he'd never seemed to have a problem before.

He pulled the automatic-transmission lever over to park and killed the ignition, then turned to me. 'You don't remember being in my truck this weekend, do you?' he said.

I opened my mouth and closed it again. Memory flashed, but only dimly. I'd been dancing Saturday night, as usual. I'd gotten a ride home from friends. Hadn't I?

'That's when you told me about wanting to buy a car. I didn't know if you were serious. You were saying a lot of things. You were drunk.'

I looked around the cab. 'I didn't throw up in here, did I?' It was the only reason I could imagine for the disapproval in Kenny's pale-blue gaze.

'No,' he said. 'But you were staggering when I saw you walking. You were drunk out of your head.'

'I had a little too much,' I said. 'It happens.'

'I saw a girl once, died right on her porch, key in her hand. She was too drunk to get it in the lock. Laid down to sleep it off in ten-degree weather. I had to tell her parents,' Kenny said.

'I can take care of myself,' I said. 'We're into spring, anyway.'

Kenny watched Silva cross the parking lot. 'This isn't much of a job for you, you know,' he said. 'Do you ever think about the future?'

'Actually, I do,' I told him. 'I might want to work in the field.' *The field* was where the real mining was done, where miners ran shovels and drove production trucks so large their tires were taller than I was.

'You want to work in the field,' Kenny repeated, his voice skeptical.

'Women can be miners,' I said.

Kenny shook his head. 'That's not what I mean. This isn't about women's lib, Sarah. Don't pretend that it is.'

'Someone's got to do that kind of work,' I said. 'The money's a lot better than what I'm doing now.'

He sighed.

'Don't worry about me, okay?' I said. I pulled the strap of my purse back up over my shoulder. 'I've got to go in.'

⋆ ⋆ ⋆

In early June, a freak storm dumped five inches on us in the middle of the day. A Thursday, with the weekend coming on. The fresh snow occasioned an impromptu snowball fight among those of us on the 8-to-4 shift. I hit a rangy young mechanic, Wayne, square in the face. He caught me and put a handful of snow down the back of my shirt. Screaming, I yelled to Silva to help me, but she was laughing too hard.

On Monday morning, Silva was in a more sober mood.

'What's wrong?' I said, when she didn't respond to my attempts at light conversation.

'Aren't you worried about Wayne?' she asked.

Wayne. I'd danced with him Saturday night, I remembered. More than one dance. After that, my memories jumped ahead to Sunday morning. Cheryl Anne had come into my room, angry. *Someone* had knocked her hair dryer from its hook on the wall into the toilet bowl last night; did I have any idea how that might have happened or why *someone* just left it there?

'What about Wayne?' I asked Silva.

'You don't remember?' she asked.

That was fast becoming my least favorite question.

'You broke his nose,' Silva said.

I shook my head, stricken. 'No way,' I told her, but already I was uncertain of my own words.

'He's saying a guy did it, and his friends are backing him up, because he's embarrassed that a girl did that to him. But it's all over that you did it. They say he was hitting on you pretty hard all night. You don't remember any of that?'

My hand rose to my upper arm. I had a bruise there, since Saturday night. I'd written it off as the result of stumbling into something, perhaps in my encounter with the bathroom wall and the hair dryer. Now I realized it was the right shape for fingers, squeezing hard. Wayne's grip. I heard a young man's voice hiss in my ear. *Rigid*, he was saying. No. *Frigid*. The general shape of events was beginning to re-form in my mind.

'Maybe,' I began defensively, 'if he'd listened when I said — '

'You don't even remember how it happened,' Silva said, cutting me off. 'You don't know what you said or what he said.'

She was right. She saw through me. But in the

moment, her voice reminded me of Cheryl Anne.

Prissy bitch, I thought, and looked away, leaning down to yank the laces of my boots tighter and knot them.

★   ★   ★

Wayne never confronted me about the incident, and his lack of righteous anger confirmed my suspicion that he bore at least some of the guilt for what happened that night. Still, I decided to cut back on my drinking.

That resolution lasted a few weeks. Not long enough.

★   ★   ★

'Probably half the young people in town are drunk on Friday or Saturday night. Why aren't you lecturing them?'

It was summer. I had followed some of the maintenance guys on a cliff-jumping trip to one of the pit lakes. *Cliff* was a bit of an understatement, but jumping from the bluffs over the water was a local tradition among young people. The mining companies tried to chase kids away, because of liability issues, but it never really discouraged anyone.

I couldn't swim, and had only hooked up with the guys because I'd expected that in light of the summer squall we were having, they'd call off their plans to go to the lake in favor of something drier and safer. Not true. The worst of the lightning had passed, they told me, and they were going to get wet by swimming anyway, weren't they?

So I'd gone along, and as we'd all progressed in our drinking, their encouragements to jump began to make more sense to me. There's really nothing to swimming, they said: once you're in, instinct will take over. We'll come get you, if you get into any trouble. Besides, you're already wet.

In addition to my whiskey courage, I was beginning to dimly perceive some kind of slur on my gender if I didn't do the things the guys could do. So I was very near to jumping when a white light lower to the ground and of longer duration than lightning splashed over us. The headlights of Kenny's truck.

He'd sent the guys on their way, but I was sitting wet-haired and sobering fast in the cab of his truck.

'Tell me you never went cliff-jumping as a kid,' I demanded.

'That's not what bothers me,' Kenny said. 'It's your drinking. You're getting something of a reputation, Sarah.'

Reputation. That word had a connotation beyond drinking.

'What are you trying to say?' I demanded. 'I haven't slept with any of those guys. Not a goddamned one. If anyone's saying so, they're lying.'

'No, that's not what they're saying,' Kenny said. 'They're saying you're a lush and a tease.'

'That's not fair.'

'You drink and dance with these boys, Sarah,

go out to the lakes with them with no other girls around. What do you expect them to think?'

'That I like drinking and dancing and going to the lakes. If they think I owe them anything, that's their problem.'

'If you get hurt, it's not going to matter whose fault it is,' Kenny said. 'You're a tall, strong girl, but one day it isn't going to be enough. One morning you're going to wake up and be the last person in town to know you pulled a train the night before.'

Never would I have believed that Kenny knew a phrase like that. It was like a slap in the face. I was a child to chiding, at least with him. I swallowed hard and didn't let the hurt show. 'I can take care of myself,' I said thinly.

'You keep saying that, but you're not doing it,' Kenny said.

★   ★   ★

Later that month, coming home drunk, hot, and thirsty late on a Friday night, I knocked a glass from the kitchen cupboard. I thought I was being a good roommate as I got out the broom and dustpan to clean up.

But in the morning, Cheryl Anne and Erin noticed a few shards of glass my clumsy efforts had left behind. They also inspected the kitchen trash and found the broken remains of a champagne flute that had been a keepsake from Erin's sister's wedding. They suggested it was time I found a place of my own.

I found a vacancy in a three-story rooming

house. Kenny's big truck would have made the move a lot easier, but he and I weren't speaking much.

★ ★ ★

August brought the hottest days of summer, and the most humid. Everyone who didn't have air-conditioning was out on the streets. My third-floor room was a very efficient trap for the heat, so when the weekend came around, I also planned to spend as much time away from home as possible. The bar was air-conditioned, and after a certain hour, the bartenders were too busy to notice someone underage in the corner.

One Sunday morning, I woke up in a holding cell, with a pounding headache. When the jailer came down, it was Kenny.

'What'd I do?' I asked.

'If you don't remember,' he said, 'why should I tell you?'

Half a dozen possibilities ran though my mind, none of them good. I thought of Wayne and his broken nose. I thought of the beautiful deep-gray Nova I'd just bought and told myself I'd never drive drunk. *Please God, not a hit-and-run.*

Kenny relented. 'You didn't do much of anything,' he said. 'Just drunk and disorderly in public.'

'Okay,' I said, sitting on the bench with my hands dangling loosely between my knees. 'I get a phone call, right?'

I was thinking I'd have to call a bail bondsman. Who else was there? Silva? The

330

shambling old man across the hall from me at the rooming house, who smelled of layers of cigarette smoke and whose last name I'd never learned? Kenny was my closest friend, and clearly there was no help coming from that quarter.

'You'd get one phone call if you'd been arrested,' he said. 'I didn't arrest you last night. You're not officially here.'

'What?' I said.

'I brought you in here to sober up and think a little.'

I should have been grateful, but instead I just got angry. I stood up, and immediately my blood pressure rose, making my head throb. 'You think I want favors from you?' I said. I held out my hands as if for handcuffs. 'If I did something wrong, arrest me. If I didn't, then let me out.'

Kenny shook his head.

'No, arrest me if you think I deserve it. Then at least I can call someone, make bail, and get out.'

But Kenny shook his head again. 'I don't want to do that today for the same reason I didn't last night,' he said. 'I don't want you to have an arrest on your record, because it could hurt your chances.'

'Chances for what?'

'For being a cop,' Kenny said.

I let my hands fall. If he had said, *For the space program*, I couldn't have been more surprised. My voice, when I spoke, was faint. 'Are you kidding?' I said.

'You're too smart to be a miner and too mean

to be a college girl,' Kenny told me. 'You've got a lot of energy and it's all going nowhere. You need a job you can pour it into.'

'You're not serious,' I said. 'They don't need people here, anyway. There probably isn't even a vacancy in the every-other-weekend citizen's reserve program that you do.'

'No, there isn't,' Kenny said. 'But they're always looking for good people down in the Cities.'

'You're serious,' I said.

'Yes,' Kenny said.

For a moment I didn't even feel the ache in my temples. Kenny thought I could be someone like him, and this amazing realization made all my anger drain away. He was wrong, of course.

'Listen, Kenny,' I said, 'thanks, but I'm not cut out for it.'

'How do you know?' he asked.

'I just do. You're reading me all wrong.' After another moment I said, 'Really, I'm sorry.'

When he saw I meant it, Kenny fished for his keys.

★   ★   ★

Weeks passed and September came. Kenny had gone back to his work, patrolling the mines during the week and the streets and jail on the weekend. I went back to what I did best, drinking on the weekend nights.

Around 3 A.M., after a typical Saturday night, I was in a familiar position: kneeling over the toilet bowl. When you throw up on a fairly regular basis, you lose your distaste for it. Afterward, I wiped the corner of my mouth with my hand, swaying slightly on my knees, feeling the dampness of unhealthy sweat on the nape of my neck, grateful for the cool night air from the open sash window. I'd just brushed my teeth and was splashing water on my face, when outside the window, a woman screamed.

I froze, completely still except for the water droplets crawling on my face, and then I went to the window.

'Hey!' I yelled. 'Is someone out there?'

The bathroom window looked out onto a grassy slope, which led up to the railroad tracks. It was dark there, except far to my right, where I could see the signal lights on the tracks.

'Hey!' I yelled again. There was no response.

'Goddammit,' I said, fumbling for my towel. I wanted to hear drunken tittering, or a sour voice saying, *Yeah, yeah, I'm fine.* I wanted to feel irritated. It was preferable to feeling worried about someone in the dark who'd screamed and now wasn't answering.

Back in my room, I undressed and pulled back the bedcovers, instructing myself to forget about it. I told myself that animal noises could trick you sometimes. Like bobcats, for example; they sounded a lot like women screaming. Or barred owls.

It wasn't any bobcat. It wasn't any owl.

If anyone was out there, and really was in trouble, they'd have screamed again. They'd have answered when I called.

You don't know that.

For God's sake, what help would I be? I was still half drunk. Surely someone else, nearer, had heard it as well. Someone else would look into it.

You can't be sure of that. You don't know that anyone else heard. You only know that you heard.

'Son of a bitch,' I said tiredly, and started looking for sturdier clothes to wear than the ones I'd worn drinking.

My only weapon back then was a Maglite, but it was beautiful, four D-cells long with a body of anodized cherry-colored metal. As I went up the slope behind the house, still a little unsteady on my feet, I swung it in arcs, illuminating the brush and shadows. 'Is anyone out here?'

When I'd finished searching behind the house, I doubled back. The scream might have come from the front of the house, a trick of acoustics bouncing the sound waves off the slope and back toward the bathroom window. I retraced my steps down the slope and went out into the street. Walking toward town, I shined my light low onto lawns and into front entryways, careful to avoid the darkened windows beyond which people slept. Then, as I got into town, I found myself looking into alleyways and at the front steps of businesses. Nothing. There was no sign of any trouble, and the streets were quiet as a movie set by night.

I ended up standing in the town square, completely sober and totally alone in the center of town. The night was nearly gone. Dawn would come in an hour.

* * *

Kenny was dressed for church, in a coat and tie, with his hair slicked down, when I knocked on his door at seven-thirty in the morning. He took in the sight of me at his door, Maglite still in hand, with a mildly quizzical expression.

'I think I want to be a cop,' I said.

28

'I don't see a case here,' Kilander said.

It was the morning after Marlinchen and I had our drinks out by the lake, and I was doing something I'd done a number of times since the morning I'd told Kenny Olson I wanted to be a cop: conferring with a prosecutor over the feasibility of criminal charges.

It was, though, on an unofficial basis. Kilander and I were spending the lunch hour in his office, eating takeout I'd brought up: a curried chicken salad over lettuce, dinner rolls, and iced tea. I'd just told him what I knew about the Hennessys: Hugh's beatings and Aidan's exile, the inexplicable animosity Hugh felt toward his eldest son.

'It's an ugly story, no question,' Kilander said. 'But the purpose of juvenile and family law isn't to punish, it's to intervene. No agency would try to prosecute a parent for past child abuse that didn't result in permanent injury.'

'I know that,' I said, tearing my previously untouched roll in half and spreading butter on it. More than anything else, I was stalling. What I was about to tell Christian Kilander, I hadn't even shared with Marlinchen yet. 'What I've told you is essentially background. That wasn't the end of the story.'

'Ah,' Kilander said. 'Should I cancel my one o'clock deposition?'

He was teasing me; I'd known he'd do that.

I'd known he'd play devil's advocate, too. It didn't bother me. That was partly what I'd come to him for, his sharp and reductive mind.

'Sarah?' Kilander prompted.

'I think Aidan shot himself with his father's gun,' I said, setting the roll down uneaten. 'I think Hugh covered it up.'

For the first time, Kilander smiled. 'You come up with the most amazing theories,' he said. 'Do tell how you arrived at this one.'

I told him about Aidan's missing finger and the explanation Marlinchen had given me for it, the neighbor's vicious dog that had supposedly bitten the three-year-old boy, causing him to be away from home for what Marlinchen had called 'a long time' and to return without a little finger on his left hand.

'Why don't you believe it?' Kilander asked.

'I've seen the area they live in,' I said. 'They have neighbors, but not immediate ones. It would have been quite a long trek for a three-year-old to make, to put himself in the path of a neighbor's dog.'

Kilander said nothing.

'At that same time, Hugh Hennessy owned some antique pistols. He kept them in his study and showed them to reporters; I've seen them in magazine photos. But at some point later, Hennessy developed an aversion to guns. He won't have them in his home.' I banished an unwelcome thought of Cicero. 'Meanwhile,' I went on, 'Hugh decided to replace the carpet in his study. He had the money to have it done professionally, and he wasn't a do-it-yourself type. Yet he did the work himself. Badly. You can see it was done by hand. The kids estimate he did this about fourteen years ago, when the twins would have been three to four years old.

'At around this time, in her earliest memories, Marlinchen Hennessy has a rather odd recollection. She says lightning struck the house, and that it upset her mother to the point of crying, and that this gave her a fear of storms for years to come. Storms and loud noises,' I added, stressing the last two words.

'Couldn't there really have been a lightning strike?' Kilander asked.

'I've seen the house from the outside,' I said. 'There's no damage from it anywhere.'

'So it was repaired,' Kilander said.

I shook my head. 'That's what I thought, but Marlinchen Hennessy can't even point to the spot where the house was hit. How could she have vivid memories of the night it happened, but no memory of seeing the damage, or workmen climbing up to repair it, anything like that?'

Kilander nodded.

'Speaking of home repair,' I went on, 'in addition to the carpet Hugh replaced himself, there are bleach spots on the carpet in the upstairs hallway, like someone scrubbed out some stains. They're consistent with Hugh cleaning up bloodstains himself, to the best of his limited ability.'

Kilander nodded, speculative. 'So you think the little boy shot himself with his father's gun, and the finger wasn't salvageable.'

'He was just old enough to be curious like that, and disobedient. He'd probably seen guns on TV,' I said.

'And Hugh lied about what happened to cover it up,' Kilander went on.

'It would have been professionally disastrous,' I said. 'Imagine what the media would have made of it: 'Negligent Father Leaves Loaded Gun in Unlocked Desk; Adorable Tot Shoots Self with It.' Hugh was a bigger name in those days; the press was interested in him. It would have been bad publicity for any writer, but worse for Hugh. He'd written two popular books on family and love and loyalty. Being a family man was his — ' How did marketing people put it? 'It was his brand.'

Kilander scraped the rest of the chicken salad onto his plate. He was eating more than his share, but I kept quiet. There was something endearing about his unabashed greed.

'So Hugh tried to keep it quiet,' I said. 'The twins were just young enough to have their memories reprogrammed like that. If your parents tell you something long enough, you believe it,' I said. 'But if you talk to the Hennessy twins, their memories don't line up. Marlinchen remembers lightning striking the house. Aidan doesn't. Marlinchen says Aidan was in the hospital a long time. Aidan doesn't think he was. Something's screwy there.'

Kilander sipped his coffee, thinking. I got up and walked over to the window, looking out.

'It explains the abuse,' I went on. 'Hugh cleaned up the house as best he could, but Aidan was the one thing Hugh couldn't sweep under the rug. He was always around, with his maimed hand, and it probably just got under Hugh's skin. I think things might have been okay if his wife hadn't died, if he didn't have a bad back and an ulcer . . . I think he was just under a little too much stress, and Aidan became the scapegoat. Because of Hugh's guilt.'

'Do you have any physical evidence for this?'

'No,' I said. 'Not yet.'

'What about ER records?' Kilander said. 'Sounds like the kid got some kind of treatment, if the finger was removed neatly.'

I shook my head. 'Medical records from fourteen years ago? I'm sure they're in a box, in a warehouse, somewhere. But I'd need a subpoena to get at them, and that's not going to happen with the evidence I have.' I paused. 'That's why I haven't told either of the twins about this. I don't want to shake them up, not until I have some proof.'

'When will that be, exactly?' Kilander asked.

Touché.

'Right,' Kilander said. 'And here's the million-dollar question: So what?' He didn't wait for me to answer. 'Even if you found incontrovertible evidence in support of your theory about the gun, it was still an accident. If Hugh lied to his children, that's not a crime. And that's just the grounds part of it.'

'What's the other part?' I asked.

'You said this guy has aphasia, from the stroke?'

I nodded.

'That's probably the worst possible handicap he could have sustained, from a legal standpoint. If he can't communicate, he can't participate fully in his own defense. Even the most hard-core of judges would throw the case out so hard it'd bounce.'

'I wasn't talking about a prosecution this month, or even this year,' I said. 'He's recovering. He could recover completely.'

'Or he might not,' Kilander said. He put his plate and napkin into the plastic bag the food had come in. It was time for his one o'clock deposition. I put my plate in, too, and tied the top of the bag shut, planning to drop it into a trash can in the outer office.

'You make a hell of a case for it, Pribek,' Kilander said. 'If it makes you feel any better, I believe you when you say something's screwy out there. But even if you're correct on every single point, I just don't see a courtroom in this family's future.'

* * *

That afternoon, my onetime partner John Vang called me. He was investigating a rape case, but the 16-year-old victim had been nearly monosyllabic in front of a male detective. Vang thought follow-up questioning by a female investigator would help. Was I available?

It took me nearly thirty minutes to break down the wall the girl showed to Vang. Later, I almost wished I hadn't. Three assailants, all known to her, in an apartment-complex laundry

341

room. Five separate assaults, three vaginal, two rectal. I left feeling numb in the bright sunlight of midafternoon.

My conversation with Kilander, too, still weighed on my mind. I knew he was right, but it was at times like these that the system truly baffled me. I wasn't sure what anyone could have done differently, yet the world had pretty clearly failed Aidan. I knew there were plenty of child and family programs that put a great deal of money and time into their efforts to protect the young, but sometimes it seemed like rain falling directly onto the ocean, nothing getting where it needed to go.

My cell phone rang. I picked it up, one hand on the wheel.

'Detective Pribek? This is Lou Vignale at the First Precinct.'

'Hey, Lou,' I said. 'What can I do for you?'

'I've got a girl here who says she's one of your informants. Her name's Ghislaine Morris.'

'Ghislaine?' It wasn't a name that had been on my mind for a while. 'Yeah, I know her. What's the arrest for?'

Vignale hadn't specifically said she'd been arrested, but I'd had a premonition. Nothing else that had happened today was wholesome or inspiring.

'Shoplifting,' Vignale said. 'She was at Marshall Field's, jamming stuff under the blankets in her baby stroller. But she says she's helping you on something, and you'd want her released.'

'She said *what*?' I ran my free hand through

342

my hair. This, on top of everything else
. . . Maybe Shiloh was right, and I shouldn't
even have kept her phone number.

'Ghislaine is *confused*,' I said. 'She is not
helping me at the current time on anything.'

'She said you might say that,' Vignale said.
'And she said to remind you about the guy in the
Third Precinct. Some kind of doctor?'

I opened my mouth to speak and then closed
it again, thinking, *Oh, hell*. Ghislaine was
manipulative, but she wasn't stupid. Now I had
my work cut out for me.

'Field's caught her in the store, right?' I asked.
'So they got all the items back undamaged?'

'Right, but they want to press charges.'

That was fairly common procedure — department stores always like to discourage shoplifters
— and trying to dissuade the manager from
pressing charges probably wouldn't be easy, but
it would have to be done.

'I'll be down to get Ghislaine as soon as I talk
to the store manager,' I said. 'Tell her to sit tight,
okay?'

'Uh-*huh*,' Vignale said. There was more than a
little wry disapproval in his voice, but he said no
more, except 'I'll tell her.'

★ ★ ★

Forty-five minutes later, I was waiting at a side
door while Officer Vignale went back to retrieve
Ghislaine.

The heavy door swung open and Ghislaine
came out. Despite her everyday clothes — a

343

T-shirt and cutoffs and bright plastic flats — she smelled of an only-for-evening scent; she'd been sampling at the perfume counter.

'Bye!' she said brightly to Vignale, who did not respond. Ghislaine turned to me. 'Thanks for coming down so fast, Sarah.'

'Don't worry about it,' I said pleasantly. 'Where's Shadrick?' All Ghislaine had with her was a bag from Sam Goody.

'Oh,' she said. 'My friend Flora lives near here. I got her to pick him up for me and take him home.'

'Did you take the bus down here?'

'Yeah,' she said.

'You need a ride home, then?'

Ghislaine gave me a slanted look. She sensed that my generosity was out of place, given the circumstances. 'Really?' she asked.

'I'm going that way anyhow,' I lied.

'That'd be great,' she said, her good humor bubbling up again.

As we headed out of the station, she hefted the Sam Goody bag at her side, and said, 'Don't worry, this stuff's legit.'

'I know,' I said. 'Generally, shoplifters don't bother to steal the bag.'

'Oh, listen to you,' she mocked, opening the car door to slide inside. 'The stuff at Field's was, like, chickenshit, not even a hundred dollars' worth of stuff. Otherwise you wouldn't have been able to fix it.'

We pulled out into the street and began to navigate the one-way interchanges of downtown Minneapolis. I headed toward Ghislaine's

344

neighborhood — Cicero's, too — but I took us down several side streets, moving away from the city's center and from streets on which the buses ran.

'This isn't the fastest way to my place,' Ghislaine said, flipping down the sun visor to look for a mirror.

'I know,' I said. 'I thought we could use an extra couple of minutes to talk.' I damped down the noise from the radio.

She glanced over at me. 'About what?' she asked, shifting in her seat.

'We need to talk about what you told Officer Vignale, about you being my informant and helping me with the 'doctor' in the Third Precinct.'

'Well, that was true,' she said.

'Right. I asked you about him, you told me what you knew, I compensated you. That was the extent of your help. You're not assisting me on an ongoing basis.'

Ghislaine looked ahead, as if the traffic were fascinating.

'So unless I'm mistaken, when you told Officer Vignale to 'remind' me of it, you were threatening to give up Cisco unless I came down and bailed you out.'

Mixed feelings flickered in her eyes; insecurity turned to a determination to counterattack. 'Well, I just thought it was interesting,' Ghislaine said, her voice rising in imitation of harmless surmise, 'that I never heard anything about him getting arrested. I was like, 'I told Sarah about him, I wonder what happened.' So I thought maybe I should tell someone else.' Ghislaine smiled, all innocence. 'I mean, what better place for an agoraphobic guy than prison? He wouldn't have to go outside for years.'

'Cicero's not agoraphobic,' I said.

'*Cicero?*' Ghislaine repeated, and there was a world of speculation in the one word. *Oh, hell*, I thought. I hadn't meant to use his real name.

'What is this guy,' she went on, her tone brightly insinuating, 'your new best friend?'

Ghislaine had seen me around the neighborhood; I knew that from our encounter on the bus. And she heard things, which was what made her a good informant. I wondered how much she really knew about my repeated visits to the towers. Obviously she knew enough. She'd guessed that threatening Cicero would get her what she wanted, and I'd unwillingly confirmed it by fixing her shoplifting bust.

I pulled to the curb.

'What are you doing?' she asked, looking around at the side street we were on, brown brick apartment buildings on each side.

'This is where you get out,' I said.

'But we're a mile from where I live!' Ghislaine protested.

'Yeah, I know,' I said. I turned in my seat, one elbow resting on the steering wheel. 'You could use the walk, Ghislaine. You need some time alone to get your head straight and think about how smart it is for you to try to jerk me around.'

Her coral lips opened slightly, in shock.

'I'm going to say this real loud and clear for the cheap seats: I don't explain to you how I do

346

my job, and you don't ask,' I said. 'You don't drop my name to get out of petty-theft busts, and you're never going to mention Cicero Ruiz again, not even to a meter reader. You forget that, and I'm going to make sure you end up in an agoraphobe's paradise.' I put my hand on the gearshift. 'Now get out.'

Ghislaine's lips tightened, but she climbed out of the car, her plastic bag rustling. She didn't close the door right away.

'I didn't know you were so hard up, Detective Pribek,' she said bitterly.

I reached over and pulled the door shut, put the car in gear. She yelled after me.

'If you dig crippled guys, Sarah, the Cities are full of white ones! *Why don't you just go down to the VA Hospital and pick yourself one out!*'

29

Several days passed. Comfortable now with Aidan's presence in the Hennessy home, I spent less time there, and my nights at home.

There, late at night, I found myself restless, surfing late-night TV. Occasionally, pausing on one of the educational channels, I'd see a show on forensics: techs observing the glow of Leuco Crystal Violet stains or peering at fibers under a microscope. I'd switch away quickly. Other than that, I kept my mind off Gray Diaz. Likewise Cicero Ruiz. My aborted letter to Shiloh remained buried under newspapers and unpaid bills. Work, in general, was uneventful.

One such workday ended with an errand out toward the lake country, reinterviewing a witness in an old case with leads sputtering out. On my way back, I passed a bus stop and a very familiar figure waiting there: Aidan Hennessy. I pulled over; he recognized my car and came to meet me.

'What's up?' He shielded his face against the setting sun.

In that moment, I was surprised to realize how much I liked him. Somehow, I'd gotten more comfortable with Aidan Hennessy than with anyone else in his family, which was remarkable, given how we'd started out. I'd spent much more time with Marlinchen, and I did like her, but I could never quite get comfortable around her. Her shifts in mood, her endless caution, always weighing her own words and those of people around her . . . Sometimes she made me tired. Aidan Hennessy was laconic, uncomplicated. More than anyone else in his family, he reminded me of myself.

'Thought you might need a ride,' I said, and Aidan climbed in.

'I'm not going home,' he told me. 'I'm going to the store. I promised to make dinner tonight, but I need a few things.'

'Okay,' I said. 'I can drop you off there, but I could also probably give you a ride to the store and then home, if you'll go downtown with me first. I've got to check in before I leave for the day.'

'Okay with me,' Aidan said. 'I'm not in a hurry.'

I accelerated, trying to slide onto the 394 in advance of a moving van traveling at a good clip. When I had, Aidan spoke again. 'I just got a job,' he said.

'No kidding?' I said. 'That's great. Where?'

'At a nursery. Of plants, not kids. It doesn't pay that great, but it'll help out at home.' He lifted his ponytail and shifted it to the other side of his neck, cooling the skin underneath.

We drove a few miles in silence. The rays of the lowering sun hit the windshield, which turned its new purplish color. 'You've got a weird haze on your windows,' Aidan said, rubbing it with his finger.

'I know,' I said.

'It's not coming off.' He was still worrying it.

'Don't bother,' I said. 'It's permanent.'

'You must really like this car,' he said.

I didn't say anything.

Downtown, Aidan went up in the elevator with me to the detective division. He didn't say anything while we were up there, but I saw him craning slightly to look around, perhaps surprised at how much it looked like any other office setting. I switched my voice mail over to forward to my pager and spoke briefly to Vang, then Aidan and I left.

At the store, he found what he needed: a cheap whole chicken, several potatoes, an onion. He also bought us each a Coke, and paid with money from the Hennessy household fund. Then we walked back outside, into the early-evening heat, and stopped in our tracks, looking around.

The Nova was nowhere to be seen. Out of laziness, not wanting to cruise the aisles for the nearest possible parking space, I'd simply parked at the edge of the lot. Now the car seemed to be gone.

'What the hell?' I said.

'There it is,' Aidan said.

He was pointing at a truck and horse trailer at the edge of the parking lot. I'd simply assumed that it was parked along the edge of the lot, with no other cars behind it. Now I saw, through the windows of the big Ram truck, a slice of the Nova's roof was visible.

'I think that guy's illegally parked,' I said. 'I don't think he's supposed to have a vehicle this long parked over two spaces. Maybe I should cite

350

him.' We were headed across the parking lot, toward the trailer.

'You have a citation book with you?' Aidan said skeptically.

'I'm an officer of the law,' I said as we circled around the rear of the horse trailer. 'Anything I write on will hold up in court. I think.'

'You *think*?' Aidan said, and snorted with laughter.

'Sure,' I said. 'Where's your receipt for the groceries? I'll — *Jesus!*'

I jumped, and a thin brown waterspout of Coke leapt from the can. A dog had sprung up from the bench seat of the pickup truck, barking and snarling, safely behind the closed window, but only inches from our faces.

'Holy shit,' I said. The Doberman continued to bark at us, its sharp-snouted face mashed up against the saliva-smeared glass, teeth bared. Then I got a good look at Aidan. He had dropped his bag of groceries and was half bent at the waist, his hands on his thighs as if for support.

'Are you okay?' I said.

'Yeah,' he said, nodding, his face pale. 'I'm all right.' He tried to laugh. 'I'm a real tough guy, eh? Scared of a dog locked in a truck.'

'It startled me, too,' I assured him.

He bent and picked up the grocery bag, taking a deep steadying breath as he did so. 'Let's go,' he said.

When we were out on the road, Aidan spoke again. 'I've just got a thing about dogs,' he said. 'Because of my hand.'

I nodded. 'Do you remember the day you lost your finger?' I asked him, steering us onto the highway. 'I mean, really remember it?'

'I have this snapshot image,' he said. 'I can see my hand with the finger half torn off, and the blood just starting to flow. The dog didn't take it off cleanly. It was semiattached, but I guess it wasn't . . . what's the word? Viable. So a doctor must have finished the job.'

Aidan checked to see if I was okay with this grisly story, and apparently I wasn't turning pale, because he went on.

'At the base of the finger, below the main wound, there was a separate tooth mark, I guess from where the dog gripped and let go before biting down again and taking the finger. In my memory, it's a dent, just starting to fill up with blood. Now it's a scar.' Aidan extended his left hand, slightly tilted, so I could see the pink mark just below the stump.

'What kind of dog was it?' I asked, returning my gaze to the highway.

'A pit bull, I think,' Aidan said. 'That's what I remember most, the white face with pointed-back ears.'

'Pit bulls just don't seem to fit with your neighborhood,' I said.

'Yeah,' he said. 'It's weird, I know.'

After a moment, I spoke again, asking Aidan what most likely seemed to him an unrelated question.

'When you lived in Georgia,' I said, 'what did you do for fun?'

'Fun?' Aidan said. 'Not a lot. There wasn't

much to do out where Pete lived.'

'Did you ever hunt?' I asked. 'Go target shooting?'

'Hunt, no,' he said. 'I went target shooting, once. We knocked cans off a fence.'

'How did it make you feel, handling a gun?' I asked.

'It was boring,' Aidan said, shrugging. 'Once I'd done it, I didn't feel like doing it again.'

'Did it make you nervous?' I asked.

'Not really,' he said. 'Why? Are you recruiting for the police academy?'

'No,' I said, shaking my head in amusement. 'My job isn't really about shooting, anyway. They make you learn to use the gun before they turn you loose with it, but if you're lucky, you never have to shoot anyone on the job. I never have.'

'I was going to say, you should be talking to Colm,' Aidan went on. 'I think he'd probably have about eight guns by now, if Hugh weren't so opposed to them.'

'Yeah,' I said. 'Colm mentioned that, about your father.'

The Hennessys were like a family viewed through a prism. Nothing lined up. Hugh loved his antique pistols and had kept them in his study; no, Hugh hated guns and wouldn't have one in his house. Marlinchen was afraid of loud noises, but Aidan wasn't scared of guns. On the other hand, he really *was* afraid of dogs. It didn't square with my theory about the study. I didn't know if I could make sense of it at all.

'What about you?' Aidan said, breaking into my thoughts. 'Did you ever hunt?'

'Me?' I said.

'Well, you grew up on the Range,' he said. 'Lots of people hunt and fish there.'

I shook my head. 'When I lived in New Mexico, for a while I was infatuated with my older brother's crossbow. Then I shot a deer with it. I can't even remember if it was deliberate or a whim or even just an accident, but I know after that I never wanted to hunt. Couldn't stand the idea.' I tucked a strand of hair behind my ear. 'But my anti-hunting morals don't run *that* deep. I mean, I eat meat.'

'Good,' Aidan said. 'You can stay for dinner, then.'

★ ★ ★

Aidan's meal — baked chicken and mashed potatoes with a green salad — was simple and satisfying, not quite as well seasoned as the dishes his twin sister prepared. At the table, the kids talked about final exams, summer coming, and their plans to visit their mother's grave on her upcoming birthday.

After we were done eating, Marlinchen said, 'Donal, maybe you want to go watch some TV? We're going to talk about some boring stuff.'

To a lot of kids, a phrase like that makes the radar go straight up; they know the truly interesting grown-up issues are going to be put on the table. But Donal accepted his sister's words at face value. He left.

When he'd gone, Marlinchen said, 'I talked to Ms. Andersen today, about Dad.'

354

I recognized the name, after a moment: I'd seen it on a bulletin board at Park Christian. She was the medical social worker in charge there.

'How is he?' Colm asked.

'Good,' she said. 'He's been steadily improving. You guys knew that. In fact, Ms. Andersen says he can live at home.'

Beside me, I felt Aidan shift in his chair, but he said nothing.

'He still needs physical therapy, and speech therapy,' she said. 'But all that can be done here. Ms. Andersen's going to help us with all those things. I agreed that we can move him home next week.'

'Wait a minute,' Aidan said. 'Just like that? This is something we need to talk about.'

'I would have discussed it with you guys before I said yes,' Marlinchen said, 'if we had any alternative. But we don't. Dad's insurance won't pay for his hospitalization if the hospital itself has recommended outpatient treatment.' She speared a stray piece of lettuce on her salad plate, but didn't eat. 'You know what the money situation is like. We can't pay for it ourselves.'

'Isn't physical and speech therapy and home care going to cost us, too?' Aidan pointed out.

Marlinchen straightened confidently. 'That's the thing,' she said. 'Dad's insurance is pretty good on paying for outpatient services like that. The therapists can even come out here. Home care is a little different. We won't have someone live in, but Dad's at moderate-assist level.' When no one seemed to know what that meant, she explained. 'That means he needs help with 50

355

percent or fewer of daily activities.'

If anyone was bothered by my presence at a family discussion, they didn't say so, and I made no move to get up.

'That'll improve as Dad keeps up with his rehab,' Marlinchen went on. 'It won't be a big deal, especially since there are five of us here with him. We'll all pitch in.'

'I won't,' Aidan said.

Marlinchen looked politely confused, as if she'd misheard.

'I've got a job,' Aidan said. 'I'll help with money. But I can't bring him his meals or sit with him and pretend . . . pretend that . . . '

Liam was looking down at the carpet, as if embarrassed. Colm's face was unreadable.

'Aidan,' Marlinchen said softly, pleading. For a brief, golden time, all had been right in her world. Aidan had returned, and her father was ready to come home. Now that façade was crumbling.

'What do you want from me, Linch?' Aidan asked. 'You want me to say it doesn't still bother me, or pretend it didn't happen?'

That was exactly what Marlinchen wanted. She wanted to lay psychological Astroturf over everything ugly.

'I know you have legitimate grievances,' she said. 'But Dad's had a stroke; he could have died. That changes people, profoundly. It might soften him, in a lot of ways.'

Could. Might. So much of what Marlinchen said was wishful, divorced from hard evidence.

'If you can just keep an open mind,' she went

356

on, 'I think maybe we've got a chance to start over here. All of us.'

Aidan shook his head. 'He won't change, and I won't share a home with him.'

'I don't understand,' she said. 'Where else could you live?'

'I'll live out there,' Aidan said, pointing to the detached garage.

'No, you won't,' Colm said, unexpectedly entering the conversation. 'That's my place. I'm not moving my things out to make space for you.'

'Colm, your workout space is hardly the issue here,' Marlinchen said.

'Yes, it is,' Colm said, and there was unexpected heat in his voice.

'Maybe I should be going,' I said, but no one seemed to hear it.

'If he doesn't want to help with Dad,' Colm went on, 'then he shouldn't even be here. And if he doesn't want to live with Dad, then he should — '

'Will you stop talking about your brother like he's — '

' — get his own goddamn apartment or something.'

' — not sitting right here!' Marlinchen finished.

'No!' Colm said. There were patches of red in his cheeks, like he'd been running in winter cold. 'He talks about Dad like that, like Dad's not even his father. He calls him 'Hugh.' If he doesn't want to help us — '

'He is helping!' Marlinchen interrupted. 'He's got a job, and — '

'Who cares about his fucking job!' Colm's voice rose yet higher. 'We don't need his money! We were doing fine!'

'*We?*' Marlinchen echoed. 'What do you do around here? How would you know? It's not you balancing Dad's checkbook. You're not clipping the coupons and buying the groceries!'

'Linch,' Aidan said, his voice low. 'Cool it.'

'I didn't ask him to come home! I don't care if he stays here or not!' Colm leapt up with a noisy backward scraping of his chair, and left. The room was so quiet in his wake that I could hear the ticking of the old Swiss clock, all the way from the living room, and then the start of a commercial from the family-room TV filled the silence.

'That went pretty well,' Liam said dryly.

Aidan pushed his chair back from the table and said quietly to Marlinchen, 'Yell at me if you have to, but I'm going to have a cigarette.'

Marlinchen shook her head numbly, meaning no, she wasn't going to lecture Aidan about smoking. He got up and left the table.

'I'll clear the dishes,' Liam said.

When it was just the two of us, Marlinchen wiped away a tear. 'I just don't get it,' she said. 'Aidan taught Colm how to swim. He taught him to catch. Colm used to want to *be* Aidan.'

I looked out through the window and saw Aidan, pacing on the back deck. He tipped his head back and exhaled smoke.

'Why don't you let me talk to Colm?' I said.

* * *

358

A dull thudding, like an irregular heartbeat, came from the other side of the garage wall. I heard it before I even opened the door.

Inside, the heavy bag that hung from the rafters was jumping steadily under the blows Colm was laying into it. He was still wearing the Adidas sweatpants he'd had on at dinner, but from the waist up had stripped to a narrow wife-beater undershirt, and his hands were protected by black bag gloves.

I wasn't a fight fan, but I knew enough to see that Colm was pretty good. He didn't make the amateur mistake of standing back from the bag, thinking the point was to strike with your arm extended as far as possible. He stood close in while throwing his hooks and uppercuts, getting his body weight into them. He didn't hyperextend on his jabs, either, so they were quick, like they should be.

'You want me to hold the bag for you?' I asked. His blows were hard enough to make the bag dance.

'I like to let it move,' Colm said. 'It simulates a real opponent, one that could evade you.' He moved back and aimed a roundhouse kick at the bag.

'It simulates an opponent with no arms who can't run away,' I pointed out.

Colm's eyes narrowed slightly at my words, and the uppercut he followed the kick with grazed the side of the bag instead of digging in. I stepped in to hold the bag, laying my hands on each side, about level with my shoulders. 'If the bag is still,' I said, 'it's easier

359

for you to work on your form.'

I was comfortable in gyms, and comfortable with guys who hung out in gyms. Colm and I probably had a lot in common, under the surface. It could so easily have been pleasant.

But Colm was scowling. He executed a powerful front kick, pushing hard through his heel. It was supposed to rock me backward, off my feet, and nearly did. It was only because I saw him set his feet, preparing for a powerful strike, that I knew what he was going to do and had leaned my full weight against the bag so he didn't dislodge me.

Colm shifted tactics and spun a high roundhouse kick into the bag, hitting my right hand, up where I thought I'd positioned it out of reach. It wasn't a hard strike. If he'd wanted to, he probably could have broken bones, since I wasn't wearing gloves. He was just showing me what he could have done, a point he underscored by not meeting my eyes afterward.

'You've got amazing flexibility,' I said. 'Have you thought about ballet instead?'

Irritated, he shifted back, to launch a kick even higher and strike my hand again. This time, I caught his heel and yanked. He lost his balance and fell.

'What's your problem?' Colm glared up at me.

'Do you ever think about what your father did to Aidan, when he was living here?' I asked, without preamble. 'The way he used to hurt him?'

Colm scrambled to his feet. 'Maybe Aidan deserved it!' he said. 'It didn't happen to any of us, just to him! Don't you think that's kind of weird? Don't you think he did something to deserve it?'

'Like what?' I said. 'Tell me what he did.'

A muscle worked near Colm's jaw; above that, his face was mottled with exertion and anger. 'I don't want to talk about this,' he said. He stalked to the door and out of the garage.

Another triumph by Sarah Pribek, the great communicator. Well, I'd started this. I couldn't leave it unfinished.

I found Colm sitting under the magnolia tree. He'd already taken his boxing gloves off and was starting on the flesh-colored wraps around his knuckles when I reached his side.

'If there was a Hennessy family crest,' I said, sitting down next to him, 'the motto on it would be, 'I don't want to talk about this.''

Against his will, a small, wry smile began to play at the corners of Colm's mouth. I realized how handsome he was when he smiled, and how rarely I'd witnessed it.

'Back there, in the garage,' I said, 'you were off-balance physically, and I knocked you over pretty easy. You were also off-balance emotionally, and I got you to walk out on me with two questions.'

Colm let the last of his right-hand wrap fall to the earth.

'You were off-balance because you were angry,' I said. 'Few things make us angrier than our own guilt.'

The half smile fled Colm's face, and there was

361

a guarded light in his eyes. 'What are you talking about?'

'When your brother and sister were hiding Aidan out in the garage, you were the one who turned him in to your father,' I said. 'You got him exiled back to Georgia. Before that, you let him take the blame for a window you broke. And when Liam and Marlinchen were expressing reservations about my arresting Aidan, you went and got my handcuffs.'

'I get it,' Colm said bitterly. 'I'm the asshole here.'

'No,' I said. 'But sometimes the hardest thing to forgive other people for is the wrongs *we've* done *them*. To protect yourself, you have to tell yourself that there must be something wrong with Aidan.'

Colm pulled up a handful of grass, which made a low *thrrip* sound as it came up, exposing black, loose soil.

'Something else, too,' I said. 'I think you're angry at Aidan for letting you down.'

Colm pulled up another small handful of grass. 'Saint Aidan?' he said sourly. 'The hero who came home to bring in another income and help Marlinchen take care of everyone? What could *he* have done?'

'He scared you,' I said.

Colm gave me a quizzical look.

'Years ago, you idolized him; he was everything you wanted to be. Then you saw him powerless before your father's rages. That was frightening. You couldn't blame your father; Hugh was the only parent you had. So you

362

switched sides. You agreed with your father on everything and aligned yourself with him, and you told yourself that there must be something wrong with Aidan, that your father treated him that way. Because if what was happening to Aidan wasn't his fault, then it could happen to anyone. Maybe to you.'

I saw the muscles of Colm's throat work. I wasn't expecting tears, but that uncomfortable stiffness in the throat, that was promising.

'Then you made yourself into a caricature of toughness,' I said. 'You wanted to be stronger than you'd ever thought Aidan was. But that wasn't the point. Aidan couldn't have solved the problem by being taller or stronger or faster or tougher. You know that.'

I tore up my own handful of grass, uncomfortable in the role of armchair psychologist. Between the two of us, Colm Hennessy and I would defoliate the whole patch of ground under his mother's beloved tree.

'I like fighting,' Colm said. 'Wrestling and boxing and weightlifting, I like those things for themselves, as sports.'

'I believe you,' I said. 'But they have their limits. If you want to feel better about Aidan being here, I think you need to go talk to him, instead of retreating into your gym with your heavy bag.'

'Yeah,' he said quietly. 'Yeah, okay.'

I felt relieved. I'd done what I'd come out here to do. Now I wanted out, before I said the wrong thing and undid it all. 'Come on,' I said. 'Let's go up.'

30

Dr. Leventhal, the department psychologist, was an approximately ninety-nine pound woman with lovely iron-gray curls and a very faint British accent long eroded by life in America. I'd never had the chance — or rather, the requirement — to work with her. So I was mildly surprised that she knew my name when I stuck my head in her door.

'Detective Pribek,' she said. 'You can come all the way in; I'm not busy.' She was impeccable in a pale-rose suit and a small gold Star of David around her neck, and even though I was in clothes and boots suitable for the job, I suddenly felt as rumpled as a bloodhound.

'I only wanted to ask you a quick question,' I said. 'I don't really need anything.'

'Please go ahead,' she said. 'I'll help if I can.'

'Let me run a hypothetical situation by you,' I said. 'If someone was told repeatedly, from the age of three or four, that he'd been badly bitten by a dog at that age — even if it never happened — could he develop a vivid memory of the incident? One that's almost visual?'

Since she was a psychologist, I was expecting a wordy and inconclusive answer. I was wrong.

'Yes,' Dr. Leventhal said. 'It helps that the child in question is so young. Age three to four is generally accorded to be the threshold of recall. But even adults have been known to fabricate

364

memories when psychologists encourage them to.'

'Why would a psychologist encourage that?' I asked.

'For a study,' she said. 'Sometimes a subject's brother or sister is called upon to prompt the subject to remember a 'childhood event' that never happened. Under those circumstances, the individuals being studied tend to agree the event took place, and some even add details that they 'remember.'' She paused. 'A subject's likelihood of doing this depends somewhat on how imaginative or credulous they are. Significant also is who's trying to convince them: an older sibling's word is more likely to have the ring of authority than a younger sibling's. Who's doing the persuading in your case?'

'A parent,' I said.

'That would definitely qualify,' she said. 'Memory can be the servant of emotional needs. If a child had a strong desire to believe what he or she had been told, then certainly, he or she could construct a memory and develop a related fear.' Dr. Leventhal uncrossed and recrossed her legs. 'I should have asked you, did the child in question have any sort of help from a hypnotherapist in sorting out his memories?'

I shook my head. 'Is that a bad thing?'

'Well, improperly practiced hypnotherapy has been implicated in the construction of false memories. Most often, we see that from therapists who specialize in sexual abuse. When the patient wants to 'please' the practitioner, often she'll agree to leading questions under hypnosis: for example, 'Is there someone else in the room with you?''

'Not this time,' I said. 'This boy didn't have any therapy at all.'

Dr. Leventhal nodded. 'I don't mean to denigrate hypnosis altogether, but there's still so much we don't understand about it. Or about memory, for that matter. It's a truly amazing field. Do you know what a screen memory is?'

I shook my head.

'Psychologists don't always quite agree on the definition, or on how common it is,' she said. 'But at its core, a screen memory is a defense mechanism. Some patients who have been through traumas can't remember them at first. They remember simpler, more acceptable events.'

'Like what?' I said, interested despite myself.

'For example, a patient might say, 'I looked out the window and saw a pair of crows in my neighbor's yard,' when in fact she saw a man beating a woman. The mind replaces an unacceptable image with an acceptable one. A screen.'

I must have looked amazed, because she smiled. 'The mind is very powerful in its own defense,' she said.

'That's fascinating,' I said.

'I can tell you're interested,' she agreed, 'because when we started talking, you were hanging back in my doorway, and now you're halfway to my desk.'

I realized it was true.

'You seem quite skittish in here, Detective

366

Pribek,' she said. 'I assure you, I don't strap people into one of my chairs and force them to discuss their childhoods.'

'Well, that's good,' I said. 'You'd be bored with recollections of my personal life. I had a pretty dull childhood.'

'It's a common misconception that psychologists are only interested in the abnormal,' she said. 'Healthy minds are often as fascinating as troubled ones.' Then she tilted her head slightly. 'I wonder, though, if you're being entirely honest with me when you call your growing-up years boring.'

'Well,' I said lightly, 'I don't remember seeing any crows, if that's what you mean.'

★ ★ ★

A co-worker's unexpectedly bad summer cold forced me into the slot of on-call detective two nights in a row, and I didn't visit the Hennessy place either of those evenings. On the third day I glanced at the calendar, wondering why the date seemed to stick in my memory. After a moment it came to me: today was Marlinchen and Aidan's eighteenth birthday.

The summer solstice was less than a week away, and the day was still bright as midafternoon when I drove out after work, parked, and went up to the French doors. Normally, Marlinchen was making dinner at this hour, but the kitchen was empty. Some pots and utensils were out on the counters, but no one was to be seen. I went around to the front door and knocked.

When Marlinchen opened the door, she looked years older than her age, wearing a silky cinnamon-colored shirt and a straight black skirt. Before I could comment on that, though, or she could speak, I noticed something else.

The Hennessys had never, in the time I'd known them, used the formal dining room. Generally, the kids ate at the kitchen table, where I'd first looked for them tonight. But now the family was grouped around the long table in the dining room. A pair of candles glowed between serving dishes, and faces turned to look at me.

The long and lanky form of Aidan, though, was not among them. Instead, at the head of the table, light gleamed off the metal of a cane that leaned against the chair. I lifted my gaze and met the pale-blue eyes of Hugh Hennessy.

'Sarah,' Marlinchen said, her voice light and surprised.

'Hey,' I said awkwardly. 'I didn't realize you'd be eating this early.'

'An earlier dinnertime is better for Dad,' Marlinchen said. 'He's tired from the move home, this afternoon.'

From his place about eighteen feet away, Hugh was still watching his daughter and me. He probably couldn't hear us, but even so, I felt uncomfortable, and moved away from the open door. Marlinchen, being polite, followed me outside.

'I didn't expect to see your father home quite this soon,' I said.

'We did the conservatorship paperwork this afternoon,' Marlinchen said, 'and I signed him out. That's why we're celebrating tonight. The birthdays and Dad being home.'

'I'm in awe,' I said. 'When do you run for the state legislature?'

Marlinchen laughed, pleased. 'All of this is thanks to you,' she said. 'Do you want to come in and join us? We've got plenty of food to share.'

'No,' I said. 'No, that's all right.'

'Are you sure?' Marlinchen said.

They were obviously halfway through their dinner already, but that was only partly the root of my refusal. Something about the scene — the family together, the way Hugh watched me silently from his place at the head of the table . . . Things had changed. The circle had closed, and I was an outsider.

'I'm sure,' I said. 'Thanks for the offer.'

'Well, thanks for coming by,' Marlinchen said. 'Really, I can never thank you enough for what you've done.'

It was impossible to miss the note of valediction in her voice. *It's been great knowing you*, it said.

★ ★ ★

Gravel crunched under my boots as I walked not to my car but toward the detached garage, the current living quarters of Aidan Hennessy.

I wished I fully understood my discomfort with Hugh. I'd spent plenty of time around individuals who had done a lot worse than

369

mistreat their children. Why, then, did Hugh's baleful blue gaze have such an effect on me? It was as if he knew what I knew about him. I had to be imagining it, I thought, the idea that his cold stare said, *My family is none of your business. Leave us alone. The past is the past.*

The door to the garage was open. I knocked on the frame and looked inside. What I saw surprised me. Aidan was working on the old BMW. Its hood was raised, and a drop light glowed over the engine. He looked up at the sound of my knock.

'Happy birthday,' I said.

'Hey,' he said. 'Come on in.'

I did. 'What are you doing, there?' I asked him.

'This is the ultimate project car,' Aidan said, looking not unhappy at the challenge. 'It hasn't been run in fourteen years.'

'Fourteen?' I repeated.

'That's what Linch says. She's got access to all Hugh's records.' He ran a hand along the roof. 'I may be in over my head. I'm going to have to drain the fuel line. I can't even list it all yet, everything it's going to need.' He shrugged. 'But what a great car it'll make for Marlinchen, when it's finally done. She hates that Suburban.'

I peered through a window at the interior, just as I'd done the night of Aidan's return, when I'd checked out the property.

'It's fairly clean inside,' he said. 'Except the spiderwebs.'

He was right. I saw nothing unusual, the leather seats not torn or damaged.

370

'Where'd you learn mechanics?' I asked.

'I was always interested in cars,' Aidan said. 'Most of it, though, I learned in Georgia. Pete had farm equipment, and an old truck I used to work on.'

'Useful skill,' I said. 'But it might be better for you to buy a secondhand car that runs, rather than count on fully rehabbing this one.'

'Maybe,' he said. Straightening, Aidan went to a nearby shelf. Among the tools lay his pack of cigarettes and lighter. He took one out, flicked the lighter, and ignited the slender white cylinder.

I took the opportunity to look around. The setup inside the garage had changed. At the far end, Colm's heavy bag still hung from the rafters, but the weight bench had been moved out to make room for a cot, which was covered with a motley assortment of blankets. Nearby, a cardboard chest of drawers had been set up, with a single photograph in a frame atop it. Overhead, a bare bulb illuminated the whole place.

'Does it bother you,' I asked Aidan, 'being exiled out here?'

Aidan hesitated before speaking. 'Hugh gets kind of weird when he sees me. Like he did at the hospital,' he said. 'Otherwise, no; I like having my own space. Don't forget, it was me who didn't want to spend a lot of time around him.' Aidan tapped ash into a Mason-jar lid he was using for an ashtray. 'Besides, it's not like I can't be in the house. I just have to stay downstairs. Hugh doesn't do the stairs very well with his cane, so he's going to be upstairs a lot.

At least for a while.'

'I see,' I said.

It was hardly an ideal arrangement, but more and more I was coming to understand what Judge Henderson had told me: you can't dictate how families order their affairs, or run their lives.

The framed photo on the dresser caught my eye; I gave it a closer look. In it, Elisabeth Hennessy sat under her magnolia tree, holding a boy of about two or three on her lap. His hair was lighter even than hers, and I doubted very much he was Liam or Colm.

'Is that you with your mother?' I asked him.

'Yes,' Aidan said.

'It's the photo you and your dad fought about?' I asked.

'Yeah, it is,' he said.

'If you don't mind my asking,' I said, 'where'd you hide it, that Hugh never found it?'

Aidan smiled. 'With Aunt Brigitte,' he said. 'I mailed it to her that same day, and she held on to it for me.'

He'd carried it with him thereafter, even on the streets as a runaway. His reverence for his mother was palpable, and I thought that Hugh had been perceptive, if cruel, the day he'd banished Aidan from a visit to Elisabeth's grave.

'Your mother's birthday is coming up, isn't it?' I said. The kids had mentioned it, the last time I'd eaten dinner with them.

Aidan nodded. 'Sunday,' he said. 'We're probably all going out there.'

Taking out my billfold, I fished my card from it. 'Listen, I've got to go,' I said. 'I know

372

Marlinchen has these phone numbers, but now you'll have them too, in case you ever need anything.'

'You're not going to be around anymore?' Aidan asked.

I smiled ruefully. 'I seem to have become obsolete.'

And indeed, as I pulled down the long driveway, I watched the old weather-beaten house fall away in my rearview mirror as if it were for the last time.

* * *

But when I slept that night, I dreamed that Hennepin County had put Hugh Hennessy on trial, on the condition that I would be his prosecutor. In court, I stood to do my cross-examination.

Mr. Hennessy, I said, *please tell the court what happened in your study on the night in question.*

I saw a pair of crows, Hugh said.

That wasn't the response I'd expected. *Could you please restate your answer?* I said.

Lightning struck the house, he said.

Someone among the spectators snickered. The judge said, *Control your witness, Counsel.*

But Hugh would not stop. *It was a pit bull,* he said. *I saw a pair of crows. Lightning struck the house. I saw a pair of crows. I saw a pair of crows. I saw a pair of crows.*

31

At the cemetery where the Hennessy children's mother was buried, a marble angel stood guard over the headstone, either serenely reflecting or grieving. Below, the stone read, *Elisabeth Hannelore Hennessy, Beloved Wife and Mother.*

It was a bright Sunday afternoon, and I was sitting at the graveyard's highest point, a mausoleum with a half flight of stone stairs leading up to it. Two pine trees offered shade from the western sun, and it was here that I'd staked out a spot to watch Elisabeth's grave and wait for the visitor I hoped was coming on the anniversary of her birth.

For the past two days, I'd tried to put the Hennessys out of my mind. Early on, when Marlinchen had come to visit me, asking for help I'd thought I couldn't provide, all I'd wanted was to be shed of these people. Now Marlinchen, the official head of her household, had given me leave to forget about them, and I couldn't. I was maddened by a contradiction that I couldn't resolve.

Dr. Leventhal had supported the idea that a young child's mind could be so malleable that it would fabricate a memory, even a visual one. But the detail in Aidan's story was so realistic: *the finger was just barely attached . . . blood was dripping off it.* From the little individual tooth mark he'd seen, filling up with blood, to the fact that his finger hadn't quite been severed — it was *You Are There*, documentary realism.

Somehow, I didn't think Aidan would be able to conjure such a detailed, lurid image of his injured hand. He didn't seem that imaginative to me. It was one of the things I liked about him, that he was simple and straightforward. I wasn't the world's biggest fan of hidden depths. Shiloh had plenty of them, and they'd ended up ruining his life.

Besides, to fabricate a memory was one thing, but a fear? Aidan was truly afraid of dogs. That indicated my theory, about the study and the loaded pistol, was wrong. I could deal with that. I'm semipro at being wrong; it's a correctable situation. That wasn't the problem. The problem was Marlinchen and her memory of what she thought was a lightning strike, but sounded to me like an accidental shooting in the house. A memory Aidan didn't share. Either Marlinchen was mistaken, or Aidan himself was, and yet they both seemed convincing when they told their stories.

Then there was the old BMW. Hugh had locked it away for fourteen years. It fit in the same time frame as the carpet replacement in the study and Aidan and Marlinchen's mismatched early memories. It was one more thing that occupied that fourteen-years-ago plateau. The threshold, as Dr. Leventhal had called it.

My first idea was that Hugh had put the car away because Aidan had bled copiously in it, and unlike the study, Hugh couldn't get it properly cleaned up. But if Aidan shot himself in the hand, the universal first instinct would be to wrap the hand in a towel and keep pressure on it. Certainly it would have bled, but I couldn't see it bleeding so much that Hugh couldn't clean it up. And had he believed that someday someone would examine his car, looking for evidence that his son's accident didn't happen the way Hugh had said it happened? I'd seen some paranoia in my day, but that seemed outlandish.

It wasn't impossible, though. The problem was that I knew so little of Hugh's character. I couldn't talk with him, and there were limits to what his children could explain.

What I really needed was the memories of an adult who'd been close to the Hennessys early in their marriage. One who'd known Hugh and Elisabeth well during that time of their lives. One who, like Aidan, had been banished from the Hennessy home. Whose banishment, like everything else, had happened on that fourteen-years-ago threshold.

It was two hours later when he came, a tall, thin man heading up the path, toward Elisabeth Hennessy's grave, holding a small bunch of white narcissus in his hands. Time had changed J. D. Campion little. His black hair was still long enough to be caught back in a small ponytail on his neck, and he still wore a beard. There was no gray in either. The flowers he slipped into the recessed holder were wrapped in the clear cellophane that florists provide.

Campion had good hearing. He turned to watch me coming while I was still ten feet off.

'Mr. Campion,' I said. 'My name is Sarah Pribek,' I said. 'I'm a friend of Marlinchen Hennessy.'

'Marlinchen?' he said, surprised. 'Then you know Hugh?' he said.

'Not exactly,' I said. 'I'd like to talk to you.'

'You've been waiting for me here?' he asked.

I acknowledged it. 'You're hard to track down otherwise. I tried to find you through your publisher and phone listings, but I didn't have any luck.'

Campion watched a pair of squirrels fight over a perch high in a tree. 'That seems like a lot of planning just to meet me,' he said, slowly. 'You're not here to talk about Vedic references in *Turning Shadow*, are you?'

'No,' I said. 'I'm not.'

'So how is it that you know Marlinchen, but not Hugh?' he said.

'I met Marlinchen only recently,' I explained. 'Hugh had a serious stroke two months ago.'

'I didn't read about that,' he said.

'It wasn't in the news,' I said.

'How bad is it?' Campion said.

If I satisfied his curiosity right here, I'd give up an incentive for him to talk with me. 'I'll tell you all about it,' I said, 'but I was hoping we could talk someplace more' — *private* wasn't the word, as no one was within earshot — 'comfortable.'

Campion didn't bite right away. 'I'm sorry,' he said, 'but I don't really understand who you are.'

'I'm a Hennepin County Sheriff's detective,' I said, 'but this isn't an official investigation. I'm helping Marlinchen with a family situation.' I

377

looked down the hill, to where I'd parked. 'Like I said, I'd like to talk to you about it, but this might not be the place.'

'Maybe not,' Campion said. 'Would you have a problem with a bar?'

★ ★ ★

I'd been curious what sort of drink a poet might order in a bar. The answer wasn't very exciting: Budweiser. I had a Heineken to keep him company. We sat at a table near the back of the bar, next to a pair of unoccupied pool tables.

In my line of work, you usually have the luxury of saying, *I'm asking the questions here*, even if you don't have to say it in so many words. Either you're interrogating suspects who are under arrest, or you're interviewing witnesses who are intimidated by the gravity of the situation they've gotten involved in. In those situations, the answers generally flow one way, toward you.

With Campion, I had to give information to get information. It wasn't that he was unfriendly. But he hadn't been in contact with the Hennessy family for nearly fifteen years. He wouldn't even understand the questions I was asking until I explained a few things about the Hennessys' situation. Nor, I thought, would he be inclined to. He didn't know me, and he only had my word that I was here on Marlinchen's behalf.

I told Campion about Hugh's stroke, Marlinchen's quest to find her brother, and Aidan's return, keeping quiet only about Hugh's child abuse. When I was done, Campion said, 'It's been fourteen years. I don't know what I can tell you that'll help.'

'Tell me about fourteen years ago.' I drank a little of my Heineken. 'What'd you and Hugh Hennessy fight about?'

'I don't know,' Campion told me.

'Of course you know,' I said levelly. Campion didn't seem the type to be offended by straight talk. 'Friendships don't break up permanently for no reason.'

'You'll have to ask Hugh, when he's better,' Campion said. 'I know how it sounds, but to this day, I don't know what he was so angry about.'

'Tell me how it happened,' I said.

He settled back in his chair. 'I was on the road a lot back then. Minnesota was like a home base for me, because Hugh and Elisabeth were here.' He drank. 'One night, I got into town late and went by their place. I hadn't seen them in about four months. When I got there, Hugh wouldn't let me in.' Campion shook his head, as if freshly baffled. 'He said I was a bad influence on his kids, I'd always been jealous of his success, and he didn't want me coming around anymore. Then he shut the door and didn't open it again.'

'And then what?' I asked.

'I left,' Campion said. 'I wasn't going to mope at the door, like a dog who'd been bad. I called him a few days later, to see if he'd gotten over whatever it was. He told me not to call again, and hung up on me.'

'Did you ever talk to Elisabeth?' I asked.

'No. I tried, but she never answered the phone. It was always Hugh.'

'Do you think Elisabeth was at the root of Hugh's anger?' I asked. 'Was he jealous?'

Campion stiffened, as if about to take offense. Then he relaxed a little. 'I guess when a guy's bringing flowers to a woman's grave ten years after she died, it's not a big secret he's hung up on her,' he admitted. 'But Elisabeth made her choice, and I respected that. And she would never have been unfaithful to him. Hugh *knew* that.'

Campion shook his head again, as if letting go of a mystery that would never be solved. He drained the last of his beer.

After getting us another round, I asked, 'If it wasn't about Elisabeth, could it have been about her sister?'

'Brigitte?' Campion said. 'What about her?'

'You had a relationship with Brigitte, didn't you?'

'It didn't last, but yeah, I did.'

'Hugh didn't seem to like her. She never visited the family or vice versa.'

Campion tilted his head, thinking. 'You have to understand,' he said slowly, 'that Hugh was a rigid guy. Morally rigid. Brigitte did some drugs; she did some guys. Hugh didn't like that. In contrast, he and Elisabeth were married at 19. That was almost medieval, for the times.'

'I know,' I said. 'If Hugh disapproved of her so much, why do you suppose he'd send Aidan to live with her?'

Campion frowned. 'I have no idea,' he said. 'You're asking me to make a guess, and I've already proven I don't understand what makes

Hugh Hennessy tick.' He watched as a woman in her early twenties, with brilliant coppery hair, half jumped onto the bar and kissed the bartender hello, supporting herself with the heels of her hands. 'I'm more surprised that Gitte would have taken the kid in. She never had much money, and she was a single mother herself by then.'

I had been lifting my glass toward my mouth, and stopped midway. 'Really?' I said. Aidan hadn't mentioned living with a cousin.

Campion nodded. 'She let me stay at her place once, several years after we had our quick, flame-out affair. She had — it's a dated term, but I thought of this guy as her common-law husband.'

It was an old-fashioned term, one that some of the grizzled veterans used around the squad room, as common in its day as *baby mama* is now. Generally, it was used in describing the affairs of slum dwellers whose idea of couples counseling involved frying pans or screaming matches. Campion didn't sound like he meant it that way.

'You know how some people are really *together*, even when they're not married? You can just tell it's a serious thing?' he said.

I nodded.

'That was her and Paul. I forget his last name. Something French. They were obviously good for each other.'

'Well, they couldn't have been *that* good together,' I pointed out, 'if she was a single mother years later.'

Campion shook his head at my assumption. 'Paul never left her. He died.' His voice dropped a little lower. 'I was there.'

I wasn't prompting him at all, by this point. There was a story inside him that wanted to come out.

'Paul wasn't threatened by an old flame, so when I came to visit, I planned to stay for a week,' Campion said. 'They'd been living together for three years. Gitte was happy. Paul did something in construction. God, he was a big guy. Maybe six-four, and tough. But a good guy. Thought the world of Gitte and the kid. Their son, Jacob, was two years old.

'Toward the end of the week, I went out drinking with Paul. We went to this bar he liked, a real bucket of blood. I've been in some bars in my day, and even so, I was glad to have Paul at my side. We were fine until Gitte's neighbors came in. These guys — I don't use this kind of language lightly, but trust me, I'm a word-smith — these guys were douche bags.'

I smiled to let him know I wasn't offended.

'Gitte's neighbors raised pit bulls to fight,' Campion said. 'The dogs scared the hell out of Gitte, not just for her sake, but for Jacob's. She wanted the neighbors to pay their share of a better fence between the two yards, but these guys' attitude was 'You want the fence, you pay the whole nickel.'

'Paul was willing to ignore them that afternoon, but they starting getting in his face, making remarks about Gitte. Then it was on. Half the bar jumped into the fight. Me included.

382

I'm not much of a fighter, but Paul was my drinking buddy at the time. Them's the rules, you know?'

'I know,' I said.

'I got my clock cleaned fairly early, but Paul ... I've never seen anyone fight quite like that. The thing is, he looked happy. Incandescent.' Campion shook his head, remembering. 'It took four cops to subdue him and get him into the squad car. I walked outside after them. They left Paul to sit there while they mopped up the rest of the fight. But as soon as Paul was in the backseat, he put his head down, against the window, and closed his eyes, like all the fight had gone out of him. Like he was at peace.' Campion paused. 'The cops didn't question it either.'

'Question what?' I said.

'He was dead,' Campion said. 'When they got to the police station, he didn't have a pulse. It was one of those rare, undetected heart conditions, the kind that sometimes makes an athlete drop right after a race. Some lawyers called Gitte afterward, talking about a negligence suit against the cops, but it wasn't the cops' fault, and she knew it.' Campion sipped a little more beer. 'I stayed around another month afterward, with her and the little boy, Jacob. I wanted to help out. But I wasn't Paul, and Gitte and I weren't suited for each other. We'd been down that road before. I moved on.' He shook his head. 'I'll never forget that afternoon, though. I remember walking out of the bar after Paul

and the cops, and the sun was setting, and I
was standing in that dirt parking lot, and Paul
just laid his head down and died. I've always
wanted to write about it, but I've never been
able to.'

32

At eight-thirty Monday morning, I was waiting outside Christian Kilander's office. It was my day off, and I'd dressed for it, in old Levi's and a loose cream-colored shirt that belonged to Shiloh. Seeing me at his door so early, Kilander arched an eyebrow. 'To what do I owe this honor?' he said.

'I already owe you a favor,' I told him, 'but I need another one. You did law school and your first clerk's job in Illinois, right?'

'I knew putting my résumé on file was a bad idea,' he said, balancing coffee and his briefcase in the same hand while he unlocked his door.

I followed him inside. 'You've still got contacts down there, right?' Kilander was a master networker; I doubted he'd let any useful association grow too much moss.

He set his briefcase down on the credenza and his coffee on the desk. 'I see where this is going,' he said. 'What do you need, and from whom?'

'Vital records, from Rockford,' I said.

'You know those are public,' Kilander said. 'You don't need to pull strings. Just call and ask.'

'Or I could just call Dial-a-Prayer,' I said.

Government records — birth and death certificates, marriage licenses and decrees of divorce, property records, school enrollments — are documents of public record. They also frequently get misfiled. Or names are misspelled.

Or the computer is down. It's best if you can hunt for what you need in person, taking your time and employing all your patience.

If you can't be there, you need someone who can go the extra mile to help you, someone who recognizes your voice on the phone. If not, you're condemned to a day of sincere disembodied voices. *I'm sorry, sir, I'm sorry, ma'am, we don't have that information. There's nothing I can do.*

The bottom line: if you want to be able to say you tried, you can call an anonymous clerk. If you really want the information, you find a personal connection.

'All right, kid,' Kilander said. 'What are you looking for?'

'Birth, death, school, change-of-name . . . I'm not sure exactly what I need.'

'So you're trawling, not spearfishing,' he said. 'Okay, I'll dig up a couple of phone numbers. In fact, I'll make a few calls, to get you started.' He sat behind his desk, flipped through a Rolodex, spoke without looking up. 'Is it casual day over at the detective division?'

'No,' I said. 'It's my day off.'

*   *   *

I staked out an empty conference room and spent the day making follow-up and return phone calls to Rockford. When my cell rang at 4:25 in the afternoon, I was expecting another call from Illinois. That was why I couldn't place the masculine voice on the other end. 'Detective Pribek?'

'Speaking,' I said.

'This is Gray Diaz. I know it's your day off, but I was wondering if I could have a few moments of your time today. I'd need you to come downtown.'

The BCA. The tests were back.

'That's fine,' I said slowly. 'Where are you? I'm downtown right now.'

★ ★ ★

Diaz had made himself fairly comfortable in the office of a vacationing prosecutor, Jane O'Malley. He'd spread out his materials on her desk, so that pictures of her two children and her nephews and nieces looked out over the Royce Stewart paperwork.

'Thank you for coming,' he said. 'Please, have a seat.'

O'Malley had good wide armchairs she'd bought herself, low and soft, that guests sank deeply into. I was familiar enough with them to know that they'd be too comfortable to be comfortable, particularly if Diaz continued to stand, thus towering over me. I settled onto the arm of the chair, a half-standing position, instead.

There was a beat while Diaz accepted this. Then he walked over to the window and looked out, although I doubted he was really looking at anything.

'Sarah,' he said, 'I haven't told you anything

387

about myself.' Pause. 'I came to work in Blue Earth because my father-in-law is ill. My wife doesn't want him to have to move, at his age. He's lived in that town nearly all his life. He'd probably stroke out from the stress of packing everything up and moving out of his farmhouse. You know?'

'I know,' I said.

'I'd much rather be up here, working with you guys, in Hennepin County.' He paused. 'If I were, you and I would be colleagues, Sarah. We could have been working cases together.' He turned from the window. 'I wish that were the situation here. I wish I didn't have to meet you under these circumstances.'

'So do I,' I said.

'Because of that,' Diaz said, 'because we're virtually colleagues, I want to give you an opportunity. I'm getting close to the end of my work here.'

I said nothing. Diaz walked over to stand between me and O'Malley's desk.

'When I first interviewed you, Sarah, I asked you if there was any reason someone might have seen you outside Stewart's house the night he died. You said no.'

'I remember,' I said.

Diaz sat on the edge of the desk, like a teacher having an informal moment with a student after class. 'I'm asking you now,' he said, 'would you like to reconsider your answer?'

Don't hesitate here. 'No,' I said. 'I wouldn't.'

Diaz looked away, toward the window, then back at me. 'We found blood in the carpeting of your car,' he said. 'There's also a diagonal groove in your right rear tire, damage caused by something it ran over. It's as distinctive as a fingerprint.'

I didn't say anything, but felt the muscles in my throat work, swallowing involuntarily.

'Sarah, I know what Royce Stewart did to your partner's daughter. I know that the night Stewart died, you believed your husband was dead and that Shorty had an opportunity to help him and didn't. There are highly, highly extenuating circumstances here.' He leaned forward until his half-folded hands almost touched mine. 'I'm familiar with your record. I know you're a good cop, Sarah, and I want to help you. But we've come to the point where you need to tell me what happened that night. If you don't come out and meet me halfway, I can't help you.'

In that moment, I wanted to tell Diaz the truth, and for the worst of all reasons. Not because I feared what would happen to me if I continued to obstruct justice, as I had been doing since that night in Blue Earth. Not because he had forensic evidence that might convict me whether or not Genevieve returned to confess. I wanted to tell him solely because I wanted so badly to believe what Gray Diaz was telling me with his words and tone and posture: that he wanted to help me.

I cleared my throat. 'I'm sorry, Gray,' I said. 'I have nothing further to add to what I've already told you.'

Diaz sighed. 'I'm sorry, too, Detective Pribek,' he said, standing. 'I'll be in touch.'

Back in the conference room, I couldn't remember what I'd been doing before. I looked at my notes, and they made no sense to me.

'Are you all right?'

I hadn't heard Christian Kilander come in. 'I'm fine,' I said, turning from the window.

I wasn't lying. Calm had settled on me unexpectedly, and I understood why. Gray Diaz had made it pretty clear that this was my last chance to level with him. Maybe I should have taken it, but now it was too late. First-time skydivers must feel this way, just after they jump. There are a dozen chances to back out of a dive, but once they've stepped out into the air, they're committed. Whatever happened, safe landing or bloody impact, the weight of decision was off their shoulders. Like them, I'd made my choice. Whatever happened from here on was out of my hands.

Kilander held out a fax. 'This came for you, from Rockford,' he said.

I took it from his hand. *Certificate of Live Birth*, it read at the top.

'Sorry there wasn't anything else,' Kilander said.

'No, that's okay,' I said, still scanning the text. 'Sometimes one thing is all you need.'

★ ★ ★

In retrospect, it might have been better if I'd taken some time to think, to sleep on what I'd learned. But I didn't. At five-thirty that evening, I drove out to the lake.

The weather really was beautiful, a sunny day without a hint of the humid gray scrim that takes the bloom off many of Minnesota's summer days. I wasn't surprised that the Hennessy kids were outdoors on this bright evening.

All four boys had divided up for a football game by the lake. It was an oddly matched game, but probably the best they could do: Aidan and Liam against Colm and Donal. Above them, Marlinchen presided over a grill on the porch, painting sauce onto chicken breasts and wings. She was wearing a white T-back tank shirt, cutoffs, and sunglasses with a copper-wire frame and greenish-silver mirrored lenses, a Discman on her hip. When she saw me, Marlinchen pulled the earphones off her head, to rest around her neck. 'Sarah!' she said, looking pleased. 'We're having a little barbecue to celebrate school being out. We'll probably have plenty to spare, if you can wait.'

She seemed in excellent spirits. That was going to change.

'I'm afraid I'm here on business,' I said.

'What kind of business?' she said.

'Your father has limited ability to answer yes-and-no questions, right?' I said. 'That's how you did the conservatorship hearing, as I understand it.'

Marlinchen glanced immediately up at the high window. 'Dad's resting right now,' she said. 'What's this about?'

'I need to ask some questions only he can

answer,' I said. 'About your cousin, Jacob Candeleur.'

'I don't have a cousin named Jacob,' she said. 'We don't have any cousins, period.'

I took the birth certificate from my shoulder and gave it to Marlinchen. I saw Marlinchen absorb the names: Jacob, Paul, Brigitte.

'See the birth date?' I said. 'He and you and Aidan were born only months apart.'

'How bizarre,' she said. Puzzlement had washed away the polite anxiety in her voice. 'I never met him.'

'Your father didn't like your aunt Brigitte, and kept her away from his children,' I said. 'But it isn't true that you never met your cousin Jacob. You grew up with him. He became your closest friend.'

'What are you saying?' But Marlinchen was beginning to understand. Her eyes went to the tall blond boy beneath us, who was letting Donal outrun him for a touchdown.

'That's not your brother Aidan down there,' I said. 'It's your cousin, Jacob. Your father didn't give him away to Brigitte when he was 12,' I said. 'He gave him *back*. Aidan, I mean Jacob, said that Brigitte was affectionate and clingy, as if she'd always wanted to be a mother. And she *did*. To her own son.'

Marlinchen took off her sunglasses to make eye contact. 'Is this some kind of a sick joke?' she asked. She enunciated as if speaking to a child. 'There's a rather gaping hole in your theory, you know. If that's Jacob, where is the real Aidan?'

This was the hard part. 'If I had to guess,' I

said, 'I'd say he's buried under the magnolia tree.' I pointed. 'I think he shot himself with your father's gun, fourteen years ago, and your father buried him under your mother's favorite tree. The choice of burial site was probably a misguided way of comforting her.'

'No,' Marlinchen said.

'You have memories of it: a loud noise, your mother being upset and sleeping in the same bed with you that night. For comfort.'

'It was a storm that upset her,' Marlinchen said.

'No,' I said. 'You all say your father didn't have any interest in cars or home improvement. Yet he laid the new carpet in the study himself, and he's held on to a car for fourteen years saying he might fix it up someday. Fourteen years, Marlinchen.'

'What's your point?'

'When Aidan shot himself, your father rushed him to the hospital in that car. The carpet in the study he simply replaced, because it was soaked in blood. The smaller splashes, in the hall carpet, he scrubbed out with bleach. But the car, where Aidan lost most of his blood? He couldn't ever fully clean that up. That's why he was afraid to ever get rid of the car. Afraid that a buyer might find remnants of blood, under the seats, in the carpet and floorboards. Ditching the BMW and claiming it was stolen would only have made it worse; it would have made the car of interest to the police if it was ever found. No, the safest thing was to clean it up as best he could and lock it away on his own property.'

Marlinchen glanced at the garage, but only quickly.

'None of those cover-up methods was particularly adept,' I said, 'but they didn't have to be. As long as Hugh didn't sell the house or the car, no one would ever get a close look at what evidence remained.' *Until now*, I thought. 'Hugh replaced Aidan with his sister-in-law's son,' I went on. 'I don't know how he persuaded her. Maybe he played on her concern for her grieving sister. Maybe he paid her off; Brigitte was poor, and a single mother. It could be that she thought Jacob would have a better life with her older sister and Hugh. But if she hadn't gone along with it, imagine the consequences. Hugh's career would have been terribly compromised. Your mother might have been labeled unfit along with him. You and Liam might have been taken away by Family Services, for who knew how long?'

'Okay, okay,' Marlinchen said, holding up her hands for me to stop. 'I see where you got your theory, but it's all impossible. He couldn't have just been *switched*. I was four years old. I would have known.'

'You weren't quite four. Kids are susceptible at that age, and their parents' word is like God's word,' I told her. 'Hugh brainwashed you. He told you that Aidan was away. He stalled for weeks. Then he brought home Jacob and said 'This is Aidan,' until you and Jacob both accepted it.'

'But Mother . . . ' Her voice was very soft.

'Your mother was in on it,' I said. 'I suspect it

394

wasn't her idea, but she went along with it.'

That had been the difficult part for me, too, acknowledging the complicity of the woman who slept under the marble angel in the cemetery. Elisabeth had also borne a share of guilt in Jacob's fate. But where guilt had poisoned Hugh, it had softened Elisabeth. She had adored her sister's son, sharing with him a bond between two wronged souls.

'It wouldn't have worked at all, except that the two of you weren't in school yet,' I said. 'Aidan had no teachers, no playmates that came to the house, and no older siblings. There was no one else to trick. J. D. Campion was the only other person who'd seen both Aidan Hennessy and Jacob Candeleur. Later that year, your father inexplicably and flatly refused him entry to your home.'

Marlinchen's lips parted very slightly, and I thought perhaps that last detail, which her own knowledge of her parents' lives confirmed, had convinced her. Then she straightened, as if relieved. 'Aidan's missing finger,' she said, the three words like a syllogism. 'If there was no attack by a dog, how do you explain that?'

'There was a dog,' I said. 'His neighbors in Illinois raised pit bulls, and there was a shoddy fence in between the two properties. Jacob really did lose the finger to one of the pit bulls, which is why he's scared of dogs to this day.'

Below us, Colm took Liam down with a hard tackle. Marlinchen appeared to watch, but I doubted she was really seeing it.

'There's more.' I said. 'This birth certificate is

all the paper there is on Jacob. He never registered for school. There's no death certificate. No adoption papers. He just drops off the grid. Because he was in Minnesota.'

'So you've got a piece of paper. It doesn't prove anything,' Marlinchen said. Then her eyes lit with a new idea. 'Did it occur to you that maybe Jacob was the one who died young? Maybe our aunt Brigitte let him drown or something. She was always drunk, or stoned — '

'Don't do that,' I said, shaking my head. 'Don't let your father think for you all your life. You never met your aunt Brigitte, but you never questioned your father's account of her. You're more willing to think ill of her, a stranger, than of your father, whom you saw firsthand hurting Aidan physically and psychologically.'

Despite all her denial, the truth of these words hit home, and she was silent.

'I'm not saying your father is a monster,' I said. 'He made a mistake, probably in haste, in the hospital parking lot, and it snowballed and ruined his life. By the time he realized that guilt and grief were destroying your mother from the inside out, it was too late to fix it. Imagine how it would have looked to the world, months or years later: burying his own son in an unmarked grave on his own land? Taking someone else's child and erasing his identity? Hugh's esteem and career might have survived his son's accidental death, but his behavior after that crossed all moral and legal lines.'

I wondered if I'd spoken too frankly; but honesty was overdue here. The Hennessys' world had been short on it for too long.

The boys were still playing below us. If they'd noticed my presence, they hadn't read the body language. They probably thought Marlinchen and I were having a civil conversation.

'Your father's guilt, first over Aidan and then your mother, ate him up inside. Literally, in a way.' I didn't need to remind Marlinchen of her father's ulcer. 'Did you ever wonder why the photo of your mother and Aidan bothered your father so much?' I asked her. 'It was the real Aidan, at age two. Jacob didn't know it, but your father did. It incensed him to have to see it every time he looked in that bedroom. It reminded him of how his plan worked out. Your mother never recovered from her guilt over it. She died of it, either by accident — ' I cut myself off.

Too late. Outrage was heating Marlinchen's delicate skin. 'Or what, on purpose? Are you suggesting she *killed* herself?'

I was, but of course it was too much for Marlinchen to handle at this point. 'No,' I said quickly, appeasing her. 'No, I'm not saying that.'

Still too late. 'I think you should leave now,' she said.

'Think what you asked me to do, when we first met,' I said, getting desperate. 'You asked me to find your brother. That's what I'm trying to do. You're the legal head of the household now. If you won't let me talk to your father, give me permission to dig under the tree and look for your brother. Like you wanted.'

'My *brothers*,' she said, pointing, 'are all home. My father is home and getting better.

397

We're coming together and healing our wounds. That's hard for someone like you to watch.'

'Someone like me?' I repeated.

'You were kicked out of your home by your father and raised by a virtual stranger. You wouldn't understand what it's like to be part of a real family.'

'I'm sorry?' I said, though I'd heard her clearly.

But if Marlinchen saw that she'd stung me, she didn't ease up. 'That's why you can't accept that we're happy now,' she went on. 'You'd rather my brother be dead, my mother a suicide, and my father in prison.'

'That's not true,' I said.

'Go away,' she snapped. 'I'm tired of your morbid mind and your sick theories.'

There was nothing left for me to do here. She wasn't going to cool off. I headed down the steps.

'Don't come back.' Marlinchen threw the words after me. 'I'll call the cops if you come around here again.'

I wanted to say, *I can come back with a warrant*, but the truth was, I probably couldn't. I didn't have enough hard evidence. Besides, sometimes you have to relinquish the last word. I understood the root of Marlinchen's anger. It was fear. If she hadn't heard a glimmer of truth in my words, they wouldn't have poured acid onto a vulnerable spot in her mind. Stiff-limbed, I climbed into my car and headed down the drive.

The top of the little rise at the end of the

Hennessy driveway afforded me a good view of the field where the boys were playing, and I paused there before pulling out onto the road. I looked back.

Aidan, as I couldn't stop thinking of him, stood conferring with Liam, holding the football in his hands. Exertion had raised a fine sweat on his bare chest and his face. The boys got into position, and Liam threw the ball to Aidan. Aidan caught it easily and started to run. His blond ponytail swung crazily in the afternoon sunlight as he ran. Colm, determined, raced to intercept him, but Aidan dodged easily and poured on the speed, outpacing his brother, heading for the unmarked end zone.

The high window was empty; Hugh was not watching, and for a moment I wished he were. Maybe for the first time he'd recognize something he'd failed to see for so long.

Hugh believed strongly in family. In his writing and his life, he'd pursued the ideals of the close-knit, loyal, and loving clan. He'd never been able to see it, but Jacob Candeleur, without a drop of Hennessy blood in him, represented the best of those ideals. From a young age, he'd had a strong instinct to protect those he loved. He'd pulled Marlinchen from the freezing waters of the lake, when she'd fallen through the ice. He'd fought with the bullies who'd picked on Liam. He'd come home from his new life in California to be with his sister and brothers.

With Colm on his heels, Jacob gained the ground of the predetermined, invisible end zone and spiked the ball. Colm, giving up gracefully, extended his hand and gave Jacob a low five, scooped up the ball, and went to regroup with Donal.

Jacob didn't follow. He stood a moment, breathing hard. Then he dropped to his knees, and from there he lay down on the grass.

There was something evocative about that action, something that stirred a recent memory.

'Oh, God,' I said.

I put the Nova into reverse and backed down the driveway at 40 miles per hour, skidding to a stop ten feet from the deck. Marlinchen stared at me from her place at the grill.

'Call 911,' I yelled to her as I jumped out of the car.

I expected some kind of resistance from her, but she looked down at the grass, where Jacob was still not moving, and her brothers were standing around him, and believed me.

'What should I say?' Marlinchen called.

'Cardiac arrest,' I yelled back, plunging down the slope.

Maybe it had never occurred to Brigitte that the heart defect that killed her lover Paul, the father of her child, was hereditary. Or maybe she'd never found a way to warn the son who wasn't supposed to know he was her son. Maybe she'd meant to, someday, but her own death had caught her unawares.

Liam, kneeling at his cousin's side, said, 'I don't think he's breathing.' He sounded puzzled, like he wanted to be contradicted, wanted someone to tell him that healthy 18-year-olds didn't just stop breathing.

'Move,' I ordered, dropped to my knees, and rolled Jacob onto his back. I shifted the tigereye leather necklace off the hollow of his throat and laid my fingertips there. The great arteries did not pulse under my touch. I tipped Jacob's head back, checked the airway. Clear. I closed off his nostrils, breathed for him. Pumped his chest hard enough to contuse the flesh. Breathed again.

When the paramedics came, they asked who was going to go with Aidan, as the kids identified him, to the hospital. I opened my mouth to volunteer Marlinchen, but she shook her head. 'You go, Sarah,' she said frantically. 'Please, please, you go with him.'

The furious defender of the Hennessy family, who'd chased me off her property, was gone. Marlinchen was a scared teenage girl again, and to her, I was Authority. She still believed I could help her brother when she couldn't. Numbly, I climbed into the ambulance.

I stayed with Jacob Candeleur all the way to the ER. Among the hectically laboring doctors and nurses, nobody noticed as I trailed along behind them, stood against a wall, watching their futile efforts. I was there as they called the code at 7:11 P.M. and as they dispiritedly filed out.

The last one out, a male nurse, turned to look at me from the doorway. 'You gonna notify the family?' he said.

I nodded assent. 'In a minute.'

For some time, Hugh Hennessy had been hiding behind the wall of his illness and his privacy, hiding from the people he'd hurt. That ring of people just kept getting bigger. Aidan, whose death his carelessness had long ago caused. Elisabeth, whose suicide he helped bring about. Brigitte, whose child he had taken. Jacob, whose loss of identity had ultimately been fatal. In a way, even Paul Candeleur. Paul the loyal, ready fighter, who'd somehow given his son his values through blood alone, who'd never lived to see how his son's life would go so wrong. I couldn't believe this death didn't hurt Paul, too, somewhere.

33

Marlinchen, already no stranger to adult responsibilities, learned a new set that day, the kind many people don't have to deal with until their thirties or forties. I guided her through the process of releasing a body to a funeral home, making the necessary choices. I advised her to have all the kids, even Donal, look at Jacob's body.

'It makes it real,' I told her. 'It'll help them through the denial, and later they can feel like they said goodbye.'

All the kids seemed numb. None of them cried.

Outside, in the hospital parking lot, Marlinchen sat in the passenger seat of the Nova, stared straight ahead, and asked dully, *Can you stay over tonight?*

You have to be American, I think, to understand how middle-class Americans grieve in modern times. Elsewhere, when people die unexpectedly, there is wailing, there are tears, there is recrimination; you can see it almost every day on CNN. In other places, liquor flows and the telephone doesn't stop ringing; neighbors come by with food and consolation.

In the Hennessy household, the wide-screen TV held court all evening. Even Liam surrendered to it, his knees drawn up against his chest, seeking comfort in the electronic opiate of modern times.

I cooked for them, keeping it simple: spaghetti with tomato sauce, green salad. Marlinchen made up a tray for Hugh, and just before bed, she gave him a pill. 'It helps him sleep,' she said, 'and I don't think I can stay awake tonight, to help him to the bathroom, or read to him if he can't sleep.'

'That's probably a good idea,' I said. She seemed to want my guidance on little things like that.

Just before going upstairs, Liam went to stand at the window. He couldn't see the place where Jacob had died, but in the black glass, he was looking in that direction.

'I don't get it,' he said. 'I just don't fucking get it.' His sharpboned face was pinched with something that would blossom into pain, when he stopped trying to fight it so hard and let himself feel it.

I laid a hand on his shoulder and said nothing. Marlinchen and I hadn't discussed what I'd told her that afternoon, about Jacob Candeleur and the real Aidan. I couldn't begin to guess when she'd be ready to talk about it again, or to tell the other kids.

Restless, I didn't fall asleep right away. I was only drifting off, on the family-room couch, when the click of the French doors woke me.

Marlinchen, outside in the moonlight, was dressed in a practical long-sleeved white T-shirt and faded jeans. In her hand was the spade Liam had used to bury Snowball. She was heading toward the magnolia tree.

I'd had no solid evidence for that part of my theory — that Aidan was buried there — but it just seemed so clear to me. What else on the property had that look, of a monument? Why had Hugh walked down there, years ago with Marlinchen, to tell her something he'd said was important? Why were the Hennessy kids drawn to the tree, going there to talk and reflect and be still, as if called there by the whisper of the dead?

I got up and dressed.

Marlinchen didn't hear me approaching, so intent was she on her work. Slight as she was, she put her body weight into every thrust of the spade, like a tiny backhoe. She was crying as she dug.

'Marlinchen,' I said.

She looked up, tear tracks silver in the moonlight, her face beautiful even in grief.

'Let it go for now,' I said. 'We can do this later.'

'No,' she said, her voice wet. 'You've been right about everything, from the very beginning. I didn't listen.' She looked up at Hugh's high window. 'Do you think he could see me down here, if he were awake?' Without waiting for an answer, she said, 'I hope he can. I hope he sees me digging out here and has a heart attack on top of his stroke. I won't lift a finger to help him, this time.'

'It's not your fault,' I said.

'No, it's *his* fault,' Marlinchen said, vehement. 'I've been protecting him for years. I didn't tell anyone how he treated Aidan. If I'd told

405

someone, anyone . . . ' She trailed off and wept, but didn't stop digging. Out on the lake, a barred owl screamed, sounding disturbingly human.

'It's not your fault,' I said again. 'You're hurting, and you want to be doing something right now to make things right. But it's better, legally, if you let a technician do the digging. You could break bone hitting it with the spade, and then the evidence is damaged.'

'Evidence!' Marlinchen laughed, a high sound not unlike the owl's. 'There's no need for *evidence*. He'll never see the inside of a courtroom. He'll be too sick. That's how he'll beat this.' She laughed, bitter. 'It's his fault Aidan's dead, it's even his fault Mother died. But he'll never pay.'

She thrust again with the blade. 'Nothing sticks to him. Nothing ever hurts him. Aidan's teachers, who were supposed to be looking for abuse? They wouldn't have recognized it if Dad had beaten Aidan right in front of the school! They brought his *books* to parent conferences for him to *sign*.' She sniffled. 'I protected and defended him. I didn't give you the information you needed, because it made him look bad.' She wiped her nose with the back of her hand, a child's gesture. 'Even before that, for years, I took care of him. After Mother died, I cooked and took care of the house and the finances, all so he'd have time to write and teach and think, and do everything but be a father.'

The wind kicked up unexpectedly, bringing a lingering scent of the afternoon's barbecue.

'And just when I was nearly clear of all the responsibilities, he has a stroke. It's perfect. He's trapped me again. He'll get better, but never completely well. I'll be here until I'm forty, making his meals and keeping track of his medication.'

'It doesn't have to be that way,' I said.

'Yes, it will. You don't understand,' she said.

The smell of smoke was stronger, and the problem was, Marlinchen hadn't actually lit up the barbecue pit earlier.

'Do you smell smoke?' I asked her.

'I'll take the bones up and show him that I know. I'll make him look at what he's done.' Not listening to me, she spiked the blade viciously into the earth. I turned to look up at the house. An uneven reddish light flickered in the darkness behind several windows.

'Son of a bitch,' I said.

As I ran up to the house, Liam emerged onto the back deck, Donal beside him.

'Where's Colm?' I demanded.

'Inside,' Liam said, his voice slightly hoarse. 'Getting Dad out.'

Hugh, I realized with a sinking heart. *A goddamned invalid on the goddamned second floor of a house with a goddamned staircase.*

'We have to get Dad out,' Donal echoed, his voice cracking.

Behind me I heard footsteps and barely reached out in time to catch Marlinchen on her way into the house. 'No way!' I told her. 'You stay out here. I mean it,' I said, seeing refusal in her anxious face. 'I'll handle things.'

407

The air inside the house was hot but bearable, as though someone had simply cranked up the thermostat recklessly high. But there was also a scent of smoke in it, and I felt a thrill of nerves run through my body.

The smoke was thicker in the hallway of the second floor, where Colm was in his father's doorway. 'Come on!' he said. 'Help me with Dad!'

For a moment it was tempting; Colm was strong. But I felt the heat on my skin, growing uncomfortable, and I knew that fires get out of hand so fast, become unsurvivable without warning. I couldn't take the chance that Colm might die because I'd decided to let him help me and we were both trying to get Hugh out when the whole room flashed over.

'No!' I said, half yelling, even though we were standing fairly close together. 'This is no time to be a hero.'

Colm shook his head. 'It's Donal,' he said miserably. 'He was smoking in the basement. He started the fire. If Dad — '

'The firefighters will get your father down,' I said. 'They have the equipment and the training.'

I spoke with more confidence than I felt. By the time the fire crew arrived, it would probably be too late for a 170-pound invalid to be borne out of the house. Colm saw that truth in my eyes. He opened his mouth to speak again, but then succumbed to a fit of coughing.

'This is how rescuers get killed,' I said.

With one last, agonized glance into his father's darkened bedroom, he nodded agreement. I put a hand between his shoulder blades and urged him toward the stairs.

Out on the deck, much of my skin felt as though I'd been lying down on a giant skillet. It was likely that Colm felt the same way. I pushed him down in front of the spigot and turned it on, and he splashed water on his face, chest, and arms. When he moved back, I was about to do the same, when I noticed something that troubled me.

'Where is Marlinchen?' I asked.

Colm, hair dripping, straightened up to look around. Liam had his hands on Donal's shoulders, and he too looked mystified.

'No! *Fuck!*' I was so angry, Colm flinched at the sound of my voice, even under the circumstances. Marlinchen had gone in for Hugh. Her words by the graveside — *I won't lift a finger to help him* — were just words. When push came to shove, she'd fallen back into the old patterns. Sacrificing her welfare for his.

I faced the three boys. 'Okay, you guys get back,' I ordered them. 'Way, way back, down the driveway, where it's safe. And stay there. If Marlinchen or I don't come out, do *not* come in after us. Understood?'

They nodded.

Moving as quickly as I could, I dropped to my knees and turned the spigot back on. I put my head under, soaking my hair, the water like ice as it scrawled along my scalp. I pulled off my shirt, soaked that, put it back on. Then I went back in.

As soon as I looked into the house again, I knew I couldn't get up to the second floor. The stairs were aflame; to try to run up them would be suicide. The only way up to the second floor was blocked off.

I went back out the front door, circled the house to stand under the high window, Hugh's window facing the lake. The grape blossoms on the trellis were tightly closed, puckered and grayish. The trellis. It had held Jacob's weight. It would hold mine.

The wooden framework groaned and pulled forward as I put my whole weight on it, but it stayed standing, and I started to climb. The leaves brushed against my face as I did, and even through the smoke I could smell a faint, sweet odor from the closed blooms.

Hugh's sliding window was open as wide as possible behind the screen. Marlinchen's work, I thought, getting fresh air in the room. Hugh was on the bed, chest quivering irregularly with what might be little coughs, from the smoke. I remembered the sleeping pill Marlinchen had given him, and wondered how aware he really was.

Light spilled from the master bathroom, and then Marlinchen's silhouette appeared in the doorway. She held a bunched sheet in her hands. She'd filled the bathtub with water, I realized, and was soaking sheets and towels to fight the flames that had already spread into Hugh's room.

'Marlinchen!' I yelled, again.

'Sarah!' she called back, and there was relief in her voice. Authority was here. 'Help me!'

She didn't want me to get her out; that wasn't

what she meant by *help*. She wanted me to come in and fight the fire with her.

'Come to me!' I yelled back. 'You're going to — ' I'd been about to say *die if you stay here*, but cut myself off, afraid Hugh was awake and lucid enough to hear me. If he was, there was little more terrible to imagine than his situation: aware but not mobile, at the mercy of circumstances, wholly dependent on someone else to save him.

I changed tactics. 'The firefighters are almost here!' I called to Marlinchen. 'They'll get him down safe! But you have to come out now!'

'I can't!' she told me, shaking her head again, then swinging a wet sheet at the flames closest to the bed. 'Come in and help me!'

Then something happened that nearly made my heart stop: she dropped to her knees, coughing, blinded by smoke. I thought this was it; she was overcome.

'Marlinchen, come to me!' I yelled. But even in her coughing fit, she shook her head.

I glanced up at the bed again. Water was streaming from Hugh's nearly closed eyes. I knew it was the smoke that was causing it, but it looked to me like tears. A mental image of my own father, dead now, flashed across my mind like a spark of static electricity, and a grief as strong as nausea made my stomach roll over.

I made a decision. I wasn't going to look at Hugh again. I couldn't look at him and tell the truth, and if I didn't tell the truth, Marlinchen might not live.

'Listen to me!' I yelled to her. 'Three things can happen here! Three people can die in here tonight. That's what'll happen if I go in and try to help you. Or two people can die. That's what'll happen if I leave you here. Or just one person can die, and two will be saved.'

Marlinchen probably couldn't see me through the smoke and her streaming eyes, but her face turned in my direction. She got to her feet. Blinded, she stumbled forward.

As she did, I pried a thumbnail under the bottom edge of the window screen, trying to keep a one-handed balance on the trellis. I forced the screen upward and loose from its track along the windowsill. It gave way, and the bottom corner of its metal frame sliced sideways across my forehead, a quick scratch like that of a fingernail, and then it was bouncing down the bowed-out trellis frame, the leaves shivering wherever it hit.

'Okay, we're cool,' I assured Marlinchen, who was wedged in the now-open window. 'I'm going to ease down a little to make room for you, but I'll keep my hand here' — I had one hand on her lower leg — 'so you'll always know where I am.'

I hoped I sounded confident. The truth was, I had the beginnings of a Chihuahua shake in my legs from holding my place on the trellis.

'Just put one leg down and find a foothold,' I said, 'and we'll just climb down easy, one step at a time.'

A fine plan, totally worthless. When Marlinchen put her weight on the trellis, the whole

412

thing gave way. I saw a flying white moon, smoke, the lake, and then the whole planet hit my back, then the back of my head. Marlinchen was more fortunate. I broke her fall.

34

The familiar smell of cyanoacrylate glue brought me to my senses, but this wasn't the lingering scent of old fumes. It was sharp and fresh. My eyes were closed, but I felt someone touching my forehead with gentle fingers.

'I should own stock in the superglue business,' I said, eyes still closed.

'Shh,' a low, familiar voice said. 'You're shaking my hand.'

I opened my eyes and wasn't surprised to see Cicero. I'd recognized his voice a second earlier. What I was a little less clear on were the events leading up to being on Cicero's exam table once again.

I remembered the fire at the Hennessy place, and scattered events after that. I remembered Colm by my side. He'd led me to a safe distance from the burning house, and encouraged me to lean on him, and I did, grateful for his young strength and his disobedience in coming back for me. I remember emergency vehicles at the fireground, and trying to help because I couldn't grasp the idea that I was at the scene as a patient, not a first responder. A crowded ER waiting room, then a quiet place, someone speaking to me in a low, calm voice. Cicero's voice.

'I can't believe you're *gluing* me back together,' I said.

'A doctor's trick, not to be tried at home,' he said, sitting back.

'I didn't think I was hurt,' I said. I remembered the sharp corner of the window screen scraping across my forehead, but it had seemed like nothing, a scratch from a kitten's claw.

'Oh, it's a pretty bad cut. *Don't touch it,*' he reprimanded as I lifted my hand toward my forehead. 'I'll show you.'

He rolled away in his chair, came back with a hand mirror, and held it up in front of me.

'Holy shit,' I said. Only now did I remember blinking blood out of my eyes, more than once. Blood that had dried now on my nose, cheekbones, even my chin.

'It looks worse than it is.' Cicero was rolling away again. 'You've got a little swelling on the back of your head, also, but nothing too serious,' he said. 'You were holding some ice on it for me, do you remember that?'

'No,' I said.

'Otherwise you're fine. I'm going to get you a little more ice. Can you throw me that cloth?'

I looked around and saw a wet, pale-green washcloth on the exam table next to me. I picked it up and started to rise, but Cicero, at the edge of his kitchen, merely held up his hand. My throw was a little off, but Cicero adjusted and caught it backhanded.

When he came back, he had the ice, as well as a clean cloth in a small, stainless-steel bowl of soapy water. I took the ice pack from him and held it to my head. It wasn't hard to locate the injury by the dull ache I felt there, as well as the dampness of the hair around it. Cicero set the bowl down and wrung out the rag.

I saw what he was going to do. 'I can wash my own face, in the bathroom,' I said.

'I know you can,' Cicero said. 'But I want you to sit still and keep applying that ice pack, and in the meantime, I'm tired of feeling sorry for you unnecessarily because you look like you just went ten rounds with Lennox Lewis when it's nowhere near that bad.'

I submitted to his ministrations, like a child, closing my eyes as he gently scrubbed dried blood from my skin.

'I need to tell you something,' Cicero said. 'The last time you were here, you mentioned my brother's death.'

'We don't have to talk about that,' I said, opening my eyes.

'Yes, we do,' he said. 'You were afraid that I equated you with the officers who shot Ulises.' His voice was soft and level, like always. 'I don't. You're nothing like them.'

'You've never seen me on the job,' I said.

'I never spoke to those men,' Cicero told me. 'They never came to me, to explain what happened. You would have come. Am I wrong about that?'

'No,' I said honestly. 'I would have.'

Cicero nodded and went on with his work. The sensation on my skin was hypnotic, as was the sound of the soaking of the cloth, the splatter of water falling back into the bowl as he rinsed and wrung the cloth, a second time and then a third.

'You weren't too clear on how this happened,' he said. 'Something about a house fire and falling from a window during a rescue, is that about right?'

'Basically,' I said. 'Why?'

Cicero let the cloth float in the bowl and handed me a towel to dry my face with. 'You put yourself in dangerous situations a lot, Sarah,' he said. 'Pulling kids from a drainage canal, and now this.'

'That's only twice,' I said.

'Twice in the time I've known you,' he corrected. 'Which is a little over a month.'

'It's part of the job,' I said.

'No,' Cicero said, shaking his head like a teacher hearing an unacceptable excuse for incomplete homework. 'I know enough about police work to know the things you're doing are not typical.'

'Who wants to be typical?' I said lightly.

'Sometimes,' Cicero said, 'when people consistently get themselves injured or hurt, there's a reason. Sometimes they're trying to draw attention to something else that's hurting them, something they can't show people directly.'

'I don't understand.'

'Sarah,' he said carefully, 'when you and your husband were living together, did he ever hit you?'

'God, no,' I said. 'Shiloh was a cop, too.'

'That doesn't disqualify him,' Cicero said. 'It's a very physical profession, and it draws

417

aggressive people who — '

'I know all that,' I said. 'But Shiloh never hit me.'

'I just get the feeling,' Cicero said, 'that someone hurt you.' He paused cautiously. 'Was it sex?'

Blame it on the late hour, blame it on the head injury . . . I was about to deny it, and instead I heard myself say, 'It was a long time ago.'

'Your father?' Cicero's dark eyes were very intent on mine.

'Brother,' I said. Then, 'I never tell anyone that. I never even told Shiloh.'

'I'm sorry,' Cicero said.

'I don't want to talk about it anymore.'

'Okay.'

'I mean ever.'

'All right.'

'Do you feel sorry for me?'

'No.'

'Okay. I don't want to talk about it anymore.'

I realized I was holding a wet rag with nothing in it anymore. Taking it away from the back of my head, I unfolded it and saw a tooth-size chip of ice inside, all that was left of a cube.

'The thing is,' I said, 'if I do extreme things on the job, it's just because I want . . . I want to . . . '

I started over. 'I met this kid recently, a paramedic.' In my mind's eye, I saw Nate Shigawa. 'I envied him,' I went on. 'In his job, he gets to stop the bleeding. My job is different. By the time I'm there, the bleeding is over. Sometimes long over.'

I was thinking of the real Aidan Hennessy, so young when he died, and of his mother, pulled from the waters of the lake.

'Just because the bleeding's stopped doesn't mean the pain is gone,' Cicero said. 'I expect you help with that.'

'When people let me,' I said. 'Sometimes — more often than you'd think — people say they want help, but really they don't.'

The day that had started outside Kilander's office had finally caught up with me. I felt tired in ways that were more than physical. I didn't know how Marlinchen was. I didn't even know *where* she and her brothers were. I thought I should find out, make sure they were all right, that someone was with them. But I just couldn't do any more. Not tonight.

'What time is it?' I said, and turned to look at the clock. It was 1:58 A.M.

'God, I'm sorry,' I said, sliding off the table. 'You need to be in bed. I'll leave.'

Cicero started to speak, but I didn't let him. 'I feel fine, I'm okay to drive — ' I stopped, realizing something. 'I didn't drive here, did I?'

Cicero shook his head. 'You don't remember?'

I closed my eyes, accessed dim mental images, but nothing would come into focus. Then I was struck by an impossible idea. '*You* brought me?'

'Yes,' he said.

'But — '

'I told you I can do the elevator when I have no other choice,' he said. 'I'm not so much surprised that I went down that damn elevator as I am that my van started.'

419

I must have looked very surprised, because Cicero was watching me with amusement.

'You called me from a pay phone near the ER. You were a little fuzzy on the details, but apparently you'd just bolted from the waiting room. I told you to stay where you were. I was going to take you back to the hospital, if need be, but you were ambulatory and not seriously injured, so I respected your wishes and brought you here.'

He went outside to find me. I wanted to say that I was proud of him, but realized immediately how much it would diminish him, like a pat on the head. 'I owe you,' I said.

'You owe me $120, to be exact,' Cicero said. 'Eighty for the doctoring, and forty for making me go down in that damn elevator.'

I almost smiled, relieved at the deft way he brought us back down to earth. 'You know what?' I said.

'You don't have that much on you,' Cicero finished for me.

'I'll bring it tomorrow,' I promised.

'No hurry,' Cicero said. 'Just try to be more careful out there, all right? There are limits to what even I can fix.'

35

At home, I slept for five hours and woke to the ringing of my cell phone; I was needed to come in and help with the matter of Hugh Hennessy's untimely death by fire. I went downtown and gave a lengthy statement, explaining my involvement with the Hennessys and describing the events of the night before.

I learned a few details, too. What Colm had told me last night had been correct, if sketchy: Donal had been smoking in the basement. Under sensitive questioning by a veteran fire investigator, the youngest Hennessy explained that he couldn't sleep and had gotten up in the night to sneak one of his oldest brother's cigarettes. He had seen Aidan smoking when upset about Colm's blowup at the dinner table, and thought that cigarettes must help in times of stress. While hidden in the basement, Donal heard movement upstairs and thought someone was looking for him. In his haste, he threw his half-finished cigarette into a trash can and slipped back upstairs. He hadn't realized the danger of what he'd done, nor that the basement was filled with flammable materials: old furniture, a foam mattress. The fire investigator told me that he was only surprised the old wooden house hadn't gone up faster than it did.

After giving my statement, I ran into Marlinchen, who hugged me like a long-lost sister in the hallway. Campion was there as well, having heard the news on WCCO. Later that evening, one of the fire department officials let me ride with him out to the Hennessy property. There I found my car covered in soot, but otherwise driveable. I hosed it down as an interim measure, and drove it directly to a car wash.

It was only as I was falling asleep that night that I realized I'd forgotten to bring Cicero the money I owed him.

★ ★ ★

The next day, around noon, I drove to the towers. On the 26th floor, I stepped out of the elevator and into a scene I'd been a part of too often.

Soleil was standing in the hall, leaning against the wall, her face a mask of grief. She was crying openly outside Cicero's apartment. Nearby, at the door to Cicero's apartment, a young uniformed officer was standing guard, trying to look impervious to the shock and dismay around him. From inside the apartment, a radio crackled. And I felt a fine tremor begin in my legs. The last time I'd felt that sensation was in the county morgue, where I'd gone to view a body a forensic assistant told me might be my husband.

I wished I didn't know the things I knew, wished that like a civilian I could kid myself that a scene like this could signal a burglary or a simple assault. But it didn't. It didn't mean anything less than a homicide. I could have turned around and walked away, gone someplace private to internalize it. But I didn't.

No one questioned my presence there. The neighbors knew me as Cicero's girlfriend; and the cops on the scene knew me as a Sheriff's detective. The uniformed officer outside the open door had me sign in on the scene log, and then I went inside.

It seemed wrong for there to be so much activity in Cicero's apartment, which I'd associated with ambient light, quiet, order, and Cicero's form, low to the ground but kinetic in its stillness. Now, every light in the place blazed, and able-bodied people moved around, looking out of proportion to the surroundings, their movements too quick, seeming random.

The apartment had been torn up. The chest holding Cicero's medical instruments and supplies had been overturned, and notes from the filing cabinet were strewn on the floor. The wheelchair lay tipped forward in the middle of the living room. Nearby were some streaks and droplets of dried blood on the short, hard carpeting, as if someone had shaken a paintbrush.

The first of the technicians, a man named Malik, was starting a sketch that would eventually capture the layout of the apartment, as well as the position of every relevant object and bloodstain. The other tech, a full-bodied, red-haired woman I hadn't met, was making notes. The detective was standing off to the side. It was Hadley.

423

He'd been my last boyfriend, pre-Shiloh. He'd worked closely with Shiloh, when they'd been on the interagency Narcotics task force, and I'd once raided a meth lab near Anoka with both of them. A black man, Hadley wasn't particularly tall, but he had quick reflexes that I remembered from games of one-on-one. His hair was shorter now than in his undercover-Narcotics days; it was a look more suitable to his new role as a Homicide detective.

His dark eyes took me in, and he lifted his chin in acknowledgment. He could do no more while talking on his cell phone.

'When the techs are through . . . Yeah, I don't know,' he said. He shifted his weight, and light flashed off the .40 he carried in a shoulder holster. 'Good, okay.' With that, he disconnected the call.

'Pribek,' he said. 'The county sent you?'

'What happened here?'

'Victim's name is Cicero Ruiz,' Hadley said, ignoring my failure to answer his question. 'Looks like a robbery-murder. Neighbor says he was doing some kind of cash business from the apartment.'

I warned you, I thought. *I warned you.*

Hadley nodded toward the door, where Soleil was out of sight. 'The same neighbor called us this morning,' he said. 'She saw the print outside the door.'

On my way in, I'd missed the sight of half a reddish shoe print, where someone had tracked blood on the way out.

'She got a bad feeling about it, so when he

didn't answer her knock, she called us,' Hadley finished.

'Have you interviewed her at length?' I asked.

'Not yet. That's why she's in the hall, waiting,' Hadley said. He took out his notebook but didn't open it. 'The rest of the neighbors say they didn't see anything.' He indicated the medical instruments on the floor. 'It looks like the guy was a doctor, but that can't be right; not in a building like this.'

'He *was* a doctor,' I said. Cicero was beyond needing my promise of silence now. 'Prewitt asked me to track him down. He was practicing out of his apartment.'

'He saw *patients* here?' Hadley said.

I nodded. 'That's what we were hearing. I was supposed to get evidence for an arrest.'

'Well, we're a little too late for that,' Hadley said.

I swallowed against the solidifying muscle in my throat.

'Sarah?' Hadley said.

Homicide detectives, more than most police, have to rely on an article of faith: that victims of crime can be helped even after they're dead. I'm not sure I ever fully believed that. But now a voice in my mind said, *Do your job*. And at the moment, I didn't question it. I swallowed a second time, and then I could function again. 'What do you know?' I asked.

'Not much,' Hadley said. 'It looks like there might have been two people involved,' Hadley said. 'I'll let the technicians decide that, based on the shoe prints and any fingerprints they find.

Like I said, robbery is the probable motive.' He rubbed the bridge of his nose. 'I don't know how much money the doc was making, but I don't think he gave it up easy.'

'He was beaten?' I asked.

'Oh yeah,' Hadley confirmed. 'I saw the body. He was worked over. Let me show you.' Hadley moved down the hall, waving me after him.

In Cicero's sanctuary, the photos on the low dresser were undisturbed, but the drawers had been taken out and overturned, like those of the filing cabinet. On the floor, at the foot of the bed, the carpet had been stained dark red in an irregular area around three feet in diameter.

'He died in here,' Hadley said. 'I think Doc knew his attackers. At least, he let them in. There's no sign the front door was forced. They make a surprise attack in the front room, get him down and out of the chair. He fights enough that there's some blood out there. Then they drag him into the bedroom. This is where the serious beating took place.' Hadley pointed at the blood spatters on the wall. 'See that? That's a lot of blunt force. Either it was personal animosity, or, more likely, he wasn't giving his visitors what they came for.'

Something was wrong about Hadley's theory, I thought. Cicero needed the money his practice brought him, but he was too practical to die for it. He would have surrendered it. If he'd been beaten to death . . . I shook my head. Hadley had suggested personal animosity, but I couldn't fathom it. Cicero had had no enemies; I would have staked any amount of money on that.

'We already bagged the weapon. A twenty-pound weight, one of a set. Are you okay?' Hadley said.

On the mirror, a dark hair was trapped in dried blood.

'I'm sorry,' Hadley was saying. 'I forget you don't see as much of this as I do. You want to go back out in the front room?'

'No,' I said, finding my voice. 'I'm okay. I want to help with this investigation, if I can.'

Hadley nodded, finding nothing unusual in the request. 'Be glad to have you,' he said.

A woman's voice called for Hadley; it was the crime-scene technician in the other room. 'Excuse me,' Hadley said.

I looked toward the photos on Cicero's altar and thought of what he'd said after he'd written me the prescription.

I do not need to get arrested, Cicero had said. But he'd been wrong. Even if he'd served jail time, it wouldn't have broken him. Cicero might never have forgiven me for turning him in, but at least he would have been alive. He was dead now because I'd overruled my better instincts and obeyed his wishes.

When he'd told me the story about the troubled young psychiatric patient and the night she'd called him to her home, Cicero had said, *I was probably pretty goddamned lonely, although I couldn't have seen it back then.* The same could be said of me. I'd needed Cicero's friendship and feared living with the memory of his anger, so I'd shielded him from arrest. At the core of it, I'd spared him out of selfishness and, in sparing him, had killed him.

From the array of photos, a younger, untroubled Cicero and his brother Ulises regarded me. Dead now, both of them. One killed by cops, the other by a cop's leniency.

★ ★ ★

For the next hour I immersed myself in work. Hadley went out to do quick preinterviews with the neighbors, in order to separate out those who, like Soleil, knew enough to merit taking them downtown for a formal statement. I stayed in the apartment and, using one of the technicians' cameras, meticulously photographed Cicero's apartment, every object, every bloodstain, detaching my mind from what I saw through the viewfinder.

I was nearly finished when Hadley strode back though the front door. 'Pribek!' he said. The tone in his voice was urgent enough that Malik dropped the pencil he was writing with. I lowered the camera.

Hadley was holding his cell phone in his hand. 'We've got to suspend things here,' he said. 'A couple of officers got a call from a drugstore over on University Avenue. A pharmacist called them about a suspicious prescription. A couple of kids tried to pass it off, but the pharmacist knew right away it was a fake. The writing on it didn't mean anything. It was just some Greek-looking scribbles.'

Of course. The prescription pad.

'And the doctor's sig on it? Cicero Ruiz, MD.'

Hadley flashed me a humorless smile, like a shark's. 'Got to hand it to the doc. He shafted 'em.'

Hadley had been mistaken, earlier. There was no hostility behind the beating, no personal hard feelings, like he'd theorized. They had needed Cicero to write prescriptions for them. When he'd refused, they'd hurt him to break down his resistance.

Hadley spoke again. 'The kids wised up and fled the scene just as the cops were getting there. There was a little footrace in the store, and one of the suspects fell. He's in custody.' Hadley shook his head. 'His friend left him behind. No honor among thieves.'

I barely heard him.

I could understand Cicero being targeted for his money. Everyone he'd ever treated knew he ran a cash business, plus everyone those patients might have spoken to about the unlicensed doctor in the towers. But the prescription pad —

'Sarah?' Hadley's voice was impatient.

'Sorry,' I said.

'They're holding the kid from the drugstore. The word's going out to pharmacies to be on the lookout for the other guy, but we've just got a description, not a name. Only his friend can ID him.' Hadley slipped the cell phone into his jacket. 'So let's go lean on him.'

★ ★ ★

From the window of Hadley's car, I watched the flow of traffic, pedestrians filing through the

429

crosswalk, the sun glinting off the high buildings in the distance. I felt as if a membrane were separating me from the outside world. Crumpled in my hand was a piece of paper: my medical history, written in Cicero's hand. It had my full name on it and, had it been found in Cicero's place, would have been impossible to explain to my superiors. Even so, I'd felt cheap and petty when I'd retrieved it from the overturned filing cabinet, like I was betraying Cicero by doing so.

Hadley touched my hand with the backs of his ring and middle fingers, the lightest of touches. 'Hey,' he said. 'I think you're taking this one too hard.' He looked away from the street just long enough to make eye contact, then veered around a furniture delivery truck. 'Is it because this guy was a paraplegic that this bothers you so much?'

'No,' I said. 'It's just . . . ' I hesitated. I had to say something, but I didn't want to pierce the membrane and let my feelings out. 'It seems like such a waste of a life.' I pushed the medical history into my shoulder bag. *Please don't let him want to talk about it anymore.*

'I know,' Hadley said. 'According to his neighbor, he was — '

'Can we talk about interrogation strategy, before we get downtown?' I interrupted.

Hadley swerved around a slow-moving Oldsmobile. 'That's probably a good idea,' he said.

★ ★ ★

It was a time-honored tactic: when two people commit a crime, get one to turn on the other.

430

Give him a chance to get a jump on his partner, implicating him in everything. Appeal to his self-preservation, and imply that his partner would do the same to him, if the chance presented itself.

It was Hadley's investigation; I'd agreed to let him take the lead. I was supposed to take the gentler, good-cop role.

The young man waiting in the interrogation room didn't look like much of an outlaw: about five-seven, with hair the color of straw and a scraggly chin beard. The lower lids of his blue eyes drooped a bit, giving him a listless appearance, but there was a glint of hostile pleasure in his gaze, as if he were looking forward to not helping us. He wore oversized jeans of dark, coarse denim and a red hooded sweatshirt. A bluish tattoo hid in the webbed fold of flesh between right thumb and forefinger, and it seemed to crawl like a spider when he moved his hand.

When he saw us, the first thing he did was yawn.

'Don't get too comfortable, Jerod,' Hadley said.

Jerod Smith, 19, of South Minneapolis. He had a prior for marijuana possession. That wasn't a serious rap sheet. It was possible that his friend at large was, in fact, the author of Cicero's death.

'You want to tell us about Cicero Ruiz?' Hadley said.

'Who?' Jerod said.

'If you're gonna lie, at least tell smart lies,'

Hadley said, perching on the corner of the table. 'Ruiz's name was on the prescription you handed over to the pharmacist, so we *know* you know who he is.' Hadley took a deep breath, just for show. He was nowhere near losing his temper. 'Ruiz is dead, and then you're trying to fill prescriptions he wrote. That looks very, very bad. I think it's time to cooperate.'

The boy shrugged. 'He was fine when we left his apartment,' he said. Then his lips quirked, as if he were holding back amusement. 'Maybe he fell out of the wheelchair and hit his head on something. Maybe he had some kind of seizure, like those people do.' Jerod raised his arm, with the hand flopped over, and banged it against his chest in imitation of a spastic.

I leaned forward. 'Listen, you little prick,' I said, 'do you think that you're safe because Minnesota doesn't have a death penalty?' I couldn't stop myself. 'That's no cause for joy. Runts like you don't have girlfriends in prison, they *are* girlfriends. By the time you get released as an old man, that jumped-up clitoris between your legs won't have gotten any action for fifty years.'

Jerod's eyes first widened, then heated, and his jaw set. Behind me, Hadley said smoothly, 'You gotta admit, that's something to think about, Jerod. Why don't we give you some time to mull that over.' He stood, and I followed him out. I knew what was coming.

Out in the hallway, Hadley rubbed his forehead and said, 'Okay, there was a lot of engine noise in the car and maybe I misheard,

432

but I thought we were clear that I was going to be the heavy, and you were going to be nice and give him someone to confess to.' He didn't sound as upset as I knew he was. He had the control over his emotions that you need in the interrogation room.

'I know,' I said, ashamed. 'He pissed me off.'

'Well, now we have to regroup,' Hadley said. He watched as a file clerk rolled a cart past us down the hall. 'All right, I'm just going to cut to the chase in there. Then you get impatient and give up, and I'll agree. We'll see if that works.'

Jerod looked mutinous as we came back in, but he didn't actually sneer, and he didn't say anything. Maybe he would crack.

'Okay, let me lay it out for you.' Hadley pulled out a chair and turned it backward, straddling it. 'This is how it's going to work. We need to bring in your partner. That's our main concern. If you assist us with that, it's going to help you a lot, in the eyes of a judge.'

I leaned against the wall as if bored with the whole process.

'Right now, we don't know whose idea it was to go to Ruiz's apartment. We don't know who actually killed him. We don't know if that was supposed to happen or not. All that's up in the air.' Hadley held up a cautioning hand, as if Jerod had been about to speak, although there'd been no sign of it. 'Now, I'm not telling you to say anything that isn't true, Jerod. I'm just saying that we don't know any of these things, and with Mr. Ruiz dead — '

Dr. Ruiz, I corrected Hadley mentally.

' — we've only got two people who were in that apartment who can tell us,' Hadley said. 'Now, your buddy, back in the drugstore, he ran out while you got arrested. That doesn't suggest to me a real trustworthy person. I'm just wondering, when we catch that guy, what kind of regard for the truth he's going to have. I wonder what he's going to tell us about who did what in that apartment.'

I was trying not to look involved, but I couldn't help but notice that Jerod was beginning to look a little nervous, the muscles of his face slackening.

'This is what we want,' Hadley said. 'We want your friend's name, his address, all the information you have that'll help us bring him in. If we get that, maybe we can help you some. But if you wait too long, and he commits another crime, maybe someone else gets hurt' — Hadley leaned back as if withdrawing his interest in Jerod's welfare — 'then that's gonna be on you. Because you could have prevented it, and you didn't.'

Jerod said nothing.

'What about it, Jerod?' Hadley pressed.

Jerod looked at the floor. It was time for me to enter the action.

'Forget it,' I said to Hadley.

Hadley looked at me irritably, as if we were partners who really didn't get along, even outside the interrogation room. He said, 'Do you think you could give me more than five minutes to — '

'No, I can't,' I said, my voice rising. 'Because

434

we'll catch that other kid. He'll do something stupid, because he's got all the impulse control of a goddamn leaf in the wind, and we'll catch him and then we'll have both of them.'

Hadley lifted his hands and let them fall. 'When you're right, you're right,' he said simply. 'Okay, let's call and have a corrections officer take him over to the jail.' He stood up and we headed for the door.

'Wait,' Jerod said.

Perfect.

'It was Marc,' he said. 'It was Marc's idea to go see this guy, and it was Marc who hit him with the weight, afterward. Like, four times. I said, 'What the hell are you doing?' but he didn't listen to me.'

Whether it was true or not, who could tell? It didn't matter anymore to Cicero, and not much more to me.

Hadley set the notepad down in front of Jerod. 'Give us Marc's full name and other information first,' he said. 'Then I'm going to have you write down a statement about what happened in Mr. Ruiz's apartment.'

'Dr. Ruiz,' I said.

'What?' Hadley looked at me blankly.

'Dr. Ruiz. He was a doctor,' I said.

Jerod was writing. When he finished, and Hadley had torn off the top sheet with Marc's information, we were technically ready to go, to put the information out on the radio. Hadley turned to the door, but I didn't. I was following the train of thought Hadley had interrupted at the crime scene.

There were only three people in the world who'd known that Cicero had a prescription pad in his apartment. One of them was dead, and one of them was me. That left only one other person.

I sat on my heels next to Jerod's chair. It was an intimate, rapport-building position. 'Jerod,' I said, in a quieter voice from the one I'd been using, 'how'd you know to target Dr. Ruiz?'

'I told you, it was Marc's idea,' Jerod said.

'How did Marc know?'

'He hangs out with this girl, they're from the same town in Michigan,' he said. 'She said she knew where there was a guy who had cash and a prescription pad in his apartment.'

I tried to keep my voice level. 'Marc's from Dearborn, is that it?'

Jerod blinked, surprised. 'Yeah, how'd you know?'

'Do you know the girl's name?' I asked, ignoring his question.

Jerod thought. 'Something French, kind of like Charmaine, but that's not it. She thinks she's his girlfriend, but she's not. Marc's just letting her wax his stick.'

'Thanks, Jerod,' I said, unsmiling. 'Put all of that in your statement.'

* * *

Out in the hall, Hadley said, 'What was that about?'

My hands were shaking with anger. I laced them behind my back where Hadley couldn't see. 'Marc's girlfriend is a sometime informant named Ghislaine Morris,' I said. 'She might know something about where'd he'd go in a situation like this.'

'Right,' Hadley said. He was walking down the hall, and I was following. 'But why'd you tell Jerod to put all that in his statement?'

'She set these events in motion,' I said.

'So she ran her mouth,' Hadley said. 'That's not against the law. We can't charge her with anything.'

'No, we can't,' I said. 'But I'm going to check out a motor-pool car and go talk to her.'

We stopped in front of the coffee machine, and Hadley filled a paper cup to the rim. He looked at me and raised an eyebrow in invitation. I shook my head, *No, thanks.*

'Good idea,' Hadley said. 'But why a motor-pool car?'

'My Nova is back at the building Ruiz lived in,' I explained. 'I rode over here with you.'

I'd been so numb from finding out what happened to Cicero that I hadn't even thought of my car as we'd left; I would have climbed into a spaceship if that was what Hadley had led me to.

'Right,' Hadley said. 'Wait a minute, then, and I'll go talk to the girlfriend with you.'

I shook my head in negation. 'Sooner is better,' I said. 'You've still got to look over Jerod's statement and get him processed in at the jail.'

★   ★   ★

At the motor-pool, I signed out a nondescript, well-maintained mid-size sedan, dark blue. It reminded me of something that Gray Diaz would drive. I shot it up the ramp a little faster than necessary, and two administrators, crossing the garage in rippling trench coats over their suits, looked at me with disapproval.

I'd decided what to do with Ghislaine. I was going to bring her down to the station and find out what she knew about the whereabouts of her boyfriend, Marc. But first we were going to make a little detour to the medical examiner's office.

I'd warned her that if she threatened again to give up Cicero, I'd put her in prison. It had been an empty threat. Now she'd done worse than report Cicero to the police, and my hands were tied. She'd done nothing chargeable, as Hadley had said. But I could do this: I could make Ghislaine look at Cicero, make her see the end result of her actions in a stainless-steel drawer.

36

The girl who opened the door at Ghislaine's apartment looked like her country cousin: a little shorter, a little heavier, with hair that was as white as corn silk, and small, apprehensive blue eyes. She was braless under a V-necked white T-shirt, her pale legs in cutoffs, barefoot. Behind her issued the mindless noise of a television talk show.

'I'm here to see Ghislaine,' I said.

'She's not here,' the girl said.

'You don't mind if I come in and verify that, do you?' I took out my shield. Her eyes widened fractionally, and she stepped backward. 'I was just feeding the baby,' she said as I came in.

'Shadrick?' I said.

She shook her head. 'My baby. Shad's with Ghislaine.'

A six-month-old infant, dressed in fuzzy, androgynous yellow, sat in a high chair on the border between kitchen and living room, linoleum and carpet.

'Did Ghislaine do something wrong?'

Yes. 'No,' I said. 'I need to ask her some questions. She's a material witness.'

I moved toward a short half-hallway, like the one in Cicero's apartment. The bathroom didn't take long to check out. A ghost of steam hung in the air from an afternoon shower, and creams and cosmetics cluttered the sink. There was no one behind the rippled, frosted glass of the shower door.

In the first bedroom, the bed was unmade, but not so much that I couldn't see the giant, yellow face of Tweety bird on the rumpled comforter. On the wall was a Packers pennant, and below that bookshelves with no books on them except high school yearbooks. Model horses lined two of the shelves in their entirety, and a stuffed dog lounged on its side on a third shelf. I'd come to an apartment inhabited by children.

'That's my room,' the girl said.

'I didn't catch your name,' I said.

'Lisette,' she said.

Another improbable Gallic name. Lisette's heritage, as evinced by her looks, seemed to be pure Saxon; I didn't think she was French.

'Are you and Ghislaine related?' I asked.

Lisette shook her head. 'Just roommates.'

I moved on to the last bedroom.

Ghislaine, I was guessing, was a year or two older than her roommate. It showed in her room, more feminine than childlike. Ghislaine's bed was made up, a pale-pink eyelet comforter pulled taut with cheap lace-trimmed throw pillows carefully arranged, and Ghislaine's toys were more expensive: an MP3 player, a cellphone charger, a row of CDs. The closet door was open, and inside I saw leather coats and party dresses. A bulletin board like Marlinchen Hennessy's showed photos of Ghislaine, mostly with boys or Shadrick, rarely other girls.

Lisette was still watching me from the

doorway. 'Which one of these boys is Marc?' I asked.

'None of them,' she said. 'He didn't do things like that.'

'Like what?' I asked.

'Get his picture taken with Gish,' Lisette said. 'Or act like a boyfriend. He was too cool for that.'

'Oh, yeah?'

Lisette nodded. 'Gish loans him the keys to her car, so he can go to these parties he doesn't even take her to. He leaves his laundry here for her to take to the Laundromat, and his clothes smell like other girls' perfume.'

'How does Ghislaine take that?'

'She just keeps trying harder to please him. She bitches to me, but never to Marc. And when I tell her, 'So dump him,' she does a complete turnaround.'

'Like what?'

'She'll say, 'He's changing. I know he really cares about me, inside.' Ghislaine thinks that because he gives her stuff. But it isn't anything he cares about, just things he steals. Marc likes to think he's thugged out.' Lisette rolled her eyes. 'Anyway, Gish won't quit him. She keeps trying to think of something else she can do, to impress him.'

Right. Then she did think of something, something really good, and all it cost was Cicero's life.

'Was Marc here today?' I asked.

Lisette shook her head.

'Thanks,' I said.

A more impartial observer than I would stand in the doorway to Ghislaine's bedroom and look at the pretty objects she surrounded herself with, the sweet pastels, and mistake these things as signs of her innocence and harmlessness. They'd see a girl barely out of her teens, who liked pretty things and clothes and shopping, who kept her room with its Target-brand furnishings in perfect order, and they'd wish her well. They'd say it was Marc's fault she was so desperate to please him; they'd say it was society's fault that girls her age gave and gave to the boys around them, provided them with sex and money and support and got nothing back, until they were desperate.

I'd thought all these things too, when I'd first met her. I'd dismissed Shiloh's opinion of her as grounded in his streak of judgmentalism. I'd been taken in by her chatter and her infectious warmth, and not recognized something malignant as a tumor that grew underneath it.

The truth was, Ghislaine's love of pretty things and nice clothes was at the heart of her malice. She wanted what she wanted, and if other people were hurt in the getting of those things, that wasn't real to her. Because they weren't real to her. Shadrick was, it seemed, and so was Marc. Everyone else was a resource to be used. Like Lydia, who she'd sold to the Narcotics task force. Like me, whose name she'd used to get out of a shoplifting bust. Like Cicero.

At the front door, Lisette realized her indiscretion. 'Listen,' she said, 'you aren't going to tell Ghislaine what I told you about Marc, are you?'

'No,' I said. 'I won't.'

Lisette looked relieved. 'What do you want me to do if Ghislaine comes home?'

'Nothing,' I said. 'I'll catch up with her eventually.'

★   ★   ★

'Hadley.'

'It's me,' I said, sitting in the car outside Ghislaine and Lisette's building. 'I didn't find the girlfriend. I'm coming back in. Have you thought about what you want to do next?'

'It's past six,' Hadley said. 'I'm going home.'

'I thought we were looking for Marc,' I said.

'There's not much more we can do,' Hadley said. 'A unit's been to his place, but like we figured, he didn't go back there. He's probably on the run, but his description's out there. Someone will catch him.'

Hadley didn't sound tired, but he'd probably been on the job since eight that morning. And he was right. In a situation like this, detectives didn't cruise around after hours in a radio car, vainly hoping to run across a suspect.

'Look, you want me to wait for you to come in?' he asked.

'Why?'

'Your car's still at that building, isn't it?' Hadley asked me. 'I could give you a lift over there to get it.'

'Don't worry about it,' I said. 'I might hang out downtown awhile, see if any likely reports come in. I'll pick up my car later.'

443

'Sarah, I know I said something like this earlier, and usually I wouldn't repeat myself, but I really think you're working this too hard.' Hadley paused. 'Did you know this guy? Was that not your first time up there, when you came by?'

I am sick of lying to people. I just want to tell the truth to someone I like and respect, for a change.

'I was supposed to get evidence so we could charge him,' I said, evading the specific question. 'If I'd moved faster, he'd be alive and in jail right — '

'No,' Hadley interrupted. 'This is not your fault. Those kids just blew Ruiz out like a match they were done with. It pisses me off, too. I'm angry enough at them without having to think that they've caused someone I like to be sitting around a precinct house after hours, eaten up with guilt over what she might have done differently.'

'Thanks,' I said. 'I won't stay too late. I promise.'

★ ★ ★

I stayed at the precinct for two hours that night, drank coffee, talked with the midwatch people. Garden-variety crimes, or activity that might or might not be criminal, were reported over the radio. Along Nicollet Mall, a panhandler was harassing shoppers a little too hard. At the airport, a child who was supposed to be on a flight didn't get off. On the 35W, a car was pulled to the side without flashers, the driver

444

drunk, sleeping, or slumped behind the wheel. Eventually, I gave up and asked a patrol officer who was heading out to give me a lift to Cicero's building. Before I left, I checked out a handheld radio. Just in case.

The patrol officer and I didn't talk much on the road, and we didn't talk about crime at all.

'Funny, isn't it?' he said. 'Look, it's after nine and the sun's just set.' He took a hand away from the wheel to point at the bath of golden light in the west.

'Tonight's the summer solstice,' I reminded him.

'I know,' he said. 'But I still can't get used to it. I've lived here almost all my life, and it still gives me a thrill to see the sun setting at this hour.'

When we got to the building, I didn't look up at the empty eyes of the windows above me. 'Thanks,' I said, shut the car door, and walked straight across the parking lot, where the Nova waited for me. I almost sensed a rebuke in its low-nosed posture: the Nova and I were getting separated a lot these days, a pilot and wingman out of sync with each other.

It was just as I was crossing into Northeast that the call came over the quietly crackling radio on the passenger seat beside me. In the careful language of over-the-radio communications, the dispatcher's voice reported a request for backup, shots fired at a small liquor store up Central Avenue. Not very far at all from where I was heading now.

I pressed the accelerator down.

When I'd heard the dispatcher's voice, a small shockwave had risen from deep in my body, heat rising to the surface of my skin. It was recognition.

The business wasn't a pharmacy, but that didn't surprise me. Whether or not Marc realized that Cicero's forged prescriptions were nonsense, he knew better than to try again to cash one in, at least not in the Cities. But Marc needed money, and so he was turning to a profession that he knew. *Marc likes to think he's thugged out*, Lisette had said.

He had laid low until nightfall, and now he was moving. One score, and then he'd leave town.

The Nova's front end bumped down and surged up as the car dove into a low parking lot. There was a single squad car outside.

I got out of the Nova, flashed my shield as I approached. 'What's going on?' I asked.

The officer looked up at me, and I saw that she was very young indeed. I knew her: Lockhart, from the drowning scene, who'd taken me downtown to have my statement taken. Roz had been with her then, but now she was nowhere in sight. Lockhart had graduated to working alone, but she didn't look quite in control of the situation.

She was trying, though. She responded to my question with a clipped nod, just a lift of her chin, and then cut her eyes toward the store. 'I think I've got an armed assailant in there,' she said. 'The sole customer said he ran when the shooting started. Shooter was a young white male, he thinks.'

'Where's the witness?' I asked.

'Across the street. I told him to stick around, then I yelled for everyone to vacate the parking lot and stay clear.'

She must have had a bigger voice than her size suggested, because while a small crowd of witnesses were watching us, none of them had tried to breach the territory Lockhart had put off-limits.

'The customer just saw it out of the corner of his eye, the guy drawing the gun, then he ran,' she went on. 'He heard the shots as he made the door. Didn't see the shooter come out.'

'What about the other customers?' I asked.

'He's pretty sure he was the only guy in there,' Lockhart said. 'Except the owner, who was behind the counter.'

'The owner didn't come out?'

Lockhart shook her head. Her brown hair was clipped up against the back of her skull, but a small rooster tail was free enough to shake along with the movement. 'Neither of them,' she said.

'There could be a back way out,' I said.

The store was a boxlike structure, with bars on the windows and posters for Minnesota's lottery games behind the bars, taped from the inside. Jostling with them for the attention of passersby were posters for cigarettes, for beer, for flavored liqueur, and for phone cards. I couldn't see a goddamned thing that was happening inside. If anything was.

For the robber to flee through the back and not be seen again was one thing, but the owner should have made himself known to us, if he could walk.

Lockhart said it aloud. 'I think the owner's down. I want to go in.'

'No,' I said. 'There are paramedics on the way, right? With the backup?'

'That could be too late,' she said.

'I know,' I said. 'I'll go in.'

'We'll both go,' she said.

'No,' I said again. She was young and untried, and I didn't want her on my conscience. 'Just me.' Before she could protest, I said, 'Stay here and cover the door. I'm going to check out the back.'

I was setting a lousy example for Lockhart, not waiting for the backup, but I took out my .40 and circled the building, slowly.

It was strange to think that we were coming up on ten o'clock. Even Venus hadn't been able to break through the pale blue light of the northern sky, and the store's neon sign seemed weakly lit, as though low on energy.

When I turned the corner, into the back alley, I saw a car parked there. An old blue sedan. I glanced down at the tag, the number unfamiliar to me. It wasn't Marc's.

The back door was open. This was the heart of it.

I stood to one side. 'Sheriff's officer!' I yelled in. 'If anyone inside can hear me, please identify yourself!'

Only silence.

'Okay, I'm coming in, and I'm armed!' I went on. 'I'm prepared to use deadly force if threatened. Last chance!'

I sounded like the training manual for deadly force situations. I felt like a teenager pretending to be a cop, sweat breaking out on those bits of skin that are the first to dampen, under the eyes, the back of the neck.

Still nothing. I moved inside slowly.

Immediately inside the back door was the inventory room, wooden shelves piled with cardboard boxes. There was no motion in my line of sight, no human forms. To my left I saw an open door. A bathroom, with a few cases of inventory piled up even in there, next to the dirty toilet and towel dispenser. A smell of cigarette smoke hung in the air. Otherwise empty. All this took only a second to register.

Before I even got into the salesroom, I smelled it. Not blood, but the barroom smell of spilled liquor, sweet and corrupt.

It was all in the salesroom: fallen shelves, broken bottles, disaster. A millimeter of liquid spread along the pale linoleum floor, glimmering in the light from the fluorescent fixtures overhead. The creeping spill was still moving, heading toward my feet even as I stood looking at it. Within the nearly colorless spill were rust-colored rivulets of blood.

I followed these rivulets up to their source, turned reflexively away, made myself look again.

He was young and male and white. Beyond that I didn't know. He'd been wearing a nylon stocking over his head as a mask, and now it had turned into a thin sack of blood and brain matter. There was nothing in the sack that could

449

be called facial features. His handgun, a .38, was on the floor at his side.

I turned to follow what logically was the course of the gunshot. It seemed to have come from the counter, which made sense if the owner had shot him. The owner was nowhere to be seen, but the counter was waist high. It wasn't hard to piece together.

For good measure, I spoke again as I approached the counter. 'I'm a Sheriff's detective,' I repeated, circling the far end of the barrier. 'I'm coming around the counter now. If you're hiding down there with your weapon, please let go of it now. It's all over.'

The owner lay on the floor before a wall of pint and ounce bottles, not moving, eyes closed. His clothes were sodden, but not with blood. With alcohol. Shattered glass lay all around him, and what little blood trickled from his superficial cuts obviously came from the bottles that had shattered. His chest rose and fell serenely as a sleeper's, fallen shotgun near his side.

He was balding, with light-brown Mediterranean skin. He looked a little like Paul, the frugal john, whom I vaguely remembered meeting about a hundred years ago. Here a third smell competed with the blood and alcohol. It was urine, from the stain on the front of the shopkeeper's cheap trousers.

Handgun versus shotgun. The young robber had probably pulled his piece at a decent shooting distance for a weapon like that, two feet away, on the other side of the cash register. The store owner had probably played along until he

450

could reach down on a pretext and pull out his shotgun. When he had, the boy had been startled into the wrong reaction. He'd stumbled backward first, to get away, then remembered to fire his own gun. But by then it was too late. He was too far back, and too rattled, to hit the owner. The slug had hit the wall of short bottles, which had shattered. The store owner, having been fired upon, pulled his own trigger, to deadly effect. Maybe more than once, judging by the mayhem he'd turned his store into. Then, seeing the results of his own work — the kid's head seeming to explode red behind the thin nylon — he'd fainted, losing control of his bladder on the way down.

The shopkeeper was fine; the robber was dead. The only thing for me to do was to not disturb the scene any more than I already had. I needed to go back outside and tell Lockhart everything was all right.

That was when I saw the leg.

It protruded from behind the end of the second aisle. The foot ended in a sandal, and the toenails were colored a deep scarlet, too smoothly and regularly for the color to be blood. These toenails were painted. But the little octopus arm of red that was inching slowly from behind the endcap . . . that was definitely blood. It seemed the shopkeeper had gotten off more than one shot before making his swan dive.

Coming around the counter, I went to the end of the aisle and got the full view. Ghislaine Morris lay on her back, eyes closed, one leg folded up and backward at the knee. The blood that was spreading from her body came from her chest.

Lisette had said that Ghislaine had loaned Marc her car so he could go to parties he didn't even take her to. Now he'd borrowed her car again, the blue one in the alley, and taken her to a shootout. A ragged hole at the center of the bloodstain on Ghislaine's chest bubbled noisily, and the surrounding material fluttered wetly. A sucking chest wound; they'll get you pretty quickly. I still hadn't heard sirens in the distance.

Ghislaine had set herself on this course. She'd had more choice than she'd given Cicero.

No sir, I told an imaginary future inquisitor. *I didn't see her. I was attending to the owner of the liquor store. I had no idea that there was a third victim.*

Ghislaine's wound bubbled again. Her mouth was turning blue around the lips. She wouldn't make it to the ambulance.

Yes sir, I imagined saying. *It's just a terrible tragedy.*

But all along I knew I couldn't do it. 'Goddammit, Cicero,' I said aloud, and then I ran behind the counter for a plastic bag to seal the wound with.

I'd gotten the lung reinflated as best I could when a pair of hands pulled my shoulders back. I looked up and saw the fine, calm features of Nate Shigawa.

'We'll take it from here, Detective Pribek,' he said.

Glad that he remembered me, I nodded and got up, out of his way. And since I was in

452

motion, I just kept moving back, toward the storeroom. His partner, Schiller, was attending to the store owner. Everything was under control.

I walked away, out the back door, and found myself standing alongside Ghislaine's car. This time I noticed something I hadn't before. A child's safety seat, in the back. I bent and looked through the window. Surely not.

But Shadrick was inside, his small head nodded forward. He'd slept through the whole thing.

The back door was unlocked, and Shadrick wakened as I opened it. He was silent as I unhooked the restraining straps and lifted him from the car seat.

With Shad in my arms, I walked around to the front of the store, and once again I was in the middle of the whole 911 circus. A radio coughed and crackled, and emergency lights flickered off the pavement and the front wall of the liquor store. Emergency workers trotted past, doing their jobs, but no one seemed to need me. No one was looking at me, in fact. Except for one person, standing at the very edge of the scene, inventorying me in a way that was familiar from my prostitution detail, long ago. Gray Diaz.

He was slightly rumpled, in shirtsleeves, and there were deep lines underneath his eyes. He looked tired, I thought, like he'd been working too hard. He didn't have a warrant in his hand, but that didn't mean he hadn't gotten one.

'Detective Pribek,' Diaz said, meeting me

halfway. 'I heard I might be able to find you here.' He looked more closely at me. 'What happened to your face?' he asked.

'I fell,' I said. 'At the scene of a structure fire.' Now he'd get on with it.

'I just came around to say goodbye,' Diaz said. 'I'm going back to Blue Earth.'

'You are?' I said.

'My investigation here is over,' Diaz said. 'The Stewart case will remain open, officially, but inactive.'

He looked around at the other officers, our peers, none of whom seemed to be paying any attention to us. Then he turned back to me.

'I know you killed Royce Stewart, Sarah, I just can't prove it,' Diaz said levelly. 'I guess you thought a life like Stewart's didn't matter, and in terms of the system, it seems you were right.'

He did not wait for me to respond, nor did he say anything else. That was his leavetaking.

Shadrick chose that moment to put both his soft, slightly cool hands on my face, turning my attention from Diaz's departing figure. Shad looked into my face, as if to receive instruction or counsel.

'Don't look at me, kid,' I said.

37

When you're sleeping well, the trapdoor at the bottom of your mind opens and you have deep, strange dreams: psychodramas full of symbolic imagery that you rarely remember on waking, and when you do, you tell a friend, *Last night I had the weirdest dream*. It's when you're restless and not sleeping well that you dream close to the surface of your mind, more like thinking in your sleep than dreaming.

In other words, the details of the dream that follows were just speculation, nothing more.

I was back in the courtroom. Hugh Hennessy was on trial, but this time I wasn't the prosecutor. I was just observing, or that's what I thought, until Kilander laid his hand on my shoulder.

Hugh can't speak for himself, he said. *Any judge would throw this case out so hard it'd bounce.*

You said that already.

But they've found someone to speak for him, Kilander said. *They want you to do it.*

I said, *I can't do that.*

Don't keep the judge waiting, Kilander said.

Empathetic thinking is an important skill for a detective. No matter how much you might dislike a suspect, it's useful to adopt his viewpoint, understand his motives. I kept this in mind as I settled myself behind the stand.

Whenever you're ready, the judge said.

I leaned forward and spoke for Hugh. *I know how bad it looks,* I said.

A little louder, Ms. Pribek, the judge said.

I know how bad it looks, I repeated. *But normally my desk was locked. And normally the kids didn't even go in there; I didn't keep anything in my study to attract them, no toys or candy. I kept the pistols there because there was no furniture in our bedroom that locked. My desk did. The guns would be just down the hall if I needed them. I kept the pistols loaded because the lake area wasn't as built up back then as it is now. It was pretty isolated, and I wanted to protect Lis and the kids from break-ins. I don't know why I forgot to lock the desk that one time. I just did.*

How could it happen that the one time I forgot, Aidan went in there and found the gun? And he didn't just shoot into the air, or his foot, but his chest. His chest!

I wasn't afraid to call the paramedics and have the shooting on record; that's not why I drove Aidan to the hospital myself. I know that's what it looked like, but it's not. I was afraid to wait for the ambulance. I grabbed him in my arms and ran for the garage. If there had been any speed traps on the road, the police would have had to chase me all the way to the hospital, because I wouldn't have stopped. I wanted so badly to save him. But no one chased me, no cops saw me. I got all the way to the hospital, and still no one seemed to notice my arrival. And then I looked back at Aidan, and he wasn't breathing. He was blue. And I knew he was gone.

I sat there in the car and cried, and still no one came over. When I was done crying, I thought about bringing the ER staff over to the car, getting them to take Aidan's body, but then I didn't want them to take him away from me and put him in the morgue. So I started the car up again and just drove home. I don't know what I was thinking. I guess I wasn't thinking at all.

When I got home, Lis was sleeping with Marli in the bed, and I didn't wake them. When the sun came up, the morning was so beautiful, and I decided to bury Aidan under the magnolia tree. Lots of old American families have gravesites on their property. It's a tradition. So I buried Aidan under the tree, and I said a prayer.

Marli woke up and I told her Mother was sick, and Aidan had gone away for a while. She said, 'He's coming back, isn't he?' and I couldn't bear to say no, and so I said something like 'Everything's going to be fine.' Later, I took Lis down to the little grave. I told her this was better than sending Aidan to the hands of some funeral home to be embalmed and sewn up. This way, he'd always be with us. She cried and nodded. After that she was catatonic, almost. She didn't call anyone. Not a friend, not her sister.

That's what started me thinking. There were so many coincidences here, that no one saw Aidan in my car at the hospital, that no one had found out yet what had happened . . . It was almost like it was fate. Maybe there was some way I could cover for Aidan shooting himself. Maybe I could put it off on hunters. What good would it do for Aidan's death to be splashed all over the papers? For people to point fingers at me and Elisabeth? They would have blamed her, too. What if some social worker called us unfit? What if they took Marli and Liam, too? It would have destroyed Lis. I mean, she was pregnant with Colm then, too. She was so fragile.

That's when I remembered Brigitte and her little boy, Jacob. It was impossible but perfect. Jacob was almost exactly the same age as the twins. And they were both still so young, there was time. They could both forget the past. Jacob, in time, could be Aidan.

When I told Lis, she got hysterical, called me sick. But I weathered it. I told her that nothing would bring Aidan back, but explained all the reasons. I pointed out what Lis had told me: that since the death of her boyfriend, Brigitte had been a basket case. She was drunk a lot, stoned a lot, and she'd let her son lose his finger to that vicious dog. Jacob was better off with us. I said we could give Jacob a wonderful life here, and we'd never, ever forget Aidan, we could visit his grave every day.

Brigitte was easy. She knew she was a bad mother and that her sister would be good to Jacob. A big check was all it took to push her over the edge. And once she'd cashed the check, she couldn't go to the authorities. She was implicated.

The day we got Jacob home, too, that was a disaster. I'd told Marli, 'Aidan was bitten by a dog and went away to get better,' and she'd believed it. But when I brought Jacob in, she took one look at him and started to cry. She knew he wasn't Aidan, and I was telling her he was, and she was so confused that it frightened her. I said, 'Marli, he looks different, but he's Aidan, he's really Aidan inside.' But she kept crying and saying, 'I want Aidan, I want Aidan.' And Lis was so fragile then, she sat down in the rocking chair and wept, too. Marli was in the corner, crying, and Lis was in the chair, crying, and Jacob was standing in the middle of the room like he wanted to cry, too. I thought, You're the monster here, Hugh. How'd that happen? All I ever wanted was to be a good husband and father and now I was a goddamn monster and I couldn't understand how the hell it had all happened.

Then Jacob looked around and saw Lis. She looked a bit like her sister, Gitte, more beautiful of course, but he saw the resemblance. He went over to her and said, 'Why are you crying?' and got up in the chair with her, and she let him. Then Marli saw that her mother wasn't afraid of the new Aidan, so she went over and climbed up with them. There they all were, all three of them. Looking at them, I thought, Things are going to be okay. I would have liked to have been part of their embrace, but that rocking chair was filled to capacity. I stood apart from them and thought, You're the odd man out now, Hugh. I can live with that. I probably deserve it. As long as Lis is happy.

But of course, things didn't work out that way. Marli and the kid became fast friends, and in six months I'd swear they didn't remember that

459

Jacob Candeleur ever existed. But I couldn't forget, of course. I drank too much and got an ulcer and waited for something to go wrong. Lis loved that boy like he was her own, but she also took to spending time at Aidan's grave, and I realized what a lousy idea it was to bury him where she'd always be reminded of how he died. I wanted to move, but I was too afraid. What if the new owners tore up the new carpeting in the study and found the huge bloodstain in the floorboards? What if they dug under the magnolia tree and found Aidan's bones? What about the goddamned BMW? We were stuck here, with reminders of it at every turn.

But we couldn't grieve openly for Aidan, and I think that's what killed Lis in the end. Then she was gone, and I came home from the funeral and realized that my wife, who I'd loved more than anyone, was gone, and instead I had her sister's illegitimate kid in my house. He was crying under that goddamn magnolia, right on Aidan's grave, and I went out and hit him for the first time. It wasn't the last time, but who cared anymore? I was the monster, I'd known that years ago.

I started fantasizing that I could erase his memory of being Aidan Hennessy as easily as I'd once erased his memory of being Jacob Candeleur. It took me way too long to realize that I could do the next best thing: send him back to Brigitte. When I called to suggest that, she was all for it. And I liked having him gone so much that when Brigitte died, I found an old

460

friend who'd take him.

Marlinchen didn't understand, and I hated to hurt her. Once, I nearly told her the whole story. I took her down to Aidan's gravesite, but when I was there I lost my nerve, and I only told her about missing her mother and how we'd once pledged our undying love there.

I wanted to tell her. She's so much like her mother, and for so long I've wanted to tell somebody about this and have them say, 'I understand.' That's all. 'I understand.'

Now I know that'll never happen. I've paid and paid and paid for my mistake, and I don't know that it'll ever end. I succeeded in erasing Marlinchen's memory and I succeeded in erasing Jacob's. I can't erase the one memory I most want to: mine.

Epilogue

The first headlines about Hugh Hennessy were restrained and respectful: NOTED WRITER PERISHES IN HOUSE FIRE. The media was respectful in their coverage of the funeral, where in the front row of the cathedral, Hugh's four children all wept, their arms around each other, even Colm unashamed of his tears.

But after the burial, questions began to swirl, about why Hugh's stroke wasn't reported, about the identity of the young man who'd died earlier the same day and who'd been identified as Aidan Hennessy on his death certificate. Reporters began to probe, and in time the whole story came out. The media was banned from the Hennessy property on the day that Hennepin County technicians dug under the magnolia tree, but reporters congregated at the end of the long peninsula driveway, and their lenses captured the images as the techs brought up the bones of a very small child with ten fingers and a shattered sternum.

The Hennessy children refused all comment, with Campion acting as a family spokesman, however terse. I called Marlinchen several times in those stressful first weeks. She assured me everything was under control, and I believed her, mostly because although she sounded sober and occasionally tired, her voice lacked that sharp, tense note that I remembered from the worst of times. The continued presence of J. D. Campion might have something to do with that, I thought. He apparently had no plans to leave the Cities, and I was glad. He wasn't the guardian that Family Services would have chosen for the Hennessys, but he was perhaps uniquely suited to this brainy, idiosyncratic little family.

In August, my work took me to the University of Minnesota campus to conduct a short interview. It was a hot day, humid but not unpleasant, and considering that it was only summer session, there were quite a few young people out on the great quadrangle overlooked by Northrop Auditorium. I was crossing along a path ground down in the grass when a male voice called after me. 'Detective Pribek!'

It took me a moment to recognize the student who had called my name. Of course, Liam Hennessy hadn't changed that much in the eight or so weeks since I'd last seen him, but somehow he looked older, much like a college student — ironically, largely because he was dressed so casually, in a pale-red T-shirt and cargo shorts and sandals. His hair, never short, had continued to grow out, and exposure to the sun was bringing out its lighter tones at the tips. At Liam's neck hung a familiar leather cord strung with three tigereyes. Only the wire-rim glasses were exactly the same.

'Hey,' I said, quite pleased to see him. 'Did you skip your senior year of high school?' I moved closer, into the shade of an overhanging tree.

'No,' Liam said, quickly shaking his head. 'I'm

just here for a seminar on the Greek and Roman tragedies.'

'A little light reading,' I said.

'Yeah.'

We were silent a moment. Then I said, 'I like the necklace. It suits you, like it did him.' It was oddly true, despite how different Liam Hennessy and his cousin had seemed on the surface.

'Thanks,' Liam said. He paused. 'We debated whether it was right to bury him and Aidan next to Dad, but we thought they should be with Mother,' he told me. 'Jacob really loved her.'

'I know,' I said. 'How is Donal?'

A shadow crossed Liam's narrow face. 'He's getting help,' he said. 'The fire was an accident. Donal knows that, but it's going to take time for him to come to grips with what happened.'

'I wish more than anything it could have worked out another way,' I said.

It was an inadequate way of phrasing it. The deaths of earlier this year were terrible, but the pain that Jacob and Hugh had felt had quickly been over. It's the living who hurt, and dealing with the open-ended question *What if I'd done things differently?* hurts most of all.

'J. D.'s still in town; you knew that, right?' Liam changed the subject. 'He's helping us sell the property. The house is going to be razed, but the land's still going to bring a decent sum. And we're selling the cabin in Tait Lake, too.'

'So you shouldn't have financial worries for a while,' I said.

'No,' Liam said. 'J. D. and I are trying to convince Marlinchen to apply to colleges. She's

464

been saying she has too many responsibilities right now, but we're telling her she can go someplace local, and we'll all still be together. I think we'll wear her down.'

'I hope so,' I said.

'Hey, Liam.' The girl who interrupted us was about Marlinchen's age, with long blond hair and long legs exposed by a pair of cutoff shorts. She was standing closer to Liam than to me, and her expression indicated that she was politely hoping that our conversation was wrapping itself up. I took the hint.

'It was good seeing you,' I said.

'You, too,' Liam said. And just as I moved off, he said, 'Detective Pribek?'

I turned back.

'If I ever want to write a cop story, can I talk to you for research?'

I smiled. 'I look forward to it.'

★   ★   ★

In the end, Aidan Hennessy and Jacob Candeleur, cousins in life and brothers in death, would lie under the same marker, in the shaded, elegant graveyard where I'd met Campion.

For Cicero Ruiz, it was a little different. Minneapolis has no city cemetery for the indigent, but several graveyards reserve space for such burials, and Cicero is buried in one of them, beyond the northern treeline, in a section where handmade wooden crosses and even paper signs mark the graves.

Several days after his burial, Soleil and I

465

cleaned out his apartment. With no inheritors, we sorted everything according to the charity it was going to. The contents of the kitchen shelves went to a local food bank, the furniture to a Goodwill store, the medical texts to the library. Late in the afternoon, a tall, graying woman came to the door. She identified herself as with the Public Housing Authority and gave us the key to Cicero's mailbox, asking us to clean it out. We said we would.

Soleil and I worked late into the evening; neither of us wanted to put an extra day into our grim task. The last thing I did was go downstairs to the mailbox.

Not surprisingly, it was packed to capacity, and little of it was personal. I pitched most of the items into a green plastic trash bag Soleil and I had been steadily filling as the day wore on.

Only one slender envelope, address neatly typed, looked out of place. It was from a law firm in Colorado.

The brief letter inside informed Cicero Ruiz that the miners of Painted Lady #5 had won their claim against their former employer in the matter of the mine collapse. As a member of the affected class, Cicero's share of the judgment was $820,000.

I laughed until I cried. Soleil just cried.

★   ★   ★

Kilander, who had sources for everything, gave me the inside information about Gray Diaz and the results of the tests on the Nova. It was true

466

that the crime-lab technicians found blood in the carpet, but it was too degraded from the passage of time and exposure to heat and light for extensive analysis. The tests confirmed that it was blood and it was human, but beyond that, nothing could be concluded. That was the truth behind Diaz's last effort to get me to confess.

As an investigator, I should have seen it. In our last interview, Diaz had created an atmosphere of intimacy, calling me by my first name. He'd insinuated that he had more evidence than he really did. Then he'd stressed our commonalities as law-enforcement professionals and said that he wanted to help me. He'd been holding useless cards all along, but it was a damn good try.

I admired Diaz. Like he'd said, under other circumstances, we might have been friends.

I was sorry, too, that his last words to me had been so bitter. The implication had been clear: Diaz believed that he had lost, and I had won. There'd been no way to tell him that we'd both lost. For, not long afterward, at the shooting range, Jason Stone had pointed me out to a rookie with a knowing lift of his chin. I knew what bit of department gossip Stone was about to relate to his friend.

★ ★ ★

Labor Day came with its promise of fall, and the summer ended more or less the way it had begun, with me taking on extra shifts, getting overtime, staying occupied. One early-September afternoon, Prewitt stopped by my desk and told me that the young mother I'd saved in the liquor-store shootout, Ghislaine Morris, had made a full recovery, and he was putting a commendation in my file because of the action I had taken to save her. *Thank you, sir,* I said, and when he was gone I put my head down and went back to what I was doing.

Several hours later, at home, when the unwieldy screen door refused to open wide enough to let me in, I ripped it off its hinges. Until that moment, I would have told you I was over the death of Cicero Ruiz.

The true locus of my anger surprised me. I wasn't angry at Ghislaine, or at myself, though I had reasons to be. The truth was that I was angry at Cicero. It was he who had put me in an unwinnable situation: either turn him in to my lieutenant, or let him pursue the course that led to his violent, untimely death.

I'd said compassion was Cicero's fatal flaw, but it was pride. I would have seen it earlier, had I not needed so badly a figure in my life whose wisdom and incorruptibility I believed in implicitly. So badly had I wanted to believe Cicero simply as a good man destroyed by circumstance that I hadn't seen that his life, since the loss of his license, had been one of *self-sacrifice* in the most literal sense. Surely, even after his professional disgrace, there had been better options open to Cicero than the mines, but he hadn't taken them. The underside of pride is shame, and after his ethical lapse, Cicero had punished himself more thoroughly than the system ever could have. It was that, and also his need to carry on with his life's work even from a housing project, that had set his death in motion.

Of course, it couldn't have happened if I'd arrested him, as my job had required, or if Ghislaine hadn't been desperate to hold on to a venal, brutal young man she inexplicably wanted . . . Who can ever say with certainty why one person meets an early death and another is spared? If Cicero had been down the hall with his friends when Marc came to his door, would Marc simply have returned another day? Or would he have gone, frustrated, to another job, and been shotgunned by the liquor store owner, leaving Cicero forever unaware of how close he'd come to the county morgue? The single factors were as unpredictable as currents in open water, and my own guilt was like a small amount of blood poured into that water. The individual atoms of that blood would never be gone, but they would be diffused, like my responsibility was diminished by the realization of how many small circumstances go into any one death.

A cool peace followed in the wake of the realization. I didn't move to pick up the fallen screen door. Nor did I go inside, instead sitting down on the back step. A freight train thundered past, and the quiet that it left behind was nearly as stark as silence.

Here was the solitude I'd run from all summer long, filling my hours with the Hennessys, with Cicero, even with strangers like Special K. I'd sought a hundred problems to distract myself from the ones I'd been living with since Shiloh went to Blue Earth. I hadn't been picky. Anyone's troubles would do. So long as they weren't my own. So long as they allowed me to keep my own feelings chained and unexamined.

If I had been blind to the pride and guilt that had motivated Cicero Ruiz, it was probably because I'd had a lot of practice at refusing to see it. They were the same feelings that motivated my husband. It was pride that had led Shiloh to try to balance the scales for Kamareia's death when the courts hadn't been able to. Not only that, but Shiloh believed he could do it while shielding me from complicity, or even from any knowledge of his actions. When he had failed, Shiloh had refused to plead extenuating circumstances and seek a lighter sentence; he had gone to prison. I thought I understood better now why he had fallen silent from behind those prison walls: it was shame. Shiloh saw his actions as a dirty handprint on the life I was trying to keep upright here in Minneapolis.

I was not guiltless here, either. I hadn't reached out to Shiloh, afraid of being the first to break our mutual silence and to possibly be brushed aside. I had been unable to admit to myself how much I was angered by the effective loss of my husband, a loss I'd been so, so careful to frame in my mind not as abandonment or betrayal but simply as circumstance.

* * *

I slept early that night, and it was about two in the morning when I woke up, alert and clear-minded and knowing I wouldn't sleep any more. Instead I got up, washed my face and dressed, and threw a few items of clothing and some money in my duffel bag. Last of all, I put on my copper wedding ring, retrieved from the drawer of the night table.

On the road east, to Wisconsin, the air was warm like summer, sweet with chlorophyll. I didn't feel tired at all. I'd be at the prison by dawn. Ahead, low in the southeast and preternaturally large and pale from its proximity to the horizon, Orion sprawled like a patron saint over my destination.

We do hope that you have enjoyed reading this large print book.

Did you know that all of our titles are available for purchase?

We publish a wide range of high quality large print books including:
Romances, Mysteries, Classics
General Fiction
Non Fiction and Westerns

Special interest titles available in large print are:
The Little Oxford Dictionary
Music Book
Song Book
Hymn Book
Service Book

Also available from us courtesy of Oxford University Press:
Young Readers' Dictionary
(large print edition)
Young Readers' Thesaurus
(large print edition)

For further information or a free brochure, please contact us at:
Ulverscroft Large Print Books Ltd.,
The Green, Bradgate Road, Anstey,
Leicester, LE7 7FU, England.
Tel: (00 44) 0116 236 4325
Fax: (00 44) 0116 234 0205

Other titles published by
The House of Ulverscroft:

GAGGED & BOUND

Natasha Cooper

Biographer Beatrice Bowman is being sued for libel by a new member of the House of Lords for implicating him in a thirty-year-old terrorist outrage. At the other end of the legal spectrum, a family of South London villains gags and suffocates those who try to expose their secrets. And Inspector Caro Lyalt has information from a whistle-blower that could ruin a colleague's career — or her own. In the middle of it all Barrister Trish Maguire picks her way through the maze of lies and threats and brings danger terrifyingly close to herself and the people she loves.

DOUBLE TAP

Steve Martini

When attorney Paul Madriani takes on the defence of Emiliano Ruiz, who is charged with the murder of Madelyn Chapman, all the evidence points his way. But most damning is the trademark 'double tap' shooting of a military assassin, and Ruiz is an ex-professional soldier. Madriani discovers that Chapman's company had perfected the Information For Security program, software that could monitor every citizen. And Chapman was in a bitter dispute for control of her product with dangerously powerful men. Whether he can save Ruiz only the trial will reveal, but Madriani is now the focus of corrupt elements capable of deadly revenge on those who stand in their way.